The Flight of the Maidens

The Flight
of the
Maidens

Jane Gardam

CARROLL & GRAF PUBLISHERS, INC.
NEW YORK

OCT 0 2 2001

Grateful acknowledgment is made to the Estate of Robert Frost,
Jonathan Cape and Henry Holt and Company, LLC, for kind
permission to quote from "Stopping by Woods on a Snowy Evening"
from *The Poetry of Robert Frost*, ed. Edward Connery Lathem. Copyright
© 1923 and 1969 by Henry Holt and Co., copyright © 1951
by Robert Frost.

First Carroll & Graf edition 2001
Second printing August 2001

Carroll & Graf Publishers
A Division of Avalon Publishing Group Incorporated
161 William Street
New York, NY 10038

Library of Congress Cataloging-in-Publication Data is available.
ISBN: 0-7867-0879-4

Manufactured in the United States of America

for Lieselotte
wherever she may be

The woods are lovely, dark and deep.
But I have promises to keep,
And miles to go before I sleep.
And miles to go before I sleep.

Robert Frost

1

Three girls in a graveyard. Four feet on a tomb. Tall, burnt-up grasses. The late summer of 1946.

'From now on I'm Hester,' said Hetty Fallowes: 'Hest*ah*.'

'Well, you always were Hester, weren't you?' said Una. 'Weren't you? Christened?'

'"Hest*ah*". My mother saw it in a book.'

'Well, she'd have seen it in the Bible, wouldn't she? Being your lovely Ma?'

'"Hester" is OT. Ma's pretty hard-line NT. Jesus first and always. *New Testament. Book of Common Prayer*. Anglo-Catholic. When I get to London I'm "Hester Fallowes". I shall start as I mean to go on.'

'Not for the first time,' said Una. 'It's Lieselotte who should be Hester. You're the Jew, Lieselotte.'

The third girl, whose feet were neither bare nor propped higher than her head against the flank of the table-tomb, but neatly side by side in the grass in laced-up shoes and fawn lisle stockings, continued with her knitting.

Una and Hetty but for their feet and legs lay almost hidden in the neglected grasses among the tombstones that looked down on them from every side. Stone faces of angels, balloon heads of grinning rustics with medieval ear-flaps, the odd crumbling skull watched them like crouching tribesmen. Behind stood the church and its mausoleum, a few stones lying around in the grass. Plants bloomed and straggled from its cracks and a small mountain ash flourished from a quoin. The spire seemed to be toppling across the cobalt, un-Yorkshire sky. High up in a different air stream, clouds as light as cheesecloth skirmished. The end of the summer. Exactly one year ago this week the atomic bomb had been dropped on Nagasaki.

Una and Hetty lay in exhausted bliss, eyes closed, while Lieselotte sat in a hump like unrisen dough. Una and Hetty were skinny. Lieselotte was pasty, boneless and fat, her hair in a scant little colourless bun, her eyes myopic behind thick glasses. When she at length looked up at the spire and the sky she continued to knit, but only as part of some long reverie. The air-force blue knitting wool was emerging from a coarse little bag made of something she called 'crash', embroidered with yellow and purple woollen daisies. She came from Hamburg and had arrived in England in June 1939, on the last train full of refugee children, the *Kindertransport*. She now sat silent in the sunshine, like a woman of sixty.

All three had heard that morning that they had won state scholarships to the University in October. All three had known since Christmas that they had been awarded a place, but without a state award none of them could have taken it up. State scholarships were rare, and rarer still in the small seaside school they had attended since the war began, distracted by air raids and the news on the wireless, always hungry and six years without a holiday. They were all seventeen years old.

Una and Hetty had known the churchyard for over a year. They had come to it to lie in the grass to do their revision. But Lieselotte had been introduced to it only that morning after they had all come out from the headmistress's study basking in the glorious news. Una and Hetty had been friends since they were five, but Lieselotte had been a solitary. She had not been ignored but, rather, never befriended, nobody being sure of her because she was German. Nobody at the school had ever explained Lieselotte. The teachers had perhaps smiled at her more often than at the others, but never suggested why she might need smiling at. It was taken for granted in some symbiotic way that

2

Lieselotte was dreadfully poor, but through no fault of her own.

All three girls were poor anyway.

Hetty was poor because her father, who had been four years in the trenches in the First World War, had returned miraculously unscathed in body but shattered to bits in mind. It had once been a remarkable mind but now it hid itself, looking out only now and then like sunlight between tree trunks. Malcolm Fallowes had elected to live out the rest of his life without gainful employment, as an intellectual on a small pension. By profession now he was a grave-digger and occasional washer of the town's windows, though since the beginning of the Second World War the fenestral part of his income had dwindled as most windows were immediately criss-crossed with strips of brown paper to counteract bomb blast, and quite a few were simply boarded up.

Hetty's mother, child of a profligate father long dead, had married young and for love and had never done any sort of work in her life. She hadn't a penny. To have worked for money would have been unthinkable and destroyed the last barrier between herself and her maid, who lived-in, and was paid five pounds a year and her keep. At one time to do without a maid would have been as unthinkable to Mrs Fallowes as to do without soap. Now she was having to do without both. The maid had melted into munitions, the soap dwindled into transparent strips that were rendered down with other remnants and squeezed up again into secondary greyish dollops that soon turned to jelly, and disappeared. When the last maid had departed, like the last king, into the dark, the Fallowes were richer by five pounds a year but poorer by the loss of a ration book and identity. 'Look at my hands!' Mrs Fallowes would cry. 'Just look at all our hands!' she and her friends would say in the Lonsdale Café. They had all been careful of their soft hands. Now there was scrubbing of floors.

Mr Fallowes, brooding on the News, beset by dreams of France and hints in the paper of what was going on in Europe, sometimes came down early in the morning to wash the kitchen floor. 'For my wife,' he said to himself, though neither of them told anybody about it. Sometimes in the past years, especially after the Blitz of '41 was over and in clement weather when deaths hung fire, Mr

3

Fallowes' grave-money had dwindled. He got seven-and-sixpence a grave (lined out with laurel or privet, an extra one-and-six) and relied upon it for cigarettes and beer. At these times he had grown morose and said he felt like swinging a torch about at night to lure some passing Messerschmitt, like a Cornish wrecker on the beach. 'There's quite a few I could do without. Most of the Church. What good, for example, is a pope?'

'The Pope doesn't live here,' said Hetty, 'and without the Church you couldn't dig the graves and toll the bell.'

Mrs Fallowes would shriek and cry, say that Hetty was a heartless cynic just like her father, and that she personally didn't know what she would do without the vicar. Then she would rush about and bake little cakes with a view to putting them out for sale in the sitting-room window and there'd be no marge or sugar left. She made wonderful cakes and had a multitude of friends, and she could have done well.

But somehow the cakes never made it to a trading area. Kitty Fallowes, between kitchen and sitting-room, would falter into shame. The cakes, unpriced, were left on a little bamboo table just inside the vestibule, and when friends came for tea, which meant of course that at least one cake had to be cut into, they'd say, 'You know, Kitty, you really could *sell* these cakes. You'd make your fortune in these hard times,' and Kitty at once would look thrilled and say, 'Would you like one, Mrs Brownley? Let me wrap it up for you. No, of *course* not. I wouldn't think of it. Not from you.' Some of Mrs Fallowes's friends suspected that the Fallowes were hungrier than most and brought them offerings, like turnip jam or a tin of something from America.

Once there had been the promise of something more. Hetty's godmother, a rich woman with no family, who later passed the war in hotels and spas one step ahead of the bombs, had often remembered Hetty's birthday with a pound note but had only once met her.

Before the war she had written to say that she would like to come for an afternoon visit. A cake-of-cakes had been made and Kitty Fallowes, to show that although she had married a grave-digger she was acquainted with respectable people, had invited little six-year-old Una Vane to tea. Una was a doctor's daughter. Josephine Dixon was the godmother's name. She hailed from Windsor and her hobby was royalty.

The visit was a spectacular failure. Una, an owl of a child with sober manners who always had clean finger-nails, as behoved somebody with a surgery in the house, who always said 'please' and 'thank you' and spoke only when addressed, behaved like a drunken clown. She rocked her chair, blew crumbs across the table, made noises like a wild beast. Hetty had been embarrassed and rather frightened by this unrecognisable friend.

But loyal, ever loyal, to Una, Hetty had joined in. She had blown crumbs about, too. She had made noises like a different wild beast. She had squeezed bread-and-butter in her fingers and watched it come out through them like worms. She had spilt jam. Excited tears she did not understand had stood in her eyes.

'You had both better get down,' Kitty Fallowes had said between nervousness and fury; but the little girls were already down, rolling about beneath the table, giggling.

'Una is never like this,' Kitty Fallowes told the godmother. 'She's from such a nice family. I can't understand it.'

The godmother had pressed her lips together and then the crumbs on her plate and deposited them upon the drawn-threadwork serviette. 'Is she a foreigner? She is rather dark.'

The little girls had at last run up to Hetty's bedroom, where the steady Una had continued to cavort and fool about, and then had flopped to the floor and made herself insignificant with a book.

Hetty had circled round her, and then, for the first and last time in their lives, she had put her arms round Una, there on the floor. Hetty did not ask: What was it? Why did you do it? You knew my mother wanted to show you off so she'd see how nice we all are and worth giving money to. She did not say this, because she had no need to do so. Una had tears on her face, although it wasn't a sad book. Hetty said, 'It's all right, Una. It doesn't matter.'

Una then had howled aloud and had not said, then or ever: How *could* you and your mother make such a parade? Just to get money? You are you. Why should you beg? One day you will be beautiful and famous and you will marry a prince, I wouldn't wonder, and give palaces to your parents.

She had no need to say any of it, nor could she have done so with a six-year-old's vocabulary, but she got it across somehow. She could sense a mother trading her child.

Una, at six, had been obscurely aware of dangers and deceit. Three years later her father, the doctor, walked out of the house before morning surgery and never came back. He had been a wonderful father. He had taken Una and Hetty on cliff-top walks and shown them wild flowers and birds. He had told them stories from *The Arabian Nights*. Wherever he went Dr Vane had seemed to bring lightness of heart. He had sung jolly music-hall songs quietly to himself on his rounds. He went everywhere on foot and twirled a walking-stick. People felt better for seeing him walk by, so cheerful and handsome, with his military moustache. A family doctor, a flower in his buttonhole. Then, one day when Una got up for school, he wasn't there.

For several weeks after that, Una had come to live with Hetty and it was soon in the papers that Dr Vane's body had been found down on the rocks below Boulby Head. Someone had seen a man walking proudly along the cliff-top, his walking-stick across his shoulder like a rifle. He had been a gunner in the First World War. How Una and Hetty giggled and sang at Hetty's house during the weeks after his death. Nobody told them anything. Neither child asked. Both somehow knew that, like Hetty's father, Dr Vane had suffered from something known as The Somme. Deep in Hetty there was a fear for the grave-digger's safety, even though she once heard the grave-digger say, 'Vane was a bloody clot.'

So Una and Hetty were cemented together by disappointment and woe and it was thought rather peculiar that they were so often laughing.

They had laughed together from the start. After the dis-inheriting tea-party, the godmother had been heard by the two girls on the doorstep as she said goodbye – the girls hanging invisible over the stair-rail – '*Please* don't worry about it, Kitty. The friend is certainly rather *droll*.' They had howled with glee.

But birthday presents stopped after that, and at Christmas there

6

was only a printed card, even the signature printed and the address, which, when war came, changed from one hotel to another until it steadied at the great hotel on the Yorkshire Wolds. 'Prime funk-hole for the rich,' said Hetty's father.

The funk-hole received a direct hit and blew Miss Dixon to the skies. She'd gone peculiar by then anyhow and left all her money to the Princesses Elizabeth and Margaret Rose.

And now Una was off to Cambridge to read Physics and Hetty off to London to read Literature, and Lieselotte, who had joined their sisterhood really seriously only today, this great day in the churchyard, was off to Cambridge too, to read Modern Languages.

There had been no surprise about the achievement of Una and Lieselotte, who had swum through every school examination from the start, salmon breasting the rapids. It was Hetty – 'Hester' now – who was suddenly the amazement of the world, for she'd been thought of as only a minnow splashing in a pool.

Hetty's academic bombshell was wonderful for her. Most of all she was enchanted by the incredulous faces of her teachers. She had never been thought clever, and for years had played up to their modest expectations. Recurrently she had been labelled unsteady, self-conscious and a tiresome show-off. Vaguely it was known that she came from a difficult background. Her parents' oddness and intensity and, for all the background of the Great War, their immaturity and provincialism had been a hindrance. They were known to be 'not quite normal', and her mother 'very religious'. Hetty had discovered that their undoubted love for her had been only the extension of their love for themselves ('She has my eyes') and she had been disturbed by her comprehension of them as they swam through their lives in total incomprehension of her. They loved her, but as a dear liability. They expected no talent in her. Her father demanded that she draw no attention to herself and her mother that she strove after a stringent goodness, the moral rectitude which she herself had always been expected to achieve as a child and in which, filled with High Church guilt, she

7

felt she had failed. Hester, under Kitty's surveillance, was to be Kitty perfected.

Neither parent had ever given any thought to how Hetty would pass her life. Being Hetty was enough for them. After school there would of course be a job somewhere local, a job of some nondescript kind until she married somebody nice, for ever and ever. A young man of her own class. She herself knew that other things were to be. She loved her parents even as she drifted away. From term to idle term at school she had frolicked, whistling out of tune and in the dark.

But she had one asset, the primitive gift to the timid: the ability to identify with anyone she met, to see inside their head and hear their thoughts and to imitate and, when passion struck, even to become them.

At sixteen she had met a man. He was not a boy. He was a man. He was twenty-one, and a lance-corporal in the Army Pay Corps, stationed locally. After two meetings he had told her that he loved her and that he believed she had the most unusual mind. He already had a place at the University and would be released from the Army at the same time as she would be leaving school. They must go up together.

She had met him at the vicarage over a glass of sherry when she had been wearing a pale-green dress of Mrs Brownley's cousin's. It was old, but of heavy silk. She was tall. Rationing had kept her figure thin. She had good legs. Skirts were still short. She looked languid and romantic and vague. She was dying of shyness.

It was the first time she had tasted alcohol and she had gulped down a couple of glasses of sherry before her mother's disapproving eyes had noticed, so that by the time she was introduced to the man she was able to blot out a rather terrible name and notice only that he was slender as a wand with gigantic eyes and very fair. She heard herself say, 'How tall you are,' and he had said, 'Yes. I'm said to look like Siegfried Sassoon.' She thought he had a dry wit and only later realised that he was stating simply what he thought to be true. Hetty had been reading Sassoon and other poets of his ilk, some sad, some dead. Sassoon belonged to the world her mother loved: the old century, hunting, hoar frost, early mornings in the unknown south of England countryside, timelessness, an ordered world.

Eustace asked her to go for a walk with him, and for a number of Sunday afternoons they would walk demurely along the lanes and over the fields, sometimes to the village of the country church and ragged mausoleum, and the peeping-tom tombs. Soon they held hands.

He talked always about books and sprang about on his toes with delight when he found that she was well-read, and she was warmed through with gratitude, for it was the first time anyone had noticed. He began to kiss her soon. She had been kissed before, often, at sweaty school dances and was becoming good at it. Eustace was not adept. He kept his eyes open throughout, looking over her shoulder, often breaking off to point out a feature of the landscape above her ear. He kissed her as if he was writing it all down. The air Eustace breathed, every leaf, every twig and hedgerow was, she discovered, an index for literary allusion. 'Oh!' he would cry, breaking away from her. 'Come quickly. Look at this little glade.' She felt Dorothy to brother William, never his woman. But it was new.

And she admired him. His perfect French, his Cambridge scholarship, his voice without a trace of Yorkshire in it, his excellent hands, and his belief in her. To please him, she read more and more, found herself discussing, analysing. She adored his astonished eyes when she told him she had read the whole of Shakespeare and that, no, she had never seen a play. She had read Shakespeare in the public park on Saturday afternoons, which were her father's drinking times, though she didn't tell Eustace that. She wrapped herself up in his admiration. She even managed to subdue the recent regret that he never laughed. He could titter and sort of hiss through his teeth, but he was a stranger to the guffaw. Hetty had not yet grown out of the guffaw.

And she had to stop herself imagining what he would look like in the nude. His Army uniform lay in thick folds over what might well be a concave stomach. He never ate anything. He pecked like a bird.

But he was interested in religion, and so was she, and he loved music and so (she found through him) did she. They attended Church together, which delighted her mother, and he sang like an angel. At the Church porch the blunderbuss of a rowdy vicar pumped Eustace's ethereal hand up and down, with commendation.

To keep him, she flung herself into work and found that she could almost inhabit, almost *become*, Eustace. As she wrote and read, it was Eustace's passion and precision that began to appear in her essays, Eustace's intelligent choice of source material and criticism that began to find its way to the public library, Miss Kipling the librarian watching her at first with disbelief, then helping her. Her handwriting became Eustace's handwriting, minute, tight-packed, most wonderfully level. Eustace was a classicist and effortlessly now Hetty's Latin began to flow, and, a year before she needed to, she gained the qualifications to try for a university scholarship. Eustace had changed her very nature. He had given her the chance of her life. How amazingly lucky to have found the man of her life so young. What a perfect life must lie ahead.

But how strange that she didn't feel happier. Why was it that in his presence Hetty had become so quiet and receptive and respectful, yet when he wasn't there, even in her letters to him, the Hetty she knew, the true Hetty, burst forth? She reverted to her natural huge scrawl in these letters to him, aggressively left misspellings uncorrected, defiantly wrote nonsensical rubbish.

And he corrected her spellings.

At the beginning of Hetty's last year at school there was a change of staff and a mad little woman with haunted eyes and blotches was appointed to teach General Studies. She took Hetty – who seemed to be her only pupil – aside to tell her that she knew nothing of early English literature. 'It wasn't my period,' she said, blushing carmine at the phrase. 'I'll have to ask you to get up *The Nonne's Priest's Tale* by yourself. Please tell no one.'

'Help!' wrote Hetty to the Salisbury Plain, where Eustace was now counting out the King's shillings. 'There's no hope now. I'll never do it by myself in a term. Might as well not apply.'

And back came the pages of hem-stitched excellence and an analysis of every Canterbury Tale.

Yet how can he like me, she thought, when I can't somehow stop myself writing to him like a shrieking *ingénue*? Why don't I write like the sort of girl he really wants?

She saw this girl: cool, elegant, bossy, brisk and cutting. A woman of experience. Why had he gone for Hetty? Because, she knew, she had been the only girl available.

Oh – the awful dead kisses!

When Eustace had been drafted to Salisbury Plain he had had to leave behind at a local watchmaker's a watch strap that was being repaired, and he had asked her to collect it for him. After she had collected it she wore it. She wore it every day. She wore it at school and in bed. It was broad, black hard leather, an unlikely possession for Eustace, and it made her somehow see him with new eyes. The watch strap was the only thing about Eustace that gave her any sort of thrill, and she fastened it painfully tight around her wrist. She had no idea why.

'Have you hurt your wrist?' asked Una.

Hetty smiled.

'Who is he?'

'Oh, I just met him somewhere.'

'What's his name?'

'Oh, nothing special.'

'What's his *name*?'

'It's . . . Eustace, actually.'

'Eustace!'

But, unbelievable to Una, Hetty hadn't laughed.

Hetty kept the watch strap on her wrist all the time and at night in bed held it against her face. The leather smelled male. Somehow Eustace had not smelled male. He'd smelled of Wright's Coal Tar soap. She buttoned the strap under the cuff of her school shirt. Una, who noticed all things and commented never, began to drift away.

Una, this final year, had taken up with a sharp-faced boy from the fish shop who belonged to a cycle club, and also with a gigantic girl called Brenda Flange, who had Amazonian shoulders and thighs. The three of them were to be seen together most Sundays, out and about on their racing bikes. Una seemed not to need to do any work, and Brenda had given up trying since her mother had gone off with someone in the ARP.

Una and Brenda cycled about the empty lanes and up into the hills, Ray the fish-boy at first pedalling behind them, then coming up alongside, elbowing Brenda away, and soon taking the lead. What he thought of Brenda was anyone's guess, for, like Una, he was economical with words. The trio once passed Hetty and Eustace finger-tip touching in the lane to the mausoleum and Brenda let out a great 'Yoo-hoo!' Una and the fish-boy kept their faces forward and passed in a glitter of spokes. Eustace, who had been discussing the *Dream of the Rood*, leapt a hedge to avoid the chippings.

'You don't know them, do you, Hetty?'

'She's my best friend.'

'The Boadicea?'

'No. Not the Boadicea.'

'What a creature. Rather glorious. My word! A bronze.'

'Una – the other one – is my friend.'

'She looked like an owl with legs.'

'Owls do have legs.'

'I mean with quite inordinate legs.'

There followed a lot about the place of owls in art and literature.

After these Sunday walkings-out, even once for a whole weekend of his leave, Eustace began to visit Hetty's family and sleep in the attic room that had once been the maid's and looked over Mr Fallowes's vegetable allotment, which adjourned the graveyard. The evenings of these visits, all sitting listening to the wireless, had been interminable. Sometimes, if the film were serious, Eustace and Hetty would go to the pictures together on the Saturday night and sit in the one-and-nines, Eustace paying. All Hetty's school friends, each in some boy's arms, were along the back row in the double seats – though never Una. Sometimes

Eustace and Hetty walked back home to Hetty's house by the sea behind its rolls of barbed wire. She tried not to think of the daft days when she'd run home by the back streets eating chips out of a greasy bag with Una. She missed Una.

A year later, Brenda Flange at a Domestic Science establishment in the south of England studying Army Catering, and Ray the fish-boy much busier now with a job on the railways, and Eustace away, Una and Hetty had got together again; and this last summer, school soon to vanish for ever, they had revised their various subjects in the churchyard. Today, in homage to the place, they had come back to it again to lie among the placid tombs, and with the added distinction of Lieselotte sitting with them, steadily knitting, Lieselotte who had always been too alarming, too mysterious and too brilliant to be anybody's friend. They felt themselves this afternoon to be Lieselotte's intellectual equals. They felt the equals of Einstein this hot and throbbing day.

And Hetty was clearing the decks. She had decided to chuck Eustace.

She had discovered he had been writing all the time to her mother.

Long, long letters, fifteen words to the line, saying what a wonderful woman her mother was. Hetty had found the wad of letters in the familiar midget hand, lying among her mother's winceyette underclothes and lavender bags in the drawers where she was looking on the sly for her mother's Bear Brand stockings. The letters were all about her mother's heroes – and of course Eustace's heroes – Archbishop Temple and Christina Rossetti, C. S. Lewis and *The Problem of Pain*. Just before he left the house at the end of his last visit she had come upon Eustace holding her mother in his arms by the kitchen table with the calendar of the Via Dolorosa behind them on the wall. The kisses were only the usual tight little red-lipped pecks, but her mother was looking delighted.

Well, that's that, thought Hetty.

'That feller gone, then?' asked the grave-digger that night. 'Can't say I'm sorry.'

'She owes him such a very great deal,' said Kitty Fallowes, rosy and smiling.

'She should take that thing off her wrist.'

'What thing?'

'The thong thing she's got under her cuff.'

'I forgot it,' said Hetty. 'And I am present. I am among you. I may be addressed directly.'

'Oh, darling, but he'll need it! He asked me about it. How could you come to forget?'

'Thong thing,' said Hetty, undoing it, throwing it across the table. 'It's all yours. He's all yours. *You* can send it back.'

'That would be quite wrong, Hetty. He'll want to hear from you.'

'No. I've started to feel sick when I think of him. With you. In the kitchen.'

'Whatever can you mean, "in the kitchen"?'

'He made me feel sick,' said Mr Fallowes, 'all over the house.'

2

'And so you'll soon be off, then?' Mr Fallowes said, the morning of the day they all went to lie among the tombs, the most glorious day of Hetty's life. Years ahead, when other days had overtaken it, she still felt the glow that almost brought tears in the goldness of summer sunlight, or saw a thick envelope and headed notepaper with her name on it or a blaze of snapdragons in a July flower-bed, or remembered a wide-open front door, her mother singing as she prepared the breakfast in the kitchen at the back.

Hetty had been hanging about on the front doorstep for several mornings now at eight o'clock. The polished brass doorknob, bell, letterbox, clean sitting-room curtains. The bees in the lilies. A salty breeze from the sand-hills.

Here came the postman, his loud voice calling.

'Hetty – letter from London.'

'I've got it,' she shouted, 'I've won it. The scholarship!' and she looked up into the gold dangles of the laburnum trees and thought: Oh, Eustace!

A crash from the kitchen and her mother on the step beside her. 'Oh, oh! You must run and tell your father. Oh – he's in the churchyard finishing Mary Bottomley's. Oh, I must get my coat.'

'Aren't you going to congratulate . . . ?' But Hetty let the sentence slide, examining intently the soft leaves of the laburnum tree, its olive-green trunk. Kids shouted along the street.

15

I've done it!

Her mother was running about inside the house and came out again wearing coat and hat, giving little whoops and screams. 'I won't be long.'

'But where are you going?'

'I must tell Mrs Tallentyre. We'll see about her Linda now! Then we'll have a cup of tea and you *must* write to Eustace. He knew you'd do it! You must go in and write at once.'

Hetty wandered to the churchyard and said to the grave-digger, 'I've done it, Pa.'

The toes of her old tennis shoes stood at the grave's lip on the level of her father's chin. He leaned on his half-moon spade, his back against the little beech ladder he needed to get in and out. 'You've won the money?'

'I have.'

'*Hamlet*?' he asked.

'I said I'd *won* it, Pa.'

'And I said *Hamlet*. The grave-diggers?'

'*Hamlet* had nothing to do with it. Will you listen to me!'

'I'm asking you the names of the grave-diggers in *Hamlet*, you who will shortly be giving three years of your life to English Language and Literature.'

'Pa. Don't play dumb. Don't you care? I've got the scholarship to London. A huge state scholarship. You won't be charged one penny.'

'Just as well. I haven't one. Names of the grave-diggers?'

'Oh, I don't know. Sid and Ernie. Adolf and Mussolini. Eustace got me the award, so you were *wrong*, and I have been a bitch to him!'

'You did it yourself,' he said and hop-skipped out of the grave and took her in his arms. 'The grave-diggers in *Hamlet* have no names. They are the only people of character and dalliance in Shakespeare who do not merit names. They are as nothing. They are the dregs of the world. They are called First and Second Grave-digger.'

'So what? Maybe his imagination packed in.'

'They are nothing. As your father is nothing. A failure. I don't

16

deserve you. You will forget me now.'

They stood embracing and Hetty thought: He always thinks of himself first . Everything comes back to himself. Self-referral is the blight of love.

'Don't you want to look at the letter, Pa?'

He was gazing away over her head. So she supposed. Such a tall man. Lean and long. She was proud of his looks. So was he. Oh, she loved him to hold her as much as she loathed Eustace to hold her. Did Eustace represent a disappointment after her father, and was the whole thing Freud? Oh, God! She broke from her father's haphazard arms.

'I am the Third Grave-digger,' he said. 'I too am nameless. I am of no consequence. I shall be remembered only for my daughter.'

'Don't talk such rubbish. Anyway, I'm not disappearing. You can come and see me. It's only a London College. You went to a better one.'

'Oh, did I?'

'Pa, come and see me. I'll introduce you to my prettiest friends.'

'Hardly,' he said. 'They'll be a scrubby lot in London. I was at Oxford, you know.'

'Yes. I do know. You walked out.'

'The times were out of joint. Where's your mother?'

They looked eye to eye and said together: 'Just gone to tell Mrs Tallentyre.'

'And here's the vicar,' she said and her father jumped back down into the grave. 'I'm off.'

'*Iustus. Iustus. In incipio IUSTUS. Et infinito IUSTUS. Sed in finito GRATIAS. IUSTUS HESTA MAGNIFICA*,' he sang.

Running away down the graveyard, away from the looming vicar, Hetty was now off to Una's house to see what had happened there. She heard her father's confident baritone rising from the grave, half saw the darkness of the vicar peering down into it, loved her father with passion, loved his singing, lurched within because maybe she was in love with her father as never, never would she be with anyone else, gulped briefly because she feared that she would never be sexually aroused in the natural way of things because of her father. Oh, he had ruined her! But he was

17

random and innocent and mad and she was sure he'd never read *King Lear*. She tripped and fell at the wicket gate in the church wall and saw her mother talking to Mrs Someone-or-other at Mrs Someone-or-other's gate. Heads and chins. Up and down. Their stout unbeautiful bodies.

'Just heard,' called her mother, 'Charlotte's nephew has done wonderfully.' As Hetty sidled near she cried, 'He's going to Otley and Mrs Bainbridge's niece has got into Ormskirk. You are all so *clever*!'

But when her mother came up to her and started to walk home with Hetty and saw her daughter's fierce face, she began to look frightened. 'Well, I know they aren't like you, dear. I know Ormskirk isn't like, well, where you're going, London University. But it's very nice for their mothers. And you know, Mrs Tallentyre is very nice. She'd heard about you. Top of everybody, she said. She was so surprised, dear. Nobody knew you were clever. She's got a present for you. It's something to take with you. I think it's for darning stockings.'

That midday they had ham (forty coupons). Then they had fruit salad. They had condensed milk. It was a celebration.

'I don't know how your mother does it,' said the vicar, who had stopped by and was licking about with a teaspoon. 'She is a wonderful woman.'

'But this is a celebration,' said Kitty Fallowes.

The vicar and Kitty scraped their plates.

The grave-digger closed his eyes.

All Hetty could think of was ink. There happened to be a bottle of blue-black Quink upon the table. Ink, and other things unlikely, were often to be found upon the Fallowes's board. Ink. Her father picked up the bottle. He undid the stopper. He closed his eyes and inhaled the sharp ink smell and his wife and the vicar pretended not to notice. Her father passed the bottle to Hetty. 'Life-blood,' he said. The ink smelled salty, ferrous. Like blood. It brought back to Hetty, and perhaps to her father in times past, examination rooms, the joy of easy questions, the knowledge that all the work had paid off. 'I can do all this!' No joy like it. Page after page of wet, salt ink, blotted, legible, confident. It was ink that had freed her. Blessed ink. Ink for immortality. Stronger than history. History itself. There will always have to be ink. 'Yes? What? Oh, sorry?'

'I was saying, Hetty,' said the vicar, 'that we are all hoping this scholarship business won't go to your head. I hope you'll never forget how much of it you owe to your mother.' Her father held the ink bottle out over the table. For a moment Hetty thought that he was about to use it as a libation on the fruit salad. 'And I hope that you will never forget what it would have meant to your mother to have been granted an education like yours. She would have been granted a very different life. A fulfilled life. With her own money.'

'She could have,' said Hetty. 'Women did.'

'But I had mother,' said Mrs Fallowes.

The ink bottle hung above the tinned yellow cling peaches and was at length withdrawn and placed back on the table cloth. The grave-digger hung in obeisance over it and examined the reflection of his left eye in the magic pool of winking ink. Then he stirred the ink with his teaspoon.

The vast vicar flung himself about in his chair, helped himself to more fruit salad and poured condensed milk (thirty-five coupons) round and round his pudding bowl from the flowery tin. 'Your mother has given up a very great deal for you, Hetty.'

Her mother looked down at her pretty arms, humble and assuaged, as though she was lapped in real cream.

The unspoken words around the table had nothing at all to do with Hetty. They said that her mother had married badly. And madly.

The vicar took her mother's little hand. 'I am proud of you, Kitty. She is so very much your daughter.'

Oh, bugger off, said Hetty. In her heart.

She slammed out, found her bike and went off to see Una, who was outside the back door of her house in the alley, her bike standing on its handlebars surrounded by sprockets and valves, pumps, spanners and chains. Girton's new hope was wearing the railway lad's trousers and a football shirt of her long-dead father when he'd been in the Oundle First XV. Her face was all oil.

'It's good, isn't it? Shall we go and see how Lieselotte got on? Is that your letter? Let's see it.'

The letter confirming Una's economic security at Cambridge for the next three years was as streaked with oil as her face.

'Don't you care about it? Aren't you going to put it in a glass case?'

'Oh, it's great,' said Una. 'Big surprise.'

'Oh, come on, Una. Everyone knew you'd get it. You and Lieselotte didn't even have to try.'

'Oh no? Anyway I was only offered a place at Cambridge and a county grant. You've got a state award.'

'London's not Cambridge,' said Hetty. 'London's a rag-bag.'

'Well, stay at school another year and try for Cambridge, then. You're not eighteen yet.'

'Don't be daft. I'm not pushing my luck. They've probably made a mistake and there's another Hester Fallowes rolling about on a floor somewhere in floods of tears and all her relations committing suicide. Anyway, I'll like London. I liked it at the interview. Even being met by Aunty Norah and going all the way out to Pinner for the night because it wouldn't cost anything but the tube fare. I bought a dress in Oxford Street for two pounds. Green slime. Wonderful.'

'Yes, I've seen it. You'll have all your aunties down to see you. All the Café Lonsdale. All that sightseeing. You'll have to take all of them to see Buckingham Palace and the crown jewels and the Great Vine at Hampton Court. And the Zoo. You'll have to take the vicar to the Zoo. He'll treat you to a bread roll at Church House and you'll have to take him round the lions.'

They left their bikes and took a bus, for Lieselotte lived five miles away at Shields West with two Quaker people called the Stonehouses who had no children of their own. It was not clear how she had fetched up with the Stonehouses in 1939, but they were said to be very left-wing and unconventional and thoughtful about politics. Mr Stonehouse had been wounded in the First World War in the Quaker Ambulance Service and now spent most

20

of his time in a not very comfortable Lloyd-loom chair with books and pacifist pamphlets about his feet. Mrs Stonehouse had the pale Quaker face that seems always to be attending to a secret voice. Blue eyes gazed over your head.

She came padding now into the sitting-room carrying a small tray crowded with mugs of Ovaltine. Lieselotte was sitting knitting on the brass coal-box with the beaten metalwork scene of St George and the Dragon, the only vigorous thing in the room, and her special perch. Beside her was a neatly laid but unlit fire. The room was warm and swam with sunlight and cleanliness. Hetty stirred the mushroom-coloured depths of her Ovaltine and thought about Lieselotte, who had known since Christmas that she had won a top award at Girton, and had now landed the grant to match it.

'Well, nobody's surprised,' said Hetty. 'You never tell us anything, but I bet you came out wonderfully in the interview.'

'She never said one word,' said Mrs Stonehouse. 'Not a word to either of us.' She looked at Lieselotte with great affection.

'I didn't say many things at the interview at all,' said Lieselotte. 'I thought the German accent might not be very popular.'

'But it's a German *Jewish* accent.' Hetty was still embarrassed because she was ignorant of everything to do with Lieselotte and uneasy about saying 'Jewish'. When Lieselotte had arrived in their midst with not a word of explanation, and hardly a word of English, and fat, plain and inarticulate, there had been a general unspoken belief that she was some sort of neutral German who had got into England by accident and couldn't be sent back. 'Jews' meant little except they were people you never met and couldn't know. There was, of course, Jesus, but you couldn't know Jesus socially, because He was the Son of God. Other Jews didn't want to know you socially and made you feel scruffy.

Lieselotte, 1939–1945, had made no friends at the school. None. She had sat at the back of the class producing perfect work, speaking French fast and easily and quite differently from the French teacher, who never corrected her. Each day she had plodded three times back and forth between the Stonehouses' little villa and the school. Each day she had gone back home for

21

lunch because she had to eat funny food. It was inconceivable that Lieselotte would ever take a bike to bits on the pavement or kiss in corners at school dances, or walk the lanes on Sundays hand in hand with a man. Lieselotte was apart. She was in some way full. Sated. It was as if she had come long ago to the end of experience. The bold English girls on whose empire the sun never set frolicked and giggled about her. They had heard somehow that, at sixteen, Lieselotte had had to go to the police station to be registered as 'an enemy alien', but they had never asked questions. They never offered a confidence and she seemed not to mind. They did not let themselves dwell on her and they rejected the idea that it was only the shell of her who sat there at the back of the class, smiling. Only in the last year when work and aspirations had drawn the clever ones together had she somehow become part of the trio. But even so, she was cautious of commitment. And so were Una and Hetty.

'She makes me feel silly,' said Hetty's mother, 'but I always feel silly with clever people. Except, of course, with Eustace. Eustace draws one out.'

'Now, that you must not say,' said the vicar, patting her wrist. 'Cleverness is nothing. It has no part in the soul.'

Watching Lieselotte today upon the militant coal-box, Hetty saw suddenly something not at all to do with cleverness. Some hint of Lieselotte, some prop withdrawn to leave her straight and strong. Something completed. Something unconquerable.

A few hours later, in the churchyard grasses, Hetty was saying, 'Lieselotte?'

'Yes?' She knitted on.

'What happened to your mother?'

She knitted.

'*Someone* must have told you. Has nobody ever asked you – not even the Stonehouses?'

'Quakers don't ask a lot of questions.'

'D'you find them, well, you know – a bit boring? Jews are supposed to be so, you know, argumentative. Vibrant. Hetty was trying to imagine the Stonehouses being vibrant. 'I mean, didn't they get excited when you got the letter from Girton?'

'No,' Lieselotte said. 'No, not excited,' and she began to laugh. Her laughter was very rare and not particularly attractive. It was spluttery and damp. Her eyes streamed. 'James shook hands with me and Rosie kissed me and then we had a bit of silence.'

'It wouldn't have been like that if, you know, if you'd been at home in Germany?'

'At home?' she said, and her accent suddenly reverted to long ago. 'Oh, shot *op*, Hetty. I am counting.'

Una and Hetty lay still in the grass as Lieselotte counted stitches.

'There's a queer thing walking up this grass stalk,' said Una. 'It's like a bullet. It's far too heavy for it. It is not intelligent. It ought to hurry up and split.'

'Split?'

'Into a moth. A great big angry leathery moth.'

'Thirty-two. Finish. Good,' said Lieselotte.

'Why are you still knitting air-force blue when the war's been over more than a year?' asked Una.

'There are still the armed forces.'

'Yes, but they're mostly home.'

'There are pockets in the Far East. There is great need in Germany.'

'They won't want woollen socks in the Far East. They won't want air-force blue in Germany.'

'Do Quakers always use Christian names, Lieselotte?'

'No. They use given names.'

'You could change to an English name!'

'I'm a Jew. And I am a German.'

'Maybe you'll become something else at Cambridge.'

'Like what? A Seventh-day Adventist? Oh, Hetty, Hetty! Oh, child.'

'I'm two months older than you.'

'You are child in the womb.'

'You were born grown-up, Lieselotte,' said Una.

'Hetty is clever, so,' said Lieselotte. 'And for all I know she is an angel, so. But she is babe unborn and child of babe unborn.'

'So, so, so,' said Hetty. 'If you mean my mother, I couldn't agree more.'

Una turned on her stomach, and her face now almost grazed the flaking oval disc on the side of the tombstone that told the tale of an eighteenth-century dame and her brood. 'D'you know what it says on this, Het? It's Latin. Come on.'

'It says the geyser died,' said Hetty, 'and his wife died, but before she died she had twelve children and they all died, and before *he* died he married again and the new one had eight children (he was quite a goer). And then *she* died and she was still only, let's see, twenty-seven. Nice sort of life. We're pretty lucky. Makes you want no children. They must have been scared crazy in the eighteenth century when they got, you know, pregnant. I'm not having any children. Even now, it's dangerous. And disgusting. Even if they don't die.'

'I shall marry,' said Lieselotte, 'and I shall have many children. And they will not die.'

The late afternoon sun was as hot as ever. 'That was thunder,' said Una. 'We're all going to get soaked. We'd better run for a bus.'

Lieselotte was catching a different bus from Hetty and Una, on the opposite side of the road.

Hetty and Una rolled out of the flattened grass, leaving in it for a short time the impression of their narrow bodies, like the setts of hares. Lieselotte wound up her knitting and put it in the linen bag. Big splashes of thundery rain began to fall about the churchyard. Hetty thought: We shall probably never come back to this place.

When they reached the road Hetty called across to Lieselotte at the bus stop opposite. She felt brave and affectionate with happiness. 'Sorry, Lieselotte. I didn't mean to ask about your mother.'

Then her bus and Una's came swishing up in the rain, and they jumped in and Hetty swung out on the bar as the bus swept away, calling again to Lieselotte, who was struggling with a queer grey mackintosh that looked like wet tissue-paper and kept ballooning out around her fat body. There was the impression of glittering glasses, and wildness. Lieselotte was slapping and slapping at the mackintosh, which wouldn't stay down over her stout legs. She didn't look up.

'She looks like a grey boiled sweet,' said Una. 'We won't be seeing much more of her, you know.'

'Why not?'

'She's cleverer than us. She is a Jew. She'll find her own sort. She's somebody, Lieselotte is. She'll soon forget us.'

'But we've just started knowing her.'

'You can't really *know* her. She's a Jew and we're not.'

'How d'you know we can't?'

'It's common knowledge. Jews have a secret life and they've drawn tighter together now. After, you know, Belsen and that.'

They both turned their minds from this unbelievable word. They had seen the film. They had watched in silence. They hadn't referred to it again. A blank.

And I have secrets, too, thought Hetty. My mother and the vicar, and my mother and Eustace. And my feelings in my father's arms. And sex and that. And—

But she could not on this happy day think of anything else worth calling secret. Not much. The hollow of the two wars that had shaped her. Maybe the deep thing she felt for Una, and the depth of her sadness about her own and Una's Pa.

3

The Lonsdale Café was the Versailles of Shields East, the melting pot for ideas and discoveries, the epicentre of the post-war world. It was a long, grey room with a dirty glass ceiling lately rescued from swathes of black-out crepe, a dusty piano at one end with candlesticks on metal brackets, one broken. The small tables still boasted table cloths made of cloth, though very thin, and there was, intermittently, a waitress of great age, like the last ethnic Tasmanian waddling between the tables in a black dress worn shiny and a frilled apron grown small over the war years. It had been intended for a fly young girl long gone off to munitions in turban, red lipstick and slacks.

To this establishment there came now, several times a week, in peacetime again, their other duties done, respectable survivors of the old town. They gathered here partly from a hunger they had not felt during the war. The bottled coffee looked like gravy browning but cost only a penny-ha'penny. The penny cakes were so hard they bounced, but they were metaphors for the past. The women in their shabby pre-war coats brought with them gloves which they laid upon the table like passports. They wore felt hats with a small bird or a feather or a piece of painted fish bone in the hatband. They lifted their cups with little fingers raised, as courtesans of the Regency, a secret sign, and sat discussing one another.

Most of the women of one particularly large group were Mrs

Fallowes's friends. Her friends were multitudinous, though none knew her as Hetty did. All at the Lonsdale sang a litany – as Mrs Fallowes did too – on all their friends, all appearing to concur until one or other got up to go home. Then the theme would be taken up again but played in a different key. 'No love lost in the Lonsdale' was a refrain of the grave-digger, but in fact there was no love to lose. Not actually *love*, unless it was the love born of cemented experience, love maybe of their own presence there. 'It is only contingency,' said the grave-digger, 'contingency and hats.'

But there was one thing every woman there agreed upon and that was Kitty Fallowes. A very nice, pretty-faced, good woman, a real friend. Too religious, which must be hard on her daughter these days, but somehow it suited her. The atmosphere in that house of course was very intense, Kitty often falling on her knees and weeping. She had been seen through the glass door of the vestibule, though that vicar was obviously a help to her. '*Obviously!*' They looked hard at one another. 'Now, *Mr* Fallowes—' There would then be a rolling of eyes. A husband was meant to be a bread-winner, a man who each day went to work at a certain time and returned home at five o'clock to a properly laid-up meal and a quiet evening with the wireless. Mr Fallowes had never stepped inside an office and was always covered in earth.

One of the reasons that the Lonsdale liked Kitty Fallowes was that she really did feel most deeply for them all, especially about their health. She rejoiced with those who rejoiced, though there hadn't been a lot of that about except on VE and VJ days, which somehow had been very flat. Each time it had been very disappointing weather for the street-parties.

But what she did, most superbly, Kitty Fallowes, was to weep with those that wept. As others are drawn to pleasure, Kitty Fallowes was drawn to death and dying and was an over-enthusiastic predictor of the first manifestations of both. She prepared you. Magnificently. It was said by the unkind that she'd been known to adapt her clothes for mourning for those still living. Like the eighteenth-century tombstones, she gathered to herself the fullest register of misfortunes and reacted to new information about them with very comforting excitement.

She always thought ahead, and it was always on somebody else's behalf. Her Birthday Book was thick as a train timetable. She could give only modest birthday presents – a card of pins, a handkerchief of her grandmother's, a few bread units and once, in 1945, a potato; but she never forgot. Kitty Fallowes was profoundly, most sombrely religious but, for one who looked so confidently towards the release from the sorrows of this world, she was put into an intensity of concern by small disorders. A shivering fit was always a rigor. A bad cold was a congestion of the lungs. In the air raids she had been stalwart and when it came to real sickness or a death of someone close to her she was almost nonchalant. Yet everyday indispositions were as the Black Death and, the more insignificant her acquaintance, the more assiduous she was in enquiring for them and reporting on them.

'Most of it's boredom,' said her husband. 'Imaginary illnesses. In the raids we all had to jump to it.' When her brother was killed at Arnhem Mrs Fallowes had been magnificent, and quite stern with the man's poor wife. But again, 'She didn't like either of them much,' said Mr Fallowes to Hetty. Mrs Fallowes spoke of her own ill health, indeed of everybody's, of life itself, as a treacherous river on which we are flung at birth and must struggle against until this transient miserable body, the soul's guest, merges properly into the sea of heaven.

These beliefs Kitty did not discuss directly in the Lonsdale Café, where she spent most of the time talking about Hetty, of whom she was tremendously proud and tremendously jealous. Mrs Fallowes' poor health as a child (the local doctor was famous for prescribing only glasses of water) had meant that she had had almost no education, and like many High Church women of the time, filled with the idea of making their bodies a living sacrifice and trying not to think of sex except as a method of pleasing a husband, she had thrown her passions into motherhood and Church ritual. And penitence. And Confession. And 'being unworthy'. 'Unworthy of gathering up the crumbs under Thy table,' she always intoned in church beside the kneeling Hetty with desolation, even relish. She had been brought up by holy spinster aunts of a certain social standing who had held the civilised world together in Shields East, and these long-dead women were still of great importance to her. The hazy memory of them among the *aficionados* of the Lonsdale Café, and her lack of a Yorkshire accent, set her a little apart from the other ladies there, who were mainly people most regrettably not born in the town.

On the morning of the letter about Hetty's great award, Mrs Fallowes set off for the Lonsdale at the first opportunity to inform the known world.

'I don't suppose you want to come with me?' she asked Hetty as she powdered her nose with a puff.

'You're right.'

'They'd all love to see you, you know. Miss Bland's so fond of you and her sister's very ill.'

'No thanks. I have to write letters.'

'Letters could wait for one morning. You do know that Elsie Richardson's going blind?'

'I have to write straight off and tell the College. If she's blind why don't you just pretend I'm there?'

'Oh, I'm sure they'll hold on to your place if they don't hear till the weekend. It's library half-closing and Miss Kipling will be there. Now, you do owe *her* something, Hetty. And Mrs Brownley's always wanted a daughter, poor childless soul, though there wasn't ever much hope – well, of course he was gassed – but she's always been so interested in you. And she has that bowel trouble and a really terrible leg. Whoever needs a letter so soon?'

'Oh, well, I suppose – Eustace.'

'Oh. Eustace. Well, yes, of course you must write to Eustace, if he'll ever get it on the Salisbury Plain. I'll tell them that you'll be going round to see them all, shall I?'

'What, all of them?'

'*All* the women?' said the grave-digger. 'She has to call round on all those women? Whatever for?'

'Well, they'll want to congratulate her. They're very fond of her.'

'Yes, but is she fond of them?'

'That is not a Christian attitude, Malcolm. And I expect they'll want to . . . give her little things.'

'Well, now you're talking.'

'Sounds like a layette,' said Hetty. 'A fallen maiden.'

'That will do, Hetty. It's a formality, going to call on people. Formalities are going. We used to give the telegraph boy ten shillings in the war, when it was good news. Though it wasn't very often. I think, Malcolm, we ought to have given the postman a ten-shilling note.'

'I haven't got a ten-shilling note. Not till the next commission. Have a look at Mrs Brownley's leg.'

'You're a cold man, Malcolm. Oh, I wish we had a telephone. There's not a call-box till the town clock. Now, *write* to Eustace, Hetty, and come down to the Lonsdale later.'

But Hetty had disappeared.

'Well, just at this moment she is writing to tell her boyfriend,' she told the assembled company, while the old waitress creaked among them with the thick white cups. 'Oh, well, yes, of course. She's thrilled. And so of course are we.'

'Is that the officer?'

'Well, Eustace is not exactly an officer. He's what is called "officer material", I'm told. There's not much time for these national-service boys to become officers.'

'My sister's Roy is,' said someone.

'People think he must be an officer because he's so tall. He's been a great help to her. With the exams. He has very nice manners. D'you know, he writes letters to me as well. It makes him seem part of the family. He's very good with people of our age. Mine and Malcolm's, though I'm afraid Malcolm doesn't care for him so much as I do, but then Malcolm was in the trenches. No, Eustace would do anything for us. He cuts the grass. Of course, we've given him a lot of hospitality.'

'Is it serious?' asked the public librarian, Miss Kipling.

'Oh, no. Just *great* friends. It's early days.'

'Is he well-off?' asked Mrs Legge.

'Oh, I've no idea. The family's in commerce.' (She had found out that Eustace's father managed a hat shop in Felixstowe.) 'I mean, Hetty is only at the very start of her life.'

'I've no belief in women with careers,' came from the mound of rags in the new mechanical wheelchair that was Mrs Eaves. 'It shrinks the womb.'

'The one worry I do have about Eustace,' said Mrs Fallowes, ignoring this interesting concept for the moment, 'but I don't say so to Hester of course, is that he doesn't look very strong. He has that high colour.'

'Does he cough?'

'No, I've not noticed a cough, but, yes, he is what you'd call tubercular-looking. I'd not think that he'd live very long.'

'Can Hetty cook?'

'I beg your pardon, dear? Oh, cook. Well, you know, none of them can these days.'

'Well, we should all be watching our vitamin intake, cook or not,' said Mrs Brownley, a very nice woman who was always presenting people with healthful things, especially now that foreign fruits were occasionally available. At the moment she was very taken up with grapefruit.

'I bought this for Hetty,' she said. 'A little gift of congratulation. I *knew* she'd do it! You'd be surprised how far you can stretch a grapefruit, if you present it well. First you *prise* it out of the skin, if you can find one of those curved little knives we all had once. Yes. And then you *squeeze* the flesh. Yes. And let it lie all night with the skins sliced up on top of them – it makes all the difference if they're on top. And then you pour it all – not the skins, all the nice mush – into a screw-top jam-jar. And then you shake it. Very hard. With a little saccharine.'

'Is it the Classics?' asked Miss Kipling.

'The Classics?'

'Is Hetty going to read Classics?'

'Oh, yes. I think so. Almost all of them.'

'I'm glad,' said Miss Eaves. 'I'm very glad she's not passing over the old Classics. I really loved *Jane Eyre*. I thought she was doing something boring like Latin and Greek. I hope she'll read Trollope, too.'

'And if you have a refrigerator,' said Mrs Brownley, 'which I am lucky enough to have, John working at the ICI, you can store it for several days. And you'll find it deliciously cold. I hear that Jewish girl is very ill.'

'Lieselotte?' Mrs Fallowes' eyes grew large with alarm. 'Oh, no. No, she can't be. She was perfectly all right yesterday; they were all together somewhere, celebrating. All the afternoon. Oh dear, ill? Will it be all the emotion, d'you think? And not a word from Germany, you know. There's never been confirmation, you know, one way or another. Most of them have heard by now. There must be someone left who could lay claim to her. A whole year. Oh, ill?'

'Well, she's got something, or so I heard. She may not be exactly ill. A cold. Sitting in grass and waiting for buses in the rain. She's an indoor girl of course. Hardly goes out. Jews are supposed to have strong constitutions, but they're not outdoor types.'

'We could never get her into the Guides,' said Hilda Fletcher (and thought: And Hetty only turned up twice).

'But she's German too. And Germans are outdoor types whatever else they're not. I can't think how she comes to let it be known she's German. You'd think she'd have said Austrian. I expect it's living with Quakers: they're so truthful.'

'There won't be much interest in good food *there*,' said Mrs Brownley. 'There'll be very small helpings.'

'But she never did look a *well* girl,' said somebody else, as though Lieselotte Klein were already dead.

4

'Oh, Hetty? Hetty? Are you about?' called her mother. 'I'm afraid Lieselotte's been taken very ill. It sounds like a severe flu. She caught it waiting for a bus. Oh dear – just when everything's going right for her at last.'

'She's tough,' said Hetty.

'And Mrs Brownley's sent you a grapefruit. In a bottle.'

'What an odd reward for gaining a university place,' said the grave-digger. 'Oughtn't she to have sent it to Lieselotte?'

'Yes. Perhaps you should take it round to Lieselotte, dear.'

'No, thanks, it's mine,' said Hetty. 'I like grapefruit. I can count the grapefruits coming into this house the past five years. Nil. I don't know where she gets them.'

'Perhaps she sells her body,' said the grave-digger.

'Lieselotte's had plenty of Ovaltine,' said Hetty. 'It was pretty well on tap. Covered in skin. Oh, OK, I'll go and see her, but she was fine yesterday.'

'Well, don't stand too close. She may have been harbouring something and it will have become released with relaxation after the good news. Oh – and *did* you write to Eustace?'

Dear Eustace,

Thanks for all your letters. I've been meaning to write but got rather half-hearted. I'm glad you don't put your letters to me in the same envelope as the ones you write to my mother, which she hides in her lingerie.

I've got a big state scholarship so that I can take up the award to London. Nice letter. Came on posh paper. A lot of it is thanks to you. So thanks.

Thanks very much, Eustace. You did a lot for me.

Great excitement here and I've been given a bottle of crushed grapefruit.

I hope the survival course went well. I didn't know you'd have to do that sort of thing in the Pay Corps but I suppose it does take some surviving.

I'm thinking of going away for a bit, and I'll let you know for how long when I have it organised. It will be for as long as possible. I haven't mentioned it here yet, so please don't you, when you send your next letter to my mother. I've realised I have a lot of work to do so that they don't find out that, apart from what you taught me, I'm practically illiterate.

Love, Het.

She sat looking with interest at what she had written, wondering at the louche, confident, uncaring girl it revealed. She was surprised at her plan of escape and wondered where the words had come from.

Going away for a holiday, am I? Correspondence certainly clarifies the mind, she thought. I have even remembered that I have the money.

She wondered which girl Eustace had fallen for, the easygoing letter girl or the humble maiden in the lanes. He would not find her style in this letter unexpected, for she had always sounded off like this in letters; but the physical presence of the Hetty he knew was the silent bluestocking of Sunday afternoons. He had never commented on the stark, uncaring Hetty of the letters. She had sent similar ones before. Sometimes she wondered if he ever read them.

There was a mystery about Eustace. A dichotomy. He played parts, she rather suspected. The pedant, the wooer, the grandee and the Minstrel Boy who to the Wars had Gone. 'Ye gods,' as the grave-digger would say, 'who was he?'

And who the hell am I? So thought this morning's common, flashy Hetty. I'm off to Una's.

She biked round to her friend, pausing on the way beside the litter-basket outside the post-office, the post-office windows empty except for newspapers and fly-papers. She went in and bought a penny-ha'penny stamp, stuck it on Eustace's letter and then chucked the letter in the litter-bin. 'Well, I have written it,' she said, and rode off. Then she swerved round, circled back, leaned over from the bike and retrieved it. Then she binned it again.

She sat in Una's kitchen soon, and they shared the grapefruit between two small bowls, carefully measuring the juice. Una's mother passed through the kitchen from her hair-dressing salon at the front of the house. The salon had once been the seat of the doctor's surgery and still held the whiff of anxiety and prognosis. It was not a busy hairdresser's, since it was claimed that Mrs Vane was self-taught and some of her clients were a little afraid of her, for she was an uncommunicative, mocking woman with gypsy eyes. But she was cheap.

'We're going out,' said Una, 'to Lieselotte. She's ill, or something.'

Mrs Vane hummed a tune from her lost, *thé-dansant* years.

'We ought to take her something.'

'Whatever for?' said Hetty. 'We never have before. You sound like my mother. We're not old.'

'Yeah, but we're not kids. And Germans are generous.'

'She's never given us anything,' said Hetty.

They finished their grapefruit and pedalled the five miles to Shields West, where they propped the bikes against the Stone-house kerb beside the seafront. Mrs Stonehouse opened the door and, exactly as before, shook both of them by the hand and stood aside for them to pass. Mr Stonehouse seemed not to have moved since their last visit, but there was now nobody seated on the coal-box. Mr Stonehouse laid aside the *Daily Herald*, rose, then he also shook hands, and silence found its way among them.

'We heard that Lieselotte isn't very well,' said Una at last.

'She is quite well,' said Mrs Stonehouse, 'but unfortunately she isn't here any more. She has been rehabilitated.'

'What – to Hamburg? She can't. Not in one day!'

'It is a repatriation of a kind, but not to Hamburg. No. She has simply gone away. The Award letter was quite a coincidence. Nothing to do with it. We had heard nothing about repatriation, but I think the Jewish organisations – the *Kindertransport* – may have been in touch with her. She has been getting a few letters that she has never explained.'

'But she was with us on *Monday*! She was in the churchyard, knitting. She never *said*.'

'I don't think she can have known it would be so soon. I think it is to do with something that's been discovered about her family. It was not for us to ask, we felt.'

'But what if it had happened in the middle of her exams?'

'Something to do with America,' said Mrs Stonehouse. 'A visa has been procured somehow.'

'I don't think the exams really came into it,' said her husband. 'We must just wait to hear from her.'

The quiet house that had protected Lieselotte from her early years of nightmare blazed with summer light from the sea. At the front door again, Mrs Stonehouse allowed herself to say, 'It really is very sudden. We're trying to get used to it.'

She opened the door wider and wider, holding the handle tight. 'We're *trying* to get used to it, but we feel very . . . diminished without her. And very sad.'

'Well, I should think so!' said Hetty. 'Well, it's *mad*. It can't be for ever? She'll probably walk in again tonight.'

'York,' said Mrs Stonehouse. 'They were taking her to York.'

'Well, it sounds like the Gestapo. But at least it's not far. It must be a temporary thing, York.'

'She was up, packed and away with them. All in a few minutes. She's left her books, and most of her clothes. Very nice people, but rather bossy. They weren't Quakers.'

'York?'

'We did just wonder if they'd said "New York".'

They stood on the doorstep again, saying goodbye, the sandy, salty wind blowing right through the house and out of the open back door, where sheets and pillowcases were galloping on a clothes-line in the wind. It was as if Lieselotte had been gathered up, laundered and would soon be folded away.

'She's left her mac,' said Hetty, seeing the dead grey tissue-paper bird hanging from a hook in the passage.

'She didn't care for it,' said Mrs Stonehouse. 'It was mine. I don't care for it very much either. I think she's going to be very well-provided-for now. There seemed to be talk of money, though they were all chattering away in German, which of course we have been unable to do with her. At first she just listened and looked . . . well, quite vacant. And then she began to stumble into it. And then she began to talk quite fast. She quite lit up. We heard a different voice. A new person. An excited person.'

'Oh, it's going to be a shock all round,' said Hetty.

'Yes. Yes. It *is* sudden.' Mrs Stonehouse was bright-eyed, but tearless. 'Especially having had no children of our own. I forgot to ask you if you'd like some Ovaltine?'

'Wait till Ma hears this.' Hetty was shouting vulgarly back over her shoulder along the seafront, biking home. 'She'll go over the church tower and head-first down through the glass roof of the Lonsdale. They'll all have her raped and kidnapped before the first scone. I don't know what to do now, do you? What do you want to do?'

'We could go to the pictures,' said Una.

They both knew that there was a repeat at the Palace of the Belsen film. Hetty thought she ought to go. It was on before the Deanna Durbin and she might be able to take it this time, especially since Lieselotte's relations seemed to have turned up. She'd only seen five minutes of it before, when her mother had felt faint and said they both had to come out. It had been like a sixteenth-century Masque of Death, quite unreal.

'The vicar says that the Belsen film is faked,' she said. 'He says you can fake anything on the films. He was in Intelligence in the First World War.'

'What does your father say?'

37

'He wouldn't go near it. He's not actually very good at that sort of thing.'

'We could go round and see some of the teachers, and say thank you and so on,' said Una.

'Mine will probably be in hospital being treated for shock.'

'Or I could start my reading list. Have you had one?'

'Yes. It'll take about eleven years.'

'Mine from Girton has nothing to do with Physics. Who's E. M. Forster?'

'He's an old pansy who writes about India. He doesn't write anything at all now. He just lives in Cambridge thinking of the hopelessness and sadness of the Empire. You'll probably meet him.'

'Can't wait,' said Una. 'Well, I might go and find Ray. He's off at twelve today. We could get some miles in.'

Pedalling alone towards home, Hetty stopped beside the post office litter-bin, which was almost empty, litter being in short supply. The letter to Eustace, sealed and stamped among the empty Gold Flake cigarette packets, looked conspicuous. So she sighed, and took it out.

Hetty knew that this was the moment to abandon Eustace. If it was a novel, she thought, this is the perfectly appropriate, most natural development. At this point the heroine should have the courage to leave her grateful little-girl self behind and start again towards maturity. What's more, she thought, to hell with novels, it was guilt about her false position with Eustace that was flooding and spoiling these days of glory.

But if this *were* a novel, she thought, it would be hard not to end it with Eustace. Everything about her meeting him had been so right, so perfectly timed. She had at seventeen loved a man – a man of nearly twenty-two – who had loved her, and was right for her in every way.

And tall.

And except for the Adam's apple he looked great. Such lovely hands, although they did hang down, a bit like seal's flippers. And his nails were always so clean. And he sang so beautifully and his poetry was almost exactly like Walter de la Mare's. And he had been so pleased when she'd agreed that he was like Sassoon, and often asked her if she still thought so, and she had always said yes; though somehow you couldn't see Eustace tally-hoing on a horse. Or in the trenches, at ease with his men. And loving them. Deeply, deeply.

And Eustace thought she was wonderful. He had said so, which nobody else had ever done and maybe never would. There'd been plenty of kissing in Hetty's life, at church socials and with soldiers in back streets after Saturday-night hops which her parents knew nothing about: but nobody had ever *said* anything. Just mauled and gobbled.

But there had been one moonlit night when she was fifteen on the way home from a Bible meeting (*Hosea*) and in the local park, with the railings all gone to make Spitfires. She had been in the rose garden with a devout sort of boy from Corporation Road, and they had kissed and kissed to the accompaniment of the Messerschmitts rumbling overhead in the dark towards Tyneside. The park had stood open ever since 1941 when the firemen had not been able to get in to deal with an unexploded bomb that had landed in the bowling green and turned it to a pond. By 1943 every member of the Bible class came home along the park and melted into the bushes, except for Hetty, who wouldn't go beyond the more conspicuous park benches. Other, notoriously sexy, Bible students had like nesting birds made the bushes heave and chirrup. A dirty girl from Muriel Street had once told Hetty, over school dinner, that Betty Grangely went on the sand-hills at night, and sometimes in the daytime, with soldiers.

'She can't! They're mined.'

'They're mined all right, but I've seen them at it. Going at it like tortoises.'

'Tortoises!'

Betty Grangely had disappeared in the Upper Fourth to become an usherette and was now to be seen walking slowly about the town with a big black pram.

'God has answered almost every prayer I have ever made,' Mrs Fallowes said all through the war years, 'except one: that we might somehow have afforded to send you to a private boarding school, Hetty. I know that your school is respectable and all-girls, and the only boys you know are the ones at the Bible class, but it is so *very* mixed. I'd like you to have met girls who had nannies and ponies, and to have sent you to school with them in the country. It is what I always expected. I'm afraid I was never good at finding money, and some such very extraordinary people are.'

In the early years Kitty had written all this to Josephine Dixon, the godmother, but it had appeared to hold no interest for her. She was at the time back in Windsor (Mr Fallowes said in order to move in royal circles).

'I went to a private boarding school in the country,' said the grave-digger. 'Look where it got me.'

'It got you the confidence to do exactly what you wanted. *Always*,' Kitty said. 'Reflective idleness is what it gave you. But have I ever complained? I have not. I have *never* wanted money for myself. And I married a gentleman; and I never saw another man so – d'you know your father was *beautiful*, Hetty, *beautiful*. Most gloriously handsome. When he was a boy.'

'You've told me, Ma.'

'And I believe that the English country-gentleman has always been the backbone of the country. Look at Jane Austen.'

'There were some poisonous country-gentlemen in Jane Austen,' said Mr Fallowes.

Hetty met no other country-gentlemen in Shields East except her father, however, and had made do with the Bible class on the park benches.

'"Look thy last on all things lovely, every hour",' said her father, 'and I do do a job. I am a grave-digger.'

'But your father was a contented, *delightful* country-gentleman, Malcolm.'

'My father was an old soak. I thank God he left me no money so that Het has been able to attend a good state school.'

Hetty sometimes wondered how much her father and mother knew about tortoises. She was aware that there had been difficulties in that area 'because of the trenches'. She had met a few boarding-school girls in her time, when the little town was stiff with the gentry before the war, and they had always struck her as sly and lubricious, making mysterious allusions, despite nannies and ponies. They seemed to have slender home lives and to fester with grubby school secrets. And here she was. Here she was now. This red-gold day here she was in the warm wind, needing a sail no more, biking along beside the midsummer park, Eustace's letter still in her bike basket and knowing she was as yet not even a beginner at love. She dropped the bike behind the park-keeper's bothy and set off to wander the walks and borders of her schooldays, so hugely overgrown by the kind neglect of the war. Along the dark rail-side walk she went, beside the asters and purple heliotropes, through the rose gardens where some papery roses still swung heavy on almost leafless branches; past the peeling cricket pavilion to the ornamental lake that wound away out of sight beyond the boat-house. The park flower-beds had once held ranks of weedless wallflowers and antirrhinums and chrysanthemums, trussed tight with raffia. In the war they had been left to droop and slouch, die or survive, make countless common friends. Clouds of willowherb and dandelion floated around them and the once-pruned ornamental trees had grown wild above. Lofty sycamores gloomed over the tennis courts, which had become a cracked green asphalt pool in a dark wood. Their surfaces were like creeping jenny lying treacherous on water.

There was nobody but Hetty in the park today. The old tennis nets were tightly rolled between the posts like rusted-through wire netting. The smell of lavender in the crazy flower borders beyond the courts was fit to make you weep. Tennis at fifteen with semi-boyfriends in the twilight. Gone.

She walked along until she came to the boat-house. Two or three swans idled on the water behind it and watched her. She sat down on the jetty and the wood was warm against the backs of her thighs. She looked at her legs stuck out in front of her and wondered if they were improving. She would probably have to give up wearing flannel shorts in London. Beyond her quite nice feet lapped the artificial lake. Along the winding banks lay tumbling artificial rocks, like hard black sponges. The sun blazed, the old dinghies knocked exhaustedly against each other, their oars locked together at the gunnels with an iron handcuff.

The boatman was nowhere to be seen, for it was midday and he was Boozer Bainbridge who'd had a bad First War at Ypres. Peg-leg. Glass eye.

Hetty stepped into a boat, rattled its handcuff till it fell apart, shoved off with the brittle oar and drifted out on the lake. The swans turned calm backs.

It was a shallow lake and muddy, and she easily put the boat about, prow west-facing, and rowed quietly out of sight between the wilderness shores.

As far as she could see on either side showers of roses tumbled down into the water. Forests of dahlias imitated sunsets, phloxes shone like sweet fire among spikes of rosemary and buddleia dizzy with scent. As a child she had walked here sedate between the rows of labels and sticks.

'I have adored the war,' she thought.

She steered the boat towards an ornamental island, tied up and lay down. Oh this summer! So wonderful.

To be leaving it all.

Something had happened to Hetty here, on this little boating lake three years ago, and she had told nobody. It had been pre-Eustace, but Olivier's film *Henry V* had set her upon Shakespeare and she was reading *King John*. The park had been silent, as now, and as hot. She had opened *King John* with pleasure, dreaming of plays, turned to Act I, Scene I, when the soldier appeared.

He was a regular in the Green Howards and nowhere near an officer. There was nothing of Siegfried Sassoon about him. He was a short, stocky chunk with tight curly hair in a mat and a medal ribbon on his pocket. His mouth was the mouth of Henry V. The soldier who will never take no. He stood above her in the rosemary and the roses, and jumped down into the boat, both feet together, steadying the rocking, making the water jump with little splashes, and then he came down on top of her and the boat rocked more. Some water, quite warm and pleasant, slapped in. She smelled his lovely skin and hair. The delight in him began to frighten her. And then the voice of Boozer Bainbridge came roaring over the water and the soldier disappeared.

Boozer had not seen him. He wasn't seeing anything very straight that day. He was standing far across the lake swinging a chain and calling, 'Number nine, come in. Come in this minute.' He couldn't remember if she had paid, or when she had taken out the boat, which had been only minutes before, and he was belligerent and uncertain. Up behind her on the bank there was the escaping crackle of bushes, and she shouted, 'I'm just doing my homework. I've only been out ten minutes. You've forgotten. Again.' Boozer Bainbridge grunted and slashed the chain on his tin leg. 'I've got half an hour left.'

But she hadn't wanted to stay longer. She had rowed in at once, faster than ever before, and at the boat-house she had hung about until she met some friends and gone home with them. Oh, how long ago it had been. And how young. And how dreadfully dangerous. She looked back with longing. Nobody knew.

'Did you pay the shillin'?' Boozer Bainbridge asked today. 'I don't remember yer shillin'.'

'I must have done. You wouldn't have let me have the boat.'

He looked at her with loathing, 'La-di-da,' he said, 'posh talk,' and stumbled off into the boat-house. Hetty had a sudden memory of Lieselotte's glare when anybody talked of 'little Hitlers'.

Rape. You heard people say there had been none of it in Nazi Germany. Her father had listened to Lord Haw-Haw saying rape should be automatically punished by death. 'Good thing, too,' he had said. 'There's something to be said for Hitler.' And her mother had said, 'That's enough, Malcolm.'

Hetty in the peacetime sunlight thought about Lieselotte and wondered where she was and if they would ever meet again. She felt that soon she might have been brave enough to ask Lieselotte some questions. She had the sense of Lieselotte now, quite close, beating down the horrible grey mackintosh with her fat hands. You knew that Lieselotte sat in private darkness. Even in the Quaker house.

But you'd have thought she might have left some message for her friends.

Well, I can be thought desirable, thought Hetty, which she isn't. That soldier wouldn't have jumped on her, even in Germany. But then, she decided, Lieselotte was probably too intelligent to feel the need to be desired. Too ancient and heavy with her past.

And I've got everything to start, thought Hetty. I'm going to be ruthless and positive and in charge of my own soul. And I'm going to have a good time. I think I'll start smoking.

As she biked past the litter-bin for the third time that day, there were a few more cigarette packets in it. She took the letter out, then tossed it back.

Hetty had a capital sum of her own in the National Provincial Bank. It was one hundred pounds, and had been deposited there two years ago on the death of the outraged Josephine Dixon, who it transpired had been making many wills since meeting Hetty at six years old, all of them excluding her god-daughter. These wills, however, including the one in favour of the Princesses Elizabeth and Margaret Rose, had not been proved. They had grown ever stranger. Fur coats had been bequeathed to the Princess Marina of Kent and cigarette lighters to the Prince of Wales, though this particular will was superseded immediately when the prince took up with Mrs Simpson. Thus, all these unsigned wills set aside, the one made soon after Hetty's birth survived. She and the lady's maid got a hundred pounds each and who knows how many millions went to a home for small dogs in Harrow. Hetty's father had immediately put the hundred pounds in the bank in his name, in trust. She had not even seen the letter, but she had not forgotten her fortune.

'Aunty Josephine's money,' said Hetty. 'Could I have some now, d'you think?'

'But you will soon have your scholarship.'

'Yes, but I need some money now, Pa. I've been thinking of going for a holiday.'

'I wouldn't advise ever touching capital,' said the grave-digger. 'And you are going away altogether in October.'

'I want to do some reading. By myself. People do.'

'And leave your mother? You know how she's going to be when you've gone.'

'Couldn't it make her get used to the idea? Pa, it's *my* money. I've actually made some enquiries. Even before the exams, Miss Kipling at the library said I ought to get away. So did Hilda Fletcher.'

'Childless women know so much,' said her mother. 'Oh, Hetty, this is the last chance you and I will ever have to be together as mother and child. Well, of course, I suppose I could come with you.'

'No,' said the grave-digger. 'Who would look after me?'

'Yes. Yes, I suppose that's true. I never have left you. You can't make a piece of toast. Well, shall we all go away together? Like before the war. We could go to Runswick Bay.'

Hetty's sinking heart made a lump of her face.

Unexpectedly the grave-digger said, 'No. She wants to go alone. How much of Josephine's money will you need?'

'Well, it's six pounds a week and the fare. I'd only go for about three weeks.'

'Three weeks! But you've never been away alone for a night even with the air raids, except to Granny when you were five and you cried all night and it was only Newcomen Terrace.'

'The air raids are over and so's Granny and, Ma, it's only the Lake District. It's not abroad. I'll write. Every day, if you like.'

'I should hope *not* abroad! There's nowhere *fit* yet abroad, nor will there be for many years. Vera Robertson says there's not a bite to eat in France.'

'Actually, Ma, I *have* to go. I know I have. They've sent this huge reading list and I'll never get it done here, with you and all the Lonsdale Café.'

'Oh, but, just to Scarborough? For the last time? Just you and me?'

'You make me do so many chores at home, Ma.'

'Make? That I do not. That I *do* deny. I've never expected it. I know how I suffered myself. You have never got down to a floor in your life. Look at my hands. But I do think you could do the bathroom sometimes.'

'I scrub the floors,' said the grave-digger.

'Well, I'm going. I'm nearly eighteen. All I want is about twenty pounds.'

'But where?'

'It's a boarding house near Ullswater.'

'But whoever do we know in Ullswater?'

'Nobody. Wordsworth. The reading list's all about English radicalism. Wordsworth went there, so I'm going there.'

'Yes, but he'd heard of it. He came from round there. It rains all the time, I do know that. I recited "The Daffodils" at school and won a certificate. I'm sure I've never been to the Lake District, and I'm over fifty.'

'You don't have to kill the king to understand *Macbeth*,' said the grave-digger. 'I'm quite out of money at present.'

'OK, then I'll earn it. I'll work for Boozer Bainbridge at the boating lake.'

'You'll do no such thing. No member of this family has ever spoken to Boozer Bainbridge, he's a drunk. And you wouldn't be passed by the town council.'

'OK, then. I'll borrow from Eustace.'

'Now, that', said Kitty solemnly, 'I will not allow. It puts a girl under an obligation.'

'Borrow where you like,' said her father. He was strange and furtive about money and was often seen slinking into savings banks.

'I'll borrow from the vicar,' said Hetty, watching her mother.

'*You will not!*'

'And, Pa, you *have* got money. Plenty of money for beer and cigarettes.'

'*Apologise!*' shrieked her mother. 'I will not hear this in this house. Very well. I'll sell my cameo brooch. It was your Aunty Margaret's.'

Mr Fallowes whistled a tune from *Snow White and the Seven Dwarfs*, and went out to dig over his allotment.

The next day he drew out twenty pounds of her money from the bank and put it before her, his hands hovering in the hope of getting it back.

The following day a volume of Siegfried Sassoon's *Memoirs* arrived from Eustace in a good binding and Hetty flogged it in Middlesbrough for six pounds ten.

A week on, in the public library old Adelaide Kipling left the desk and slipped an envelope under Hetty's book. Inside were two large squares of tissue-paper that turned out to be five-pound notes.

'I couldn't! Oh, Miss Kipling!'

'I heard that you wanted to go to Grasmere. Poor Coleridge. D'you know, they papered his walls with newspaper? It was all they had. Just a little extra.'

'Oh, I think it must be because Miss Kipling has always been so very fond of *me*,' said Mrs Fallowes. 'I think she taught me "Daffodils".'

Una Vane and her widowed mother were not set apart from the rest of the world entirely because of their joint tragedy, they were apparently set apart from one another. Down the Lonsdale – where Mrs Vane had never once been seen – they said, 'Whoever could imagine Una was her daughter?' But though Una and her mother spoke little to each other they were in fact enmeshed and entangled together like the roots of a pot-bound plant.

Their worst time, the worst they would ever have, when Mr Vane had called out a jolly goodbye and gone out to jump off the cliff, had been twelve years ago, and Una after staying with the Fallowes had returned home to a house standing in silent disbelief, a locked door on the medicine chest, a mother giving the appearance of being quite unchanged.

Within a couple of months Mrs Vane had set up her salon, 'Vane Glory! Where Permanent Waves are Permanent!' She had had the board raised above the front door and taken down the brass plate that proclaimed her husband's name and credentials. It was still somewhere about the house.

At first, from simple kindness, many people had patronised Vane Glory, but Mrs Vane proved to be an unreliable cutter and the procession of underpaid girls who did the shampooing tended to come from the slums of Middlesbrough and had feeble fingers and broken nails. Mrs Vane continued undeterred. She had a sardonic wit, no sense of self-pity and never referred to the past.

The house ran with cats. There were rivers of cats. They curled up in curlers and washed themselves around the wash-basins. As the years passed, odd clever Una stroked the cats, occasionally washed out the wash-basins and minded her book. Neither she nor her mother was remotely interested in cooking, so that they mostly ate out of tins; literally out of tins, spooning cold baked beans into their mouths and watching the cats pounce and spring at the blowflies against the window-panes, often forgetting an imprisoned client in the salon trapped beneath the electric drier or sitting with wet hair observed by yet more cats.

Mrs Vane was proud of her drier, which was one of the latest power-filled domes. Her mother, who had been a hairdresser too, though trained, had had to sit her clients in front of a coal fire with a towel over the shoulders and a cup of tea while they held their heads to the flames. Mrs Vane's mother's clients had looked like the victims of shipwreck. Mrs Vane's were like apprehensive pupae.

Una always kept her hair cropped short and never mentioned hairdressing at school. Since the age of seven she had been taken up with Mathematics, and since sixteen with Mathematics and the bike-boy. Her mother never referred to either. Nor did her daughter. It was clear to anyone who ever gave the matter thought at all that Una must have an unconscious as deep as the sea. However else could she have survived Mrs Vane's unconscious too? 'At Vane Glory,' said the grave-digger, who adored both Una and Mrs Vane, 'there is a *lot* going on, out of sight.'

'Not really,' said Hetty, whose unconscious was only just beginning to build up. 'Nobody goes there. They're poor as mice. It all goes on cat meat.'

'Let them eat mice,' said her father. 'At Vane Glory you might be out of the range of mice. You are beneath the sea. Six miles beneath the South China Sea – did you know? – there are blind white fish who are unaware of light? Una of course may swim up. I wouldn't think her mother would. I think she rather enjoys the shadows.'

'Half the time I don't know what your father's talking about,' said Kitty Fallowes.

And now with Ray, who had been the fish-boy, and then the milk-boy, and had become the bike-boy with a job on the railway, Una skimmed the surface of the bright world like a dragon-fly. She had seen him as a child almost, helping in the fish shop, and she had met him properly two years ago when he had changed direction and come delivering milk to her back door. Mrs Vane was his best customer.

Ray had walked up the yard each morning, cats like snipers watching him from every crack and cranny, and one day, when Una was hard at work on her bike, Ray took over. He told her of a better bike. She went to see it. A deal was made, and now they flew about the countryside together every weekend, though seldom speaking. Una changed.

'I'll do your hair,' Una's mother said to Una one empty day, soon after Lieselotte's disappearance. Una had put aside the Cambridge reading list and was absorbing the journal of the Cyclists Touring Club through the drowsy afternoon. 'I'll give you a nice perm. And a tint. What colour would you like?'

'Nothing. White.'

'Now, white's the one that nobody can do. I'll give you a heliotrope.'

'OK.'

'No,' she said, looking through her rather tired pamphlets, 'I don't seem to have the heliotrope. It was all used up on that person who complained. I'll do you a platinum.'

'OK.'

Humming a slow tune from Nelson Eddy and Jeanette MacDonald, Mrs Vane washed her daughter's hair in the stifling front room. 'Oh, Jeanette MacDonald has a lovely head of hair,' she said. 'Well, so has Nelson Eddy. Beautiful ripples.'

'Beautiful eddies,' said Una.

They laughed.

49

Mrs Vane began to sing with a strong baritone, her face becoming male, square and fervent. She picked up a hairbrush and waved it about, giving a clever impression of managing a rearing stallion while brandishing a gun.

'Not much longer now,' she said, winding up the final roller and clipping it up into the electric charge that dangled with twenty-nine more from a lethal-looking mechanism that suggested Death Row. From Una's small head sprouted all the rollers wrapped in waxy, horn-coloured papers like shreds of vellum. 'I'm very highly strung today,' she said.

'*Switch on!*' cried Mrs Vane. There was a sizzling noise and a sharp hot smell. 'Well, that's fine. I'll go and get us a cup of tea.'

Una stayed in position and looked out of the window. The angle of her unhappy neck made it impossible to read a magazine and her mother had not switched on the wireless, as she said that one cannot be too careful with electricity about. 'That's why I've never bought a second drier,' she said. 'My mother taught me that. She wouldn't have anything with a charge in the house. There's a flash-point that can strike at random.'

A perm took three hours. Clients became so exhausted that they had to go home and lie down. They were told not to *touch* the hair for three days, not even with a comb, or it would turn all to frizz. 'Like not approaching velvet after it's washed,' said Mrs Vane. 'Not even run your hands over it.'

The sun shone peacefully and yellow on the garden. It was a childhood day. A radiant, southern day. She imagined Cambridge – Una who imagined nothing – like this. Day after golden day, and no more north-east wind. And Cambridge would be good on the bike. Flat. Open and clear. Unlike the jungle of Vane Glory's garden, where among the twelve-foot-high hollyhocks standing in clumps around the foot-high grass somebody could be seen approaching now, through the gate.

It might be Ray. She did not want Ray to see her like this. Strung up.

How curious. Why not? Ray had no interest in what she looked like. (Except he likes my thighs, she thought. I know he does. He looks them over for design faults and doesn't find any. 'You'll have stamina,' he says. 'You'll never have full speed, but you'll get there. We might try the Osmotherly Twenty.')

A face appeared through the hollyhocks and vanished. It was her father's face. She must have fallen asleep. Don Quixote's beautiful sad face. She jerked upright and electricity fizzed. Her eyes ran with the warm lotions, or with some memory.

'What is it? Ma? Ma? You've forgotten me.'

'No, I haven't. What d'you think I am – an amateur?'

Una knew that her mother was not qualified to dress hair. 'Ma!'

Her mother dabbed the parchment rolls and leaned Una's head over the basin. 'Here's the messy bit. Sloppy-slops.' Water flooded the floor. The curlers were drawn out slowly, one by one, the loose hair rinsed again. A cat caught a strand of it from among the hairnets behind the taps, and then spat it out.

'Interesting colour,' said Mrs Vane. 'Did we say we'd do it eau-de-nil?'

'No. Platinum.'

'Oh.'

'Well, I'm not going to look,' said Una. They looked at each other instead, and began to laugh. Down she went for another warm rinse and up she came like a horse from the trough, and saw again the melancholy, lean man at the window. He was now walking away.

'There's someone looking in, Ma. It looked like—'

'Like who?'

'Like, well, Dad.'

'It's Hetty's Pa. You've forgotten.'

'You saw him? You didn't ask him in?'

'He's a law unto himself. He's not just anyone. He's getting worse.'

'He'll have come round about Hetty. Or – Ma? Does he come round here?'

'Never. He never would. He's a gentleman.'

'You are hopeless. You're a *non sequitur*, Ma.'

'Now that would be a good name for a shop. A shop selling fast cars.'

'And what are you talking about? Mr Fallowes is a sexton.'

51

'Sexton Blake of the Ace of Spades. Ha ha.'

'Mother, I must go out and find him. It may be one of his bad days. Hetty's decided to go off for a bit.'

'Oh, well. Put your head back. Hmm. Very strong-coloured water. Makes me think of my dear old Dad. He could lower a pint.'

'You'd better not talk like that when you come to see me in Cambridge.'

'Mirror . . . There now. Mirror on the wall!'

'Help! I say, it's rather good. It's like burnt toast.'

'Call it caramel. Caramel cream,' said Mrs Vane.

After the last rites, the final shampoo, the final drying beneath the helmet with the sparking wires, Una was combed out.

'I look older,' she said, turning her head about. 'Do I look like Jeanette MacDonald?'

Mrs Vane began to trill like a curlew. '"I'll see *you* again, Whenever spring *breaks* through again".' A cat made a dash for the door.

'You'll break the glass,' said Una, but she began to sing too.

The voices of mother and daughter floated down the street, where Mr Fallowes stood with his old leather-saddled bike, listening and thinking.

She is not mine, he said to himself, and so I am allowed to say, 'What thighs.' And, 'What *hair*.' The mother is mad, though good-looking.

He chose to walk home slowly beside his bike, giving it a rest; but at home there was nobody. Church again, he supposed, and went to his allotment. If this was Peace, it was almost unendurable. He drifted to the trenches.

And no black-out any more as winter comes. No girls to collide with in the dark, and then slip away from, unknowing and unknown.

5

The grave-digger had forgotten that the house would be empty when he reached home because Hetty and her mother were on a valedictory outing prior to Hetty's Lakeland holiday. There had been several of these, Hetty suggesting most of them and being pleasant and sweet. Once they had gone to the Lonsdale, where Mrs Fallowes had sat proudly beaming as the group all said how they had always known that Hetty was clever. The woman who had been her kindergarten teacher said she remembered how ambitious Hetty had always been. 'Oh, *very* ambitious. And you told such stories about yourself. We thought you really believed them, and we had to make you stand in the cupboard. *So* clever.'

'Yes, and so quick to read. Of course *I* taught you to read.'

'My mother taught me at home,' said Hetty. Her mother shifted about and became nervous.

'Loyal to Mummy!' said the teacher, crooking her finger, and her mother mopped and mowed.

'Well, that *was* nice,' she said, after they'd left. 'Darling, do you *have* to wear that varnish?'

('Did you see the nails?' said Mrs Finch when they were well away. 'Shape of things to come. Well, she always had that look. She was *deep*.')

'And tomorrow we'll go on a bus. We'll go and see somebody and have tea. We might go together to Wilton Woods, darling.'

These were the woods where Mr and Mrs Fallowes had done their courting. They had been engaged for four years ('And of course we never *did* anything. I think the engagement was a bit long, actually') and had once been surprised by a wandering cow. The sad little story had gone down the years. Hetty heard it again. She herself had passed a terrible afternoon with Eustace in Wilton Woods, and had been wary about woods hereafter.

'I'd rather not.'

The vicar had called in unexpectedly and taken Hetty aside because, he said, her mother was looking hurt.

'You must realise that you are going away to a *new* place and *new* friends, and for your mother there will be *nothing* new. Only the loss of her daughter.'

'She'll have you, of course,' said Hetty.

'I hope you are not already growing hard, Hetty. I hope you will never turn against your mother.'

'Why ever should I?'

'There are things you cannot understand.'

'If you're talking about Pa, then don't worry. There's no one like Pa for Ma. Nobody else could muscle in for long. They love each other.'

'Hetty, I don't like that look. You understand nothing. It's my fate – I'd say luck – to have met your mother and I flatter myself I've brought her a little happiness. She talks to me, of course, and a great deal of the time about you. And your . . . difficulties with the young man.'

'I'm going on Saturday,' said Hetty the minute the vicar was out of the door. 'I wasn't going to tell you yet, but now I am. I've fixed it all up, even the train times.'

'But however shall we know you've arrived safely? I don't suppose there is a telephone.'

'Well, since there isn't one here—'

'Oh, but I'm sure Mrs Brownley would take a call and come down.'

'It's three miles away and she's only got one leg or something.'

*

There was a tight-lipped, huffy evening, the grave-digger uncon-
cerned, reading *Heidi* and remembering holidays on the Rhine.

'I'll write as soon as I get there,' said Hetty. 'You'll have it by
Monday.'

'Oh, my, Hetty! But you know I shall be taking you. Settling you
in.'

'With my party shoes in a bag?'

'But there are such queer people about, now that the war's
over.'

'They weren't all that ordinary then. And, Ma, the *Lake District*!
It's full of old trouts.'

'*Which* lake is it?'

'Well, it's not all that near a lake, it turns out, but it's near a
mountain called Robinson.'

'It doesn't sound very Wordsworthian.'

'She's a nice woman who keeps the place. She's well-known.
Mrs Stonehouse has been, just last year.'

'Is this woman a Quaker? I really ought to come with you to see
her if she's a Quaker. I've never been happy about Quakers,
everything in black and white. They have renounced the
Sacraments.'

'She's very hospitable. She cooks these massive puddings and
she's often had students. I'll be reading all day . . . Oh, Ma! What
can go wrong? Hilda and Dorothy have been there. Hilda actually
knows a lot of other people there!'

Mrs Fallowes stopped ironing shirts and said, 'Hetty! Hetty,
why ever didn't you say? Well! Now you have made me happy.
Hilda and Dorothy!'

6

When Lieselotte Klein had stepped off a train at York in the late summer of 1939, a splendid sanity that had not been known to her in Hamburg or during most of her childhood flickered back to life. Standing on the platform had been two women officers of the British Red Cross Society resplendent in dark serge, polished leather, brass and footwear; unsmiling, daughters of Empire, aware of their national significance yet utterly different from their counterparts – if by now there were such – in Nazi Germany.

Neither of them had ever travelled far from their home county, yet the Red Cross had stiffened their lives and given them a sense of the world. Since 1919 these two women had lived together, needing nobody else for any emotional fulfilment, sexual appetite being of little consequence to either of them. The First World War had deprived their lives of brothers and cousins and friends but had drawn them together into a harmony that made men unimportant.

The First World War, which had shattered bodies and spirits, had been the making of Hilda and Dorothy, and on 11 November every year since 1919 they had come into their own, striding together at the head of their local organisation in the November Armistice procession, to the sound of martial music often out of tune, as they were – or Dorothy was – sometimes out of step. Eyes-right to the war memorial, Hilda and Dorothy had saluted.

The mayor always stood on the cenotaph steps. He was both

mayor and bank manager of the town, the bank where Hilda worked as chief clerk. The mayor had left the bank entirely in her care for years, knowing that as a woman she could never be manager and that she would never disloyally go elsewhere.

On these occasions Dorothy, less militant than Hilda, gave little smiles at people as she marched along. Dorothy was a teacher of small children, who all adored her, and when she marched, plumper and bouncier than Hilda, the children ran along the pavements beside her waving flags and shouting, 'There's Miss.'

Dorothy and Hilda sometimes doubled on these patriotic occasions as Girl Guide captains, which they had also been for many years, and then they appeared in cockaded hats, their left arms a tapestry of badges for proficiency. For twenty years on several evenings a week between the two wars they had continued in their different uniforms and never missed a meeting. Within minutes of the news at eleven o'clock, at the outbreak of the Second World War and the first hysterical (mistaken) air-raid siren, they had scrambled into uniform and in moments were organising shelters and first aid, casting people out of school-rooms and parish halls, setting up depots for making and winding bandages. They were ready for anything. Except perhaps for the rehousing of unguaranteed Jewish children escaping from the Nazis who were arriving in Britain with nowhere to go.

Hilda and Dorothy had little real knowledge of Germany or what was happening there. They saw it through the pages of their old school books. The word German meant, simply, evil. The word Jewish meant something a little shady and quite apart. There had been no Jews in their Red Cross or Girl Guide com-panies. They would, however, do their best, and their duty.

On York railway station then, in October 1939, they were awaiting a large contingent of *Kindertransport* Jewish children, rather nervously.

But out stepped, in the care of a woman who introduced herself as a member of 'The Movement', a pale wisp of a child holding a small, neat suitcase and a paper bag, who seemed possibly to be deaf and dumb, or even retarded.

*

57

In the little car with the Red Cross regalia in the windscreen and on the back window, old squashy leather seats and blinds with strings and pompons, Hilda Fletcher in 1939 had driven the child across the Vale of York. Dorothy had sat next to her in the front and Lieselotte crouched in the back, so hunched and small that she could scarcely be seen by either of them in the front mirrors. She seemed to have placed herself determinedly out of sight and when Dorothy brought out her compact to powder her nose the mirror in it had gleamed on Lieselotte, who at once slid down on to the floor.

From the floor she had looked up at the two uniformed backs and thought that though the hats were very dull and ugly they were not menacing. The conversation of the two women was incomprehensible and not at all like the English she had been learning at her Volkschule school. Since 1936 she had been forbidden school.

Outside, the country rolled flatly along on a sorrowful day of rain, one of the few wet days that summer. The stubble fields bristled like pewter, the farmhouses were a raw, rough red. Airfield after airfield came into view with lines of waiting bombers standing in the rain.

The car was being driven slowly, the lady driver changing down at every bend, an orange carrot shooting out on either side of the front windscreen to indicate which way she would cautiously be turning next.

At a railway level-crossing there was an incident. A truculent woman carrying a bucket in one hand was trying to lower the crossing gates with the other, the sound of a goods train steaming ever nearer. The sillier of the two ladies got out to help. The little engine with its blacked-out hood and a long line of covered trucks went clinking by, and the surly woman, who was in semi-railway uniform, raised the barrier and set down the bucket. 'Doing my bit,' she said. 'I can't manage the signal-box yet. Are you lost? I can't help you, I'm afraid; it's me first day and I don't know the area. But, then, I never did know much.' She looked without much interest at the dark, pale child crouched in the back of the car, like a cold puppy.

Lieselotte thought that the woman had a very coarse way of

speaking but quite liked the laughter of the Red Cross ladies, and after a time she scrambled up and sat on the leather seat. The little one turned round and said, 'Are you all right, dear?' Then: 'I don't think she understands English!'

'I don't see why she *should* understand English,' said the driver. 'They've been having lessons in the depot down south. But poor little things. She has dreadful dark rings round her eyes. What does it say in her papers? Did I have them or you?'

'I saw none. The Movement woman rushed away. I'm glad she's going to the Stonehouses. I think they've been down south to meet her once already. The Quakers know all about the *Kindertransport*. They're about the only ones who do.'

'Not long now, Lieselotte,' said the tall one, and Lieselotte jumped with surprise at hearing her name.

'I wish I had a sweet for her,' said the fat one.

The three of them stood on the Stonehouse threshold and after a time Hilda and Dorothy left. Lieselotte felt sorry to see them go and wished they had shaken hands with her instead of saluting.

Mrs Stonehouse hung up the child's coat and unpacked her small bag and set her down at a table, where she looked at the food but did not eat it. Before bedtime she was able to play about with a piece of bread and margarine. Mr Stonehouse showed her some children's books. One was a German edition of *Strewelpeter*, which failed to move her. The sun came out just before it set and the house, filled with light, was silent and grave. Lieselotte was very polite and did not look much about her, but Mr Stonehouse took a photograph of Winston Churchill off the wall and replaced it with one of the sensitive, reluctant King.

'We won't switch on the News,' he said.

'She wouldn't understand it.'

'No. But she must be spared the tone of it. And the music. It's all patriotic at the moment and she'll have heard enough of all that.'

That night Mr and Mrs Stonehouse went to look at Lieselotte in her bedroom to say good night. The old rag doll she had had in her suitcase was not in bed with her, but bravely put at the other end of the room, and Lieselotte was already asleep. But even in sleep

59

the pale face gave nothing away. It held an expression of sugary sweetness, almost complacency, but not peace. They felt that had Lieselotte awoken at that moment and looked directly upon them, she would still have been far away. Though she would have smiled and smiled. At the refugee camp at Dovercourt, for the past months, she had become an expert in invisibility.

The weeks had come and gone. No relatives had emerged as promised, for they had grown tired of waiting and hurried on to America. At last the Quaker guarantors of the unguaranteed had come through. Lieselotte had heard nothing of her parents.

With the Stonehouses Lieselotte's appetite quickly revived and she had soon put on weight and her colour had become less ashen; but her sleep had continued unnaturally deep and they never once saw her without the cat-like smile, nor broke through her elderly, almost obsequious manner. It was the only thing that they found difficult about her.

From the start, the Stonehouses had taken her to Quaker meetings on Sundays. The Quaker way of asking no personal questions, not even one's name, had suited her; but when the other children left the meeting after the first fifteen minutes, to play outside, Lieselotte had chosen from the first meeting to sit with the Stonehouses, in the silence. During one Sunday dinner, she asked suddenly why there were so many young men at the meeting not in uniform.

'They're called "conchies". Quakers have to be conchies. We don't believe in killing and so we are not able to join the armed services. It's hard to get accepted as what is called "non-combatant". Non-violent. It's very hard for us. I don't think there's one of us who doesn't feel guilty.'

'You *should* feel guilty,' said Lieselotte, still smiling, but her eyes were now like coals.

'It's hard,' Mr Stonehouse said. 'We serve in other ways. In the last war I drove an ambulance in France.'

'And now?'

'I'm old now. I haven't been called up. I read, and try to understand.'

'I see.'

'I'm in the Fire Service. You sound as if you don't think it is enough?'

'No. I should choose to kill. I shall always want to kill, and kill.'

On Remembrance Sunday for the First World War, the mayor of East and West Shields, in scarlet and gold, with his boots showing under his robes, one sole flapping (cobblers now being in short supply), inspected the town's opposition to Hitler as it went marching past the cenotaph, more or less in step. Brownies, Boy Scouts, Boys' Brigade, the Fire Service, the Women's Voluntary Service in purple and green, the Observer Corps. The Home Guard carried pitchforks and broom handles. When Hilda and Dorothy came striding at the head of the Girl Guides to the sound of drums and tin whistles, Lieselotte on her way home from a Quaker meeting, stopped and her smile left her. She gave a sharp cry and burst into tears. Dorothy saw her and waved and nodded in sympathy. Hilda of course did not turn her head or break step but contrived somehow a sympathetic wink. That was six years ago.

7

Hester left for her Lakeland retreat at the end of August 1946. It was a very wet day, a day so soaking that a taxi had to be ordered which would break into the first of Miss Kipling's five-pound notes, to the annoyance of a driver with no early-morning change. Hester was prepared to walk to the station in her mackintosh and pixie-hood, her great sack of books on her back and lugging her suitcase; but she was not – after many a contretemps and storm of maternal tears, and then at last the most awful accepting silence – to be allowed to travel alone. Her mother was to accompany her as far as Darlington and wave her off from there.

It was a poor compromise Kitty Fallowes had won and it did not comfort her. She still had many momentary panics at Hester's three-week seclusion and defection into the intellectual life.

But when the day came, wet though it was, Kitty Fallowes had reached an almost holy calm. She had made arrangements to meet a friend in Darlington for lunch at Dickson and Benson, before returning home; and the rain, the unrelenting rain, and the low autumnal skies were only proving what she had been saying all along: that the Lake District would be a wash-out. It had always been a wash-out. Mrs Brownley had said she thought Hetty should have chosen Torquay.

'Well,' Kitty said, 'at least this Mrs Satterley sounds a perfectly good sort of woman and it's a clean farm.'

'How on *earth* do you know, Ma?'

There was silence. 'Oh, well. Well. I got the vicar to write to the vicar there. *You* gave me the address you know, Hetty. He's going to come and see you.'

'He's *what*! A vicar? There? Come and see me? That's it, then. How *dare* you, Ma! Right. I'm going by myself. You can stay here and stuff Dickson and Benson's. If you go, you go in a separate carriage.'

But her mother in the taxi caught up with Hetty thundering along to the station beneath her haversack, like Quasimodo along the Excursion Walk.

'Oh, Hetty!' she beseeched, through the taxi's window. 'Oh, Hetty, do let me come. Hester? I'm so sorry. I do keep doing the wrong thing. I always did. Do just let me come so far on the train with you. I'm so sorry to have butted in again.'

The wet mountain of Hetty avalanched, sopping, into the cab and her suitcase after her, but she was in a steaming rage.

In the train her mother, now thoroughly damp from standing on the open platform, sat in a corner, penitent, Hester ignoring her. Soon the train passed her home and she saw the grave-digger standing hatless in the rain, regarding his leeks on the allotment. He did not look up to salute the train as they went by.

'He has already forgotten us,' said Mrs Fallowes, and a quarter of an hour later – it was an empty carriage except for the two of them – as they steamed through the bombed Middlesbrough slums, 'Oh, don't you see how I *need* the vicar?' She was crying into a pretty handkerchief and looking red and bloated. 'Oh, I'm so sorry, Hetty. I shouldn't involve you!' The weather lightened a little over Northallerton, and a ray of sunlight pierced a green field. 'So pretty – look, Hetty. So lovely!'

Mrs Fallowes had been taught, and believed, and had always impressed upon her daughter, that remorse is a sin. Repentance and apology are the thing. Our Lord has taken away our guilt. 'Oh,' she said, 'I'm so sorry, dear. Now you say sorry to me. It's all we need to do, you know. Though I've always believed in Confession to a priest as well.'

'I've nothing to confess.'

'If you think that, dear, then I'm afraid you're in rather a bad way.' (The sweet thing about Mrs Fallowes was her uncertainty whenever challenged, but sometimes she spoke from automatic reflex.)

'Someone's said that to you, haven't they? You're just quoting. So who do I confess *to*? The vicar? Knowing what I know about him?' Hetty could never expatiate upon the vicar; the mere thought of his love for her mother revolted her. She could not bear to see him touch her mother's hand. 'You've never given the matter a moment's rational thought, have you?'

'How can I have rational thoughts? With you and your father? Oh, I'm sure nobody else gets spoken to like you speak to me,' and Mrs Fallowes wept again.

Hetty's love for her mother made her crueller. 'So who *do* you suggest I confess to? And what? You – you actually checked up on me. Got the vicar to write and see where I was going. Without telling me. And *when*? *When*, for goodness' sake, were you doing all this? Christ!'

'I will not have Christ's name taken in vain,' cried Mrs Fallowes. 'And I will not have you speak to me in this way. Do you think Una speaks like this to her mother? Or Mrs Black's Nadia? I got the vicar to find out where you were going the minute you told me – your father caring nothing. And I've checked up with the Stonehouses, and with Hilda Fletcher, of course. You know I have to be ahead of myself. Always. It was the way I was brought up at the convent.'

'But so *secretive*! You're not quite straight, Ma.' Hetty as usual had no handkerchief and so she pressed her pixie-hood up against her mouth.

And so they carried on, all the way to Darlington, and left the train exhausted. Hetty's train for Carlisle was to leave from the same platform.

'You look worn out, dear,' said Mrs Fallowes nervously.

'No, I'm OK. I'm sorry.'

Mrs Fallowes put away her handkerchief and put on her gloves and a brave face. 'You really do look poorly, dear. Oh. I'm sorry. I'm so sorry. Have we time for a cup of coffee? I do get worked up,

I always did. I can't help it. It's my blood pressure.'

'No. We can't leave all this luggage standing around.'

'Oh, you're crying too! Oh, Hetty! You do know how much you mean to me?'

'The train's coming.'

'Oh, no. No, it can't be. Not yet. Oh, yes!'

They stood with long faces, side by side. 'Oh, come *on*, Mum,' said Hetty. 'You'd think you were never going to see me again.'

'Oh, Hetty!'

'I hope Joan Thing's all right and you get a good lunch.'

'Oh, Joan's always all right. She's *always* well. I haven't seen her for years, but we write of course. This is such a chance. It's quite an occasion.' The tears that had been on her face like dew were gone and she was smiling. 'Now write, darling, won't you? Can I have a kiss?'

But Hetty was bending to the knobbly haversack and arranging it on her back.

'Oh, Hetty, you look terrible. Please forget everything I've said!'

As Hetty straightened up carefully and picked up her suitcase before turning to kiss her mother, some people, another mother and daughter, came laughing and pushing into the carriage ahead of her.

'Oh, hurry, dear. I'll feel so dreadful if you miss it now.'

Hetty scrambled in and as the door shut and she turned back to wave, both the people who had pushed past her on the platform pushed past her again, flung themselves at the window and leaned out. They were laughing and hooting and waving at whoever it was who was seeing them off and they filled not only the open window but darkened the windows to either side. All Hetty was able to see of her mother as she bobbed and twisted among the arms and legs and waving hands was a glimpse of a blotched and seeking face, a handkerchief in a clutched-up gloved hand and, for an instant, her mother's small feet in her old shoes and the zip-bag she always carried when she went anywhere where there might be nice shops.

There was no point in calling out goodbye.

*

65

The predatory mother and daughter fell back in their seats, laughing as the train gathered speed way past the end of the platform, and when Hetty looked out of the window the train had rounded a bend and her mother was out of sight. She sat down, aware that the two people knew exactly what they had done. They were good-looking, well-dressed, confident and smiling. Pearls. One string each.

Hetty waited for them to apologise for shutting her out, but the woman only smiled at her.

'Valentine and I are going to a *concert*,' she said.

Hetty wondered what to say. Valentine must be the daughter. Valentine stared at her.

'We have *fun* together,' said the mother. 'Tonight it's Mozart. It was to have been Beethoven but thank goodness it's not. It's not the weather for Beethoven, we think.'

Valentine did not comment. Hetty hadn't a notion what the mother was talking about.

'*Great* fun,' the woman repeated. 'Are you going far? What a mountain of luggage! Is it your first time travelling alone? Your Nanny looked quite upset.'

'She is my mother,' said Hetty, with a look that brought the woman up short as if Hetty held a gun. The woman's face and Valentine's became as stone. Hetty looked out of the window and said no more.

When the pair got out, from the very corner of an eye she saw the girl glaring at her mother and on the platform turn back to give Hetty the ghost of a wave.

Oh, Ma. Oh, Ma.

At Carlisle I'll buy a card for her and post it on the station. 'Arrived safely.' Then she'll get it on Monday morning. Oh, Ma!

Oh, Ma!

But suppose she did not arrive safely? It would confuse the police. If after three weeks she did not return home, instead lying dead somewhere in a siding, tossed into bushes or in a shallow grave, her mother would show them the card and say, 'Oh, but it *can't* be Hetty! Look, we had a card. I know that she would have

66

posted it the minute she reached her destination. At heart Hetty was [was, oh, *was!*] a very *warm-hearted* girl.'

Death.

A number of flashing visions. Mrs Satterley of the farmhouse questioned by the Lake District constabulary. Eustace seeing it in the national press. Eustace writing a poem about her. Eustace's biographer interviewing him in the years to come in Eustace's book-lined study. The bachelor slippers, the blazing logs, the clenched pipe, the faithful dog. 'Marriage? Ah, no. It did not come my way. Well, there was a girl once, a girl of seventeen. I was only twenty-one myself. She disappeared on a train journey to the Lake District, in 1946. Never seen again. Yes, she was the inspiration for the Hetty Poems. No, I'm afraid that even now I cannot speak . . .'

The train for Penrith came rolling along into Carlisle station and seemed reasonably clear of murderous faces, although so packed that she had to stand in the corridor looking into the eyes of some sweaty and none too clean Scotsmen. A ticket inspector, full of wrath, came cursing down the packed corridor. Beer was being swilled, bottle-tops removed with teeth and ex-army expertise. Everyone was smoking.

'Gi's the War,' said a man in a demob suit and a pre-war pork-pie hat. 'There was more laughs.'

'And more grub,' said his pal.

Hetty fell out of the train at Newcastle dragging the sack of books behind her.

'Got a body in there?' asked the pork-pie hat, but didn't help her lift it out.

It was a dreary platform here, and no trains. A gormless youth sat regarding her from a seat across the line. He was eating something in the nature of an Eccles cake and the crumbs were all over him. *The Idiot Boy*, she thought. Would he have written that poem if— She remembered she had a picnic with her and burrowed in her handbag to retrieve it as an express from Edinburgh passed through. But then, at the first bite, her own train was signalled and everything spilled about her.

In the carriage she tried to assemble it again and saw that the picnic consisted of a huge chocolate cake, and no knife. How on earth did her mother think—? And how had she found the marge and sugar? She must have made it weeks ago, on the quiet, and it would be stale. Why am I crying?

'Grand cake,' said the other occupant of the carriage. 'You don't see them sorts of things any more.'

She thought, And so I'll have to break a bit off for him.

He was a ferrety farmer with a sunset complexion and a mouth that hung hungrily open exposing a single, dangling tooth.

'Would you like a bit?'

He began to cackle and she thought, Oh God! What have I said?

He took the fragment of cake and mumbled it about around the tooth. 'Where yer off at, lass?'

Should she say, 'The next station,' and get out, and then get back in again further up the train? He smelled of drink. 'Robinson.'

'Oh, aye. Robinson, eh?'

The train slowed.

'Well, I's gittin' out 'ere. Good luck, then, lass.'

Station after tiny station. Dozens of them. The train stopped and steamed and sighed and waited, and puffed on.

It was all of a sudden the most beautiful afternoon. And, oh my! Oh, my goodness! Oh heavens – a vast, bright purple mountain.

Nearly there. On my own.

8

Ray, the ex-fish- and milk-boy, had never been inside Una's house in nearly three years and from habit did not even call for her now, after having been appointed clerk on the London and North Eastern Railway. For years he had waited in the back street astride his bike, whistling and thinking. Since his elevation he had permitted himself to wait now outside the front gate, the occasional clients of Vane Glory passing him with suspicion. Since Nagasaki he had waited, still balanced on the bike but not whistling, reading books and the daily papers. He would look up now and then at the Cleveland Hills inland, frowning. When Una came out with her bike to join him, he would fold the literature away in his bike bag and they would ride off as usual, without a word.

Since gaining her place at Cambridge last Christmas, even before the necessary money to accept it had come through, changes had occurred in Una. In the horrible years between childhood and maturity she had not shown any physical signs of puberty: no menstruation, no spots, no stomach cramps, no bulges, no sulking, no lethargy – particularly no lethargy. When at thirteen, and even up to sixteen, her friends, Hetty particularly, had frowsted in bed at weekends till dinner-time, picked their teeth, pricked the palms of their hands with pins, drooled over lipstick advertisements and shoes, grown heavy bosoms, Una, hairless except for her head and flat-chested as the milk-boy, had remained alert and brisk, ever on the move. Though she was never seen doing much work, except in the last year by Hetty among the tombs, and never once spoke of coming examinations, her light in the attic window, observed by the grave-digger on his late-night wanderings, told another story. But, since the evening of the day of golden contentment, the day of the scholarship letter, Una had slumped.

Una could slump. It was uncanny. She must be ill. She missed breakfast and rose at noon to loll on the horrible cat-strewn sofa, to live as it pleased her. As the summer went on, she grew for a spell morose and apart. Ray never remarked on it, Hetty and Lieselotte had now both vanished and her mother continued in her separate dream. As August drew into its second and third week Una gave the impression that she would now sleep, sleep and sleep. Sleep and die. Or wake when the time came for her to start thinking of Cambridge in October. Or to choose not to go. There was time yet.

One morning she woke with a bad stomach ache and her bed in a mess of blood. She did not get up. For three days she seemed to release the tensions of years, bleeding and bleeding. Her mother toiled up the stairs with gin, but she said, 'No, I wouldn't like it.'

'Go on,' said Mrs Vane. 'I know best. I'm that relieved. I thought you were peculiar. I was thinking of telling a doctor.'

Three days later Una felt well and triumphant and alive as never before. She lit the old greenish encrusted geyser in the lonely bathroom and had the bath of her life. Afterwards, downstairs, she found Mrs Vane looking at the well-stacked fire which she kept at a roar even on the hottest days because of the cats.

Una confronted the idea of not going to Cambridge as she drank tea. She analysed the concept of the felicity of getting in there. I got in, and therefore I need not go, she thought. I can't leave Ma, can I? At length she said, 'I might not be going, Ma. To College.'

Mrs Vane moved into the scullery and began to wash the salon towels. She often just hung the damp ones out in the yard and used them over again, but there was a nasty summer cold going about, and the time had come. They were threadbare and grey; but who'd use good coupons on a new towel? Most of her clients brought their own.

'You mightn't go? Oh dear.'

'You can't mean that, can you? Just "oh dear"? Did you hear, Ma?'

'Oh dear and oh dear and oh dear.'

Una bumped into Hetty's father as she wandered about by herself on the prom one evening. His lanky figure looked romantic and young in the gloaming, but desiccated when you came near. The First World War, she thought. It may have turned him loopy, but it didn't get at his looks. He must have been wonderful. Outside the Lobster Inn the grave-digger towered over Una and looked down on her with his bright green eyes.

'Not go?' he asked. 'To Cambridge? Refuse the place? To what end?'

Una flung off down by the sea. His eyes frightened her. Her genie of misery had for a second sprung from its bottle and confronted his. She was confused. She wished Hetty was here.

'I'm off cycling,' she told her mother, 'tomorrow, with Ray – did I tell you? We're going youth-hostelling for the weekend.'

Her mother was eating bread and marrow jam at the kitchen table, which was covered with pages of the *Daily Mail*. 'It doesn't bear thinking about, the news,' she said.

'We'll be back Sunday night. He's got to work on Monday.'

'Staying over Saturday night? Who else is going?'

'Just us, but there'll be others when we get there.'

'Well, he's but a child. Have you read this about Germany? They're starving. I never put much store by that American Aid. They say half the boxes are empty. D'you ever read the papers now? Once you took an interest in politics. You worked too hard at unnatural things. On the sly. Physics. Your heart was never in the progress of mankind, though your mind was. You may have burnt yourself out just as you should be rising to things like the morning star.'

This extraordinary speech was the longest Una remembered her mother ever having made.

Mrs Vane gazed at the leathery ivy growing across the window, blowflies droning. A wasp or two near the jam. She continued, 'You could wash that window rather than go flaunting off on bikes. Now you're a mature woman.'

Her daughter's silhouette, the spikes of singed hair standing up around it like a tousled halo, was still. In all the years of their struggle together, Mrs Vane had never suggested housework. Una was too clever for chores.

'It's OK, Mum. There are separate dormitories. I know what I'm doing. I'll wash the windows when I get back.'

'I do not pry,' said Mrs Vane, 'I say not one word,' and she began to sing, 'I'll Gather Lilacs'. 'He's a child, I dare say. He's never conversed with me. Now I shall say something. I shall say it once. Then I shall never say it more. Don't you think you could do a bit better? Than him?'

Una said nothing.

'After all, you're going to the University of Cambridge. You might even decide to be a doctor. Doctors have to be careful who they marry. Your father made that mistake.'

'He did *not!*' Una slid from the table and circled her mother's chair as if she would pounce. And embrace her. But it hadn't come to that. 'My Cambridge friends, if I have any, would never meet him.'

'But when you invite them here, to stay in your home, then they would.'

A pan of mutton bones boiled over on the stove. A cat yowled and fled.

'Ma,' she said very early the next day. 'I'm going now.'

'Where?'

'I told you. Off biking. I'm all packed. He's calling for me. He's probably sitting at the front gate now.'

Sorrow shadowed Mrs Vane's gypsy face. 'He has never rung the bell and faced me,' she said. 'Not since he was delivering fish at the back.'

'I've got to go, Ma, or I'll never go. What about when I'm at College? You'll have to do without me then.'

'I'm working that out. I might close the salon and start a cattery. I thought you weren't going to College?' She paused. 'And what about rations?' she cried, as Una pushed the bright, ticking bike down the hall.

'I've got some.'

'And money?'

'I only need six shillings, and Ray's got it.'

'You would never take money—'

'Bye, then, Ma.'

But Una hung about the vestibule. It was a fine old house. There was an inner door, half-glazed, with a pattern of ferns and birds in the glass. 'A real, doctor's house', her mother had called it. But so big. Far too big to keep clean.

'Bye, then, Ma.'

Mrs Vane sat on, her eyes on the kitchen table, her plump hand smoothing the photographs of famished German children. Una hung in the vestibule until she was sure her mother wasn't coming out to wave her off.

Ray did not turn as she came down the path but folded his paper away and began to arrange his feet under the pedal straps. 'Yer ready, then?'

She said, 'Yep.'

Mounted side by side, heads down, rear ends up, the two skinny figures rode their bikes away. Only once did Ray call to her, signalling the turning they should take for the hills before the one-in-three corkscrew bank that led up on to the moors. He didn't look back to see if she followed.

Halfway up the bank she had to get off and push, but Ray surged forward, standing at last doggedly upright on the pedals as he rode out of sight, far out on the moor. There was still some morning mist from the bright dew that was making the fields seem to run with green milk. When she reached the heather, sheep were sleeping here and there about the road, which was warmer to lie on than the hard heather to either side. Twice they nearly toppled her. Another, unknown animal flashed across, almost under her front wheel, an orange streak. She tottered. The mist suddenly rose with a single swirl of its skirts and revealed the map of fields below and the heather above them, to every horizon, raspberry-red. The road across shone silver, and the air smelled of fresh laundry.

She free-wheeled for miles down the next long curling hill, swinging her legs, gulping the lovely air; then, pulling herself together, she dragged her fingers against the brakes and came flying round the final bend where the trees began. Over the stone bridge she flew and found Ray perched up on the wall by the pub, smoking a Woodbine.

'Great run,' he said.

She pulled herself up beside him and he lit a Woodbine for her.

'What she say, then? Your Ma?'

'What about?'

'Us? Tekking off for the night?'

'Not much. But she minded.'

'What you say?'

'I said there'd be a lot of others. In the hostel. And it's not as if we'd be alone.'

'There's not many ever at High Dubbs,' he said. 'Not after the school holiders.'

'I said there'd be separate dormitories.' She didn't look at his face as she said it, but at their four feet hanging down in a row from the wall. He had small feet, like a kid's.

He was like a kid. He's only doing this to prove he's not, she thought. He's just using me. Afterwards he'll boast he's done it. With a College girl. He looks fifteen.

Ray jumped off the wall and looked up at her. 'You can go back if you like. It's still a fair way to High Dubbs and it's afternoon already. Go on back if you want. Yer know t' way back. I'm not telling you.'

She thought of the return to Vane Glory alone. Her mother complaisant. Complaisant rather than relieved. No greeting, as there had been no farewell. No kiss. Her mother never kissed. Her teasing and cunning laughter. Cruel. She heard again her father crying in the night. I have never, never felt this about my mother before, she thought.

'I'm not going back now,' she said, and in a moment they were away through the village, up the hill and out of it again on the other side of the river, and up to the more open moor.

Una was now keeping up with him. She began to sweat deliciously in the hot sunshine and as sweat trickled down her back she began to laugh. She rode faster, overtook him, and he wagged his head at her in commendation as she flew by.

She noticed that he was now smiling, and her heart thumped. Nobody could say he hadn't a handsome face. And she laughed aloud.

His face was a man's face. A working man's face. She was going away with a working man, and his legs were beautiful and strong.

The wide moor spread wider. Plateau on plateau opened in front of her, with long, navy-blue pencilled horizons retreating before her as they covered the miles to come. Now it was she who was leading the way.

9

Mr Fallowes on his rainy allotment listened to the train taking his wife and daughter away to Darlington but did not look up to watch it rock by. The leeks looked spindly, yellowish. He gave them up, and was soon pedalling along on his very heavy old bicycle beside the sea towards Shields West, and the Stonehouses. He stopped *en route* to look over the wall of Vane Glory for a while.

All at once it had become a sunny day once more, which might have been the reason why at this moment the hairdressing-salon's blind was being urgently pulled down. He pushed his bike round the back, where, over the high yard wall, he watched other blinds being drawn down one by one, though the back part of the house was quite out of the sun. He imagined for a moment that Mrs Vane was preparing the house for romantic daytime assignations, which gave him a small thrill of excitement. Then he remembered that he knew Mrs Vane, and that she was a good woman. She would have no liaisons during working hours.

He disliked the sight of a descending blind and said to someone coming out of the post office, 'It's all curtains for me.'

Already he was missing Hetty. Soon Una would be gone, too. He had watched her grow from a small, fat bulb to a tall narcissus. She had always been about the house. All the young maidens departing. But of them all it was Una who stopped his heart.

And the Jewish girl gone too, and nobody seemed to know

where. Sometimes the tide came in and took a whole generation. You didn't see it coming until it was above you in its terrible power. He heard the screams, the senseless suicide of the guns, and the great wave curled and crashed over all.

He got off his bike and carried it down to the sea-shore, where he remounted and rode for several miles along the hard wet sand, and behind him his tyre marks made a beautiful deep pattern that was soon obliterated by the lacy, bridal sweeps of water spreading in arcs along the shore. He reached the esplanade of Shields West and rode among its streets until he found the Stonehouses' address, where he sat down on the kerb beside his bike.

'I think it's a tramp,' said Mr Stonehouse.

'Does he want food?'

Mr Stonehouse went to the gate and leaned against it. 'Hello? Have the Friends sent you?'

'I have no friends. I am a grave-digger.'

'Then you must be Hetty's father. Come in.'

They sat with cups of tea. The silent room pleased Mr Fallowes.

'I have decided', he said, 'that I should become a member of the Society of Friends. The Company of Quakers.' The silence continued. 'I expect you're missing the Jewish girl,' he said. It was not put as a question, 'You will have heard of the explosions in the Far East? Tens of thousands have been killed in Japan?'

'Just over a year ago,' said Mr Stonehouse

'So long? How the time goes. They say that the result will be enforced kinship throughout the world. From nuclear fission will come nuclear fusion. So violence has done the trick. Nevertheless, I should like to fill in the necessary forms to become a Quaker. Peace at *any* price.'

The Stonehouses sat on, waiting for a leading. Mr Stonehouse said at length that Mr Fallowes would be welcome at the Meeting House but that membership was not a matter of forms.

'I was in the last war,' said the grave-digger. 'I was in the trenches for four years and I was never wounded in body. Can you explain that? I am good for nothing but continuing to dig holes for the dead. Now there will be no work for me at all. The

77

Bomb eliminates graves. We shall only be painted shadows across whatever walls are left. We shall be as the flat hordes of the extinct animals that stampede across the cave walls of prehistory. But there will be nobody left to marvel at us.

'We can't know that,' said Mrs Stonehouse, offering an oat cake and more tea.

'I think you must be missing your daughter too,' she said. 'Isn't she somewhere in the Lake District?'

'Oh, she's not at all political,' he said. 'But did you know she has surprised herself by getting a major award to the university? Herself, not me. She is a remarkable girl. But I could wish her home again. Of course we are at some distance from Hiroshima, but I feel it is best for those who love each other to stay together. They tell me, by the way, that my mind is getting worse, so if I have told you all this before, I apologise.'

'She'll be coming home again,' said Mrs Stonehouse, 'I expect it will feel like no time at all.'

'She's very young, you know, my Hetty,' said her father.

The Stonehouses sat thinking that their child, Lieselotte, had seemed very old, but they did not say so.

'A thousand ages in Thy sight', sang the grave-digger as he pedalled home along the virgin shore, 'are like an evening gone.' An evening gone. An evening with Kitty, if she's back. Then the nine o'clock News on the wireless and a beer. Bedtime. That's my lot.

Mrs Vane watched him pass from behind her reluctantly virtuous blinds.

'A lovely man,' she said to a cat. 'It's a tragedy. But she's lucky. He always goes home.'

10

Lieselotte, after her dazed and abrupt parting from the Stone-houses, had been driven first to York, this time in a much better car than Hilda's in 1939. She was driven by a member of a Jewish rehabilitation organisation to a brisk and busy office. After the Stonehouses, the talking and shouting was like a furious debate. On and on. A man came up and shook both her hands together up and down and began to speak to her in German. Shortly, with less expressive people, she found herself on a train travelling south – or so she thought until suddenly she was in Edinburgh. She was met by a man with a clipboard of names, one of them hers, and taken to what looked like an abandoned hut. At some points during this day and night there must have been food and sleep, but later she recalled nothing except the packet of food Mrs Stonehouse had given her, which she finished before she reached Scotland. In her purse was a one-pound note.

'I should like, please, to get a telephone message to my family.'
'Your family?'
'Yes. The family with whom I have been living.'
'Aren't you going to London?'
'I simply don't know.'

A bright, black-eyed girl came up and said, yes, they were, and she'd find some change for a phone call, but Lieselotte must have refused it. There was a surreal moment when one of the people in charge asked if anyone wanted to go to the pictures.

'What's it all about?' she asked the bright laughing girl.

'We've been linked up. They've found us some relations, hey? Oh God!'

The next day Lieselotte found herself on a train to London with two thin women, scruffy and furious, who talked endlessly in Polish. They ignored her. As the overworked old engine staggered through Newcastle station Lieselotte could have sworn that she saw Hetty dropping a picnic about on a platform; but this seemed hardly likely.

The train stopped and started, started and stopped, sighed and clattered through the English midland plain. She dozed. At one stop the Poles got out and returned with unspeakable sandwiches with the corners turning up and the content, a smear of orange paste, smelling of fish. They did not speak to her until she spoke to them in English, when they asked her where she was being sent. Something within Lieselotte cringed with fear at the word 'sent'.

She wanted to say, 'Cambridge', which she had last seen at Christmastime – the interview, the raw day, the river lashed by willows in a biting wind. For some reason she said simply, 'To College,' and this seemed to silence them.

'Have you money?'

'I'm paying for myself. I have a scholarship.'

'You'll need it.' They gave her addresses that meant nothing to her. Later she threw them away. 'How old are you? If you are not eighteen you may not be allowed to go. Not if there's an American relative turned up. You'll need authority.'

The train clanked on.

'You've had confirmation? Of which camps? You've heard nothing?'

Lieselotte decided to stare and say nothing, and then pretended to sleep, and in the dreams that came were the brass coal-box and the knitting-bag, the piles of books around Mr Stonehouse's chair, the sea light over the cliff-tops. Hetty's laughter. Una's droll face.

At Euston she was met by people who were decidedly expecting her, seemed to know her already. They shook her hand, greeted her by name, but forgot to introduce themselves. There was a tall and noble-looking Jewish woman in a beautiful coat and skirt and shining lipstick, who drove her to an address in the ruined streets of Notting Hill, where, at the foot of steep area steps and from behind a basement door, appeared a very old man with a carefully oiled and tended beard and moustache.

'This is she,' said the glamorous woman, 'Lieselotte Klein.' The man signed for her and the woman was gone.

'Come,' he said, and Lieselotte followed him down a corridor thick with dust, to a big room where every shelf, cupboard-top and sill was covered with plates. Plates, saucers, cups, cream jugs, sugar bowls, slop basins, butter dishes, little pots for conserves and honey. And every kind of teapot. They were ornate and very fine. Here and there were china figurines, painted porcelain people, cherubs and kings and corsairs and frilly ladies. An old woman was moving painfully about the room, flicking at everything with a feather duster.

'She is here,' said the old man. 'She is come.'

His finger was holding the place in a yellowed German paper-back with red and black roman script on the cover. These fastidious fingers, the curly script, stirred some far back knowledge in Lieselotte. She had a plunge of terror that these were her parents, unloving of her and unrecognised by her. They had not even greeted her. The old woman continued to flick about among the figurines and teacups, and the old man stumbled away.

Lieselotte stood among the crowded furniture, where there was not room even to set down her small case. A gilded *chaise longue* was piled high with what looked like couture dress-boxes – she saw the word 'Worth'. Again, a strand of thought trailed by. A great chair like a throne sagged on two legs and into the mountainous clutter a shaft of sunlight fell like a searchlight down from the street.

'We brought everything,' the old woman said. 'Yes? Ha? We spent our small fortune. We are not fools. In 1934. We foresaw.' She began to speak in German. 'We did not lose one single piece. We were in Art Packing. I am also a specialist in fine cloth and brocade, but our profession was in Transportation, which has

81

forever filled us with shame. The word. We transported great works of art, all over the world.'

'Give us the David of Michelangelo,' called out the old man, 'and we could deliver it safely to El Dorado.'

'As it grew more difficult, less safe for us, so we charged more,' said the old woman. 'There is no record now of what German treasures we saved from the Nazis. None. Except in *here*.' She tapped her head. 'In my head are Rembrandts, wrapped in linen. Not yet recovered. I could lead you to every one if someone would buy me airline tickets. Nobody else knows, not even my husband. He has forgotten, yes?'

'Yes,' said the old man, reading his book.

'And here, when I was established in this country I was immediately recognised as an authority. I was put personally – personally – in charge of the train that went to Wales to hide all the paintings from the National Gallery in the caves. I was *personally* commended by Winston Churchill, and I shall show you his letter. But,' she said, 'I am now poor and forgotten.'

'Excuse me. Is there a lavatory?' Lieselotte asked in German, though it sounded like English. 'I'm sorry. The train from Edinburgh was so crowded—'

'And,' said the old woman, leading the way through an obstacle course, round and round ottomans and humpties and piles of rolled-up carpets, '*and* you see what we have rescued? Do you know what remains of Dresden? This only,' and she pointed to the motes of dust in the underground dwelling's sunbeams. 'Dust,' she said, 'and what you see here on these shelves at 34e Rillington Gardens. And millions of us dust too, not yet counted, not yet properly mourned. Not only the dead of the camps. Mr Feldman and I have more to mourn than you. You have only your dead family, gassed at Auschwitz. We mourn a whole nation. It's down the passage.'

There were faded old ribbons in the WC, twisted into the chain and ending in a bow, like a child's plaited hair. So much china was stacked on the floor and on the high window-sill, it was difficult to manoeuvre oneself on to the seat. The tiny place was dark and smelled of something musky, velvety, not unpleasant. Like an old

German theatre, long sealed up. How do I know this? thought Lieselotte. Pinned down the back of the door were pages from old magazines, pictures of opera stars and dimpled blonde women gazing at hair-pomaded men with whiskers and younger men with big porcelain teeth. The women's hair had been tonged into ridges and they looked out on Lieselotte on the lavatory seat through garlands of rosebuds threaded round flimsy violins.

The old lady banged on the door and shouted something about musical comedy and then Lieselotte heard the words 'Viennese opera'. Could the old pair have once been operatic stars as well? She felt relief, certain now that these people could never have been her parents.

Some way ahead in the rambling, sorrowful basement someone had now started up a gramophone and an aria – Lieselotte's memory stirred again, this time in a wave of longing – crackled out across the listening rooms.

'Is there . . . excuse me, but might there be a bedroom some-where?' she asked the old man, when she had at last found him standing in a cupboard, the old woman having vanished. He was watching a small kettle on a smaller gas ring.

'No,' he said, 'no,' swinging a little Meissen teapot between finger and thumb. 'No. But there is a variety of sofas. We ourselves do not sleep very much now. We sit up most nights. We have our music, thank God. We took up the habit during the Blitzkrieg, five years ago, and then the doodle-bugs. We never suffered. You are not from Dresden?'

'No. My father was a doctor in Hamburg.'

'And when did you have the confirmation? When we applied to adopt a child from the *Kindertransport* we insisted on a child who was a certified orphan. Auschwitz was certainly where your parents died. It is better for you to be told. I see you have not been told. Yes?'

'Could you,' she said, calmly, 'by any chance tell me how long I shall be staying here?'

'We should be happy for you to live with us for ever. If of course the suggestion of a relation in the USA is found not to be true.'

'I've heard nothing,' she said. 'I go to the University in October. To Cambridge.'

'Then you shall live here with us.'

'I have no money. I'm very sorry to mention it.'

'You shall share our bread.'

'Thank you. Actually, I'm sure the people I have lived with in Yorkshire must have had some allowance for me.'

'Weren't they the Quakers? Then I think not. And now in this house you will also share our bread. We eat and pray together – though Lena, poor soul, does little praying now – and we shall be your parents and you shall be our child.'

On a tin tray he had arranged exquisite cups of gold and rose, a cream jug and teapot frilled and encrusted with tendrils and flowers as limpets and corals decorate rocks. The tea was laced with more sugar from a thick blue paper bag than Lieselotte had seen in such bulk for many years. The jug was for ornament only. Condensed milk was poured from the tin into the cups and all was stirred round with a communal silver spoon. 'This is, after all, a celebration,' he said, tidying up the rim of the tin with his fingertip which he then licked.

'I am so sorry,' she said, 'that I have less than a pound in the world, but would it be possible to telephone some friend of my Yorkshire family?'

'We are quite penniless ourselves,' he said. 'There is a call-box in the street, but a trunk-call can take up to an hour.'

The old woman came by and stopped to watch Lieselotte drinking tea. She made the odd flick with her duster here and there. She said, 'Oh, how she is like Berenice!'

'Aye, aye,' said the old man.

'She's got her very eyes.'

'Now, now. It's time to go to bed.'

The old woman, Mrs Feldman, began to remove piles of newspaper and old blankets from a sagging sofa. 'Here's your bed, girl. Lieselotte.'

'But,' said Lieselotte, 'it's only seven o'clock.'

The Feldmans stood considering, as those who have forgotten clocks.

'It can't be more,' she said.

'But you must be tired,' said Mr Feldman. 'I'm sure we always seem to be tired. We hardly ever go out now. Well, where is there to go? And yet we are always tired.' He took a stool and climbed on it and began to draw several heavy bolts across the door.

'The china,' said Mrs Feldman, addressing Lieselotte: 'we have to be vigilant. London is not what it was before the war. There are a great many foreigners.'

'We never went down to the shelters,' said Mr Feldman, 'and, as you see, here we are quite safe, and so is the china.'

They muttered and pottered and grumbled at each other in German, clattering in the cupboard of a kitchen, and brought her at length a piece of cold meat on a plate and then a honey cake out of a tin, some bread and a glass of wine. The honey cake was like wood but the wine was sweet.

She lay down on the sofa, which smelled the same as the WC, of old theatrical violet scent and dust.

Dust, dust, she thought, and slept at once. To find herself in the Yorkshire churchyard, in the happiness and sunlight beside the sad old tombstone; the tossing of the English trees, the cold rain after unexpected thunder. Hetty's laughter. Hetty swinging from the bar of the bus. 'Sorry I asked about your mother, Lieselotte.' Una: 'There's something climbing up this stalk. It's like a bullet. It wants to explode.' The soaring clouds, the Christian steeple.

She heard the old man talking in some cluttered corner. 'I'd say this was a *good* girl.'

'She's like Berenice,' the old woman answered from some nest of rugs. She seemed to be having trouble with breathing.

'Don't upset yourself now, *Mutti*. All's past. We're doing right to have her. We're not finished. And she's a Jewish girl.'

85

11

As Hetty came staggering out at Robinson Halt station with her unwieldy luggage, she looked about the surrounding mountains and hills for the taxi she had been assured would be waiting to take her to Betty Bank and there it was, but surrounded by several forceful-looking people in the process of hiring it. A lumpish oaf of a driver was in charge, and seemed to be negotiating deals. It was a broken-down conveyance, and the only one in sight.

The other candidates for the ride were large and taciturn, wearing shorts and bearing packs. They were being ungenerous with their vocabulary, but also unbending.

'Two pun,' Hetty heard. 'That's t'price. Tek't or leave't.'

Heads muttered together.

'Thee an' all?' asked the driver. 'Where til? Oh aye, I heared tell. That's Betty Bank. Beyond Robinson. Aye, I can tek five.'

Everyone climbed in. Nobody spoke. Hetty thought that the Lake District must be greatly changed since Wordsworth's day. They were silent folk in the poems, but not belligerent. The war must have changed them.

Not that anyone can have suffered anything up here, she thought, they never had a single bomb. Wordsworth had never had a bomb either, she thought, though he must have had some nasty memories of the French Revolution. They couldn't get him home, he was so taken up with it. But his manners never suffered, she thought, he was always a courteous man.

Inside the taxi it was very cramped, with five rucksacks, a suitcase and five people. Hetty's pack full of books was twice the size of any of the others, and the cumbersome shape of it seemed to be causing her fellow passengers to look thoughtful.

'You climbin' with yon thing?'

'No. No, I'm studying.'

'Yer off toward Grasmere? Well, yer off course here.'

'I know. I'm going to a guest-house. To do some reading.'

The information was lugubriously received. They shifted their great feet about in their great boots.

'Yer 'ere.'

The boy had stopped his taxi in a lane where nothing was to be perceived on either side except fields. They had driven scarcely a mile.

'No,' she said, 'it's a guest-house. Called Betty Bank.'

'It's yon.'

'But there's nothing here.'

'There is. Up yonder. Through yon yat. Straight on, turn right, throught trees. Saves yer two mile.'

She clambered out.

'Two pun.'

'But we've come no distance. I've got luggage.'

'Two pun.'

The other four sat staring, face forward. She thought, They'll be travelling free now.

'It was to be two pounds between the five of us.'

'They's goin' on. It's two pun each.'

She handed him, slowly, two one-pound notes.

'A tip's usual,' he said.

'I can't afford it.'

The rotten little car drove away down the lane, not one head turning, and she was alone. Though the station was not very far behind her, there was not a sound. Two trains a day, and hers the last. There was not a car, not a cart, not a bike, not a person about in the fields.

She anchored her rucksack against her backbone with care and tightened the straps over her shoulders, and then had to take it all off again to throw it ahead of her over a gate. She heaved it on once more, picked up her suitcase and started crunching up the steep field, which was silver stubble decorated with slanted prickly stooks of corn, tied with twine. There was a dark hole within each long stook, and she thought of sliding off the book-bag from her shoulders and thrusting it inside a stook until she could return tomorrow with a wheelbarrow, or something. She had no idea how near or far she was from Betty Bank. And so she toiled on.

The steely field ended. There was another hedge, another stile. The stile was narrow and high, and took time to negotiate with suitcase and bag. The second field, like the first, had no path crossing it and was freshly ploughed. It seemed an indignity to sully the furrows but she could see no alternative, and she stepped across them, trying to step lightly on a neat, straight line. Looking back, she saw her footmarks winding up the field behind her like machine-gun fire, or as if some splashy hippopotamus had lately passed. At the high top of this second great field the woods began, oak and beech just starting to turn from green to pale rose-madder and rust. Gold gorse bushes stood along the edge of the woods in a long barrier and she had to wander up and down until at last she found a thin place she could struggle through. In front of her now was a green alley running straight upwards again to a ridge.

She plodded and climbed, stopping once to slide off the swaying books, to drag them along behind her through the grass. It was very hot. No birds sang in the beeches. Where the hell am I? thought Hetty.

Emerging from the trees, she found that the grassy alley she had walked between them came out upon a wider, grassy lane that crossed in front of her, left and right. The track continued up through more woods ahead. The wide lane, left and right, was overhung with bigger trees. There was a ridge of grass down the middle of it, and wild flowers and ferns on either side.

'So I turn right, do I? Well, so he said.'

And she turned right, now embracing the great muddy pack of books in her arms, the suitcase hanging below, painfully, from her thumbs. The lane became narrower and more shadowy but, as it wound on and on, it widened again, the trees thinned and late-afternoon sun shone levelly through them, splashing the lane with light.

Quite soon there appeared, standing alone in the middle of the lane, a long trestle table and a chair. They stood not across the lane as barricade, but sideways on, as if expecting people to file past, as at a frontier post. There was grass in tufts about the ankles of this furniture. The table was spread with a very old, worn length of oilcloth patterned with blue flowers, on top of which lay, face-down, a paperback book and, beside it, a jam-jar half full of money. There were several pennies, many shillings and sixpences and at least two half-crowns.

Hetty regarded the table. There seemed no possible way that it could have come here. It was a heavy thing and the track had clearly not been made for motors. There were no cart ruts. Hetty imagined two hefty men, one walking backwards, each carrying a table-end along the lane that wound both in front and behind the table, on and on. On and on. It had clearly been there for a very long time. The legs were bleached and warped, the oilcloth split and stained. The stains were reddish as if they might have been blood.

Hetty felt, as she stood in the silence, that it was necessary for her to be severe with this table, to accost it in some way, to confront its idiocy this idiotic afternoon. She heaved up the rucksack and rested it on the table, which swayed a little with the jolt. Then she picked up the face-down book, opened at a particular page.

The book was called *The Perfumed Garden*. She remembered a *Scented Garden*, about a nasty child from India who had been made delightful when confronted by the wonders of Nature; a book which she had never found convincing, a book— No! Wait a minute. Not *Scented*, but *Secret*. That was *The Secret Garden*.

This book, it appeared, was also some sort of whimsy about the East, and so the owner of it changed in Hetty's mind from a nice toothy schoolteacher on her holidays, reliving her childhood, to a William Morris type in a floppy dress and wedges of hair, smelling a lily. Somehow neither woman would have been a surprise sitting in this lane. Hetty flicked about through the book, and wondered now whether it had been written by a man. She read—

Wow!

Ker-ist!

Unbelievable!

She slapped the book down on the table on its face, gathered her luggage and thundered along the lane, almost running.

At the lane's curve she looked back, expecting to see nothing. She had dreamed it all.

But there stood the table and chair.

As she looked back at them the trees through the length and depth of the wood suddenly tossed about. There was a rushing of wind and more bright rays of sunlight blazed through the trees above the lane, like torchlight. She saw that the trees of the higher wood grew in only a narrow strip, and on both sides, ahead of her, they were now thinning all the time. Back behind her, though, she could still see the table in the shadowy part of the lane; just make out the pages of the book, riffling about.

Around the next bend there stood to her right, on the lower slope of trees, the backs of some stone buildings and a small white gate. There was nothing to say that this was Betty Bank but she went round some bushes, and a grindstone standing in nettles, and came upon a flagstoned terrace with marguerites and hollyhocks and a black-and-white sheepdog lying looking at her. It wagged its tail and appeared to be interested.

Beyond and below lay all the fields she had climbed, the corn stooks now each with its own shadow, the wind agitating the saplings growing in all the hedges.

With her back to the dog and Hetty, on the farm flagstones, stood a woman with the broadest back Hetty had ever seen, criss-crossed by white apron bands fastened to her skirt with big linen buttons. The skirt was long, but rucked up over her haunches to reveal the backs of knees the size of pork knuckle, and feet in huge black clogs. She was surveying the road from the railway station, which stood directly below the farm, and quite remarkably close.

'You never! Up them fields . . . Never! He *never* sent you! Two pound? I'll see to him. I'll fettle him. Mark Watson. It's the war. We never knew of exploitation before the war, never. He'll have tekken two pound from each of t'others. Ten pound! *And* he knew the taxi was booked for you: I sent instructions. He'd think you'd be from town and senseless, and never tell me. You *never* carried them great things?

'And what a climb! Are you fashed? Now here – come on. Yer dinner's ready. I was out lookin' to see ift train was late, and yet I knew it wasn't, for I heared it an hour since, but now and then there comes one you don't expect. We used to have the odd munitions go by in the dark of night and that confused us, likely. We didn't care for it, never knowing when one would tek it into its head to blow up. Sparks flying out oft funnel, well, they were brave drivers and all ought to have the VCs, but now there's just the two for passengers. Well, I saw that taxi standing waiting. You can see it now. It's back. He'll have tekken on t'others over yonder for climbing and not wanting to loophole over here ont way. Disgusting! Here's your bedroom now – small, but look at the view. Ewer and basin and the gentleman under the bed. Wash your face and come right down on. Six o'clock sharp's supper-time and seven o'clock o' morning's breakfast, and you find your own, midday.'

Find? thought Hetty. Find?

Where? Out along the hedgerows? Blackberries? Catch a rabbit? There'd been no mention of finding, in the letters. She was always hungry at lunch-time. There were certainly no shops. What do you do with water in the basin after you've washed in it – chuck it out of the window? No, there was a queer bucket with a basketwork handle. Awful.

She looked under the bed and saw a giant chamber-pot shining clean and painted with medallions and rose garlands, like the ewer and basin. She'd *never* use it. Think of the woman coming in to carry it out! Wherever did they take it? Did they fling it on the fields?

And there were a lot of people here. She could hear them. A crowd of voices. The other guests talking downstairs. The walls were thin. You'd be able to hear everything in the night.

Her bedroom walls were papered with rosebuds, the paper peeling away at the corners. It must be damp in winter.

The fireplace was painted shiny black and looked as if it had never seen a flame. There was a fan of white paper in the grate and on the mantelpiece two rose-pink candlesticks, but no candles, a pot with a spike for rings and another one with letters of gold saying 'A Present from Maryport'. Over the fireplace was a looking-glass painted almost all over with clusters of violets, and the words 'Thy Will be Done'. The bed was high as a barrage balloon, puffed up with feathers in the mattress. There was an upright chair and a small desk to read at. She'd asked for that.

On the desk were two letters – one of course from her mother, the postmark a week ago, naturally, to be sure of being on time. The other envelope showed the familiar hand of Eustace. Her mother must have sent him the address, *unasked*.

Hetty flung both letters to the floor and went down to supper, opening the dining-room door on a well-behaved expectant silence. Several people who looked like bus conductors and their wives. And here was Mrs Satterley again, now ladling out stew.

12

Lieselotte was listening for the swish of the sea and the quiet movements of the house at Shields West, Mrs Stonehouse preparing breakfast in the bright and antiseptic kitchen. The air seemed thick today, the darkness extraordinary for summer. It was stuffy and very hot.

She opened her eyes on to what seemed to be an underground furniture store and an unaccustomed high window that looked on to a line of stumps of area railings. Across this window, people's legs kept passing.

She was lying on a Victorian sofa fit only for a bonfire, and on a shelf near her face nymphs and shepherds, brandishing garlands and carrying lambs, smiled and danced good-humouredly in a chorus line.

Lieselotte arose and crept about. She found the beribboned wash-place and something of a towel. She found her case and rootled in it for a sponge-bag. She washed in cold water and dressed in the clean and folded clothes that Mrs Stonehouse had sent with her. Nobody was to be seen or heard, but a tin teapot on a hob was warm, and so she poured some of the stewed tea into a pink and gold cup with a handle like the neck of a swan. She walked over to the now-unbarred front door.

A blaze of London heat and light struck down on her and she saw, at the top of the steps on the pavement, her new landlord seated in a basket chair, embracing the morning air of Notting

Hill. He wore a panama hat, splintered grey with age. His face was lifted to the sun and he was holding in his hands some very grubby ration books.

'Ah,' he said. 'Good day. My wife is not yet about. Now that we have retired from the business she has a tendency to sleep late.'

'I didn't see her anywhere.'

'Oh, she's there. We are like birds. We perch as we can.'

'I was thinking,' said Lieselotte, 'that there must be somewhere I should be going to register myself, or something. For rations and so on, if I'm to be here until the second week in October.'

'Quite so. And perhaps you would kindly take charge of our ration books too. If we can present three books together to the shops there will be greater notice taken. Such meat we have been offered! The last chops had eight-inch shanks to one bite at the top. All the weight was in the bone.'

The books were hardly marked inside and very out of date.

'But you don't seem to have been eating anything.'

'The shops are at a distance. Our legs are not good. But we have good friends. There is a small delicatessen . . .' His voice trailed away.

'Do you . . .' Lieselotte seemed to hear an ancestor, a thousand ancestors, speak from within, 'Mr Feldman, do you use your clothing coupons?'

He removed his hat and examined the faded silk ribbon inside.

'Clothes we have almost forgotten. Mrs Feldman is very resourceful with the packaging materials we have about us. My hat I should miss. Vienna, 1928. D'you see the label? This could never be replaced. Otherwise – would you be able to find a use for our clothing coupons?'

'Oh yes.'

'Half-a-crown each? Off the record?' A quick glance.

'I could buy only seven at the moment. Until my grant comes through.'

'Very good. On account.'

'Well, first of all,' she said, feeling at ease, 'give me your ration books and tell me how to get to the town hall. And the delicatessen.'

The streets of Notting Hill, filthy and tall and red, were terrify-
ingly crowded after Yorkshire. Ragged children with dirty faces
yelled and played about the pavements, unshod. Every house was
a rooming-house, unpainted, unloved. There were gaps in almost
every street where the bombs had sliced them apart and left the
ghosts of rooms, fireplaces and picture rails, here and there, fifty
feet up, a picture hanging on a nail, staircases leading up floor
after floor and then away into space, a curtain still hanging at a
dizzy broken window. Notices embroidered with barbed wire
were nailed across doors barred diagonally with planks that
teetered above what had once been basements now filled with the
rubble that had descended on back gardens where black-currant
bushes sprouted like trees among wild flowers, sour wild privet,
forests of willowherb, even bracken. A child kicked a ball high in
the air and everyone around him watched it fall down and down
into one such place, and at once half a dozen children squeezed
and wriggled through the wire and jumped into the wilderness,
the pipes and cisterns and water tanks and gas mains. The girls
and the timid boys looked on. A little boy near Lieselotte was
watching her. He said, 'Eight was killed in there – four was in our
class. We saw 'em all – legs and arms and that. T'riffic.'

She found the town hall, queued for hours, left it with more
documents to fill in, walked on, walked on. She came to a huge,
bald park almost covered in Army huts, the noise of London
humming round. The park became another park, where men and
women in good clothes and affected voices walked and talked and
called to their expensive dogs. There were people on horseback in
bowler hats and breeches; and blossoming babies in antique
chariots pushed by tired old women with haughty faces and blue
veils floating behind them. A shop called The Moo-Cow Milk Bar
looked clean, and she went in and sat on a high stool and ate a bun
with cress in it and cream-cheese like Lanolin. It was very nice. She
ordered a glass of milk – it was deliciously cold – and a man came
in and sat on the stool near her and said, 'Hallo, where you from?'

'I'm a student.'

'Foreign, are you? What's the accent?'

'I've come down from Yorkshire.'

'You don't talk like it. D'you want to come out for a drink?'

She said she had to go back to her family, and left.

It was an amazement, an impossibility, this freedom. Nobody in the world knew where she was. Nowhere in the throng, anywhere in North Kensington, was there a living soul who had seen her before, or would ever see her again. She had sixteen-and-elevenpence in the world, and no bed to sleep on. She walked on and on.

The sun was baking Bayswater. Ducks ripped the surface of the Serpentine. She saw a rabbit nibbling in the grass. A rabbit. Young men and women, some of them in uniform and the uniform unbuttoned, lay out together on the grass side by side, and a little black eighteenth-century coach went by, the two black horses clinking silver harnesses. A driver sat up on the box, with whip and top hat. A monkey-person in knee breeches was up behind.

High above the road at Hyde Park Corner there soon appeared a bronze chariot, twice life-size, drawn by prancing horses. They appeared to be in terror, about to fall over the marble edge of a high triumphal arch. A bronze angel had alighted on the chariot, holding a laurel wreath and an orb. A tiny bronze boy sat on one of the chariot poles, and the chariot was piled high with bronze weapons of war. Living soldiers were climbing all over this mighty quadriga.

'Look,' said someone. 'They're taking down the air raid siren. It's on the block beneath the chariot.'

'What is it?' asked Lieselotte.

'It's the angel of peace,' a man said. 'The Wellington Arch. It was put up just before the First War.'

'That wasn't very good timing.'

'No. Well it will be OK now. There won't be another one in our lifetime.'

On she tramped. All thoughts of Yorkshire were gone. She had closed the door on childhood and on everywhere in the world but here. This was a city. She was a city dweller. She knew such things. In such a city she would always live.

That evening Mr and Mrs Feldman and Lieselotte sat eating from a cache of German sausage in Mrs Feldman's secret larder, on their knees among the figurines. From a rickety gas refrigerator on long, sexy legs Mr Feldman brought a bottle of Liebfraumilch. He said, 'We are glad not only of your help, Lieselotte, but of your company.' Mrs Feldman said, 'I'll make you a dress if you like. They say the winter brocades are coming in again at Harvey Nichols. I'd go and choose a nice length for you myself if it wasn't for my feet. A length of nice maroon. You'd suit a maroon. You'll be needing some dresses for your College balls.'

13

The enormous six o'clock meal provided by Mrs Satterley was followed by an equally enormous breakfast at seven o'clock next morning. Hetty, who had no watch, was down too soon.

No one was about. She had slept well and for ten hours. Last evening she had slid from the supper-table to walk around the farm for a while, wondering whether to go farther. Apart from walking back along the lane again she could only have climbed up or down the steep wood or fields, and she felt she had had enough of both. Most certainly enough of the lane.

She sidled off to bed, loud conversation and laughter coming in tuneless waves from the parlour below. Two middle-aged couples from Sunderland with Mrs Satterley holding forth to them.

She might as well get started on the reading list. She toppled out all the books on the bed and looked around for the light, but found no switch. There was no electricity. But never mind; there'd be a lamp. Wordsworth and Co. had managed by lamplight. She wondered whether Coleridge had been able to read his newsprint wallpaper by lamplight. He probably knew it by heart. He stayed long in his bed, poor Coleridge. She saw his huge, top-heavy figure flung down across a patchwork quilt, his glorious eyes half an inch from local weddings, sheep sales, auctions, agistments, grass-lettings, the Maid of Buttermere – groaning in the lamplight with his terrible constipation.

But at Betty Bank there did not seem to be a bedroom lamp, only a single candle in a blue tin candlestick in a cupboard beside a box of Swan Vestas matches.

She arranged the books in a stack on the floor, as there was nowhere else to put them, lit the candle and set it beside them, sat herself on the floor and began to make out a reading scheme.

Dullest first. Get them over with. The candle cast most of the room into darkness, blotting the fading light from the window and the lustre from the lake, illuminating the whiteness of the bed sheets and bolster, and the gilded mirror with its sombre message. It had little effect on the printed page of *Areopagitica*. The long day rolled across her mind. It seemed a different period of her life when the train from Shields East had this morning trundled past her father examining leeks on his allotment. Was it today, the shoving-aside by the dreadful mother and daughter who found Beethoven unsuitable in warm weather? Her mother's little feet in the poor shoes, the old zip-bag— Stop! *No!* Oh Ma, Ma— *No!*

Morning is the time for the brain. This day had gone on long enough. She'd start Milton tomorrow. Or maybe Thomas Carlyle. At seven-thirty a.m. Promptissimo, she would begin, and read till midday and then all through the afternoon. Every single day.

She undressed, climbed on to the bed, blew out the candle, and sank down and down in the feathers. She waited to float into sleep.

They'll be talking about me at home, she thought, and felt a pang of purest love.

Then she remembered her mother's letter unopened under the bed, written last week, probably while she was in the same room with her. Well, it was marvellous to be so loved, of course it was, but there was something devious. She'd heard her mother's clear nice voice: 'But I wanted to be sure there'd be a letter *waiting* for you. Oh dear! I've made another mistake, I suppose.' Oh *God*, will she never let go? Won't she ever release me? Oh, Ma, forgive me for whatever it is I've done – being like you, I suppose, full of sin, though I don't honestly think I've had much of a chance of it. And I'm not *like* you, I'm like Pa. Oh, you're *always* ahead of me, Ma. And you *must* have given Eustace the address and I bet he never asked for it. Oh, how dare you do that!

I will not forgive her – so *there*'s a sin. Good – I *will never forgive her* for getting into my love-life. She'll damn well have to wait for an answer to her letter now. I won't even read it. I'll chuck it. I know every word of it without opening it anyway. I'll write to Adelaide Kipling, not to her. That'll hurt her.

And so she slept and woke to a warm still morning of white fog so dense that she could see only a few yards beyond the window frame.

Hetty dressed and walked out upon the slippery flagstones of the terrace beside the farmyard but could not see the grass or the currant bushes. She had to feel her way about. Around the cowbyre were jostling shadows, let out from milking. They bumped against one another, swung about, shied off from her as they loomed towards her out of the mist. A man carrying three milk pails in two hands, two and one, came by, but did not speak. If he nodded, she could not tell. He passed into the mist beyond.

Soaked through by the mist, she went back into Betty Bank and found that she was alone in the room for breakfast, but wordlessly and at once a vat of brown porridge was slapped in front of her. It had a crust you could cut with a spoon, like bread poultice, but under Mrs Satterley's eye she found herself unable to say that she detested porridge, even with cream, though there was a great jug of that. The porridge was followed by about half a pound of bacon and two eggs. A mighty teapot was lowered on to the middle of the table, the pot muffled round with a red woollen tea-cosy in the shape of a Victorian crinoline. The torso of a very small painted effigy of a *señorita* poked up through the top.

'My daughter knits them.'

'Oh, how nice. I don't think I could—'

'Eat up. You have to find your lunch, you know. It's usual to clear off the full day for walking.'

Hetty escaped at last, bloated with food, and met the bus conductors cackling down the stairs joking about the fog. 'Whatever can we do in this? We'll have to play cards.' Hetty slithered by unsociably, wondering whether she was meant to make her bed before she started work.

The room was as dark as on the previous evening, the fog thick up against the pane. The morning's washing water had been brought up in a jug while she was in the garden and she washed her face and hands. The water was soft as silk. The soap made the bowl into a pond sealed over with white suds. She had managed not to use the chamber-pot – she had found a bush last night and an earth closet in a little wooden house by the byre before breakfast this morning – but the room had a sleazy look. She patted the bed tidy, moved the desk and chair, laid out Milton and Thomas Carlyle side by side upon the desk and sat down.

In the way of such brisk intention at this time of the morning, and full of porridge and bacon, she felt suddenly very tired. Tired, dispirited and bored. Nobody else in the school had worked these two years past as she had worked. Nobody else who'd passed the tests, finished the course, run the race, had had to. The passion to succeed, to please Eustace, to impress the Lonsdale Café, and, yes, to enchant her mother and flatten the monstrous vicar, had driven her on.

She had done it. And she was sick of it. She had written and memorised and read herself out. She cared no whit for Thomas Carlyle or for anyone – not for Shakespeare even, though she might think again if she ever got to see a play. She was being nothing but a show-off coming here, 'because of Wordsworth'. Imagine Wordsworth's view of her, sitting here in the mist, far from a woman's duty. Who gave a toss for any of them now, the 'Lake Poets', since the Bomb? Europe in ruins? Why hadn't she chosen Politics? The Lake District was for grannies.

She put her head down on her arms on the desk and, on a blast of wind, in flew Mrs Satterley bearing brooms and buckets.

'Slops?'

'I'm sorry?'

'Yer slops. I want yer slops.' She seized the china basin of sudsy water and tipped it into the enamel bucket. 'That's where that goes,' she said. Then she stretched her arm under the bed for the shaming – though untouched – chamber-pot, slammed it back again and thundered away.

'Leave that bed,' she called. 'I'll see to that.'

Hetty opened *Areopagitica* and read: 'A speech of Mr John Milton for the liberty of the unlicensed printing, to the Parliament of England (1644). They who to states and governors of the Commonwealth direct their speech . . .'

Difficult, this . . . 'the very attempt of this address once made, and the thought of whom it hath recourse to, hath got the power within me to a passion, far more welcome than incidental to a preface . . .'

Aha. Freedom of speech. French revolution. Wordsworth again.

She saw the table in the lane, the book, face-down, the extra-ordinary directions within. 'Open the woman's legs'. She read on. This country's liberty. He puts that scented lust and stuff in its place. Yet the table stood there in her head.

As good almost kill a man as kill a good book. Who kills a man kills a reasonable creature, God's image: but he who destroys a good book kills reason itself, kills the image of God as it were in the eye. Many a man lives a burden to the earth; but a good book is the precious life-blood of a master spirit, embalmed and treasured up on purpose to a life beyond life . . .

Yes, if life were all books, it would be easy, thought she. That's what I've been after, maybe.

Sounds from below, across the farmyard. Farmers whistling dogs in the mist. Long, loud halloos and lilting notes, a bit like Spain. *For Whom the Bell Tolls. I suppose* like Spain. Spanish music on the wireless, the click of castanets. Heart-breaking wails. Will I ever go to Spain? The vicar says we must never go while Franco lives. Will I ever go anywhere except the Lake District? Oh Lord, I'm going to sleep and it's only half-past eight. Free speech. *Areopagitica*. Spain. Hitler—

Crash. Mrs Satterley was now carrying a carpet sweeper and a bouquet of cleaning cloths. 'Now then, I'll have to ask you out of here. It's time to do the room.'

'Oh, but, actually, it's quite all right. It's all perfect. So clean.

And I have to work. I said I had to work every morning. I put it in the letter.'

'The rest of us works all day.'

'Yes, but this is reading and making notes. For College. I'm sure I said. The brain's best in the morning.'

'A good brain 'd tek itself outside on a morning like this one.'

Hetty saw that a golden light had now plastered itself against the window frame and was beginning to fill the white room.

'Fog's away. You get on out there and off down lakeside. *Why* is this room clean? Because it's done every day. Every morning, first thing. Away you go now. I'll be no time at all.'

On the flagged terrace the mist had rolled away but it still lay like a woollen mat lapping the edges of the farmyard and as she looked it began to rise towards her. Then she was inside it, cold and wet; then with a flourish it rose away above her, and the coloured landscape and the lake of black water were spread below. At a red sandstone water pump the man who had passed her earlier in the mist was washing out milk pails in a pink sandstone trough. He smiled at her and nodded.

'Mr Satterley.' He shook her hand after wiping his own on a rag. 'So thast bin put out oft house?'

'The room's being cleaned.'

'Ah. She can't be stopped. None of us'd call Elizabeth bookish. She'll care for you in her own way.'

'The trouble is . . .' He didn't seem what she had thought a farmer to be. He was clean and neat and calm. 'I have come here to read. For College,' she said. 'I'm going at the beginning of October and I didn't expect even to get in. I've never read half of what other people have.'

'Nobody has,' said Mr Satterley, 'but you've got years ahead. Take a short walk about now, maybe down lane. People get very attached to t'lane.'

'I walked the lane yesterday. By accident.'

'Yes. I heard tell.'

'As a matter of fact [or had it been in a dream in the night?], I saw something rather queer. In the lane. It was a big table, just standing there by itself, with money on it.'

'Oh, aye. It would be Friday yesterday, was it?'

'Friday?'

'She keeps table there all summer. Friday's strawberry day, August. It's become well known. Soft fruit later. You pay in jar. They come from far as Watermillock for her fruit and honey. Was she not there?'

'Mrs Satterley?'

'No, no. A very different spirit. She leaves money about, she's not your usual. Not wise, but it's never abused, I'd think. She'll be there again today with runner beans, if you're interested. It's all for Red Cross. If you walked on to tek a look and walked back again, your room would be righted and you could start on your lessons. There's jam and that yonder she sells, too. Elizabeth can't find a lot wrong with it. Honey and that.'

'Is she—? Who is she?'

He looked surprised. 'Well, she's Ursula. Don't know where we'd be without Ursula.'

When Hetty trudged along the lane and reached the table there was again nobody to be seen. There was a big pile of runner beans – rather past their best, thought the daughter of the horticultural grave-digger – several honeycombs and a large cake marked ninepence. There was an empty Gold Flake cigarette packet but no sign at all of *The Perfumed Garden*.

Hetty, carrying the cake and ninepence the poorer, returned to *Areopagitica* and sat reading until twelve o'clock, when Mrs Satterley exploded into the room bearing a plate of ham sandwiches and a glass of milk. 'Well, I'm sorry you saw fit to bring in a cake. People don't usually complain of small portions here. I'll put it away in t' pantry on account of flies. And tomorrow you'd better have some clocks.'

'Clocks?'

'Some calls them elevenses; we call them "ten o'clocks". It's known as a small snack, and you could have had some this morning but you went gallivanting out.'

104

14

High Dubbs youth hostel could be seen from afar as a single tall chimney sticking up from the middle of the moor on the skyline, like a pencil. It was the chimney of a disused slate quarry, abandoned well before the First World War. A short row of quarrymen's deserted brick cottages lay below it and the moorland around was still pitted and scarred by old slate cuttings. Nobody lived at High Dubbs any more and the youth hostel had been acquired long ago for almost nothing. German bombers had come trundling regularly from the east over the heather towards the industrial towns, and though there had only once been bombs on the moors, dropped by accident, during the war the hostel had been hardly used. The brick cottages out of which the youth hostel had evolved possessed one of the most spectacular views in England.

The road to it was hard to find, and unmarked on all but the oldest maps. At the outbreak of war, all signposts on the moors had been removed to confuse the invading enemy, and not yet replaced, but there had never been a signpost to High Dubbs off the moor road, the quarrymen presumably knowing where it was without one, and nobody else wanting to go there. You had to be on the watch for a place where a track slipped almost invisibly away from the road along the highest ridge to join a lower green road running away into the heather. Once it had been the single-track railway line for the slate trucks. The piles of cut slate must have stood beside the road awaiting collection, but that was more than half a century ago. Now the slate, the trucks that carried them, the lines they had run on, all had vanished.

But the track that had been cut for them remained, grassy and green and cropped by sheep and never overtaken by the heather, because of the oak railway sleepers – expertly laid by the quarrymen – that lined its floor. A layer of thick shingle between each sleeper mingled still with the wild flowers and weeds.

In the past year, since the war's end, a youth-hosteller had marked the place where you left the road on the ridge for the track with a small cairn of rocks and the stone pattern of an arrow. From this cairn, known only to the elect of the cycling and rambling world, to the black pencil chimney, the deep, quiet but very bumpy old railroad track stretched for nearly five miles.

Una knew nothing of tracks and slate quarries and was concerned today only with the wind in her spiky hair. She overshot the cairn and had to be called back by Ray, who yelled after her, then whistled to her piercingly through his fingers.

She was almost at his horizon. The sun was going down. He stood waiting for the dot that was Una and her bike to steady, turn about, grow gradually bigger. At length she came up alongside him again.

'Down 'ere.'

It was still warm as the sun set, but down on the track it was already darker, dark beyond its hour, and the wind on the ridge above could be heard blustering about. Una saw that clouds to the west were beginning to gather together, and before remounting her bike she turned back to look at them. They were piling into creamy, smoking towers.

Ray watched them, too, clouds working themselves into hysterical contortions, silently exploding, upward, upward.

'I've seen some rare old things up 'ere before today,' he said. 'Typhoons.'

'*Typhoons!*'

'Well, you know, twisters. Like in America. *Wizard of Oz*.'

'What, here? Up on the moors?'

'Oh, aye. You never know what to expect up 'ere. You have to

106

be careful. I don't like the look of them clouds.'

'It's like a mushroom. It's like the Bomb.'

'Aye.'

'Well, it's a thunderstorm, so let's get on, shall we?'

They jolted and jerked along the railway sleepers, sometimes trying to ride the grassy margins, but that was even harder going. Rain began casually, then continued in earnest.

Soon it was falling in torrents and they had to stop to climb into yellow oilskins, capes and hoods. It was noisy inside them. Their fingers on the handlebars turned scarlet with cold and within the ugly oilskins their bodies steamed. The track, after winding about, became a straight stretch of mud between the oak sleepers. The sleepers shone like glass. They slithered off their bikes and pushed.

Great booms and crackles of thunder announced their arrival at High Dubbs and a ripple of lightning fell down the sky and disappeared below the buildings.

'Just as well it missed the chimney,' she yelled.

'Eh?'

'Might have hit the chimney.'

'Chimney's stood there long enough. There'll be a conductor.'

'Is it locked – the hostel?'

'Aye, it's locked. There's a key int' shed. Christ!'

A colossal barrage of thunder went rolling round the moor, followed by another and another, ending up directly overhead.

'Give me air raids,' she said. 'Anti-aircraft stands still.'

'Eh?'

'Guns keep still.'

Standing now directly below the chimney, which appeared to have no lightning conductor though it was too dark now to be sure, Ray tipped his bike over in Una's direction and vanished into something like a dog kennel. He emerged with a gigantic, rusty key. Holding this in both hands he made an attack upon the hostel door, the lock looking more fragile than the thing it served. Door and Ray lunged forward together, blown there by wind and rain, and Una, wheeling the bikes, moved forward over a flagstoned, freezing-cold kitchen floor and then stood dripping in the dark. Another long ripple of electricity passed the window, followed immediately by the most tremendous crash of thunder so far.

'There's matches in a tin,' he said.

'I was going to say—'

'Gi's yer bike. Prop it up, then. Yer shivering.'

'I'm not cold. It's just my teeth chattering.'

'Jump up and down. Gi's yer 'ands 'ere.'

Ray had removed his oilskins and thrown them down. He undid his zip-jacket with the YHA badge on the pocket, took her hands and directed them beneath it and beneath his shirt and pressed them to his skin. He began to move the backs of her hands up and down beneath his own. But still she shivered. She shivered rather more. He pulled her nearer.

'Better? I can blow on yer back if yer like?'

'Blow on—?'

'Aye. They do it int' Arctic.'

'Arctic?'

'Turn round.'

He removed her little hands from his torso and spun her round, lifted the back of her sweater, opened his mouth between her bare shoulder-blades, and blew.

She yelped. He went on blowing.

'It's great. Oh, it's really hot! It goes all around.'

'Saves a lot of lives,' he said. 'Ski instructors do it. It's Alpine technique.'

'I feel like I've had a heater in me.'

'You should get yer 'air dry now,' he said, moving away, not bothering to pull the back of her jersey down. 'There's a roller towel on back oft'door. It's a bit claggy but, well . . . 'Ere, get this fire started, there's sticks and that and paper. Tin's int' cupboard. I'll get out overt' coal-house,' and he left her standing, the back of her jersey rucked up to her shoulders.

She had never made a fire. Her mother did all that. The room was dark as midnight but the storm seemed to be resting and she heard now the authority of the impersonal deluging rain. When the thunder tried again it was fainter. It had moved further away. Further away.

'Where's the light?' she asked when he came splashing in, slamming the door. The lightning rippled. Further away. The thunder sounded sleepy now.

'Hell!' he said, and took the tin from her, found newspaper lining a partly open drawer and sticks from a groaning side oven in the range. He arranged coals over them, and with a match from the box in the tin, he lit the twigs.

They watched the flame falter, blacken the paper, tremble, rise and, in no time, blaze.

'There's a gas bottle and ring ower there. Hast got the beans and that?'

She brought out a large tin of baked beans from her saddle-bag, and some bread. 'The bread's damp.'

'It'll do,' said Ray.

A blue flame roared in a corner, and a saucepan was illuminated near the gas ring. Ray peered into the pan and crossed to a tap sticking out of a wall above a stone trough. After great bastinados of knocking and retching, some gulps of dark brown water splashed out of the tap and he rinsed the pan.

'Get some more coals ont' fire,' he said. 'You canst do that much if you can't do owt else.'

She was appalled. Excited.

'And get yon stockins off. And some dry things on.'

Eating the hot baked beans and drinking powerful tea, they sat opposite each other, either side of a paraffin lamp placed on a bare table.

'I've a bottle of beer,' said Ray.

'I don't like beer.'

He found a tin mug and drank the beer. 'What's the matter? Why are you grinning?'

'I'm happy,' she said.

'Why?'

'Don't know. I'm glad you didn't drink out of the bottle.'

'Jesus Christ!' he said.

'You're different,' she said. 'From usual.'

He built up the fire.

'I'm tired,' she said and carried the dirty plates over to the tap and trough and wiped them over with an evil dishcloth. Put them away. 'See,' she said, 'I can be useful. I'm not just a scientist. When . . . when do we go to bed?'

'*Scientist*!' he said. He'd pulled his chair nearer the fire, turned his back on her. Outside, the rain clattered down but the thunder had stopped. '*Useful*!' he said. ''Ere, I'll get bikes intert' shed; gi's the oilskins. I'll hang 'em int' old oil-house overt' yard. It's dry there. They'll be good be morning.'

'Shouldn't we dry the bikes down?'

'I'll see t'ilt.'

While he was out with the bikes, she didn't know what to do, whether or not to go looking for bedrooms and lavatories. In films the girl always went up the stairs first. You didn't *follow* a man up unless he was a monster and you were cowed or hypnotised. And it would be very embarrassing going up entwined, side by side. The uncertainty, or the certainty, of what she was doing filled Una's whole being.

Tonight could change my life, she thought. I could go up to Cambridge grown-up. Half of them at school have done it already. Almost everyone but Hetty and Lieselotte. Well, maybe a third. Well, Mavis Braithwaite has anyway. And Ray's been my only one for years and years, and I his. And *never*. Not even kisses.

She found a clanking WC with a rusty chain that unleashed a tempest of tea-coloured water. Ray came in, slamming the door once more, and gave a savage kick at the fire as she came down the stairs carrying the lamp.

'Are we going to let the fire go out?'

'It will whether we like it or not,' he said. 'It's a small enough grate.'

'Do we lock the front door?'

'What for? Who's coming?'

'I just thought it might be a rule. A youth-hostel rule, sort of thing.'

He swung about, came across to her, took her shoulders and shook her.

'Here!' she said. 'Stop it. What's up? You shouldn't have drunk all that beer.' She thought, All the years and he's never touched me at all. Tonight, all alone, he shakes me.

'You talk about youth-hostel rules. You talk about washing-up. Do you ever read the newspapers, woman?'

'Well, not tonight, I don't. Shut up. You're hurting.'

'*What* are you proposing to do at Cambridge?'

'Physics.'

'Physics? You? Do you ever think what Physics means? Do you ever consider what 'appened a year ago this month? Una? Are you just plain, solid infantile? You're unawakened. Cambridge, hell . . . I don't mean sex, that stuff, unawakened. I mean you are politically, morally and intellectually unawakened. Do you have one, *one*, analytical area? One concept, except passing exams? Eh? Eh?'

'I'm off to bed. Let go of me.'

'At this moment in Japan there is a liquidated civilisation. Turned to air. Transformed into cinder. Thousands on thousands. Kids and women. *We* did it. *We* found it. *We* found out how, and *we* used it. No warning. Nothing.'

'We did give a warning – some sort of warning. And if we hadn't, someone else would have done it. And it's nothing to do with me.'

'The old argument.'

'Well, it stopped the war. If we hadn't done it, it would have gone on and on and killed as many, maybe more. It probably *saved* lives by, you know, doing it in one go.'

'You're obscene. What papers d'you read?'

'Ma gets the *Daily Mail*.'

'Exactly. Well, better than none, mebbe, but I wonder. And you think you can be a physicist!'

'I didn't know you hated me.'

Beginning to cry, she ran and stumbled out of the room, found stone stairs inside a cupboard door, climbed them holding the lamp high and saw two doors, one labelled 'Men', one 'Women'.

She slammed into Women, crashed the door behind her and

111

saw several stacks of bunk beds with miserable mattresses each with a metal ladder up the side. At the end of each bunk there was a bed roll.

She blew out the lamp, climbed a ladder, flung some of her clothes and her shoes on the floor, undid the bed roll and curled down in it.

It smelled of mossy autumn woods. Far away some reviving thunder began to rattle out an ominous song.

My first time alone with a man. And the man is Ray, for goodness' sake. It is not usual. It is not kind. It must be a punishment. Perhaps I am not meant to be loved. It is the punishment for expectation. I thought it would be something wonderful, and all I get is the blame for Hiroshima.

'I didn't split the bloody atom,' she shouted as he came stumbling into the room, feeling for the lower bunk. He too had slammed the door. Now he slammed off his boots. Whatever was wrong with him? She heard him scruffling about with his bed roll, like a dog; and lying down.

Both lay staring upwards, one above the other, in the dark.

Long, long afterwards, as she thought, He must be asleep by now, he said, 'Sorry, Une.'

'It's OK.'

'Don't know what I was on about.'

She said nothing. She heard him creak off the lower bunk and in a moment he was climbing the ladder. The whole scant structure swayed. She felt him staring straight ahead over the top bunk in the dark.

'You're down by my feet.' She wanted to laugh. She thought, Hetty would *die*. 'Ray?'

She felt him heave himself up on his strong arms and he was lying with her, his dear face in her neck.

'God, I'm sorry, Une. I'm jealous of Cambridge. I'm no good with women.'

She put both arms round him and said, 'You are. You are. You're marvellous and you're mine.'

They lay there in the mossy damp and she began to feel more

112

happiness than she'd ever known. Sleepy. Giving. She held his face.

Then, far away, there was the sound of a vehicle coming down the track. It was faint, but it was there. It was coming. It was certainly some sort of motor. They lay rigid, wrapped tight, speechless, Una's head drawn away from Ray, Ray's head alert, their warm legs still entwined. Then she buried her face in him.

'It's a car,' she said, her voice muffled and sad.

'It can't be a car.'

'It's coming down the track. It must be more youth-hostellers.'

'It can't be. It's past midnight. And never in a car.'

They broke apart and Ray sat up. 'There's no warden 'ere,' he said, 'never has been. Oh, Une, I was sure there wouldn't be anyone else.'

'There is, though. Here it comes.'

They lay down again and the approaching car came roaring nearer and passed the window, its lights swinging spitefully across the room, lighting the bunk, passing on. There was a slamming of doors.

'I'd better go,' said Ray. 'I'd better move to Men.'

'No,' she said. 'No, Ray. Lock our door.'

He got down from the bunk and said, 'Une? Are you sure?'

'I'm sure.'

He locked the door and climbed back and they lay in the top bunk again, together.

Footsteps were on the stairs, voices – a man's and a woman's. Nobody tried their door and the voices faded into the other dormitory. Whoever it was was not stopping for food or fire, or even the loo.

There was shuffling and creaking and the dropping of shoes and slowly, slowly, Ray and Una relaxed and began to whisper. Una started to laugh and Ray squeezed her like a vice and said, 'Shut up.' The rain outside was stopping. Only drops now splashed from the lintel. Then even the little splashes stopped. The window frame brightened up and, outside, clouds could be made out in a navy-blue sky, and a round moon appeared. Drops like tiny moons hung in a row along the glazing-bars.

113

Then from the next-door dormitory came the most dreadful shrieks and cries and a sort of quacking of ducks. It went on and on, faster and faster, and reached crescendo.

'Ray?' It was morning and she was sitting up in bed, warm, delighted, unravished, proud. 'Ray? Where are you?'

He was dressed and grinning and looking at her. 'Get up,' he said. 'Get up and come down. He's a soldier.'

'Who's a soldier?'

'Last night. The people last night. Quack, quack.'

She remembered. 'Oh, a *soldier*! I thought it sounded like a ten-ton tank coming along.'

'It's a jeep thing. He's here with his fiancée. *She*'s like a ten-ton tank – from the back anyway; it's all I've seen.'

'How d'you know?'

'I've been down. They're cooking their breakfasts. Sausages. It must be army rations. She looks awful. Maybe he'll give us a rasher.'

'Were they surprised? To know we were here? Oh, Ray!'

'He nearly fell dead. She just sat there looking at the fire.'

'I'm coming!'

She sprang out of the bunk in her bra and pants and began to dress as if he watched her do it every day.

He said, 'You should never wear clothes.'

Hiroshima faded.

They came out together from the stair-cupboard door into last night's kitchen and there she saw a tall man prodding bacon about in a pan and a large woman dreaming by the grate.

'Good morning,' said Eustace, bright of eye, fork aloft. 'May I introduce my fiancée, Brenda Flange?'

15

My darling Hetty, wrote her mother in her third letter in five days. Hetty had not opened the first two and nor for a while would she open this one.

My darling Hetty,

I realise now how very cross you will have been with me for writing to you before you had even left, in order that there would be a letter waiting for you at Betty Bank (what a pretty name) in case you had a sudden fit of homesickness. I know your father thinks 'Leave her alone', though he seldom speaks, but I just could not resist. The house is so quiet without you. Whatever will it be like when you go to London?

I hope I didn't annoy you too much. I should really have liked to send you some sweets (what was the chocolate cake like for the train?) but they are still so hard to get unless you pull strings and as you know I hate doing this because of your father's position in the Church. Well, I'm sure I've said all this before and much more, and I expect you haven't even read my other letters. I know I make you very impatient. But now that you have been there for some days (four and a quarter!) I thought that perhaps I might be allowed.

Not that there is very much news. Mrs Baxter is full of excitement because she has been given three bananas. She's a good soul. She says that she would send one to you, but for the difficulties of packing. She says that though there is the odd banana *about* now, there won't be any in the Lake District on account of the distance from the sea (your father thinks she is confusing them with fish). I'm afraid that she has a very queer look at present and I do think that she should go down to the surgery and have her blood pressure seen to, but you can't *say* so. In the café this morning before she came in I said as much to Joyce Dobson, who by the way has given me a tea-towel for you to take to College. She often goes to London and she says she'll take you to the theatre with her nice sister Ada who's a little retarded. What good friends I have. I think she's being so kind because I kept 'open house' all through the War, which gave her a chance of getting closer to the vicar, who has been such a help to her. I'm glad I insisted on having everyone in all the time in spite of your father who always finds everyone so *lacking*. But people are very understanding about him. Joyce Dobson, by the way, is looking very yellow again. It's a shame she never married, she is a jewel, but men are a little afraid of her, she has that tall, elegant figure you seldom see around here. Of course her arm will never be right – it is still in a bandage.

Oh, yes, in the café I met Hilda and Dorothy who had dropped in on their way back from a walk by the sea. They are finding retirement a great burden. They asked me to walk home with them past Bidewell. Do you know, in all these years I've never been inside their house? They don't entertain. We were always in the Guide Hall. They were shocked when I told them so, and they showed me all over it – that great tall house, five storeys just for the two of them now that all their airmen have gone. Dorothy says she wonders now how she managed, all that running about looking for pies. Of course neither of them can cook. I remember round the camp fire! Isn't it lovely to think that Hilda Fletcher was first my Guide Captain and then yours! All those years later! But you and I will always know how to make bread and how to lay and light a fire. It is instinctive to you and me. Not even Hitler could have taken this knowledge from us.

Hilda and Dorothy look exactly the same as when I was

116

eighteen. They've been in that house now for over forty years. They keep to the one bedroom. They had to move in together in 1940 when the fifteen airmen came and they say they've got used to it. It's like school, they say. They have group photographs of their schooldays above their beds. There are *two* beds. Your father was keen to know – he is incorrigible. And balanced on the photographs are their old school caps with the badges showing. There are Guide Camp photographs all over the walls – they are quite *sepia* – and I saw myself, the Patrol Leader of the Flamingos, with proficiency awards all down my arm to the cuff. Such happy days. We had no idea about the awfulness of the war in the trenches going on and on in France, exactly then – I do remember how many more women than men there were in the streets, though, in 1918, and the dreadfully grim faces. I'd forgotten I had such a fat rope of hair all down my back, but they remembered it. They said it was a 'rich chestnut'! It's so nice to go where people *like* you and remember you when young. It's very rare. The Lonsdale is all talk. I don't care what anybody says about them, they are two lovely, loving women and I only wish they weren't finding the stairs so difficult. Little Dorothy looks flushed, to me, and she's putting on a lot of weight, I'd say dangerously. Hilda of course is marvellous. She looks like a crane (the bird) though she eats very little because of the Hiatus Hernia. I said, 'There's no war effort now, Hilda. You should eat when you can,' but she said, 'We all think far too much of our stomachs. We discuss nothing but food,' and she looked quite sharply at Dorothy I thought. I suppose there must be friction there sometimes. Your father used to say that without friction there can be no warmth. (Oh, I wish he still said clever things like that!) And they are nice women. I do hope when you go to College that you'll meet some nice *men*.

The vicar's been having a bad time with a tooth. Your father's been rather better the last few days, more 'with it'. He's been wandering round to see Una and her mother, I understand, though I can't think why, it's such a dirty place. He says Una's hair has gone very peculiar, like heather on the moors when they burn it in autumn.

117

Well, *nothing* has happened and I suppose we should be thankful. 'Dear God, I thank Thee that nothing has happened today and I pray that nothing will happen tomorrow.' I am a bit *muzzy* and I am on some new tablets. I do think of you, almost all the time, and I'm sending you some sanitary towels by the parcel post as I don't think you took any and you'll need them next week. The Lake District should be looking very nice at this time of the year and I'm told by Mrs Stonehouse – she stayed there, recommended of course by Hilda Fletcher – that Mrs Satterley is very nice too. I took the bus to the Stonehouses, my breathing being so bad, lately.

By the way, it is true what you heard. Lieselotte *has* been taken away somewhere by a Jewish rehabilitation organisation and it is very upsetting. She hasn't written. I don't know what has happened to manners, to natural gratitude. All those years!

With so very much love, Mummy.

PS   Mrs Quarendon's dog has died, so perhaps you could send her a card? Number 247 Corporation Road.

XX – don't be cross with me. I'm so proud of you. You know how hard it is for me to show my feelings,

Mummy.

PPS   I'm just getting your father off to the chiropodist!

Hetty read this letter sitting on a bench in the high farm garden after breakfast, a week into her stay. The slops were being dealt with upstairs. On her lap were other letters in her mother's attractive, even writing, still unopened, delivered an hour ago. The day was deliriously beautiful, the mountains violet, the grass a technicolour green. The scarf of milky mist was moving lightly above the lake. The sun was already hot and the stone flank of the house she leant against was warm. Beside the pump, Mr Satterley unhurriedly washed out milk pails and the cows were coming crackling down the yard looking sideways at her, in a troop. Their eyes were tender. She closed her own and a cow came up and nuzzled her with a wet nose. She yelped.

'It'll never hurt thee,' said Mr Satterley. 'How's work going, then?'

'Oh, pretty boring.'

'D'you 'ave to do it? What are you reading all day at present?'

'At the moment it's Thomas Carlyle.'

'Aye – a nasty bit of work, him.'

'Is he? I never thought.'

'A sour man. Keep off him. He's disregarded now, any road. Now, Hester, don't waste this day. Don't sit to your book. Get out. "A minute now may give us more Than years of toiling reason". That's your Wordsworth. That's 'is instructions. Aye, and he was a solitary man. Why don't you tek off downt' lane, and on away roundt' lake, like t'other ones as comes?'

'They're just sightseers. And they're old, and they go round in a mob. And, anyway, I have to work. I got this scholarship just by accident.'

'You're being too grateful, Hester. I'd say the College was lucky to get you, and you're bonny with it. Now then, shut up that atheist this morning, walk down our lane, past Meeting House and Ursula's hole int' hedge, turn the hairpin and you're atop yon lake. Get off now. Be tea-time the weather'll be gone. This variety of mist says it's calling back later.'

So she put the letter in her pocket and set off. She watched her legs walking along in their lisle stockings with darned ladders, her feet in the lace-up gym shoes. She brooded about trousers and boots. She was passionate for some boots, but boots were expensive beyond desire. She'd not been able to keep her mind off boots lately. *Past and Present* was all boots, boots.

Wasn't it men, or sexual deviants, who were supposed to be weird about boots? Boot fetishists? She wonder about Hilda and Dorothy; they certainly liked marching. Well, Hilda did. Dorothy bounced. Oh, why am I thinking about these frowsty women? Will I never get away from my mother's world?

She liked watching men march. It was horrible being stirred by such a thing: the films of marching German troops, that terrible music. It made you tingle. It was wonderful, watching British troops marching and singing, half satirical, half near weeping. You wanted to weep yourself, hearing British soldiers sing, to run and kiss them. Sardonic, cynical, wise English soldiers. You couldn't imagine Eustace marching, though. Maybe they'd let him off it in the Pay Corps. Her father said Eustace couldn't even walk, he floated. He hung in the air like a Botticelli angel. He was all ether. Her mother had said once that it was possible that Eustace suffered from haemorrhoids and they were very nasty things and not to be laughed at, and her father had then cried out, 'Ye gods!'

Along the lane, beneath the trees. The table was bare today and sopped with dew. She wrote 'Hester Fallowes' in the dew. This table is getting at me, she thought. Some symbol of something, some metaphor. It has, somewhere, an algebraic meaning. Una should be here. Oh God, I wish Una were here! She walked regretfully, all round the table, thinking of Una, and then marched on. It's *Alice in Wonderland* here, she thought. In a minute there'll be a white rabbit.

There was not, but around the next bend in the lane someone was seated head-on to Hetty, on a big white horse.

The horse was standing still, cropping the grassy centre of the lane, and on its back a tall thin girl was watching Hetty coming towards her. It was as if she had reined in the horse, turned and was waiting. The girl was smiling and as Hetty came near she saw a mouth full of very small square teeth, like a baby's. Hetty did not care for her.

Hetty came up to the horse and stepped into the hedge to the side of it and the girl looked her up and down, then jerked at the horse's head. Hetty thought, I'd better say something, but the girl clicked her pearly teeth and trotted off past her.

If that's Ursula, thought Hetty, I can see exactly where they'd be without her. A lot better off.

She walked on and on. And on. And on. She had long passed the place where she had come into the lane from the cornfield on her arrival, and it wound on, never varying, a level, shadowy, compulsive trail from an old dream, scarcely remembered. Nobody passed and nobody followed.

On and on. The woods were silent. The sun shone through the

trees only in spots and blobs. She felt herself living inside a gold parcel. Outside was universal joy; inside, the endless, pointless journey.

And loneliness, she thought, though you mustn't say that. 'You're never alone, because of God. The everlasting arms,' Mum had said. Hetty thought of the stacked bodies of Belsen.

A stone wall was rearing into life now to her left, growing slowly until it was taller than she was, and in it there soon stood a tall door and nailed to it a small notice printed neatly with the words 'QUAKER MEETING HOUSE. All welcome. Key at Mrs Allason's'.

There was no sign of Mrs Allason's, nor of any dwelling. The door latch was a nice one with a dip in it like a metal pansy petal and, when Hetty pressed it, the door opened without a key. She pushed and saw a flagstoned path running between two carefully mown squares of lawn. Two wooden benches stood on the lawns, which were bordered with flowers. The tall, narrow Meeting House windows regarded her from either side of a front door.

Hetty tried this door and it opened into a room with tiers of benches around three sides of it and a table in the middle holding a Bible and a vase without flowers. The long windows were clear and clean, reflecting the tops of the trees in the lane. Hetty sat down on one of the benches and soon the silence, a stored silence, became very pleasing.

Then she got up again and walked about, found an ante-room in the back, where there was an earth-closet that smelled sweet, a stone shelf with cups and saucers, the cups turned upside-down, the handles all one way, a clean tea-towel, a shelf of devotional books and a notice-board with notices of coming events. Monthly Meeting. Meetings for Worship. Meetings for Sufferings. All weird. All alien. Yet she did not feel an interloper. She felt, most strangely, at home.

She left the building, looking over her shoulder for a moment, wishing to thank somebody. Then she carefully closed the door of the Meeting House, crossed the small garden and closed the door in the wall, again carefully, behind her.

In the lane outside, the girl and the horse stood as if they had been waiting for her; the girl, still smiling, but the horse now looking more impatient, tossing its head up and down and shaking it, as if it wanted to be off. The angular great girl was keeping the horse on a tight rein. Hetty, suddenly scared, cold from the coolness of the Meeting House, knew that she must be the first to speak or something would be lost.

'I suppose you're Ursula,' she said.

'*Ursula*! Whatever do you know about Ursula?'

They examined each other and Hetty saw the girl considering her gym shoes and the skirt that had been Joyce Dobson's.

'I suppose you're a Quaker,' she said.

'Whatever do you know about me?' said Hetty.

She walked on, faster and faster, the way she had been going before, until at length the lane began to drop down, to turn back upon itself in a long straggling hairpin and the woods behind her receded to display the open fields before and below her, and a wide hillside sloping down to the lake.

16

Two weeks later and three hundred and nineteen miles away, a curious chemical change was coming over Lieselotte. She was growing smaller.

She first noticed when she fell down the area steps.

'Ach, your shoes are too big for you,' Mr Feldman called down to her from his basket chair. 'You can see daylight between the backs of them and your ankle, girl.'

'I expect my shoes have stretched with all the walking about.'

'*Nein.* You are small all over,' said Mrs Feldman, manoeuvring herself among the overstuffed settees as she held aloft a very small saucepan in which she had been boiling a very small egg.

'This egg,' she said: 'where is the point of sending it all the way from Paraguay? And now – I must measure you all over again for the brocade.'

'You are carrying less weight too,' said Mr Feldman.

There was no sign of brocade in the underground apartment, nor, Lieselotte suspected, in Harvey Nichols of Knightsbridge, where it was rumoured that a roll or two was being secreted under the counter for customers of eminence like the Queen and Mrs Churchill. (The Prime Minister's wife, Mrs Attlee, did not wear brocade.) Yet one day Lieselotte had arrived home from her peregrinations to find that somehow a seamstress's table had been set up and a long swatch of some sort of red plush, very like the curtains, had been spread over it upside-down along with formidable scissors and paper patterns like an ancient papyrus. Lieselotte was now reassailed with tape-measures and declared to be losing inches in every direction.

'It's getting the right food,' said Mrs Feldman. 'True kosher food with friends to provide. Resourceful friends – you see this length of cloth? And there will be trimmings and buttons and dress-absorbers and linings. We shall find them. Mr Feldman has still a small connection with the East End mantle trade.'

'A healthy diet must have been difficult for you with the Northern Quakers, Lieselotte?'

'They tried very hard,' said Lieselotte. 'They were good to me.'

But she could hardly speak of the Stonehouses. In less than a month they had slipped into the past as completely as her first ten years, their faces shadows. Like childhood's faces. (Don't look, don't look! Gone. Gone.) She had not yet written to them.

As for food, food the great coagulator of the nation, the inescapable topic, Lieselotte was eating less here than ever she had done during the war. And eating at unprecedented times. Now she was never hungry. She ate with the two old people, from a little porcelain plate on a tray on her knees, and sometimes they forgot to eat at all. Frenziedly she walked the street of London all day long, from early morning, coming home still not hungry to toy with a Matzos biscuit and some tinned sardines. At the Stonehouses' there had been three – sometimes four – knife-and-fork meals a day, pale, nourishing and good as the Stonehouses themselves: Whitby cod, tinned rice in milk, tinned spaghetti, mashed potatoes, everything white except the spam and the baked beans and the speckled national wheatmeal bread. Hetty sometimes came with a cabbage from the grave-digger. Mrs Stonehouse had cooked the cabbage for several hours until it too had turned vaguely white. During the worst of the war there had been chances of black-market fat sometimes, but it had smelled of drains. Una's mother had found some miniature bottles of olive oil once, in a queer shop near the sand-hills, but it had been almost congealed and nobody quite knew how to cook with it. Mrs Fallowes had said it was used for rubbing on a tight chest. The Stonehouses, so undemonstrative in body, had spread all they had before Lieselotte, their silent declaration of love.

'We had lovely fish,' said Lieselotte. 'The boats went out whenever they could. They were very brave, the fishermen. It was good fish.'

'Only Jews know how to cook fish,' said Mr Feldman.

But privately Lieselotte knew that her diminishing body was the result of something other than the snacky food and the compulsive walking, something that only compulsive walking could deaden.

Every morning of that embalming gold September she set off up the area steps, past Mr Feldman examining the interior of his Viennese hat. She marched out of Rillington Mansions, down Kensington Church Street, then left, along the High Street, past the great bare shops, along the side of the park and towards the West End.

Sunlight stroked the pavements, the first leaves were beginning to fall from the avenue of elms that braced the long rise across the grass from the Albert Hall upwards and out of sight. Time and again she marched up and down this avenue of glorious elms, then circled the Round Pond. She watched the huge broken temple that was being taken from its wadding, the figure of a sad-looking, long-dead prince. 'We knocked the top off that one ourselves,' said a soldier. 'They'd painted him black, you know, in 1914, in case the gold attracted the Zeppelins. Ugly great monstrosity.'

She turned to gaze across the road at Albert's decrepit Hall, still placarded with notices of valiant concerts that had somehow never been silenced. Then on she strode, down Knightsbridge, along Piccadilly, and, via Holborn, on to the City.

Deep in the City ruins she sat on one of the rural-looking fences that encircled the craters of vanished buildings and streets, imagining them, peopling them – Threadneedle Street, Pudding Lane – considering the miracle of untouched St Paul's Cathedral standing above all the little, broken, burned-out churches. Inside, thick dust lay all over the black-and-white marble floor as if it would be there for ever. Outside, wild flowers waved in long country grasses, green jungle grew in sheets of creeper over toppling ruined walls. Insects hummed. There were cats and kittens everywhere. Bracken and chickweed looked indestructible. The London Fire Service had begun to grow rows of vegetables outside the London Wall.

On she went all through the afternoons, eastwards to the Pool of London along the oily tired river. It was a long time before she dared go down to the tube, or step aboard a rocking scarlet bus. From morning to morning she walked, and never spoke to a soul.

One day, looking for Covent Garden, she found herself outside King's College in the Strand and stepped through sandbags and scaffolding into a big, colourless cloister full of building works and rubble. Sandbags like solid masonry were being chipped away from the pillars of a broken colonnade. She wandered among the arches and met a young man with a twitching face who asked, 'You a student?'

'Yes,' she said.

'D'you feel like going to the canteen?'

It was underground and awful. From blunt thick cups, they drank coffee that was no more than coloured water, and she paid him back the tuppence. He said he was Polish. And Jewish. He had electric-looking black curls and excited black eyes.

'Carl,' he said. 'Been to the NG yet?'

They walked the Strand to the National Gallery with all its faded walls. Hardly anybody else was there. Their feet and voices echoed in the big sad rooms. An occasional attendant slept on an upright chair. There were very many clean squares on the walls waiting for the paintings to come back from Mrs Feldman's caves.

'They say Arnolfini's back,' he said, and she looked round for a person. 'There,' he said.

The little picture grew luminous as she looked at it. Pale Flemish light flowed over two fifteenth-century faces, the bridegroom's tall white hand raised, sideways on, in blessing, the bride with downcast eyes clutching her heavy green and silver robe up against her tiny breast.

'Mrs Feldman would love that material,' Lieselotte said. Arnolfini is not a handsome bridegroom, she thought. He is the colour of the Stonehouses' white fat. He looks like a hare. Not much fun. He's rather like Eustace.

126

And, all at once, again she was with Hetty, Hetty's feet waving in the air beside a sad old Yorkshire tomb, Hetty shouting with delight that she was Hester Fallowes. Hestah! Hetty the infantile, the innocent, the loved and greatly blessed. For the first time Lieselotte addressed herself to her parentless years.

'You German?' asked Carl. 'Nice to meet you. Nice to meet an intellectual again. See you next term.'

Intellectual? she thought. Am I? It must be my glasses.

When she got back to Rillington Mansions ('Ah – and so! The National Gallery? So empty and so sad. Ah – Schönbrunn.') she took off her glasses and blinked at herself, but had to put them on again to read some mail that had come for her. It included a cheque from the Jewish Rehabilitation Board to tide her over until her grant came through at the beginning of term.

Intellectual? she thought.

The next day she went to Lilley and Skinner in Oxford Street and bought some shoes with high heels, and on to Selfridges, with Feldman coupons, to buy slacks.

'I want some very well-cut slacks. I have rather short legs.'

The assistant said, 'Do you mind my saying, madam, that we don't wear high heels with trousers? Just as we never wear earrings with trousers. We can't be too careful these days, can we? There are so many people now who aren't English.'

She left the store in the trousers and the high heels, on the way home calling in at a Woolworth's and buying some diamante earrings.

'No,' said Mrs Feldman. 'Nein. I have earrings for you. Take off those trash.'

Mrs Feldman heaved her huge self sideways and burrowed in dark places. 'These,' she said. 'With the court shoes they are acceptable, but not the trousers. You don't see Jewish girls in trousers.'

But the next day Lieselotte set off in the trousers, the high heels and Mrs Feldman's amber earrings and beautiful amber bracelets, and got whistled at by workmen on a crane. They were demolishing part of Eaton Square, its façade both blanched and black, and hollow-eyed. Lieselotte thought this must be the slums.

She went swanking into a Lyons tea-shop, and the waitress in her little black dress and pinny said, 'Where'd you get your slacks, ducky? They're smashing.'

And when she came breezing home in the evening, pink-faced and with her hair cut for five shillings in the Bayswater Road, Mr Feldman said, 'I believe that you are getting a waistline.'

'Oh. Is there a mirror?'

'Now, that is a good sign,' said Mrs Feldman. 'I have never seen you look in the glass.'

They sat, all three, that night with their bits of supper on their knees, listening to the Hallé Orchestra on the wireless, Mrs Feldman sometimes dabbing her eyes and wheezing, the acreage of red plush still untacked, uncut-out upon the table, in case perhaps there might be further adjustments to come.

And that was the night that Mrs Feldman broke the chandelier.

Lieselotte had by now become used to the many nocturnal noises about the basement of Rillington Mansions, for 'Mr Feldman and I have both reached that age where we have to get up in the night at least once,' said Mrs Feldman. 'Mr Feldman, being sixteen months older than I am, he finds it difficult to get to sleep again afterwards, and he calls out. He likes to chat. This tends towards refreshment.'

Lieselotte had grown used therefore to thumps and grunts going on around her sofa, the pacings about, the filling of kettles, the pulling of the Niagran lavatory chain, the quiet, relentless bird-song of old-folks' arguments. A week ago she had begun to try to find a little more privacy for herself of a night-time and made space in what had once been a small store-room or larder, by removing some crates and boxes. Dragging her *chaise-longue* inside, she found that it fitted exactly, and since the door opened outwards she was able to pull it to behind her and have a cabin to herself. Above her head was a small barred window, covered with meat-safe mesh. From the ceiling an electric light bulb hung from a threadbare twist of purple flex. It was an illumination very different from the huge Venetian chandelier of rose-pink and yellow crystal drops that hung from the ceiling of the rambling main room, the Feldmans' valuable advertisement for their careers as packagers of works of art.

128

How Mrs Feldman, who was not a tall woman, managed to bring down this chandelier at two o'clock in the morning was to be a matter for vituperative discussion for many years to come. She had been carrying a saucepan of milk in one hand at the time and a Sèvres coffee-pot in the other, and it may be that she had become confused by the rearrangement of the room now that Lieselotte had shifted the *chaise*. It is also possible that Mrs Feldman in her long nightdress had mounted a sofa in her pre-war bedroom slippers, boat-bottomed and trimmed with imitation pink ostrich plumes, *en route* to the gas ring, and was walking therefore about a foot off the floor.

Mr Feldman, asleep in some ante-chamber, awoke to hear his wife wheezing and talking to herself as usual. Then there was silence for a time. And then there was the most almighty explosion and crash of falling glass, and Mrs Feldman's screams. Her screams were piercing, but as the showering waterfall of glass ceased, followed only by the sound of the neck of the chandelier swinging and creaking and groaning very slowly, were heard other screams which did not stop.

They were loud, long and terrible, broken into by a torrent of German in a child's voice. A child crying, 'No!' And 'No! No!'

—On and on, for her mother.

They seemed to threaten the building, and they came from behind Lieselotte's pantry door. This, when pulled open, revealed Lieselotte sitting upright in bed, eyes wide and open, screaming and screaming, hands over her ears. On, on, on she screamed.

Mrs Feldman tried to get to her across the broken glass and Mr Feldman, holding up his flannelette nightshirt with one hand, leaned forward in an effort to stroke Lieselotte's feet from beyond her threshold. The spate of terrified German continued, and the Feldmans took it up in reprise. But they could get nowhere near her because of the tight fit of the bed in the larder, only stretch out their arms. And on Lieselotte screamed. Someone in the flat upstairs began to thump on the floor with a boot.

Soon there was infuriated knocking and shouting at the front door of the flat, and Mr Feldman shuffled over to it in the dark, feeling for the bolts, and people came swarming in, clambering

129

over the furniture, pushing Mrs Feldman out of the way. They tried to pull Lieselotte from the bed. But still she screamed, though she was cold and rigid as a corpse.

At last, quite suddenly, she stopped, turned her head sideways, and lay down. Somebody found brandy and somebody else was making coffee. Everybody seemed to be Jewish, frantic, foreign and wide awake. Conversation raged.

'She is eighteen. She has come from Hamburg. It is *Kristallnacht* again.'

One by one, and very slowly, the visitors departed but Mr and Mrs Feldman sat on, over the one-bar electric fire, and did not attempt to go back to bed. The birds began to wake in the remains of the bomb-sites and in the trees in all the parks. 'It was *Kristallnacht* that decided them. After that, they sent the children away. She will be the only one of her family.'

'Auschwitz,' said Mrs Feldman. 'The confirmation must have come by now. A year ago it should have come. But she seems to know nothing.'

In that dawn Lieselotte lay quiet, her head on the pillow, listening to them talk. She slept all the next day and night, and would not even drink water. The Feldmans picked up the pink and yellow splinters of glass and sorted them into old shoe-boxes, but agreed that there was no way of putting the chandelier together again. They reminisced about how expensively it had once been insured.

Then, thirty-six hours later, Lieselotte got up, ate breakfast and said that she was going out. Wearing the trousers but not the shoes or the earrings or the bracelets, she set off without telling them where.

'She has no longer the eternal smile,' said Mr Feldman. 'So that is good.'

Mrs Feldman laid out the red velvet once again upon the table and began to pin the revised paper pattern all over it. 'Aye, she has lost inches,' she said, 'inches all over her body,' and she started to record Lieselotte's new measurements in a notebook in elegant and businesslike calligraphy. Professionally she was a deft and accurate woman. She pinned and measured, carefully and sadly.

17

Una and Ray ate a thoughtful breakfast at the pub in Semerdale. The woman who ran it had looked them up and down and paid attention to them only because they had been standing with their bikes so early in the morning on the moor's edge, as she was going out round the back to the pig. 'We're shut.'

'We just want a cup of tea.'

'I thowt ye said yer breakfasts?'

'Well, anything you've got, really.'

'Come on by, then. Roundt' back.'

And they sat in silence as she humped a great ham in a sacking cloth down from a hook somewhere above their heads and cut off two half-inch thick slices. Looking across at them she said, 'It'll be two shillin', mind.'

'Each?'

'I'm not that bad,' she said. 'Two shillin' the pair of yer and if there's an egg apiece, one-and-three.'

'Yes, we'd both like an egg.'

'So, one-and-three? Two-and-six?'

'Yes, please. Thank you.'

'You've got it?'

'Yes.'

'Very well, then. They're me own.'

'Your own?'

'Pigs an' chickens.'

'Thank you.'
'All ont' quiet?'
'Yes, of course.'

And quiet's the word, thought the woman, for Una and Ray sat in silence, Ray looking over at Una all the time. Once he gave her hand a stroke.

'You been turned out of somewhere? Not being married and that?'

Una blazed with blushes.

'Why do you think we're not married?' asked Ray.

'Because she's but a bairn. Are you in trouble?'

'Certainly not,' said Una, all at once the professional man's daughter. 'And might we have some salt and pepper, please?'

'So what's up, then? So early int' morning? Here y'are, and some new bread and a pot of tea. Good eggs?'

'Wonderful, thank you. Nothing's the matter.'

'We've a friend in trouble,' said Ray.

'I've heard yon before today. Now then, I'll give yer advice. *Tell yer mothers.* And go to no doctors. *Have* it. You'll nivver regret it. There's nowt like havin' a young mother. And don't have no truck with goin' out to work, you miss.'

'I'm leaving,' said Una, getting up.

'No,' said Ray. 'Eat her blasted ham and egg and forget her. She's a peasant.'

'I thought you were a Communist?'

'I am. Peasants are part of the class system.'

Clanking around outside in the yard, the woman called that she could let them have a pheasant, first of shoot, well, first of shoot be a long way, and no questions.

Breakfast had at least been a respite from the shock of the revelation of Eustace's perfidy and on her bike again Una felt much calmer. The road before her shone purple and wet in the morning sunshine, and in the dale below black clumps of trees stood on the tops of round green hills, white mist still about them.

When they reached the ruins of Rievaulx Abbey they propped the bikes against the walls of the hospitium and walked among the sunken white boulders in the grass, then down into the vaulted crypt and up the shallow old steps into the novices' dormitory. Through empty graceful windows they looked at all the rising slopes of the trees, and the sky. Then they wandered out again and lay side by side in the grass of the great cloister. Nobody else was there, and the early silence was beautiful.

They lay there for a long time in their grey shorts and old shirts. Ray offered Una a cigarette and they smoked contentedly on their backs.

He said, 'You've got to learn you can't live Hetty's life for her. You can't save her from everything. She's just a friend. You'll be losing touch next year anyway, you at Cambridge, her in London.'

'I'll have to tell her, though.'

'Why? She probably knows. He's probably written. He'll *have* to write now, whatever. Mebbe she's the one who's written to him calling it off. Keep out of it.'

'Well, maybe.'

'She's seen sense, I'd guess. She always looked thoroughly moped, Hetty, whenever I saw them dangling about together.'

'Well, it's difficult, isn't it?'

'What's difficult?'

'Knowing whether you love someone or not. I mean, it's been friends one's bothered about until now. With girls it is, anyway. Otherwise, it's been only talk about boys, nothing more . . . and, well, sex talk. And so on. Though mostly it's just being each other's friend.'

'I don't have a lot of friends,' said Ray.

'D'you have *any* friends?'

After thinking about it he said, 'No, I dare say I don't have any friends. I have mates – those as think same as me int' Union, since I joined LNER.'

'Well, friends are vital for girls,' she said. 'More than any Politics. And she's like a sister as well, because I've known her for ever, and we're both only ones. No brothers or sisters.'

'Well, let her mother tell her, then. I'd think from what's said she'll have heard already.'

'However do you know that?'

'I know things. I'm not just Politics.'

'Oh, it would be terrible if your mother had to tell you.'

'Tell you what? That someone's gone off yer?'

'Ray, yes! Unforgivable. I'd never speak to my mother again.'

He rolled over and, looking close at Una's face, began to tickle her nose with a stalk of grass.

'Get off!'

She kicked him and they began to plunge about in the holy ruins, laughing. A stone face looked down at them.

'Think of being here all yon time ago,' he said. 'Chanting music and never arguing and that. No women. Unbelievable.'

'Yes,' she said. 'Awful.'

'And think of nuns!'

She looked at him sideways and said, 'Well, now it's Physics.'

It was nice when he laughed. They began to fool and play like puppies.

'Come on,' he said, 'we'd best be off home. I'm on duty five o'clock.'

When they reached the front door of Una's house, however, it was still the early afternoon and there was a notice fastened in Vane Glory's window saying: CLOSED FOR STAFF TRAINING.

'She'll be at the pictures,' said Una. 'She doesn't mind it being Sunday. She says she has to go two or three times a week to study the Hollywood hairstyles.'

'Is nobody in, then?'

'No, but it's OK, I've got a key.'

'Shall I come in with you?'

'I don't know.'

'Couldn't we go upstairs?'

'She might come back. She often comes out before the end.'

He looked resentful, and they stood looking down together at the pavement.

But when she looked up at him next, she thought that maybe he looked a bit relieved.

'Next weekend, then? I do want to, Una.'

'Not High Dubbs again.'

'No. There's another one. It's t'other side of the country. We'd have to start out early on the train with the bikes int van. I can work it out. There'd be no worries there, it's the remotest hostel in England. Nobody goes there. Please?'

'Yes. I'd like that.'

'You're sure?'

'Yes. Absolutely.'

She had tears in her eyes, which mystified him, and he stood frowning as she ran into the garden, flung the bike on the grass, and slammed the front door behind her.

Over the cat-scented hall she went, upstairs and upstairs again, up into the attic where she slept. Her narrow bed. Her desk. Her shelf of books. Her curtains, six pence a yard from Woolworth's. (She'd bought them for herself. Blue gingham.) Scrubbed floor. Black empty grate never used. Photograph of the dead doctor. View of clouds racing. I have shared a bed all night long with a man, she thought and fell asleep immediately, alone.

When she awoke it was still hardly dark and she heard the church clock strike six and thought, He's on the station now in his uniform, and grinned. Some of her Science books lay on the shelf beside her with the letters from Cambridge and the local authority about her award. There was another letter from Cambridge she hadn't yet bothered with. It was the list of recommended reading. 'I'll do something about that tomorrow, she thought, then slept again.

Mrs Vane, home from the cinema, had brought in the bike off the grass and now began to climb up through the house to stand at the foot of the attic staircase and listen. Cats were about her feet and one in her arms. She began to sing 'I'll Gather Lilacs', and listened again. Silence from above. She wandered away, down to the kitchen, where she stoked the already overpowering fire and served out catfish to all comers.

She thought, I've lost her. She'll be different now. We won't be all-in-all any more. Oh, I *hope* she doesn't have a baby. I can't have her hurt. Why couldn't she have found a namby-pamby first beau? Like Hetty's. That long-drink-of-water, Eustace, wouldn't do anyone any harm. No fears there. He's good for nothing, that one, but the church choir. Well, now he's gone off with someone else. That Ray's not good enough. He comes from Muriel Street. Well, maybe nothing happened. Maybe it's all over for Unie too.

'Hi,' said Una, coming in, pink with sleep and uncertainty. 'Nice pictures?'

'*The Prince and the Pauper. Ever* so likely.'

'Not many Hollywood hairstyles?'

'No. But Hilda and Dorothy were there, so I got a laugh. Fancy, on Sunday! But they're not religious except on Armistice Day, Oooh, they looked solemn. They tell me Hetty's soldier's backed off. Milk and water, he always seemed to me, but safe.'

'*Oh* yes!'

'They said that all you clever girls ought to be doing much better for yourselves by waiting. They said, "Think of the Duchess of Gloucester".'

'You're making that up. You thought of that yourself. It's a real Vane Glory joke.'

'I may have done,' said Mrs Vane, eating a slice of bread and dripping, 'but I'm a bit of a thought-reader, you know. I'm sure they are of my opinion. What do you think?'

'I don't think very much at all about the Duchess of Gloucester. I'm going to the library. Miss Kipling's there on a Sunday night, dusting round.'

'Yes. Oh . . .' Mrs Vane said, following Una out of the house, 'I forgot to ask you if you had a nice time.'

'Fine, thanks. Bit of a storm last night up on the moors, but we got through. Got pretty wet.'

'I hope you took care of yourselves.'

She stood looking at where Una had been standing. Untiringly she stood, stroking the cat in her arms.

In the library Miss Kipling, very pleased to see Una, took her over to be introduced to *Anna Karenina,* saying that in her opinion – was

Una a fast reader? Good – it would be better to start here and then go on to *War and Peace*. 'But don't be daunted by it when you do begin. It's three volumes, but the last one is all theory. A theory of history, and most people don't bother with it.'

'My boyfriend would read it,' said Una.

'Is that the railway porter?' said patrician Miss Kipling.

'No. My boyfriend is a trainee guard. And he's very high up for his age in the Union.'

'I see,' she said. 'And when do you go up to Girton?'

And so that night, the night of her long and beautiful day, Una lay reading *Anna Karenina* on her narrow bed, continuing it next morning without bothering to get up. Monday and Tuesday were passed in Moscow and Pokrovski, and Wednesday and Thursday and Friday morning too she spent with Anna and Vronsky, Levin and Kitty, at the balls and on the sledges, at the harvests and in the snows of all the Russias. On Thursday Una was back in the library for *War and Peace*.

'Not yet, I advise,' said Miss Kipling and handed her *Madame Bovary*. 'And something modern? A little Jung, perhaps?'

'Thank you,' said Una, and when Ray appeared at the gate at midday to talk of their next sortie she hung about in the doorway and did not look at his face. She called out from the doorstep, 'Could we go another weekend? I've just found a whole lot of work I have to do for October. They've given me all sorts I never heard of.'

'OK. Fine.'

'I'm getting scared,' she said. 'I'm ignorant. You were right about me.'

'OK, I've Union business, anyway. Another week?'

He waved with a clenched fist as he rode off and she thought how much and how long she had loved him, but how, after Tolstoy, the love was now perhaps all draining away.

I'll find time to write to Hetty, she thought. I shan't mention Eustace. She wouldn't want it, she gets so hurt. But she's ahead of me in so much, though she'll never believe it. I'll go round to see her Ma and hear how she's getting on.

But all that night she passed with *Madame Bovary* and suffered and suffered, not for love but for the helplessness of a woman in love. I shall escape that, she thought.

It was Sunday morning again. Last Sunday she had been lying in the grass of the abbey ruins.

His face.

His hands.

I was never so happy. And I could cope. I wasn't embarrassed, not even by the egg-and-bacon woman. Now I just want to yawn. I'm shredded. I'm purged. God, what a way to behave!

'You look wild of eye,' said her mother and began to sing (but watching her daughter) 'Oh, Margaret, art thou grieving? Not worried about anything, are you?' she asked.

Una waited for her mother to say, Aren't you seeing Ray today? but she didn't.

Una said, 'All that worries me is what you're going to do when I go away, Mum. Otherwise, I'm very happy. Very.'

'"I'll walk beside you",' sang Mrs Vane, wondering at the sudden tears in Una's eyes, '"through the lane of dreams". I'll kick up my heels and out with the castanets, you'll see. I'm easily pleased. I like being by myself.'

They did not meet each other's eyes.

Another mother and daughter might have hugged each other then, but fat Mrs Vane and skinny Una, her wary, clever, honest daughter, did a little bit of heel-and-toe together round the kitchen. Later Mrs Vane brought out an enormous bottle of *crème de menthe* and two goblets.

18

Mr Satterley had been right about the weather at Betty Bank, and the rain and wind started about tea-time, blotting out the lake and tossing the trees. The storm began, and rain struck Hetty's window like handfuls of gravel.

'All right?' called Mrs Satterley. 'Is't comin' in?'

'Just a bit round the sill.'

'Well, muff it up with a towel, will you? Ist' ceiling right? We get this. It won't submerge you.'

All night the rain fell, and the morning looked exhausted by it, grey and soaked, too cold and dreary for anyone to find pleasure in going out of doors even while the room was being cleaned. Hetty took *Biographia Literaria* into the parlour, where she could have done with a fire. The paper fan was all that stood in the fireplace, bloated and spotted with sooty drops. The upright chairs round the walls were of horsehair, prickly to the thigh. She opened out Coleridge upon the mahogany table with its diagonal, cross-stitched table-runner and glass vase of paper roses. The marble-columned clock on the mantelpiece clanked on.

'You can come and fetch your drink clocks-time,' called Mrs Satterley, 'int' kitchen.' Hetty was the only guest this week.

So, at ten-thirty, she went to the kitchen and was handed her tin mug of tea. Two men were sitting over the kitchen fire, its kindling branches sticking out a good three feet into the room, wagging their fingers at each other. One was Mr Satterley and the other an ancient of gnarled aspect with a large nose and shabby clothes. Some shepherd. He rose courteously as she came in and bowed and sat down again.

Hetty took her tea back to the parlour and after a time thought that she might try upstairs again and sat to her desk wrapped in the sheepskin rug off the floor. At midday when she went down to family dinner – the finding of her own lunch being forgotten – the old chap had gone. Maybe he was the postman, except that they'd said the post might not get up the Bank today in the rainstorm.

'I never knew such a one for getting letters,' said Mrs Satterley. 'Three more today and one delivered.'

'Did he get here, then? The post? But weren't they *all* delivered?'

'The postie came, yes, and then there's the one letter hand-delivered. They're on the hall-stand.'

Hetty took the four envelopes upstairs and never did *Biographia Literaria* look less tempting. Oh, so cold here! The towel under the sill was sopped through, and a great blister swelled in the corner of the wallpaper above her bed. She wrapped herself in the bed cover as well as the sheepskin and wondered however she came to be sitting in this place, all alone. 'Girls of your age should be out with their boyfriends,' the vicar had told her. 'It would be more natural, Hester.'

One letter was of course from Eustace, so she threw it under the bed, unopened, to lie with the others. The second was in her mother's handwriting, so that followed it. The handwriting on the third, she didn't recognise, and on opening it found a postal order to the value of ten shillings and a card signed enthusiastically by Dorothy and tidily by Hilda. Hilda had written on the back of the card in fastidious script ('Hilda is well-connected, you know,' said the Lonsdale café) that this was a small congratulatory gift on account of the scholarship and also to say how much she and Dorothy admired her for so bravely going off to study on her own. To her surprise, on reading this, Hetty found herself flushing with pleasure. Nobody until now had ever suggested that her adventure at Betty Bank was anything but affectation. Hilda also said that she very much hoped that she had

140

not been intrusive, but she had written to a distant relative of hers who lived near Betty Bank and who might perhaps invite Hetty to a meal, just in case she felt like a little change. 'Of course she may not be at home, or it may not be convenient, but we thought we should warn you, just in case. Dorothy and I do not want to interfere in your grown-up life. We saw your mother yesterday and she is bright and cheerful as ever, but had not then received more than the postcard from you telling of safe arrival. Sincerely yours, Hilda B. Fletcher.'

The fourth, hand-delivered, letter was not stuck down, and thick as cardboard, with By Hand written across the top left-hand corner in spluttering violet ink. The writing paper inside was embossed with a coat of arms and the address said The Hall, Betty Forest.

Who's Betty Forest? she wondered. What a waste of lovely paper. It's woven with linen threads. Oh no, it's not a person! Betty Forest must be here. It must be near Betty Bank. And it's from Urgle MacGurgle, whoever that is.

My dear Hester (if I may?),
Your Girl Guide captain, Miss Fletcher, has just written to tell me that you are staying with the beloved Satterleys, all alone, and we so very much hope that you will be able to spare a moment from all your homework to come to see us this evening at six o'clock. We shall be having a few people here for drinks.

Now, how to reach us: Behind Betty Bank there is a LANE, which you may have found already. Along the LANE there is a TABLE, which you may already have noticed. It is often there in the care of my granddaughter Patsie, or her cousin Rupert, and is covered sometimes with all manner of things for sale in aid of the Red Cross, *et al.* It is my market-place, but pay it no attention. Turn your head to the RIGHT when you reach the table, and up in the hedge you will see a GAP. Go through the GAP and you will come to a small gate. Go through this gate and there we are, BELOW you, down the other side of the forest ridge. You will be looking down our chimneys, and once you have made your way down the slope you should find us in the

SALOON. If the rain has stopped all the doors will be open wide. I think that I have someone here for you of about your age.

Yours sincerely,

Urgle MacGurgle.

PS   Please do not dress.

What a very curious document, thought Hetty, and reflected that the surest way to drain an introduction of any relish is to promise it will be with someone of your own vintage. She wondered at what age this reflection ceased and decided, never. 'Eighty-two! My dear, how wonderful! You must meet my mother, she's eighty-three!' And so on. Well, if you've any sense you just don't turn up.

And there is no reason, she thought, actually, that I need turn up to this thing at all, since it is patently obvious I'm to meet sexy-square-teeth on the horse. Maybe Cousin Rupert's the horse? And Urgle MacGurgle must be Ursula. Do I answer it? Not enough time, since it's tonight. Well, I needn't go. Forget it.

But, hey, how nice of the Girls' Guildry – ain't they sweet? Ten bob. Dorothy and Hilda. I love them. Kiss, kiss. I'll write back *now*. Well, maybe I'll write to Ma first.

Dear Ma [she wrote, straight off, from within the sheepskin rug wishing she had some gloves],

Thank you for all your letters. I'm sorry I've taken so long to write back but I'm reading my head off, morning till night. It's fine here for work, though I don't think they have a clue why I'm doing it. They keep trying to get me out climbing about the mountains like the other PGs, who are middle-aged and keep shops or drive public transport and come from Lancashire. There's a new lot coming in on Saturday may be a bit younger but they'll be mad on rock-climbing again, which means that it'll be nothing but hand-holds and chimneys and crampons and pass the salt. They are all intensely uninteresting.

Mrs Satterley is very obliging but rather noisy. Mr Satterley's a Quaker, which must be how the Stonehouses know all about it here. There's no one else about much, but I've been asked somewhere tonight for drinks (don't look like that) by a friend of Hilda Fletcher. She and Dorothy have sent me a ten-bob p. order. I hope you didn't say I was short, or anything. *You really ought to be careful.* I'd thank you, actually, Ma, if you *didn't* discuss me at all with your friends. You'd get more and better letters if I could trust you not to read them out. Some hope, I know. Love to Pa. I suppose he'd never bestir himself to write to me? He has plenty of time. Have you had any little billets-doux from EUSTACE lately?

XXXX Hetty.

She looked down at the unopened Eustace letters lying under the bed around the chamber-pot, quite a heap of them, all smooth and clean. Why did they make her heart groan? The mean little handwriting. They looked as though they were written by a mouse with the eyes of a watchmaker. Eustace the clockwork mouse. No question of his signature reading like Urgle MacGurgle.

Oh, she thought, in real terms there are, today, no attractive men.

'I've been asked out,' she said, back in the kitchen for the next intake of nourishment. 'But I don't think I'll go. I'd miss supper.'

'You'll not do that: we're keeping it hot for you. You can have your can of hot water five o'clock for your wash and you're due there at six.'

'You know all about it?'

'His Lordship brought your invitation this morning. He told us what it was, and you could never not go!'

'I could if I was previously engaged.'

'That wouldn't please Ursula.'

'But who is she? What do I call her?'

'She's Ursula Fitzurse, and you call her "Lady Fitzurse".'

'But you call her Ursula.'

'Of course. Not to her face. To her face she's My Lady to me, and Lady Fitzurse to you. But she's Ursula to everyone, for all that.'

'What does she call you?'

'She calls us Mr and Mrs Satterley, though she knew us in our bassinets. It's based on mutual respect.'

Can you beat it! thought Hetty, washing in the hot soapy water from the brass can. She stood about thoughtfully and went down to the kitchen wrapped in a towel. She was getting to be rather at home at Betty Bank. In fact she'd never get away with this at home. She was decent of course but, still, there wasn't much under the towel.

'Oh, Mrs Satterley, I was told not to dress—'

'Were you thinking of going *naked*?' (She pronounced it as a single syllable.)

'No, but what does it mean? What do I wear?'

'Oh, she'll never notice. Just don't dress up like lamb and salad. But you'll need clean shoes. Give us them 'ere.'

'But they won't be clean by the time I get there. Through all the mud.'

'No, but you'll be walking-on there in clogs. You can tek mine. And your shoes go under your arm.'

Hetty dressed in a clean aertex blouse and a cashmere cardigan of Joyce Dobson's and her grey school skirt. The only shoes were the gym shoes, which, though Mrs Satterley had whitened them and hung them on the recken to dry, didn't look much like footwear for a cocktail party. Hetty slid her feet into the clogs and went clumping over the yard, a gym shoe in either hand.

At the yard gate she turned and saw Mrs Satterley looking non-committally at her through the window.

'Ought I to be taking her something?'

'It's not done,' said Mrs Satterley.

'Not a flower or anything?' (She was her mother's daughter.)

Mrs Satterley disappeared from the window and then returned with a small soft parcel which she passed through. Hetty made for the table, and the hedge.

Hetty came out of the trees above the gap in the lane and looked down, expecting a mansion. She had imagined a pale stucco palace with a terrace, and tall Noel Coward people drinking martinis, conversing acidly in the evening sunshine. Nothing of the sort. Below her was a huge platform of lead roofs surrounded by several acres of weedy gravel below them, and the house was of grim grey stone, a tessellated tower at either end, all very much the worse for wear. Trees watched the house from the ridge from three sides. Above them, shining in her eyes, gleamed a yellow, ragged sunset.

She slid and stumbled down something of a path from the ridge and found herself beside a stack of milk churns and a broken field-gate. Inside the gate a miserably maintained drive swooped round a corner and down a further hill and there the sunset disappeared and it was quite dark. Down an even steeper drop there stood a medieval gateway, where chickens were running about, waiting to be put to bed. A string of buildings attached to either side of the gateway ran along for some distance, with boarded-up doors and windows, the slits in the walls sprouting tufts of hay. Nearby was a poor-looking little green car and some farm worker pulling sacks of pigswill towards it.

'Excuse me, I'm looking for the Hall.'

'Through yon yat.'

Through the gate she came to what might be a chapel, but its stained-glass windows were patched here and there with cardboard, and some of the windows of the Hall itself looked suspiciously clear, as if the glass in them had long ago been ditched. But then, to her right, she saw an archway into gardens, and, beyond, other gardens, and she could make out trimmed grass paths between roses. Coming down one of these in the twilight and now stepping upon the gravel sweep was a small old woman carrying a washing-up bowl full of brambles.

'My dear!' she said. 'My dear child, you must be Hester Fallowes! The Girl Guide. Who has won a scholarship to Queen Anne's in London! How *clever*. How sweet of you to come. How my little granddaughter is looking forward to seeing you. Now, we'll take off our clogs, dear, and – yes. Here are my bedroom slippers, and there, I see, are your nice white shoes under your arm, and you'll meet Mabel. She's longing to see you.'

Hetty felt surprise. The horse-girl could never be called Mabel.

'Mabel,' said Lady Fitzurse, 'is not a very pretty name, but it is

145

an old name in our family. An old Cumbrian name. The Fitzurses are all Vikings – but everybody knows that, and I've never known why it should be interesting. You probably know much more about Vikings than we do. Schoolgirls today know much more than we ever did. Now here we are – lots of Mabels!'

They padded across a marble chamber in their soft shoes. A stone staircase rose from it to a minstrels' gallery that looked a bit like a Methodist chapel with faded coats of arms, and then to another great room, where the fireplace was almost the size of Hetty's bedroom at Betty Bank. A giant dead animal lay collapsed upon the flagstones and heads of multi-horned hoof-stock with glass eyes observed them from the walls. Lord Fitzurse, the shepherd of the morning, was drinking whisky round the fireplace with several other people, and a child of about ten with the corners of her mouth turned down was slumped across a tartan sofa.

'Awful tartan,' said Ursula Fitzurse. 'Not ours – we haven't one, thank goodness – some dubious Scotch cousins (always say Scotch, dear, like the Queen. Never "Scots". But of course, you know). They know we're hard up, so it's very kind of them really, sofas are such a price in the shops. Now, this is Mabel. Mabel, this is such a coincidence! Hester is going to school with you next term: she's won a scholarship. *So* clever. And so young! Now, how old are you, Hester? Hilda Fletcher didn't say – just that you are one of her Guides. But you and Mabel must be much— Well, you are very much taller than Mabel, but the Fitzurses have always been undersized.'

Mabel continued to lie on the sofa. After a moment a large pink bubble of gum ballooned from her mouth and popped.

'It's the Americans. She goes to the films. Get up at once, Mabel, and take Hester to play with the puppies.'

'Grandma!'

'Who's that?'

'Grandma – *Ursula*. Ducky. You've made a boo-boo, Grandma.'

And Hester saw the horse-girl undoing herself from a cushioned window-seat.

'Grandma, look at Hester. How old is she?'

'My dear, I haven't the least idea how old anybody is. I forget at once. Myself too. Just when you've got it in your head, it changes.'

146

'Look, *Ursula*, lousy Mabel is eleven. Look at this one. Is she eleven?'

'Well, she *is* very tall. I said she was tall. But she's not wearing make-up. And she is in school shoes.'

'Grandma, *could* she be going to school at Queen Anne's, Caversham, with Mabel?'

'But isn't Caversham London? I'm hopeless on the south. I've simply no idea. I've not been to London for years, and I never went to school at all. Neither did your mother; I made sure of that.'

'That was quite obvious, if I may say so. Grandma, will you look at this girl and give her a double gin and tonic. Now,' she said, turning to Hetty, 'I'm Patsie. We've met already.'

The heavy Mabel vanished with a glass of orange squash.

'So where is it you're going with this scholarship?'

'To the University of London,' said Hetty.

'Grandma! She's probably twenty-eight and ex-service; three-quarters of students are ex-service this year. That's why I couldn't get in anywhere. She's probably *brilliant*.'

'Oh, my dear, I'm so sorry. Ex-service? Were you in the war? The ATS? I'm sure she said the Guides, but of course she may have said Red Cross, she's a great supporter there. Tell me, dear, were you in enemy hands.'

'No, I was at Shields East High School. I'm not eighteen yet.'

'My dear! I was right. You are no age at all, though I have to say that I was married and pregnant before I was eighteen. But seventeen today is a strange age. It means that you came through the wars as a mere child. And always at home? It all seemed just fun, I expect, so long as you had no one in prison to worry about, of course. And Mr Churchill to keep us going. And victory in the end. While my poor Patsie – now, I don't know how old you are, Patsie, though you are my granddaughter, but—'

'It wasn't exactly fun,' said Hetty. 'The bombing wasn't fun. Twenty-six people were killed in Shields East one night, down the road from us. It wasn't fun. We knew everybody!'

'Oh, and here we had *nothing*!' said Ursula. 'We were blessed, but we do sometimes feel guilty, you know. But we were *stiff* with German prisoners, of course. I've got some here tonight.'

147

'Here?'

'Yes. It's one's Christian duty, and they're so useful about the estate. There's not a Nazi among them and one of them went to Eton. It's so *strange* that you never ever meet a German who was a Nazi. One wonders if . . . Well, would you like to meet a German?'

'Oh, not much, actually, thank you.'

'My dear!'

'I've a great friend who's a German Jew.'

'My dear! How pink in the face you are. Please don't be upset. I hope she is safe with us now? *Now*, we must get you something.'

'Gin,' said Patsie again. 'She'd like three gins in one glass and so would I.'

Hetty saw the child Mabel watching her from behind a stuffed bear. The bear was holding a plate of cocktail titbits on a shelf between its paws.

The silly granny. The angry bear. The Good Germans. The nasty Patsie . . . Who would be Mabel?

Hetty went across to Mabel and said, 'I'll come and play with the puppies as soon as I can.'

At this, Mabel glowered and fled, leaving Hetty more mortified than before. They stick together, thought Hetty; you can't woo them. These people. You can never join them. They only want their own sort really, although they hate one another most of the time. Her mother was wrong. The aristocracy do *not* 'have something wonderful about them'. And yet she had felt mortified on behalf of the idiotic Ursula, so sorry for the demolition of the old woman by the unspeakable horse-girl that for a moment she had even thought of saying she was only twelve years old.

The horse-girl was obviously as vile as she had sensed at first. The horse-girl was a monster. To call one's grandmother 'Ursula'. And 'Ducky'.

Hetty had been more than ready to dislike Ursula, because she had seemed to be the goddess of the feudal Satterleys – or of Mrs Satterley, anyway. She had expected a bulging Lady Bountiful in Ursula. Instead here was a dotty little child of eighty, unself-conscious, unworldly, innocent, tolerant of both Patsie and Mabel, and unwise – or brave – enough to invite Germans to a drinks party with the war ended scarcely a year ago.

Maybe Ursula had been a Nazi sympathiser? They were thick on the ground among the aristocracy, or so the grave-digger often said. 'The aristocracy and the working class,' he said: 'oh yes, they had the swastikas ready in Muriel Street, you know.'

But could Ursula ever have been clever enough to understand any ideology? You couldn't see her reading Thomas Carlyle. Or hamming herself up. All that about having no education and mixing up schools and universities. All showing off. You could bet she spoke French. And German too – oh yes! Governesses galore, and finishing schools. But so pretty and nice still, at eighty. The comical nose. The giant eyes in the tiny face. The silk top worn over what looked like a woollen laundry bag and bedroom slippers, but oh so very correct, somehow.

Why, thought Hetty, are my gym shoes wrong and Ursula's bedroom slippers OK? Why are Ursula's innocence and sweetness delicious, when my mother's innocence and sweetness make me squirm?

She pushed away the thought that her mother was herself, always. Then wondered whether Ursula was nothing but an actress, trotting round the guests, raising her loving face to them as she walked here and there, with her little plate of cheese straws. Such charm! Her mother's charm was similar, but behind it all, here in this house, oh, the comforts of wealth.

On her feet Ursula wore old slippers, but upstairs were wardrobes full, no doubt, of tiaras and coronation robes and rings like rocks. Diamond necklaces hidden in the water jugs (Hetty had read romances). Ursula all her long life had had everything she ever wanted, and wouldn't lift a finger to help anyone who hadn't. She wouldn't believe in need. She would dispense nothing but gin. Totally self-centred.

Hetty remembered the small rather damp parcel that Mrs Satterley had sent to the Hall with her, and brought it out of her skirt pocket now as Ursula came trotting up again, carrying in her little claw a brimming tumbler.

'Oh, thank you. Actually, I'm terribly sorry but I don't drink alcohol. Well, I never have up to now.'

'Oh, do start some time,' said Ursula. 'But what is this? A present? Oh, let me put this down – you needn't drink it, of course, but let's put it behind something. There are those who might come upon it unawares. Behind the bear. Now – ah! From Mrs Satterley? . . . Oh, my dear!' She had torn apart the newspaper and was turning to left and right in reverent amazement, showing the contents to her guests. 'Oh, no! Oh, how very kind! Oh, however do they do it up there? Look, look, Mrs Satterley has sent us this beautiful piece of liver! Oh, how particularly kind! Now, Patsie, you must have it all for your supper. Now then, child, Esther, Hester, Eleanor, come through to the saloon and meet the rest of us.'

Hetty at last saw some very tall people standing together but they were not like Noel Coward, for they were almost silent. They stood in the bell of the lighted saloon, in the last moments of the day, and beyond them stretched another long room, exactly like the one she had come from. They were making desultory noises that were not particularly like words, but quite soothing, like a group of heifers at eventide.

'Herbert,' introduced Lady Fitzurse, 'Hester Satterley. And George. And Edith and Freddie Er— This is Ethel Satterley – and now then, Lord Fitzurse you know, for he brought you your invitation to Betty Bank this morning.'

'Actually,' said Hetty, 'I'm not a part of Betty Bank, I'm just a paying guest there. Good evening. Hallo. I'm not called Satterley.'

'Hallo!' The tall kine, way up near the ceiling, turned their backs on her almost at once, and went on droning. She could see up their nostrils. They didn't look like German prisoners, but you never knew. Prussians, maybe, if there were still such things.

Lord Fitzurse was another matter and she turned back to where he was sitting by the fireplace in a shabby chair and shabbier smoking jacket. He nodded and said, 'Nice to see you again. Good of you to come. Is there any news?'

'News?'

'About the cow.'

'Cow?'

'Trouble with the Friesian. The breech birth. Been lying there all yesterday and in trouble already two-quarters.'

'Oh, I'm afraid I don't know.'

'He'll not try to sell her, you know. Lying there three days. Won't have her slaughtered. Some would. Not Dick Satterley, he's a good man.'

'Oh, yes. Yes, he is.'

'Got a glass?'

'Oh, no. I'm all right, thank you.'

'Met Rupert?'

'Rupert? No. No, I don't think so.'

'Grandson. Patsie's cousin. He's about your age; you might like each other. He's nearly thirty but not over the hill. Just approaching the hill. Rupert?'

'You're not very flattering, Grandpa. I'm twenty-six.' The voice came from behind the archway of the saloon. There was the clink of a decanter.

'Hester Satterley,' said Lord Fitzurse. 'Satterley's girl.'

'Hallo.'

'No. No, I'm not. I'm Hester Fallowes and I don't live anywhere near here at all.'

'Don't mind Grandpa,' the voice called. 'One person's much like another unless they're American or French and then we have to wheel him away and cool him off.'

'I know good stock, though.'

'Ah yes, you know good stock, Grandpa; that we won't deny.'

A young man came round the side of the archway, carrying two glasses of wine. One he handed to her. 'Rupert,' he said. 'Good evening.'

Hetty knew nothing of parties. During the war, as she grew up, there had been none. The word 'party' was therefore associated with childhood; with team games and jellies and frills and being taken home skipping with a present and telling your mother all about it. Later on there were the frugal school parties and the church socials with wet kisses with unknown boys, occasions that seemed to have a set of rules known instinctively to other girls but not to her. When these feverish gatherings broke up they drifted into cinemas and back-row kissing, even while the raids were on,

151

and into languorous walkings-home, two by two, the snufflings on park benches, the uncertainty about rules. The word 'party' persisted, still recalled gramophone music and musical chairs and ring-a-roses, but it was a front now for something more threatening and exciting. Then, at sixteen, there had been the sherry at the vicarage and everybody very old, except fresh-faced Eustace. She never dared tell them at school about that party.

But the alternative had been to rebel and go in with the tortoise parties on the sand-hills, and this she knew she could not do. Or to find someone close, close to one's soul, like Una and the bike-boy, and this she knew she had not yet done. She had observed all the other girls in their solemn embraces, and rather forlornly had returned to English literature.

She had sunk into books, she had wallowed in books, and when she occasionally met up with passion – the visitations of the vicar, her father's mysterious peregrinations along the shadowy promenade – she had turned from them. To her a party would always mean being six.

So that when Rupert came round the pillar of the saloon, two glasses in the fingers of one hand and a wine bottle swinging from another, she was unprepared, for she saw a face that had seen everything there was to see, and knew it. Curiosity had died in him. His manners were perfect but his expectations were nil. Nearly thirty – he's an old man, she thought. How old he looks too, with his shoulders all hunched up behind his head and his thin arms. How terribly skinny he is.

As he smiled at her and came forward she thought, But pretty marvellous eyes. There was a faint flicker of amusement in them, then it was gone. How exhausted he looks, she thought. It's an effort even to speak to me. And she almost said, Oh, it's all right, you don't have to talk to me. I'm just going.

But of course he said, 'Hallo. So glad you were able to join us. I'm Rupert and do please tell me your name, because I think I heard Ursula making a mess of it.'

She thought, How pale he is. His face is not an English face; it is like a Spaniard or something. He's out of another landscape. How black his eyes. He is very wonderful. And mysterious and clever.

And he will never look at me. He is the man the other girl gets. Oh, he'll cause havoc always.

Then she thought, What do I mean, 'get'? Do I want him? Or any man? What is it about this ancient stooping totally beautiful creature with his cheek-bones and his despising look behind the smile? Is it love, then? At first sight? I am in terrible clothes.

To her enormous surprise, one of the willowy creatures to whom she had been previously introduced now came drifting up and stood between her and Rupert and said, 'Hallo again. I was just wondering if you might be interested in a point-to-point this autumn? Didn't I meet you earlier on the Kyle of Lochalsh?'

'Oh. No. No, you couldn't have done. I've never been to a point-to-point.'

'Would you think of letting me take you to one?'

'Well, I'm going away. To London. To the University. I don't live near here at all.'

'Oh, rotten show,' he said and moved off.

Rupert's face was dark with disdain. He was looking at her bulky feet and Joyce Dobson's skirt, and her beastly bosom sticking out.

'Lord Fitzurse,' she said to the kind old man, 'I must go now. Thank you so much for inviting me.'

'Good of you to come. Meant to ask about that cow at Betty Bank. Now then, who shall see you home?'

Rupert looked at her for a moment, then moved away. Funny little Mabel reappeared and said she'd come as far as the gap in the trees.

There was no sign of Lady Fitzurse. Across the glassy spaces of the lovely room in the darkening evening she saw Rupert go nonchalantly up to Patsie, who was lounging around on the tartan sofa talking to someone. Without looking round she stretched out her arm towards Rupert's wine bottle, and Rupert filled it to the brim, and stayed standing near.

Yet as she said goodbye to Mabel, passed through the hedge and into the lane, squelching in her gym shoes, Hetty knew that she hadn't seen the last of Rupert. Not at all. This was new knowledge – the knowledge that she could wait.

19

Of course, having thought of the party for most of the night, she was certain it was Rupert's arrival she heard downstairs the next morning when there came the knock on the kitchen door and Mrs Satterley's cries below, and her heart thundered.

And then the terrifying words, 'Hetty? Yes, I'll just see. She's very busy, you know. We don't disturb her in the mornings. She's off to College – I think it's Oxford College – in October. She was sent here for some peace – there's something amiss at home, to do with her father—'

'Hallo. I'm here.' Anything but hear more. 'It's all right. I'm not busy.'

'A friend for you.'

Hetty regarded herself in the moralising mirror, combed her hair one way and then another, looked at her Tangee lipstick, apricot-rose, smeared some on, licked it off again, went downstairs; and found Patsie sprawled about on the kitchen table.

'Hi,' said the horse-girl.

'Oh, hallo.'

Silence.

She's terribly thin, thought Hetty. We're all pretty thin now, but she's ridiculous. What strange hair. Like straw stalks with a black parting. Awful skin, when you look at it. It's all make-up, as Ma says. Not much in the way of eyelashes. Why does she give you the idea that she's beautiful?

Tea was brought and the three sat down to it at the kitchen table. It was a rainy morning and quantities of clothes were hanging from the overhead pulley-airer like a poulterer's shop at some Dickensian Christmas time. More hung on a clothes-horse round the fire. Thick woollen shirts with linen buttons steamed, and a brindled cat and kittens lay in a cardboard box by the fender, the kittens feeding in a row like a packet of sausages. There were trays of rock-buns by the fire, cooling on the bink.

'Well, each of you have a bun with this tea, then. Pass up,' said Mrs Satterley.

'How d'you do it? Where d' you *get* it?' said Patsie. 'Everyone wants to know.'

'Management,' she said. 'It's lodgers' ration books.'

'No. You're a fiddler.'

'Oh, to be sure, don't I look the part?'

'No, you don't, Mrs S. I'll say that.'

'Have another.'

'I can't. My stomach's still too small. It's too soon.'

'Lucky for you,' said Mrs Satterley, stroking her great dome. 'Never mind, Hetty will. We're building Hetty up. She'll not look bad be time she goes home. Look at her hip-bones still sticking out, though. Like doorknobs.'

'You could get a job as a model with hip-bones like that,' said the horse-girl. 'I've gone too far.'

'Have you shrunk?' asked Hetty.

'Yes. I was in a camp. In China. Only a DP camp – no real hardships.' She took cigarettes from her pocket and offered them round loose in her hand. 'Cheaper than in packets,' she said. 'Buy them in fives. They get a bit bent.'

'Never been able to tek to it,' said Mrs Satterley.

Hetty hesitated but the cigarettes were put back in the pocket.

'Well, what I'm here for,' said Patsie, 'is d'you want to come for a ride? There's Rupert's horse doing nothing. He went away this morning, so it'll be standing around getting fat till he deigns to come back.'

'Gone?'

Patsie gave a yell of laughter. 'Your voice is hollow with doom.

155

Hey-day and hey-nonny-no. Not again, Mrs Satterley! It's obscene the way everyone falls for Rupert. He must have some secret smell or something, like a saint. Everyone falls.'

'That'll do,' said Mrs Satterley, fiercely, 'Hetty has a boyfriend already. There's letters and letters coming here for her every day, army issue, postmarked Salisbury Plain.'

Patsie looked Hetty languidly over from crown to gym shoes.

'Oh, well, that's all right, then. Rupert's coming back next week— Oh my, the sun's come out again! You ought to smile more often!'

Hetty, who had been shot through first with loss and then with delirious joy, now blushed with rage. And then she found herself smiling after all.

Raindrops dazzled along the window-sash and sunlight turned the kitchen fire from red and black to something pale and silver. The skinny cat got up and shook off the sausage kittens, cuffing one of them about. They squirmed and scratched on the newspaper in the bottom of the box and turned their rosy, violin-shaped mouths up to mew. Their eyes, still shut, bulged under peanut lids. They were very new creatures. Some nasty leftovers lay bloody in the bottom of the box.

'Ain't Nature beautiful,' said Patsie. 'You had a decaying lamb in here last time I was round.'

'Aye,' said Mrs Satterley. 'The spring. We had quite a few in February but t'one you saw did die. I knew it had died whent' cat started eating it. Still warm, but they know. It's Nature. Now, what's wrong with Hetty? Dear, oh dear, d'you want a bit of air? I'll opent' door. She's gone white.'

Patsie watched Hetty holding the door and Hetty knew it, and thought, She thinks I'm wet.

'Anybody hungry would have done the same thing,' said Patsie. 'And thought nothing about it. You don't know what you'd eat. Or what you'd do to get it, come to that. It's crazy, this country: none of you starved and yet all you ever think about is eating. Grandma with that liver made me puke – sorry, Mrs S, but we'd never have done that in the camp. There's no one in this country suffered a thing.'

156

Hetty again had nothing to say. At least Patsie didn't know she was reading Wordsworth. Wordsworth didn't speak much about eating the newly dead. Patsie's eyes followed Hetty back into the room. She was weighing Hetty's degree of ignorance, not liking it, treating it with ferocity. The cat who would eat the dead sheep. Well, thought Hetty, we shall see.

'I think I'm glad I wasn't in the camp with you,' she said.

'Yes? Interesting. I don't suppose you can ride, can you?'

'Don't you?'

'Well, can you? Rupert's horse is quite lively.'

'I can,' (she scarcely could) 'but it depends if I want to.'

Patsie seemed to like this. 'You won't need anything special,' she said; 'just jodhpurs, or trousers if you like.'

'I haven't any.'

'I'll find some of Mabel's.'

'No, *thank* you. I'll ride in a skirt.'

'And the gym shoes?'

'They're all I have.'

'Oh well. OK, then, I'll come and get you. We'll go round the lake and stop at the pub.'

Mrs Satterley said, 'Well, I'm not sure about that, Patsie. Hetty's not eighteen yet and Mr Satterley wouldn't like it.'

'Oh God, of course. She's a Quaker.'

'No,' said Hetty, 'I'm not. I was just looking. As it happened.'

'OK, then. Nine o'clock tomorrow?' and she slid off the table, took up a couple of rock-buns and flung away across the yard, tossing her black and yellow hair.

'The Honourable Patricia,' said Mrs Satterley, with love and displeasure. 'Well, can you wonder? She's been through China.'

'Great for China.'

'Now then, Hetty, were you ever in prison camp and saw everyone die, your mother disappeared?'

'I'll bet she was difficult, though.'

'She was in hospital six months after they got her out. In Australia. Malnutrition. That's why her hair's gone that nasty colour, and she walks so lofty.'

'Sounds like a kangaroo.'

Mrs Satterley did not smile. Whatever she thought of Patsie, Patsie was one of her tribe and Hetty was a foreign paying guest. Mrs Satterley stood up and began to drive her great arms into a mound of dough. 'Well, next week will be your last week,' she said firmly, 'won't it?'

'I'm sorry,' said Hetty, 'I was forgetting. You all belong together.'

'I knew her before the war. As a bairn. She was canny then. She'd sit on your knee, all smiles. If her grandmother were a usual woman she'd be broken-hearted about her now, but Ursula won't see changes. The picture she has first is the picture she keeps.'

'She thought I was eleven years old.'

'Then eleven you'll remain for her.'

'He – Lord Fizzle – thought I was thirty.'

'Oh well. That means less than nowt. And what about Rupert? What had he to say? Now, Hetty, I say to you direct: I don't want you to think of him. Hilda Fletcher would never forgive me. I can't at present tell you why, for someone has made me promise. But through my life I've rued that people haven't been warned when someone else sees a thing coming, just out of shyness, and I'm not shy. And there's others I've warned off Rupert and never regretted it. Mrs Stonehouse, for one.'

'Mrs *Stonehouse*!'

'I like you enough, Hetty, to save you making a fool of yourself.'

'But I hardly said a thing to Rupert. Or he to me.'

'Well, then, keep it so. With luck you'll never see him again. He is not a normal man.'

'Oh, I suppose— I'm not interested. I have work to do. But I suppose what you're trying to tell me is that he's a homo.'

'A what?'

'A homosexual person.'

'What a ridiculous—! Good gracious! Never such a thing! That's a word never spoken in this house. And very much the reverse. I'm not at liberty to tell you because it's a family matter. Why don't you go and read all them unopened love-letters and forget him?'

'Oh, *I* know! He's got TB. Or he's a haemophiliac, like the Czars of Russia. Too much Viking blood.'

158

'Certainly not! Land's sakes! He's fit and well. He was through the RAF, which meant he had a lot of fresh air. He led a charmed life. Like a saint. I'm saying no more. He has the Distinguished Flying Cross. Not even Fergus got that.'

'Who's Fergus?'

'His cousin in Scotland. A grand man. Nobody for Rupert like Fergus, nor ever will be.'

'Oh, of *course*. They're all Catholics! I'd forgotten. *That*'s it! He's in line for being a saint, and he's got the stigmata.'

'They are Catholics, just so,' said Mrs Satterley. 'The Fitzurses are cradle Catholics, always have been, but I didn't say Rupert was a saint, and I never heard tell he had anything the matter with his eyes.'

20

When in the late summer of 1939 Hilda and Dorothy had driven Lieselotte crouched in the back of the car across the Vale of York and had come upon the woman in hair curlers under her railway worker's peaked cap struggling with the gate of the level-crossing; and when little fat Dorothy had climbed out to help her, nobody had noticed that a brown-paper envelope, which Lieselotte had had with her since Hamburg and which had been handed to flustered Hilda by the woman from the refugee movement, had slipped from her lap and out of the car on to the railway line. When Hilda had driven across the line and stopped the car again to ask the way to Shields West, and the woman had said she didn't know much because she came from Hull, it had ended in laughter. Dorothy had looked round and said that she wished she could give Lieselotte a sweet.

What she had in fact given her in that moment was six years of anonymity and invisibility that had wrapped her around, a second blanket to tuck her in the blessed security of the Stonehouses. About twenty minutes after the car had driven on, the brown envelope had been plastered against the line by the first of many passing trains. Squashed and unrecognisable, it had found its way to the side of the track and had become a leaf of pulp in the detritus around the signal box. One day in that autumn the woman who didn't know much had gathered the rubbish together and burned it on a bonfire, which had caused her to be reprimanded for lighting a conflagration that might alert enemy planes and cause the liquidation of the branch line between Brafferton Halt and Hutton-le-Moulds.

So the envelope was gone. There had been other Lise Kleins from Hamburg and the exigencies of placing several thousands of other children had caused this one to disappear. She had her passport from the *Kindertransport* journey, which assured her of a ration book, and that was all.

Towards the end of the war several mysterious documents had begun to arrive addressed to Lieselotte, suggesting that she might like to apply for an American visa. She had opened them in her room. Only the Stonehouses would not have asked her what they were. She herself was mystified. But, behind her closed bedroom door, she had filled out forms, taken them to school and asked two teachers to vouch for her, and returned them to the address supplied. She said nothing about them to anybody.

She had lived on in Shields West, knitting, working, smiling, passing into puberty with commendable calmness, her childhood bandaged over and never mentioned. She heard nothing. She knew nothing of Auschwitz. She was not told that all verifications of deaths there had been confirmed. Until the night of the chandelier in Rillington Mansions, her past might never have been.

And so, on the first of September, 1946, the day after her great sleep, after her second *Kristallnacht*, she had met up with the Polish student, Carl of the twitching face, and told him that her family might be dead in the gas ovens. The Feldmans must have known, she said. Worse, the Stonehouses must have known. It was treachery.

She had told him this as the two of them were going round the Wallace Collection in Manchester Square, which had just reopened. They were among the first visitors. Their feet echoed on the marble floors and again they stared at the pale spaces on the walls that were waiting for the treasures to come home. A narrow Bonington of Venice shone with gold light and a single vermilion blob. An amethyst sky.

'Come on,' he said. 'We'll get a cup of tea.'

*

161

'Didn't the Stonehouses ever . . . bring the subject up?'

'No. Quakers wait and see. They follow leadings. They weren't led towards telling me anything. They liked me, I think. They didn't want me to go.'

'You ought to write to them. You haven't, have you?'

'I can't. I don't know why. It's terrible. They are so good.'

'Well, then, I'll write. I'll tell them you're OK. Look, they may not even know where you are. It's savage of you. You were theirs for seven years.'

'There's another thing.'

'What?'

'I heard Mrs Feldman saying, "Her mother, her father, her sister, her brother . . ."'

'Well?'

'I never had a sister or brother.'

'You don't think there may be another Lieselotte Klein?'

'Well, but there may be someone else out there. Some relative somewhere. My parents may have survived, even. They won't know what became of me. I did actually get some papers a bit ago. About America.'

'But then—?'

'No. I didn't tell anyone. Yes. I did fill them up and send them back. Look. I don't *know* why I kept it to myself.'

He took her to the first of many agencies and they discovered that there had indeed been another Lisa Klein, who was now with relatives in Canada. And Lieselotte herself at last was found. It was Carl who found her, and he went at once to Rillington Mansions to confront her with herself; but Lieselotte was out.

'She's walking, walking,' said Mr Feldman, urging him down the steep steps. 'Walking, walking.'

Mrs Feldman passed him some illegal salami, a very old Marie biscuit and a cup of black tea in a Sèvres teacup. The Polish refugee did not know when he had felt so much at home.

'There is news?'

'Yes. Her parents are dead. This is certain. It will be bad for her, but she must immediately be stopped from hoping. She has never admitted to hope, but she must now not hope. I must do it. But there is, it seems, a great-aunt in California.'

Mrs Feldman commented that his face was all atwitch and he replied that it had this habit. She said, 'I think you have your own story.'

'Hey, hey,' said Mr Feldman. 'I wonder in what age are we living?'

Carl took Lieselotte the next day to see the College Hetty was coming to, in Regent's Park, for it was somewhere new to them both. It was a beautiful day, and they walked across green lawns, past tennis courts and through Botanical Gardens. They looked up at the College library. Older students were already there. Serene faces in a row were looking down at books along a line of Georgian windows.

'She's going to like this,' said Lieselotte. 'Oh, she will adore it!'

They asked to see the students' rooms, which had just been painted for the new academic year, and there were coal fires laid already by a maid, and polished floors and armchairs and empty bookshelves waiting. One long stretch of rooms looked over a rose-garden. London hummed pleasantly in the distance.

'She can't grumble,' said Carl.

'Hetty never grumbles,' said Lieselotte. 'She's of the ecstatic kind.'

'An English girl? Ecstatic?' he said.

'She's Hetty,' said Lieselotte.

In the rose-garden in the grounds of the College by the lake, he told her what he had discovered and that her family was dead. She said nothing.

She said nothing. And she said nothing all the way back on the bus. He took her hand for the first time, and lifted it and kissed it. She stroked his face and said, 'Why is your face twitching so today?' and kissed his cheek. 'So she *wants* me, does she? This aunt? Who is she? I've never heard of her. She probably belongs to the other one, the one in Canada.'

'No. She's yours all right. I've made quite sure. She is

163

remarkably rich and I am tempted to ask you to marry me, for she is a widow and she is childless, and she swore an affidavit for you years ago if you should ever turn up.'

'Let's get out.'

They left the bus and walked together through Bayswater towards Notting Hill, at first apart, but, soon, holding on to each other tight.

'There's an enormous queue for the United States,' she said.

'Not if you're sponsored. It appears you can just go. You'll need a visa, of course, and that takes time. There will be plenty of money.'

'I have a visa.'

'*What?*'

'Oddly enough. Maybe it was meant for the other one, but I think that it might do. I got one.'

'This is unbelievable! You have a visa?'

'Yes.'

'And you go to Cambridge in exactly one month?'

'On the ninth of October,' she said. 'I go on.'

He took both her hands and then kissed them, one after the other. 'It appears that she is your only living relative in the world. It is her dead husband who was your blood relative. He was a Jew and she is not. She is a little strange, but she wants you.'

One week later, before she left for California, Lieselotte wrote letters for many hours. The letter to the Stonehouses was the hardest, but she battled through. The need for gratitude fought with an astonishing, nameless distaste. She saw her passive self, sitting on the coal-box with her knitting, all the unbelievable dispassionate years, the absence of curiosity, the rejection of lusts, the acceptance of whatever befell. The thing she saw most clearly was the beauty, the certainty, of the pacifism of the Stonehouses' religion, the folding of hands as the details of the death camps broke over the sane world. The solemnity and lack of comment after the Belsen film, the determination not to hate, the insistence on passive love.

'I couldn't be Quaker,' she said. 'The silence would extinguish me.'

'You do realise,' Carl said, 'that the Quakers did more for us than everybody else? Without them you and I would be dead now. They got thousands out. They were wonderful.'

But she couldn't forgive them their forgiveness, and it read as a cold letter to these mystical but practical people. A cold letter from a stranger. She saw them as they passed it across from one to another in the clean and perfect puritan house, the flower vase on the window-sill that held, summer and winter, only one flower. I preferred the High Anglicans, she thought. Hetty's mother's gorgeous vicar. I wonder why Hetty so hated him.

She decided that her letter to Hetty would be next.

Well, maybe not next. But soon.

When she had finished ten letters she asked Mr Feldman if he would post them and left the money for stamps.

She left the Feldmans no presents, she left no forwarding address. She left Mrs Feldman ruminating at the work-table over the spurned red plush, and Mr Feldman walking up and down on the pavement, signalling for a taxi, his arm still raised absent-mindedly, but now in farewell, as she was whirled away. He looked tired, she thought. But she forgot him.

Away she went, with only two small bags, to join the ship in Southampton that was to cross the Atlantic. She was not travelling steerage, but with a cabin to herself and a wad of money in her purse. The days passed. She was not seasick. She lay watching the waves tipping into swells and points through her cabin's porthole. Other passengers moaned and heaved and fasted, but Lieselotte ploughed through four colossal meals a day and impressed her steward and the crew. For hours at a time she sat hunched upon the deck like a small, angry-looking otter in Mrs Feldman's spiky black coat that trailed about her ankles. It was hot, delicious, salt-sprayed weather, but she wrapped the coat about her. Her tight little mouth that now did not smile was surrounded with a pattern of draw-string lines like somebody old. An otter's whiskers. She did not read, nor write nor talk to anybody, and completely ignored the fancy-dress parades, the deck-quoits, the swimming pool and the dancing, though once or twice she attended the concerts, sitting at the back with closed eyes. Afterwards she would march about the deck trailing the fur coat that almost extinguished her, and people thought she was unhinged.

From New York she flew to San Francisco, north first, then south, thrice sitting at airports she had never heard of. She delighted herself by the discovery that she was a natural traveller, finding lounges and ticket booths, documents and flight numbers with ease. Once she sat for six hours looking out of the windows of an airport – maybe Kansas City – over a vast elastic plain. On one hop of the flight she looked down on an underwater landscape, like a waving ocean floor. But these are forests, she thought; hundreds of miles of trees. It was the Fall, and the forests were crimson and yellow, sharp rust and bright gold. On the plane everyone was gazing down and exclaiming, and the pilot announced that he, personally, in all his experience had never seen the Fall so beautiful, and that he would go down a little nearer. Lieselotte sat unsmiling, and watched on.

On the second flight they came upon a mighty wound. The colours changed. She thought of tiny coloured wagons crawling like ants towards the barrier of mountains. Stopping. Making camp. Far enough. Never moving on again. Corn and wine and turkeys and Indians. The Stonehouses had sometimes allowed her to go to the pictures. The world now was beginning to break out into great swathes and peaks. Rivers were flung down in lead and silver loops. And then snow. Snows! 'The High Chaparral,' she said aloud, and the person next to her said, 'That's right, honey,' so she turned her black fur shoulder on him and said no more.

The Pacific Ocean. The ocean of peace.

The plane swung and dipped and straightened and dropped over hard blue bays and pink and yellow hills. Clusters of towers humped on an island. Building blocks for children. Were these skyscrapers? And now . . . down, down, sway, bump, down they floated over a huge bay towards an island. A glowing bridge with a rose-red rectangle at either end stood in the water, caught together by rose-red threads. Someone had flung handfuls of houses over the hills, away and away, wherever you looked. And all over the water were boats like minnows and newts and water-rats and floating white butterflies. They had landed.

She clambered off the plane and out into warm air. There was a cheerful, battering wind and unimaginable light.

In the taxi she handed the driver the address, and found it was thirty miles off. 'Do we cross the bridge?'

'We cross the bridge. It'll be a few dollars.'

'I have plenty of money,' she said. 'I've been sponsored.'

'You been sponsored? Is that a fact? Well, let's *go*.'

Over the bridge for nearly a mile, up and then down, blue, blue, blue on either side, blue of sky and blue below, the red of the bridge leaving an afterglow on the hills. There were streets and streets of light-hearted houses saying, 'Earthquakes, come and get me.' When she had told Mr Feldman where she was to live he had said, 'I am sure that you have heard of the San Andreas Fault?' Lieselotte said, 'I have never been afraid of anything in my life,' and Mr Feldman had looked grave and sad. But nobody in America was afraid of anything. Here they were all, in their hundreds and thousands, walking about in the little coloured cardboard towns, idle and happy and talkative.

Now they drove into the hills and fields. One old horse. An old-style farmhouse, then swoop and dash, up, then down. A port like toytown. Big black leathery birds flying slowly along over the water. Down, down and to a long, long seaside street with all the backs of the houses blank, their hidden fronts turned to the shore, watching the sea. The fare was huge but she felt nothing. She added five dollars for a tip, which he took as a right. I am a natural traveller, she thought again. I know how to do it.

'Good luck, honey,' he said. 'Stick around.'

He left her standing in the road beside her two bags.

Everywhere looked new. The road was not even properly finished, but every perfect, painted blank wall had its perfect, painted small gate and flight of coloured ceramic steps going down from it and round the side of the house, and out of sight. There were important garage doors on the road-level, all painted white or pale coffee-cream. The windowless backs of the houses had creepers growing on them in stylish patterns, like giant

167

pointed hands. The leaves had been made to sprout at exact intervals, like a patterned plate. Here and there along the silent street was a cistern full of lilies with flowers like leather parrots.

How quiet it was. She could see that the road had been cut through an ancient wood that had covered the hillside and was still there above her. She could not see the sea below for the houses. No people here. Not a dog. Not a leaf fallen. Not a rubbish bin. Not a bike propped up. Not a yawning cat. And not a wall that did not speak big, big money. But not a breath of exertion, experiment or endeavour.

She had expected something different. She had expected the ramshackle and outrageous, bogus like Hollywood, gardens full of vulgar statues, jokey fountains playing Coca-Cola. Big-hearted, easygoing, sharp-witted American millionaires, boasting and sleek, confident and guileless, like the GIs had been at the Shields West hops on her very occasional Saturday nights out. There was nothing here but a great hush, and understated design, the sun shining on and on, as if it would never stop. As if it had nowhere else to go.

At last she picked up the bags and took them one by one down the steep steps. Down there, round the corner of the house, the tiles turned into smoother, paler ones covered in cabalistic signs. There was a thick metal plaque on the wall depicting the awful, irrepressible sun. The door of the house stood sideways to the steps with a blank wall above it. The house must hang halfway down the cliff-side. She rang the bell. There was no sound.

There was a little balustrade in front of her and she looked down over it and saw the tops of feathery trees, moving a little. Their roots must be far, far below, clamped in the rocks on the shore. She could hear the sea down there now, swishing slowly and softly. There seemed no way into this house, no windows, no second door. She stood with her two cases in the deep shadow of the bastion wall above and wondered what to do.

The door opened and a woman looked out and said, 'Oh my! Well, hi! You've come. You're early.'

Lieselotte stood looking at her, her mouth pinched into the otter's whiskers.

168

'Well, great. OK. Come on in. Come on in and sit down. We'll not be long.'

Lieselotte dragged the luggage into a high narrow hallway that opened on to a huge white room flooded with the light from a wall of glass that was filled with the ocean and the sky. In front of this backcloth sat three women, exquisitely painted: eyebrows, lips, nails, lashes. They were playing cards round a glass table and drinking something out of long glasses. Their hair was dark, cut sharp and neat, like metal bathing-caps.

'Just you sit there,' said the woman who had come to the door. 'We'll be with you in no time at all.'

So Lieselotte sat on a long, low banquette upholstered in white leather. The carpet spread to every corner, deep white wool, like a field of snow. The chairs were white leather and steel. On the white walls were white pictures. The white painted edge to the window left no room for curtains and must have been especially glazed, she thought, for through the glass the vast blue sea did not even whisper. One of the women lit a white cigarette with a gold tip. Another smoked a black cigarette and tapped it out in a blue lapis ashtray. The smoke from the cigarettes twirled up blue against the white walls. The four fans of cards were as immobile as sculpture in their fingers. The women were dressed in navy-blue, magenta and fuschia-pink and all were hung with gold chains. Their ears were blobbed with gold and their faces were lacquered to the smoothness of their helmets of hair. But as she watched she saw that their complexions did not quite disguise the spider-web of lines, like a craze on porcelain. All four women were most immensely old.

21

Between Hetty's eyes and the pages of Spenser's *Faerie Queen*, into which she had lasciviously swooped to counteract Thomas Carlyle, there arose every two or three minutes the face of Rupert Fitzurse. It was not so much an image of his features or his stature, for he was rather apologetically stooped. It was, she thought, his regard and sweetness, his kind grace. You felt that *he* would be exactly the same for everyone – man, woman, child – but at the same time *you* would be, to him, unique. There was a peaceful animal in him, but an animal, and once he moved away from you, his mind, you knew, would return to its own meridian, its happy world. Oh, that's what he was. He was happy!

Yet he was not unworldly. The first sound she had heard from him was the drawing of a cork. He enjoyed wine. He had looked at it and twirled it about in the glass, knocked it back, the bottle swinging from his hand. She'd never seen anyone do that. Actually, she had not before seen anyone drinking wine.

Love, she thought, that's it. That's what he knows about, universal love, and no prudery. He'd be able to love you all in all, and out and out. I want him, she thought, and then, even more astoundingly, And I'll get him.

Struggling with Canto I, Book One, she felt herself in Rupert's arms.

Wouldn't Ma die from joy if I brought him home? Just walked in with him: 'Oh, Ma, this is Rupert.' Her mother's shining delighted eyes, her pretty manners. I'd certainly not be ashamed of Ma's looks either. Blushing bright pink. And saying later to the vicar, 'She's met rather a *nice* man. I believe he is an Honourable. I'm afraid he's a Roman, but he seems *very* taken with her.' Her mother's voice, always so obsequious to the vicar, would now be strong and confident. 'Well, of course Malcolm's family were not exactly *nobodies*.'

How would Rupert get on with the grave-digger? Well . . . not so certain here. The grave-digger could be a hard man.

Rupert reminds me a bit of Christ, she thought, and felt suddenly shocked, and sick.

The vicar didn't think her father was a somebody, he thought her father was a dud. He was sure, too, that Hetty took after her father. Any chance the vicar had of seeing her on her own – he didn't like her, he didn't find her attractive – he would start on about how she should look into herself, confront her soul's shortcomings. 'You're clever enough, Hester, but spiritually, *spiritually*, you have work to do.'

'Darling,' said her mother, 'I don't want to butt in, but I have often found Confession a help.'

Off we go again.

Hetty had been to Confession once, just after her Confirmation. The vicar had looked pleased with himself all the time and she couldn't think of anything to say. And once he had farted.

Then another time, after her O levels, she'd gone into the sitting-room one night, her father out on one of his ramblings, and found the vicar tousling up her mother on the sofa. She had dealt with this burly vision with a sophistication that had astonished everybody. 'Just looking for a pencil,' she said, withdrawing from the room.

Her mother had been lying there, looking languid, not herself at all, but had later burst into Hetty's bedroom, saying, 'You don't understand, you *beastly* little thing.' The following Sunday the vicar had not preached on morality as usual, but on the complex character of the Japanese.

So much for Christian love, thought Hetty, and it's no wonder I've not liked the idea of the other kind.

She had buried this awful memory until this instant. So much for Mother Church. Yet something of Christian love that didn't make you sick about sex she had seen in Rupert, and all she could think of was being with him again.

There was no further sign, however. No sign of Patsie either. No ride on Rupert's horse, no further gesture from the Hall. As to that, why should there be? She'd been asked over to meet them because of Hilda Fletcher, that was all, and more than a paying guest at a nearby farmhouse might expect. It had all been false. By the following weekend even Mrs Satterley had forgotten the subject of the Hall and the dangers of Rupert. To Mr Satterley Hetty's relationship with Rupert was no subject at all.

It was the beginning of the second week of September now, the straw all stacked, grouse-shooting at full strength, rowan berries blazing in the lane and the suspicion of 'Back-End' in the still, blue air over the mountains. Holiday people were disappearing and during the week Hetty was now the only guest at Betty Bank, and it was not fully booked sometimes even at the weekends. One day Hetty realised that this was the date when her school would be beginning the new term, and felt strange. She wondered who'd been made Head Girl. Would I have been if I'd stayed on and tried for Cambridge next year? I wonder who has my desk. Then she thought, How pathetic – I've left. It's over, and thank goodness.

Hetty ate always now in the flagstoned kitchen with the Satterleys, the kettle swinging from its chain, the row of painted tea caddies along the high mantelpiece, the cattle-cake calendar dangling from a nail on a beam, with only four pages left. The kitchen door was still left standing open on to the yard, for it was going to stay warm this autumn. A hen would appear now and then on the worn sandstone step, and put its beak round the doorpost to make enquiries. Each evening, after six o'clock supper, Hetty helped Mrs Satterley wash up, wiping each fat cup round and round, setting it down on the pink stone. Then Mrs Satterley would walk with the tin basin to the door and fling the washing-up water in a sparkling sheet at the hens, who would scream and run. The sour-sweet smell of the midden floated in and the sun went down behind the orchard. The apple trees were small and knobbly, silver-leafed, and all the little apples took the colour of the red sky.

'No rain again tomorrow,' said Mr Satterley, 'but the oats is in. Never been such an early year as '46. We'll remember it. It was the rain did it, June and July.'

'You'd not have been harvesting tomorrow, oats in or out,' said his wife: 'it's Sunday.'

'Aye, well,' he said. 'Now then, Hester, will you be coming to Meeting?'

'She might prefer Church,' said Mrs Satterley, who did, though she only went at Christmas and Harvest Festival.

The next morning Hetty walked in silence along the lane to the Quaker Meeting with Mr Satterley. The lane was a darker, deader green now than when it had first enclosed her with her load of luggage, and there was a yellow branch here and there in the ash trees, and berries shining nearer the ground. Skeletons of willowherb and thistles floated off tufts of silver silk as if sheep had been leaving gleanings. There were some wonderful brambles.

'I'll send Lizzie with a basin tomorrow,' said Mr Satterley.

Hetty wondered why he couldn't bring a basin here himself, and rather bravely said so.

'Woman's work,' he said. 'I'd never ask Lizzie to muck out a byre.'

'I'll come for the brambles,' she said.

'You have your lessons.'

'No. I'd like to. Really.'

Round the bend in the lane the table was gone. You could see where it had stood from the four tufts of darker grass that had grown up round its legs. No chair. No provender. No jam-jar. No book. Hetty felt unaccountably sad.

They walked along in the ruts between the last of the summer flowers and the hum of insects. A red squirrel watched them neurotically from a tree.

'The table's gone.'

'Aye, she takes it in around now. There's not the call by late

173

September. The walkers is mostly gone home and the summer's done.'

'Oh, don't say that.'

He looked at her, pleased. 'Come on now, Hetty, you've plenty summers left to come.'

'There'll never be another summer like this one,' she said. She had a fantasy of Rupert suddenly appearing round the next bend.

'Thou'st happy here?'

'Oh, yes. Well, it's been like arriving somewhere at last.'

'Getting away from home?'

'Oh, yes.'

'Is home not to thy liking?'

'Oh, it's not that.'

'You mean, you're not going to say it's that to me, and that is only right. But I hear there's sadness at home?'

'My mother's lovely,' she said (and thought, She's awful, too). 'And so's my father. But he's on the Somme. All the time.'

'Aye, well – here'st' Meeting House.'

They sat in the silence, Hetty wondering how you learn to say prayers just sitting, not even thinking, and, hardest of all, thinking without words.

This will be no good at all, she thought, and opened her eyes on the five or six Quakers sitting at peace, faces upturned, eyes shut. One old man had a beard like a snowball. One of the women wore a black dress with a brooch at the throat and a sort of white bonnet. They're antiques, thought Hetty. Not one of them went through the First War. Not one of them was as brave as Pa.

I should have gone to Church, she thought. I might have seen him there. They'll all sit in the family pew up in the chancel, like in the eighteenth century— Oh, no, they won't, they're all Catholics. They'll be in that Chapel with the broken windows. One thing, none of them'd be seen dead in here.

The door of the Meeting House opened suddenly with a push and a groan showing a slice of gold light from the garden, and the sullen child, Mabel, came in, glaring about her. She closed the door and sat on the nearest bench. She seemed a resentful disturbance to the silence, but then, after a minute, the silence took charge again.

Trying out religions, thought Hetty. I did that round her age, mostly to get at Mother. She looks old, somehow. Older than eleven. She looks older than Patsie, and she wasn't in a prison camp.

Some people are always in prison, she thought. She was surprised at herself. She listened to the silent words. It was not exactly a thought, it was a statement. It had been offered to her. It held the conviction that you sometimes find in dreams. It had been announced, and it must be what the Quakers call a 'leading'. She stood up and said, 'Some people are always in prison.'

The silence thickened and the words were absorbed into the room. Nobody looked at her. Nobody moved. She thought, Crikey, I've testified in a Quaker Meeting the first time I've ever been to one! Whatever'll Mr Satterley think?

They'll think I'm aggressive. Pushy. Like Patsie. Mr Satterley knows I'm not a Quaker. The only Quakers I know are the Stonehouses, and I don't know much about them, except they seem pretty dull. They're like two glasses of cold water, really. Though I suppose that's OK.

She thought of Church at home. The solemn, booming hymns, the ghastly vicar, the wonderful words and the mystery of the Sacrament. Oh God, I don't know *where* I am. I know *nothing*. She sat with bowed head and felt tears come.

Nobody else testified, and at the end of the hour they all stirred and swayed a little and shook hands with one another, and the woman in the white cap went out to put the kettle on. Mr Satterley said, 'Stay for your tea, now, Hetty, but I've got to get back to a sick animal,' and Hetty said, 'Oh, I'd like to come home now too.'

A minute or two later they were walking back along the lane, and she heard thumping feet behind them.

'Now then, Mabel,' said Mr Satterley. 'All right?'

Mabel fell into step beside them and looked up at Hetty intently.

'Hallo,' said Hetty.

Mabel mumbled something and marched alongside. When the site of the invisible table came into view, she broke away and humped herself off through the hole in the hedge, without saying goodbye, or another word.

'Yon's a sad lass,' said Mr Satterley. 'Ugly duckling.'

'Mabel at Meeting?' asked Mrs Satterley over the roast beef.

'Aye. All be herself. She looked in a rare old paddy, poor throstle.'

'Well, it's Patsie. And that Rupert. Nobody normal couldn't but be unsettled over there.'

'Patsie never came for our ride,' said Hetty. It had not been mentioned before.

Mrs Satterley looked reticent and displeased. 'Likely she forgot. It's a rare flathery family. All owert' place, as they say. No food but Chinese all the years has starved her brains.'

'Mabel wasn't in China.'

'Now then,' said Mrs Satterley briskly, 'this grand day, are you really going again to them books? I'm never easy to see you working on a Sunday.' Perhaps she noticed Hetty's look of despair, for then she said, 'Oh dear me, is it homesickness? Or is it boredom?'

'Well, I have never been homesick in my life,' said Hetty. 'I was thrilled when you said I could stay on longer and Ma was OK about it, so I haven't felt guilty. And if it was boredom I'd not be here, would I?'

Of all times, home on a Sunday afternoon was worst. Her mother, wearied by two church services, at eight and eleven o'clock, Eucharist both times, and a sermon, and by somehow managing to cook a dinner of roast meat, two kinds of potato, gravy and white sauce, Yorkshire puddings, steamed pudding and custard and perhaps a semolina on the side – the only real meal of the week – usually went to bed. Her father disappeared into his greenhouse, where a row of wellington boots each held a bottle of beer.

Later in the afternoon Hetty could hear him singing and conversing with his tomatoes or chrysanthemums. There had been nothing for her to do, since she wasn't supposed to go far from home throughout most of the war in case of the sirens. Nothing to do but homework.

It was Eustace who last year had rescued her. The front doorbell would ring after Sunday dinner and there he'd be in his uniform and his nice smile, and they would walk and talk and look at glades and he would say lovely things to her.

She began now to think about Eustace, and to remember the first excitement of him. Apart from the way he wore his beret, he was really rather beautiful. And he was brilliant. And he was a man and not a schoolboy; he could have been all of twenty-five, to look at him. He had rescued her from the hell of Sunday afternoons. He had rescued her from prison. And he had loved her. He had told her so, twice. He'd back-pedalled a bit later, but at sixteen she had been loved. And he had got her into a London College. The least she could do now was try to tell him how much he had meant to her. She would read all his letters, now, this minute – he hadn't written for nearly a fortnight, come to think of it. She gave a sigh of pleasure and decision.

Mrs Satterley flicked the tea-towel over the wooden rack on the kitchen ceiling to dry and took up the bowl of dish-water. 'So, must you really go to them books?'

'Here, I'll do that,' said Hetty and took the basin from her to throw the water at the hens. She laughed as they ran about in a squally fluster. 'They must be fairly stupid,' she said. 'A douche of cold water three times a day and they always look surprised.'

'They've short memories,' said Mr Satterley. 'They're like people. Not like cows.' He was looking pleased to see her laughing and she knew he was thinking of what she'd stood up and said in Meeting. He was thinking, She's not in prison now. This is much better.

'So, would you not like to go off walking now?' he said. 'You've years for the reading and you'll not be doing any other come October.'

'I'll write a few letters first,' she said.

'And maybe open a few?' said Mrs Satterley.

Hetty set off up the stairs with their red and blue Turkey carpet and shiny brass rods, past the artificial lupins in a jar made from a painted baked-beans tin standing on a lace doily, into her white room. The sheets and walls were blue-white in the shadows, the

177

stiff lace curtains white as the white of an egg, tied back with stiff blue tapes. The blue and white and green of Beatrix Potter mountains shone through the window.

I'm happy, she thought.

'And write to your mother, too,' shouted up Mrs Satterley.

'I will.'

But first, Eustace. She scooped all his letters from beside the chamber-pot under the bed and arranged them on the desk in date order. They were all very solid, except the last one. The last one was quite light.

Start with that, she decided. All the rest will be English Literature.

22

Lieselotte sat in her bedroom in the white house beside the Pacific Ocean. The room did not look at the sea but at the rock wall between the back wall of the house and the window, the wall completely covered by rich ferns and trails of yellow ivy. A face looked in on her from among the greenery. It watched her all the time. It was the face of a half-naked goddess, dancing and holding on her shoulder the crescent moon. Lieselotte was grateful to have been released to her room away from the huge, watchful ocean that menaced most of the other rooms, but she was not altogether at ease with the goddess.

She had been now with the aunt in Belvedere for nearly a week. The first peculiar state of her mind was past but she was still unable to accept that she was neither dead nor dreaming.

That first afternoon, after the four porcelain women had finished their Bridge, she was shown the kitchen, her bathroom and her bedroom against the rock by the minimally younger woman who had first greeted her. She had been told that the door of her bedroom must at all times be left open in case her aunt should call on her for something during the night. 'You will have no domestic duties,' said Mame ('Now, I am *Mame.*') 'and here is my telephone number in case you need me. The cleaner comes early in the morning, and the cook, but you will do the marketing. It is less than two miles to the shops and you will be given your own transport.'

'Transport?'

'There's to be a dinky little car.'

'But I can't drive.'

'Oh, she'll get you some lessons. Until you can drive, we'll get them to deliver. Now, you'll be in charge of her clothes, just washing and pressing. Underclothing and scarves, handkerchiefs and washing and stretching her gloves. The rest goes once or twice a week to the automatic cleaners. Do you play Bridge? We play every afternoon and twice Saturdays. You could make up a four sometime and let one of us off. I guess I could do with seeing to my own life now and then. Though this is between ourselves.'

'I'm afraid I don't play.'

'Oh? Well, she'll get you some lessons. Her standard is good-to-excellent but she can be a poisonous partner. Wouldn't you know? C'mon!'

'I'm sorry, I haven't been introduced to her yet.'

They returned to the great white room. The other helmeted pair had disappeared and the fourth woman, the great aunt herself, was seated staring out through the glass wall.

'D'you have my carffee?' she asked the sea. She was a tiny skin-and-bone woman with giant blue eyes. On her finger was a gold and amethyst ring, the size of a purple sugar lump. On her feet were fuchsia-pink silk slippers.

'Alice, she's here. D'you remember? Lieselotte has arrived. From Britain.'

'I don't turn easy,' said Alice. 'Come on rouaand and stand in front of me. My!!'

'Guten Tag, Tante Alice,' said Lieselotte.

'Well, my! Let's just stick to English, huh? My German's before the Prussian War.' She stared at Lieselotte a long time and coffee was brought, one cup on a black tray with a bowl of sugar and a jug of cream. 'From Hamburg?' said Alice. 'Ahl that way – and by your own self.'

'I have lived in England for six years.'

'England? Now who were you with in England – Leonard?'

'The family is dead,' said Lieselotte. 'I never heard of Leonard.'

'No loss. But why did he never write about you?'

180

'Leonard's dead, Alice,' said Mame, pouring cream on top of the coffee and putting the cup to Alice's lips. 'He died that first war. You remember if you try.'

'I get muddled. Give that cup in my hand. D'you play Bridge?'

'I'm going now,' said Mame. 'Alice, are you listening? I'm going. Can you get her to bed, Lotte?' She was watching Lieselotte all the time.

'I don't know. I could try.'

'D'you want me to show you? She don't walk good. C'mon, I'll show you where things are.'

Alice's bedroom had a bed of satinwood with bottles and jars around it in clusters, like minarets. There were flowers on little shelves, leathery orchids and lilies. There was a knock-out, funeral smell.

'Here's the nightdress. Now she has to have her padded panties. She eats nothing. Just a bite of jello or a little sandwich. She's crazy for peanut butter but never let her even see a nut or she'll choke. Don't forget her hair. It goes on a stand.'

'A *stand*?'

'A stand for the hair to stand on.'

'Oh yes. I see. I think.'

'You have looked after old people before, haven't you? I'm sure you have. Weren't you looking after some old people in London?'

'No. Actually, they were looking after me.'

'No! Oh, my! Is there something wrong with you, then? Oh, that's terrible.'

'No, I'm perfectly well. They are just Jewish and paternalistic. I was their lodger.'

'Oh, that's great, then. I wasn't sure you'd get this job, I might as well tell you, but I guess you'll be just fine. I can see she likes you. You know you're the only relative?' Her eyes watched Lieselotte. 'She's no one else to leave it to.'

'I . . . Mame, I don't think she knows who I am. She thinks I'm someone to nurse her. I was told she wanted to adopt me. I didn't know it was going to be a job.'

'Oh, *sure* she knows. She *said* that. I heard her say "adopt". She'll be ready to have you if she takes to you. Well, it'll give me a break.

181

I don't get paid for a thing I do, you know, but I guess you'd see I got the jewellery? We're like sisters, Alice and me. And it's a nice bit of luck for you.'

'Luck? *Nursing*? I was just going up to the University.'

'Oh, there's plenty of nice Colleges out here, you know, and I dare say it won't be for long. She's . . . we won't say *how* old. I wasn't against you. I was for you. I thought it wasn't one of her worst little notions. I'm married to a solicitor, a retired solicitor. He can do plenty about wills,' she said with a whiff of menace.

She was winding a long chiffon scarf round her neck, slowly round and round, not disturbing her necklaces, looking and looking at Lieselotte. 'She has these tantrums, you know. You should hear her go for some folks. She's all there for a bit yet.' Mame stared and stared at Lieselotte, whose eyes could hardly stay open.

'I'll just step back in and say goodbye to her. You know where to find me. Next door. I'm in all evening – well, unless I go to a little bit more Bridge in Tiburon. I'll look in. In the morning.'

Lieselotte heard her shouting at Alice. 'Well, *sure* she's ash-pale. They got no vitamins over there. She'll be great. She's eighteen goin' on forty. That *coat*! And you know I'd never leave you, Alice.'

The door on to the perilous step slammed shut and Lieselotte was alone with her great-aunt.

She was thirsty and rather hungry. But there was worse. There was a deadness, a hollowness, a deep, deep, shivering exhaustion. 'I am a natural traveller,' she said, but the throbbing of the ship had not left her and, when she forced it from her, there came the roar of the aeroplanes. Snapshots of airports flashed before her. All the different planes, all the faces, all the magician's carpet of the world unrolled. And then the roller-coaster of the taxi ride. Part of her still paced a deck, listened to Rachmaninov and Ivor Novello in a slightly-moving hall, swayed with the underwater fronds of New England, danced with their eerie movements, rumbled across prairies in bonnet and shawl huddled against a mother and a father driving a little cob that pulled a covered wagon. Whatever time was it? It felt like morning but it was getting dark.

She was so tired.

She was so tired that she could hardly move her feet, pick up her luggage. She watched her feet in their tottering, high-heeled shoes walk out of the bedroom and towards the ancient woman who was still sitting like a waxwork, looking at the sea.

I shall say – say now – that there has been a terrible mistake.

'What say you to a great big *fry*?' said Alice, still staring at the black horizon.

'A fry?'

'C'mon, just heave me around, let's look at you. Oh my Gaaad! It's Nina! You're the spit of Nina!'

'I'm like Nina?'

'Nina's my daughter, but I guess she's gaan.'

'Oh, I'm sorry.'

'Do you know how to make a *big* fish fry?'

'But she said – your friend – I had to give you a little jelly and put you to bed.'

'Take my stick,' said Alice. 'Pull me up. Stick back. Thanks. Now, give me your arm, kiddo!'

Alice was lighter than a child, and quicker than Lieselotte across the white carpet on her fuschia-coloured feet. She balanced herself down into a kitchen chair and pointed the shoes out in front of her. They sparkled here and there and the floaty bits of ostrich feather moved in the breeze. She tapped her stick smartly against the huge refrigerator. 'Open it up.'

Lieselotte beheld the land of Canaan. Shelves stacked with meat and fish and cheeses, packages of eggs and butter, huge flagons of milk, ice cream in fifty flavours and unnervingly clean vegetables all technicolour green. Fruit juices like Goblin Market.

'Changed my mind: we'll have steaks. Steaks top shelf,' she said, pointing her stick. 'Grill over that way, first knob left. We'll have them with plenty of ketchup, and one helluva big salad. Now, do you eat chocolate cake? With chocolate fudge topping? Now, I'm a spirits drinker but we'll open a bottle of the red and I might just take a glass. I won't corrupt you, you know, Nina. We don't want another Gilda, do we?'

183

'I'm not much of a cook,' said Lieselotte, looking at the giant steaks and wondering who Gilda was. It was the entire meat counter of the Notting Hill butcher. 'I've never seen anything like this. It'd be a month's rations at home.'

'Your home's here now,' said Alice, 'and don't listen to Mame. She's a terrible cook, that's why I get only jello. It's why I sent for you. You don't have to get the lunch; we've got a black girl for that and I've got her bribed.'

'And,' she said when Lieselotte was sitting on a high stool, eating at a counter, and feeling much better, and when she herself was seated with a tray on wheels in front of the steel chair, '*And* we'll hear no more of these padded panties. Unnecessary. I've done exercises all my life, every woman should. You should start now and you'll never know the meaning of enuresis. I'll show you. Flat on your back.'

She wiped her bird-bone fingers with a paper napkin as thick as linen. Lieselotte had never seen paper napkins. 'Bring me a flannel and I'll go over my face; and I'll brush my teeth, which are all my own. Apples do it. And my nightie's where it always is, under my pillows, and I get into it myself. She's trying to frighten you off, Nina-Lotte. She wants my money. She has so much already she doesn't know what to do with it but she's after mine. D'you want a small cheroot? No? Well, then away to bed. Even if you don't sleep you can pretend it's bedtime, it's the only way to deal with airplane fag. I should know. I've been around. Kid the body and you'll live for ever. Goodnight. You look a real good girl. I knew you'd be just like Nina.'

'Do I . . .? There was something I had to do about your hair, Tante Alice.'

'What was that?' The blue eyes turned to ice and fire.

'I don't quite know. I had to put it—'

'Let her speak for herself. She may have to lift off certain portions of herself at night. I don't.'

In the small hours of the night Lieselotte awoke. Her body had been only temporarily kidded. She had slept deeply but for just

184

four hours. The light was on in the passage outside her bedroom door and she sensed activity.

She got out of bed and padded across the white wool to the kitchen with its almost adolescent mess of unwashed dishes. Then cautiously, gently pushing the slightly open door, she looked into Aunt Alice's room. The centre light was on and both reading lamps, and Tante Alice was sitting up in bed with the newspaper and brandishing a gold pencil, not a hair of her head out of place. She looked over her spectacles at Lieselotte, and nodded.

'Can I get you anything, Tante Alice? A drink?'

'No, thank you. I'm busy with my investments. Can't you sleep?'

'I feel very wide awake. It's still so dark. It doesn't feel like morning. Or like any time.'

'We might have a hand of cards if you've a leaning that way?'

'Well, I've been living with Quakers for seven years. I never learned.'

'You don't seem to have learned very much, Nina-Lotte, if you ask me. I guess I'm going to have my work cut aaht. Go to bed and if you oversleep you oversleep. It's gonna drive Mame up the wahl. Then later on we can look at the photographs.'

When Lieselotte awoke, it was late afternoon of the next day and growing dark again and her aunt and her three companions were hard at it over the Bridge table by the window. Behind her hand of scarlet and black Tante Alice stared out to sea. The other women smoked their sleepy-smelling cigarettes.

The blue-black sea seemed to be eternally at rest, filling the acreage of window. Twenty-four hours could surely not have passed? It was still yesterday. Or it might be tomorrow. It might be in the far future, or long ago. It might be eternity.

I can't stay, thought frowsty Lieselotte, rolling back to bed in Carl's parting present, his yellow pyjamas. The dancing goddess plugged into the rock wall seemed to look her way. Oh, but there is no hope of getting out. These people are too much for me. I am without money except for her change from the journey. There is no possible hope of getting away.

As she drifted into sleep a queer hollow voice said to her, at the edge of a dream, 'This is your greatest danger yet.'

There was a dream next, and inside it she knew she had dreamed it so many times that it had become a depth of dreams, layered and flaked, interleaved like a stack of cards, melded, a thousand dreams yet all the same. It was a spyglass view of a figure at a great distance, growing smaller all the time. The figure was the size of a pin but she knew it was a man. Behind it there was a smaller shadowy figure, greyer, with sloping shoulders, but it was the man who mattered most, and from and for him – even as he grew so small as to be only a spot on the lens – she felt a terrible love and grief. Then he vanished in a roaring of wheels and steam that blew across her vision.

The dream had never woken her before. She knew now, sitting up in bed in the dark, that it had never followed her into consciousness until now, but she had had it countless times. She felt her face and it was wet. She got out of bed and climbed into Mrs Feldman's coat, although the house was very hot. Then she climbed back into bed and sat bolt upright looking at the dark wall in front of her. She must not sleep again, for the dream would come back. She sat for an age, until her eyes could keep open no longer, and as she fell, slowly and sideways, back on her pillow, her bedroom door opened a little wider and one of the skulls of the Belsen films looked round it, and then disappeared.

The next day she stayed in bed. She did not take off the coat. Mame arrived and from a great distance Lieselotte watched and listened to herself being harangued. Alice did not appear. Somebody shut her door and the day moved on, the sculptured figure outside her window hung in shadow among the ferns until it merged with the dark wall and became the night. The servant looked in once, bringing a glass of milk, standing about, talking a nice singsong. Had the black fur in the bed put her off? Through her thoughts Lieselotte heard voices raised, telephones ringing. Maybe a doctor came in.

The next day she went to her bathroom and ran a bath, but sat

186

looking at it, not removing the fur coat. The servant came to her room with a plate of sweet cakes, and sat on the end of the bed and did a sort of crooning at her, but all Lieselotte could do was stare. Mame came in and slammed about and gave her views on many things.

After her bath, Lieselotte climbed back into the bed and gathered everything around her from her cases, and began to write a letter which to her surprise she found was not to Hetty, but to Hetty's parents. It was a formal letter and she thought, This might have been written in Germany and be from some old woman.

Dear Mr and Mrs Fallowes,
You will be surprised to get this letter from me, and also to see the address from which I write. I have recently arrived in America to join the aunt of my father, my only surviving relative, who has lately been discovered. She intends to adopt me. My decision to accept her kind offer was taken very swiftly. Before I left England I tried to write to a number of people who have been so kind to me during my English childhood, but the nearer they had been to me the less possible I found it to tell them.

So now I am trying again, drawing nearer to the most important letters. I practised first on those I knew less well. Soon I shall be writing to Hetty, but first I should like to say how much I owe you, her parents, for your unquestioning kindness all the time I was at the High School. Perhaps you can imagine how much I envy Hetty her great love for you, as well as your love for her.

Here she stopped. She wrote the next sentence with tight-shut eyes.

Here is like the very faint memory of my own childhood in Germany.

She sat still. Then opened her eyes and wrote:

187

Of all the people I knew in England, your warmth and open-ness, Mrs Fallowes, and your silent and humorous watchfulness, Mr Fallowes, will always stay in my heart. Before I left my London friends, I received a surprise. Una's mother wrote to me. I have no idea how she found my address, for I was remiss about sending it to anyone, but she says that she has 'connections in Scotland'! Why this should have helped, I don't know, unless it means that she is blessed with second sight. Hetty told me Una never knows what her mother will do next! I have been out of touch with maternal feelings, I regret to say. She told me that Hetty is on a reading course in the Lake District and that she is to be married to Eustace. If this is so, I must beg you to tell her to write to me at once, for I am now very aware of the folly of a leap in the dark.

Very sincerely yours, and with very good wishes from Lieselotte Klein, who misses you with all her heart.

23

Mrs Fallowes had been in two minds about going down to the Lonsdale. The rain was dreadful.

'It's the rainiest summer I remember,' she called to Mr Fallowes. 'I don't feel at all well. Why don't you answer me?'

He was watching raindrops on the pane.

'Have I upset you, Malcolm?'

'There's nothing to say.'

She put on her coat and hat and then a transparent mackintosh and pixie-hood over both, and went to the front door, where she found Lieselotte's letter lying on the vestibule mat. At once the world shone with delights.

'Malcolm! It's a letter. From America. Who do we know in America?'

'Theodore Roosevelt?'

'Don't be silly. Though Eustace's cousin once saw him in the flesh, but then he lived in Washington, and he had no legs.'

'What, the cousin?'

'No. Mr Roosevelt. He hides it so well. It's why he's always sitting down. At that Yalta business they were all wearing aprons.'

'Aprons?'

'Well, travel rugs, even that Stalin, whom I *cannot* like, I'm afraid, whatever they say about him being a Colostomy.'

'Colossus.'

'Yes. Well, look at his cruel little eyes . . . Goodness gracious! It's from Lieselotte! She's in California!'

'To us, not to Hetty?'

'No, it's addressed to you and me. *California*, it's where the syrup of figs comes from and by the way we need some more. You're having trouble again.'

'Don't talk bilge. Read the letter.'

'Well!' she said, having finished it to herself. 'Well! I'd never have guessed any of it. What an eye-opener. She feels us real friends, Malcolm, and yet she never opened her mouth about it before. And we'll have to put her straight about Eustace. I hope she's wrong. That Dolly Vane's an imbecile. Engaged. Where did she get that? . . . Malcolm?'

'Yes?'

'Malcolm, you don't think it's true? And Hetty's told Dolly Vane before she's told us? That's something I'm afraid I could never forgive a daughter. Never.' She began to cry. 'Never. It would be a public declaration. To tell a stranger about your engagement before your mother. And . . .'

'And what?'

'To announce that she does not love us. Oh, Malcolm, read this letter, so full of love and appreciation and I'm sure we did nothing for Lieselotte except pay for her at the pictures once or twice because those Quakers were so pure. Didn't we take her to the terrible Belsen film? Though I never thought that was wise.'

'No,' he said, 'I didn't take her!' and read the letter. 'She's in a real old tangle. A real old snuff-out. She's sure that Eustace is the wrong one,' he said. 'I take to this girl.'

'My heart is beating so hard I can hear it,' said Kitty. 'Look, you can see it going up and down inside my mackintosh.'

'A heart doesn't go up and down,' he said.

'I must go to the Lonsdale. They'll want to hear all about this. Oh, I do feel red in the face. I might look in at the surgery and get my blood pressure done.'

'You can get me a cup of coffee instead,' he said, 'while I read this through. Can you not see how you talking to all that lot of silly rubbish at the Lonsdale is a betrayal of trust?'

'Trust? Why trust? I'm sure I always keep my word. She doesn't say we're not to talk about her. She'd want me to tell them all that she's all right. And they'll want to hear about America.'

'She's not all right,' said the grave-digger. 'She is clearly not all right. But then I don't know who is. Our Het's not. They never had enough fun, any of these girls. Never, since the war, and they were only kids before it started. They don't know where they are.'

'I'm sure I never had any fun at their age, either. They suspected I had a fractured heart.'

But she took off her outdoor clothes and put the kettle on, thinking all the time of Lieselotte's praises. 'Open-heartedness'. 'Love'. Hetty would never have said anything like it. But then Hetty was English. The Germans were very flowery.

'Of course the Germans are very flowery,' she called through, and walking in with the Camp coffee, the last in the bottle, she said, 'and although we shouldn't say it, the Jews *do* exaggerate. I mean, look at their music. Though I'm very fond of Mendelssohn.'

The Lonsdale café that morning looked like a chamber under the sea; the windows were steamed over and the glass roof darkened by the machine-gunning rain. The ladies had not been daunted, however, and arrived one by one, shaking drops about as they took off their noisy mackintoshes. Today, Mrs Lonsdale herself took the wet things to a tall mahogany clothes-stand, ceremonially, for she had once been town mayor. Since the war, waitresses had been hard to find and she had to appear herself sometimes, though always in pearls and a nice dress and a perm. She was in no awe of the proprietorial group who gathered at their special table every Wednesday. Some of them may have been schoolmistresses but she felt superior to all of them in her knowledge of the world. Nothing about the war had shaken Mrs Lonsdale in the least: not the air raids, not the bomb on the Gentlemen's Club, not the films at the Palace cinema of the German concentration camps, which she had thought unreal and probably done with models, if they were honest. That woman who went over to see them with the Commission from London ought to have been ashamed of herself. Belsen was no place for a woman.

191

There was an optimism about the gathering this morning. Each woman sitting with her handbag on her lap. One of them was even stroking hers.

'I don't think Mrs Fallowes will be coming today. She doesn't have a very easy time,' said Mrs Brownley.

'You mean Mr Fallowes?'

'Well, yes. Though, of course, he's not just anybody. He's a highly educated man.'

'I'm never sure that's an advantage in a marriage,' said Mrs Pile. 'There's so little for intellectual men to practise it on at home, unless of course they are married to a similar wife.'

'I'd not say that,' said Miss Colne, who had been to teacher-training College and had an affair with a married man in Middlesbrough, but didn't admit to either. 'Kitty Fallowes is so nice, and, after all, they have Hetty. And she's very *lucky* to have Kitty, now that he's so peculiar.'

'Well, of course. But, you know, I can imagine *Hetty* not being all that easy. She can look a bit surly. You know, as she went up through the school, she wasn't *anything*. *How* she got that award to University! Lily Coulter tried to teach her Domestic Science and she was miles away all the time. The school staff even wonder if the examiners got the papers mixed up.'

'No. I'm sorry, no . . .' said Dorothy, growing flushed, and Hilda said, 'I'm afraid that is *not* fair.' Dorothy added, 'And Hetty's such a nice, pretty girl, too.'

'Well, yes. She's nice enough. Well, I'd say *attractive* rather than pretty; she doesn't have an outstanding feature of any kind, not like her mother – all that lovely hair. She doesn't give *out* much.'

'She never thanked me for the grapefruit,' said Mrs Brownsley.

'This coffee is very weak,' said Joyce Dobson.

'We're waiting for the new bottles to come in.'

'It tastes like acorns,' said Mrs Pile. 'The Germans are having to drink acorns.'

'I've never tasted acorns. Anyway, so they should be.'

'I don't expect they are,' said Joyce Dobson, whose sister was working for the Control Commission. 'They'll have plenty of black-market stuff. I expect they've got cream back.'

'When I was in Vienna before the war, you should have seen the cream,' said someone else.

'Vienna isn't Germany.'

'Not far off, from what I read between the lines. Oh, and the hat shops! Beautiful soft felts.'

'Bobby, my brother, says he prefers the Germans to the French and he doesn't mind who hears him. He said it all through the First War, and he was out there facing on to them with a bayonet. He says a lot of people did, on the quiet. He says the French think nothing of us, and never did. The Germans were always nicely mannered, though not very humorous.'

'Did you ever have to do with any Italians?' asked Ada Fisher.

'Bobby has no time for the Italians, either, I'm afraid. He said they ran away, but when they didn't they were cruel-hearted. Look what they did to that Duce.'

The women looked into their coffee cups and saw blood on the piazza, the great pale upside-down face, the feet tied together with ropes, the baying crowds.

'There'll be beautiful coffee in America,' said someone. 'They're partial to it. It's the national drink. By the way, I've had a letter from the German girl. She's in London. She's going to America to be adopted by a remote relative.'

'I've had a letter too. She thanked me for my friendship—'

'I'm sure I didn't *expect* a letter. I only gave her a little dish once Miss Wilkinson brought back from Czechoslovakia in the 'Thirties. I'm not sure that's strictly in Germany now, but she was polite about it. She didn't seem the type to gush, though.'

'Well, I've had a letter too,' said somebody else.

'And so have I.'

Four women, mothers of girls, looked at each other and each one took out of her handbag a sheet of paper covered in Lieselotte's flimsy flowery script.

Dorothy and Hilda looked stony, for they had received no letter; but happier when it was discovered that these letters were each one the same, word for word.

'I expect they're just formalities,' said Mrs Bainbridge. 'The

Germans are very formal people. And the Jews are all for rituals and keeping up the social niceties.'

'The Jews we used to see in Harrogate,' said Mrs Lonsdale, butting in as she went by, 'would never have anything to do with us. They just made us feel badly dressed and not well-off. Oh, but they did do their nails beautifully, like mussel shells. Though they weren't our colours, of course.'

'She's a funny girl, Lieselotte Klein,' said Mrs Bainbridge. 'She didn't address one word to us for years when we went to the school for things or gave birthday parties and that sort of occasion. If she'd said more we'd have done more.'

'Well, but she lived with Quakers. They probably got her out of the way of talking. It's a pity. She was a girl I couldn't take to somehow, I'm afraid. She was always smiling.'

'They say Hamburg, where she came from,' said Joyce Dobson, 'is a paste. Just a paste.'

'A paste?'

'My brother Bobby went there – he's still in the merchant navy, old as he is. He's seen it all. Bobby's been to Hamburg lately on a coal boat, carrying them potash, or maybe taking it away. He was below deck when they docked and then he came up in the morning, and it was a paste.'

'You mean flat? Flattened?'

'Miles and miles. As far as you could see on the landscape. Only rubble. We pulverised them, Bobby says.'

'Like Coventry, then?'

'Well, I dare say. Yes, of course. Exactly. Let's not forget that.'

'She'll be happier in America, then. Nobody can deny that.'

They put the letters, that were now proven to be only some sort of foreign valedictory formula, back in their bags. They were no longer interesting. Joyce Dobson alone said that she wished she had done more for Lieselotte. She didn't mean money, for the Jews always had money – it was in their veins – but she would have liked to have given her some little thing. She had a party bag at home covered all over with Maltese embroidery, black silk with a long gold chain, the sort of thing you don't see now.

'But she never told you *anything*,' said Mrs Pile.

194

*

On the same morning, however, Miss Kipling had unlocked the door of the Public Library and found another letter from America lying on the mat. She went to the Reference Room and lit the gas fire, for the rainy day was cold. September was getting on now. Then she went to the wash-place, to take off her mac. She put a kettle on a gas ring for tea and then went back to the desk to remove the cloths from the card indexes and to dust the counter. This was not a job for a qualified librarian, but she was always the first to arrive. Her library was her natural home. She went into the bright room with little tables and chairs, the new children's library, and laid out *Chicks Own, Victor, The Children's Newspaper*, and rearranged some pale, beautiful new editions of Alison Uttley, who had disappeared during the war and just returned. She smelled and stroked them in welcome.

Then she took the letter with Lieselotte's name and address on the back and saw that it had been posted only a week ago. This is what is so unnerving about America, she thought. The inconsistency. This letter was all the way from California, the far side, and should have taken weeks. It must have come by non-stop plane. How amazing! Letters locally could take five days if your writing wasn't clear. There was no rationale in the world.

'Dear Miss Kipling,' she read – and then, with growing amazement, read on.

Lieselotte wrote letter after letter hunched up on her bed. Sometimes the bed was a boat and she was being taken across the ocean upon it, letting it wander where it wished. The ocean became ink. She floated on ink to the ink-blue horizon. She wrote in frenzy and sometimes, behind what she wrote, images broke the surface of the sea.

She had locked her door. There was her own bathroom off the dark bedroom, and a glass there for water. 'I must measure my water supply,' she said to herself on her raft of paper as it tossed and drifted and spun her away over the ink ocean. The pages of the letters were covered with writing, and flowed away from her on the bed and across the floor, drifting down and away on the white waves of the carpet.

Going north, she thought. Into the ice-cap.

There came a moment when the supply of writing paper ran out and she stopped to listen to a long, patient tapping at her door. She got out of bed and opened it a crack. The black servant stood with a tall glass full of raspberry-coloured something with cream and nuts. Behind was the sharp face of Mame, her throat wrapped round in pink silk. There was no sign of Alice.

The end of that day was muddled then. By nightfall Lieselotte seemed to have taken off the coat. Soon it was next day and she washed and dressed and looked at her bedroom door, and unlocked it. She went through it, to find Alice sitting alone playing patience, with her back to the sea.

'Well, hi,' said the midget figure. 'How are ya feeling? Better? It's terrible how travel destroys. You been away two days. You need the sun, girl, now. Are we going to look at the photographs?'

Lieselotte sat down. 'It is not a success, Tante Alice. I shall have to go home.'

'Not look at the photographs?'

'I can't.'

'You can. You just must.'

A tray of coffee was brought. The great sea swooned outside the window, two huge currents meeting. Islands of dark trees. Far, far away the red bridge glowing.

'It's so still,' said Lieselotte. 'It's as if it's waiting. It is terrifying.'

'Y'know,' said Alice, 'it's the earthquake. There's a feeling we should none of us be here. We're just *too* small. You couldn't do any *work* in this place, y'know. Not in Belvedere. It's a waiting room. You just get sucked into this wet-an'-dry great beautiful *globe*. There's never winter here nor summer. It's never cold. And there's so much, so much that's out of sight. I've seen a whale out there, y'know. It's that deep. Sitting here with Mame screeching, behind the cards I seen a whale. It rose up out of the sea just there – see? Just there. A great black mountain. A warm creature that suckles its young. The sea went slahdin' off its sides. And then it *rolls* away, rolls away and down it goes. D'you know, we don't

196

know what goes ahn here yet in this world? In the air and in the earth and in the waters under the earth. That's the Bible, Nina.'

'I must go back. To Europe, Tante Alice.'

'Do nothing yet, girl. Take it slow. I'll leave ya the albums. I'm going out this afternoon.'

'Going out?' Lieselotte couldn't think for a moment where she was. This jewelled little old creature's life was like the existence of a Venetian princess, watching the water, watching Venice embracing the sea. She remembered the halls of the Wallace Collection in Manchester Square, the Bonington with the sun full on a balcony on the Grand Canal. Carl's brilliant eyes. 'It's a sort of Venice here,' she said, 'but it's the size of a world.'

'Venice is the size of a hazelnut,' said Alice. 'Do we know yet whether it's still there? I'd guess it would be under the lagoon by now.'

The room grew still.

'My father loved Venice,' said Lieselotte. 'He loved the sea. Mother loved the trees and forests. We were going to travel the world. I decided, before I was nine, that I would travel and travel. I don't know why. It might be because, if you see everywhere in the world, you won't get this feeling that you belong to any of it. Maybe that's what's been wrong. Patriotism. Nationalism.'

'No promised land,' said Alice. 'Make no promises. All you're saying is you're Jewish. You are always on the move.'

Lieselotte did not look at the albums that day but returned to her room and slept. Then she gathered up all the letters and put them in their envelopes and addressed them. When the servant left the house next day Lieselotte gave them to her with the money, and some money over. It was her last money.

Alice was being collected today by a chauffeur for a lunch and Bridge, taken up from the main room in a lift to the road, disappearing behind the lift doors like an oracle departing.

Lieselotte was alone, and slept again and the photograph albums lay unopened on the glass table.

The next day she got up at a proper time, dressed and went to prepare her aunt's breakfast. She knocked on her aunt's door and carried in her tray.

'So you are rested and you are here at last,' said Alice, 'and today I go out again. I'm saarry. Mame is coming to see you.'

'Oh.'

'I can't tell her not to. Keep very cool.'

'Oh, hi,' said Mame during the morning. 'Well, so here you are, all fixed up? I would just like a little word with you before Alice and I go out.'

'We've had it,' said Alice. 'The word is said.'

'Is this crazy scheme gonna work?' asked Mame.

'We are thinking about it,' said Alice.

Mame had brought a marketing list and now flung herself about the kitchen looking in cupboards to see that all was adequate.

'There's a pack of steaks missing,' she said. 'Better stock up there. We don't agree with too many steaks in Belvedere, Liese; it's not appropriate for a healthy locality. It's a Wild West concept, and an East Coast fad. This has been a Spanish city. There's goin' to have to be big withdrawals from the Bank if it's always gonna be steaks. Now, you have to go out today, downtown. Help get your bearings. You just leave the orders in the shops, so they know your face. They'll deliver it all here till you can drive, no worry. Get yourself a caaffee an' a muffin while you're down there. There's plenty of drugstores. There's a cinema over in Tiburon.'

'Is that far?'

'Oh, you can take a cab.'

'But I haven't any money.'

Tante Alice later, being wheeled round again by the chauffeur to disappear into the steel coffin in the wall, said, 'Nina, you can walk round there. No cabs. Get yaself moving. There wasn't a day your age when I didn't play a game of tennis an' a *raand* of golf.'

'Have a heart, Alice,' said Mame. 'It's two miles.'

'I was walking ten miles,' said Lieselotte, 'twelve miles, twenty miles, all over London.'

The two enamelled faces turned to her, quite blank.

'I forgot you knew London.'

'I didn't know there was anyone *walked* about London,' said acid Mame.

'What's left of it. I should know. I've only been away less than two weeks. It is in ruins!'

'Now, that's a real shame,' said Mame.

'Is Gatty's there, and Gunter's?' asked Alice. 'Did they get the Trocadero? I learned to gargle the tune of "Garn are the Days" in the Café Royal – I heard that was garn all right – gargle with champagne; I was famous for it.' The lift doors closed and the two women vanished.

Later, after cutting her finger-nails and toe-nails and washing her hair and examining and inhaling and spraying herself with some of the scents in the minarets, Lieselotte fell back on the white sofa and picked up the photograph albums. But then she put them down again and went out.

She walked down the cold-shouldering street of cement and lilies and castrated vines, until the houses stopped and she was on the wet, salt jetties licked by the sea. The inescapable glowing bridge floated across the water, like a rose-tinted error. Along from the buildings were go-downs and stores and an iron jetty for trucks, and already a few urban-looking shops with expensive clothes. The place was developing. She came to an old bar with a sawdust-covered floor, mahogany and brass, cowboy-style. A lean man in a trance stood there, in front of mirrors and bottles. Painted signs, like flags, were draped about, saying how old the place was. Lieselotte read them, but could not understand. Two men lazed in a corner drinking spruce beer from dark bottles. They didn't serve no coffee, the drowsy man said.

She found the general store and handed over the shopping list.

The woman behind the counter smirked at her accent and said, 'Oh, *fine*. Right. Sure will,' put the list on the counter beside her and continued: 'So. You from Canada, honey? Or Britain?'

'Hamburg,' said Lieselotte.

'Is Hamburg Britain?'

'Hamburg's Germany. It's been blotted out.'

'Now, is that so?'

*

She took the road that ran along the shore, and soon became a track. After a mile or two it became a road again and she looked down on long grey sheds and a gleaming mesh of railway lines and rolling-stock – two huge yellow steam-engines all polished domes and levers – and men standing around. The day was hot and lively but the men had arranged themselves with a languor she had not seen in her life before.

One of the men shouted at her, 'You goin' to Sacramento, then?'

'Could I get across America to the east side?'

'If you take your time. We ain't in no hurry here. Where you from?'

'Britain, England.'

'What language do they talk in Britaininglan?'

One of the men started whistling and he whistled very well. It was a new kind of tune to her. Another began singing. It was a lament of some kind, a sort of Spanish, she thought. Maybe. Maybe this was flamenco. And she walked on and on by the sidings until she reached the rising ground east where there was a turret on a knoll. She climbed this slope and walked around the turret. It had a plaque saying that it was a historic monument. It looked Norman-French, like Yorkshire. It had survived the 1922 earthquake, it said. She walked on until the road divided, upwards and downwards. Up the hill the track ran between hills of covered furze. The hill beyond was like a pudding basin. The road down the hill was the one she had arrived by, down to the sea again, but maybe she had got lost somehow, because the houses below her looked older. They were wooden and stood with their feet in the water, on props, wooden piles standing in the sea. There was a smell of fish and a man was fishing from a rock by the shore, a man with a stubble beard. A long man. He looked a villain. He took out of the water a big, lashing white fish and he yelled up to her with pleasure. She could see the hook in the fish's face and its hating, cruel eyes and bars of ratchet teeth. 'I gotta shark!' he shouted, 'I gotta god-damn shark!' and he began to knock its head with a club on the rocks. She looked up at the furze of the higher path and then decided to go downhill towards her own silent, safe road again, and passed along it until she reached

200

the back of Alice's house. Looking ahead, though, she saw that Alice lived at the very end of this street of silence, and that, two or three houses beyond, the road dwindled and led up again to join the furzey moor.

She passed Alice's house and climbed upward, and soon the road became a track again and the furze became trees. From up here on the pudding basin you could see how the forest had been sliced apart to make the wonderful houses, and you could also see how tiny the street of wonderful houses was in relation to the great forest stretching away and away beyond, all along the edge of the ocean, mile after mile.

For many hundreds of miles.

She walked on, and soon the sides of the track became dense forest. Mixed trees. Very black. But here was a single car standing on the right-hand side of the track, an open, dark-blue car with dark-blue leather seats and round, silver headlamps. Somebody had left a briefcase and the keys in the ignition. But nobody was to be seen.

The car had stopped just outside a gap in the trees and a little track led down through them. Up to the left there was a glimpse of a big house, set back among the trees of the forest, which was presumably where the car had come visiting. At the gap in the trees there was no gate, no notice saying PRIVATE, no mailbox, no house name like the houses had on Alice's street below. The gap led only down to the shoreline. Someone must simply be visiting this house.

She could see a track through the trees going precipitously down into the seaside forest, and she took it.

The trees began to look old. Lieselotte started to zigzag down through them, trying to keep to the narrow path. It became quite dangerous, and she found herself scrambling and stumbling among the knobbly roots, launching herself from one tree trunk to another, arms outstretched. It was a clear track. It was used, established, important to someone. It began to lead this way and that way in parallel lines, a corniche among the gnarled, dead-coloured trees. After a time there was a shack to the side of the path, built in a cleared bit of plateau, a big wooden shack with blue curtains in the windows and funny faces painted on coloured paper against the glass. She put her hands against a window and found that she had been disrespectful, because this was not a shack but a good, large, one-storeyed timber house crammed with tables and chairs and books and children's scattered toys, paintings and paintbrushes flung down, dirty paint-water in the jam-jars. There were papers folded into darts, and trains and aeroplanes and paper kites. There was the whole of a childhood that Lieselotte in some way knew.

In a corner there was a German upright piano. On the piano lay a violin. On a chair reclined a guitar with ribbons. The bookshelves – she pressed her face harder against the glass – were full of old and battered childhood books, and again she seemed to know them, even though there were Disney comics everywhere, too, all over the floor, and a Mickey Mouse face hung from a wooden post. There were crumby plates everywhere, and Coca-Cola bottles.

And there was a sagging day-bed, a paraffin stove, a rocking-chair. Everything said, 'Come in and get me. Eat me. You don't have to ask.'

The half-glazed front door of the wooden house opened when you turned the knob. Lieselotte walked in. On a small table behind the door, behind a transfer screen covered with cut-outs of Transylvanian castles, dovecotes, the Kaiser, opera singers, fat blonde children garlanded with roses, was a battered-looking gramophone with a black trumpet. The record lying on its felty deck was 'Tales from the Vienna Woods'. All about the floor, like pools of black moonlight, were gramophone records. Swing. Jazz. Sinatra. Bing Crosby. Scott Joplin.

Lieselotte shut her eyes and breathed in fast to try to seize quickly, quickly, something that had for one moment repossessed her. She thought, A smell? A sound? Or a taste, a breath in the air? A voice? I looked up somewhere at the glass of a rainbow doorknob. I was two feet high.

But it was gone. That old room was gone. Reality was a timbered playroom in a wood in the middle of the west coast of America where they play cards and worship moon goddesses.

She guiltily closed the door and left, carefully continuing down the steep, hairpin track. The playhouse quickly disappeared.

But now, before her, she could see a sparkle and caught something in the air that might be the sound of the sea. She came slipping and swinging out through the last branches of the descending wood, the lower branches of the sort of feathery trees that waved about below her aunt's front door. She found that the trees grew straight out of pale silky sand around a tiny bay below her, and had scattered sharp and short needles everywhere. The hard black needles bore no relation to the waving, febrile branches above.

She walked out from the trees on to a little white patch of beach. The ocean sipped at the semicircle of sand methodically and gently. A seal's black head bobbed up, only a few yards into the water, looked affronted, and disappeared. A few feet above the water a string of pelicans flopped along.

To her right, almost on the beach, was a tree with a rope swing, a long rope swing so that you could sit on its wooden seat and swing away out over the water like a bell. In the tree, up in the branches, a boat seemed stuck. It was trim and painted and tied to a branch, so sometimes the water must come seeping in, deeper and deeper, to set it afloat. Lieselotte turned her head left, and then hung tight to the last tree in the forest she had just broken away from, because she was looking into a small oval disc about six feet from the ground. Its sides were nothing to do with a lens, but the space inside the ropes – for it was an oval of white rope, very small – showed a man to be lying. The rope-work oval medallion was one that fixed a white rope hammock tied to a forest tree on the bank. The other end of the hammock was attached to a hard, crooked beach-comber of a tree on the shore. The hammock itself was of heavy white sailcloth, and lying along it was a tall old man, a yachting cap over his eyes. His feet in brown and white leather shoes were crossed at the ankle, his large quiet hands were crossed upon his chest over an abandoned open book, and he was asleep.

As the sea in the teaspoon bay splashed softly and then waited, then exhaustedly splashed again, the man sighed and the book slipped. He pushed back the yachting cap and opened his eyes. He looked unspeakably sad.

She thought, It is my father.

The man lay still, observing her.

'I'm so sorry,' she said. 'I think it's private property, but there was nothing to say so. I didn't know. I'm afraid I don't know where I am at all.'

'It is Illyria, lady,' said the man.

24

At Betty Bank, after she had read Eustace's letter of rejection of their past two years ('I think that, after all, we are not really suited to each other'), Hetty felt light enough to fly up to the ceiling. Up to the ceiling, out of the window and over the lake. She crumpled the letter up, then smoothed it out, tore it into little bits and looked about for somewhere to put them. The Present from Maryport on the mantelpiece had a good tight lid that probably hadn't been lifted for a generation, so she sprinkled the pieces into it and dropped the lid back. Then she took all her mother's letters and ran downstairs with them and out of the house. The Satterleys were not about.

She took a new path, down to the road, the one the taxi should have taken, and then continued along it until she came to a track up into the fells to the north-east. The afternoon sun, as it began to go down, was making the lake rose-coloured. After about a mile, she sat down on a stone in the bracken and looked around her. All was grey and white and pink and gold. The crags looked soft, almost fluid. They shone like the bodies of soft pink seals. She felt the smallness of the Lake District, its constriction. Such a few miles holding all this grandeur. Wordsworth had been one of the Lake District crags. Man and mountain. A pinprick, an insect on the water, sometimes, but he had ended up a crag. A crag that looked out over eternity.

Hetty sat in the warm sunshine on Betty Top and considered eternity, and found it helpful. She sat until she became invisible to herself. I am not going to try to interpret Nature, she thought, I'll just sit here and be part of it. The rolling pink mountains seemed to shift and stretch before her and a long silver shudder passed across the lake. She remembered Eustace saying that the Lake District mountains were not extinct volcanoes, but volcanoes resting.

Eustace had said good things. Well, this was the end of him.

Enraged. How could I be? I wish I'd written first. I thought I'd hurt him so if I told him. I thought he'd think he was sexless – that's what he is, too, when I think of that boy in the rose-garden. Now, in a way, I know that he'd been finding me sexless. I wish he'd known about the soldier in the boat. He never will now. I wonder who she is? I'll bet she's old. I'll bet she's old and scrawny and desperate for it like a tortoise.

Yet he taught me Wordsworth. He was much better than Miss Baker at school. I wouldn't be here but for him.

She sat looking at the landscape before her, steadily, steadily. Quite tearless. Then, as she wondered who had taken her place in Eustace's affection, she realised in a flood all at once that she knew nothing at all about anyone or anything. Major state award to university, but she knew nothing at all.

She watched a man and a dog walking far below beside the lake and then turn towards her into the fields. They appeared and reappeared here and there in the bracken up into the heather, then out of sight. A farmer out looking for sheep.

There were no sheep. He wouldn't be wandering by the lake after sheep, anyway. The man came in sight again much nearer to her, then disappeared again, and all at once the dog was upon her and jumping round her, not a sheepdog but a big soft loose-skinned labrador. He pounced and pawed her.

She didn't like dogs. 'Get off, get off.' She flung up her arms against it.

'It's all right. You're quite safe,' the man shouted from just below.

She looked down and saw that it was Rupert.

'Here. Heel.'

The dog ran back to him and followed nicely.

'Has he made you filthy? . . . I know you, don't I? Yes, I do,

206

you're Hester Fallowes, friend of Granny.'

She had flopped down on the grass and he sat beside her, all her mother's unopened letters strewn about her on the grass, besmirched by the dog.

'Sorry!' he said. 'He's muddied your dress and he's muddied your letters.'

'They're still in their envelopes, it's OK. I was just going to read them. It's my mother. She writes rather often so I leave them till there's a batch.'

He looked sideways at her. He took off his cap, hung on to the dog with his other hand, put his gun down on the hillside.

'I was out rabbiting,' he said. 'Rabbiting on. Like your mama?'

She said nothing and did not smile.

Then he half-put on the cap again on the back of his head. 'I'm sorry. I'm being far too clever.'

She thought again, What very strange eyes. Gathering up her letters, she said, 'I'll take them back to read at Betty Bank.'

'I'd guess that privacy is not of the essence around there?'

'Well,' she said, 'I'm getting plenty of work done. I'm going to University in a few weeks and I'm badly educated. I've pretty well only read the set books.'

'I didn't even read those.'

'Where did you go, Rupert?' (And she thought, If Ma could hear me, so easy and free: 'Where did you go, Rupert?' – and he's nearly thirty. She'd *die* with joy. She'd faint with rapture.)

'The House,' he said (Wherever was The House?). 'For a short spell.' Then he picked up her hand, examined the fingers one by one and kissed them. Then he dropped the hand, stood up, looked away over at the basking seals. 'Then I tried to read Theology. A bit of a challenge for a Catholic. Bit of a drunken subject, too.'

'Drunken?'

'Yes. We got through a lot of wine. Vat upon vat. And other things we did – seems a very long time ago. I did a year and a half in the war. I must be nearly ten years older than you.'

'You can't be!'

'Yes. I am twenty-eight. So they tell me. I don't do a lot of anything at present.'

'You remembered how old I am.'

'Of course. And I remember there was considerable discussion about it at Ursula's horrible party. I had to speak to her about it. Told her she never looks at anyone, just into her own worried silly head. It's the worst of manners. I told her that next year you will be an extremely beautiful woman and won't be bothered with any of us. Didn't she try to send you off with Mabel? Playing hopscotch?'

'Oh never mind. It was all right.'

'It wasn't,' he said. 'It was a put-down. She was trying to keep you away from me. She's not in the least stupid.'

'I wasn't in the least likely to be swept off my feet,' said Hetty. 'I'd heard of you before.'

'That I am a Lothario? Or that I am vitriol and ashes?'

She thought, What play's Lothario in? 'It was just—' she said. 'Rupert – who is Fergus?'

'None of your business or anyone else's. He was my cousin and he is dead.' He paused. 'Lock yourself inside your childhood. I must go, the dog's bored.'

He made off up the fell behind her and she did not look round. After a time she heard him shooting. Great cracks echoed across the evening and although she knew he was somewhere above her and behind, the shots seemed in front of her and all around, bouncing and wailing across the mountains over the lake as if he was lord of the world. The sun faded and it grew cold. 'Back-End,' she thought. End of summer. Back home again.

I don't like him, she thought, in exactly the same way that I don't like the conceited Patsie, but he's worse because he makes you feel you know him utterly and he knows you. And he watches and despises you. I wish Eustace had seen him kiss my fingers.

Her mother's letters lay all together around her feet, but it was nearly dark now. They were patterned with labrador paws. With sadness and reproof. I'll read them inside, she thought, and went back to Betty Bank.

In the bedroom, the present from Maryport regarding her from the fireplace, she arranged her mother's letters by postmark and read them through. On and on they went. The same people and their boring misfortunes, the same pathetic physical woes. Mrs Someone's grandchild had had a seizure and somebody else's cleaning woman had frightful ingrowing warts on the soles of her feet. The vicar was not quite himself and had had a turn in the pulpit, and Mrs Baxter had run up to him with smelling salts. Her father was 'just the same as ever, perhaps rather sadder, though goodness knows why but we have to bear our crosses'. Una had been off youth-hostelling with that rather nice boy.

When she reached the last letter Hetty sat up rigid, and stared at it. 'Oh my darling,' it began, 'my dear darling, I must come to you! And *Brenda* of all people! *Brenda Flange!* Oh, Hetty, that great coarse *animal.*'

Hetty turned to look at the door, wishing she could lock it lest someone should come in and see her shame.

My darling – I have had a letter from him and, of course, or so one hopes, so have you. In the letter to me he even suggested bringing her *here*! For coffee! (Does he know how little coffee we have I wonder, probably not when you think how much of it he's drunk in this house all last year.) Your father was wonderful. Immediately, immediately on reading the letter, the same sort of letter as always in his nasty little mean writing, your father said, 'Coming here today? Get your coat on Kitty, we are going out to lunch.'

And, do you know, we did! We went to the Lobster Inn and although it was whalemeat which I can't manage and I had to have the cod which was rather a disappointment because it's all we ever have at home these days, I was touched. He's never taken me out since the war. While we were out he and Brenda – I can hardly write her name – did come round. Hilda and Dorothy saw them on our step. They said that Eustace's 'companion' was very big indeed and had legs like dumb-bells made worse by being in army stockings – he met her of course at the camp where she was 'catering'. But it is not for me to tell you what you must know.

Darling, please take comfort. She always looked a very *male* sort of girl to me, and Eustace always had a bit of the 'green carnation' about him. (That terrible Oscar Wilde business.) I'll say no more. You are so utterly feminine, dear. Oh, and you'll be home on Saturday. Your letter came. I have crossed off every single day you've been away on the kitchen calendar. It will be so exciting. Things are very slow here without you to tell things to (by the way I may just be out on Saturday as I have another appointment at the surgery, I have a gathered thumb). I long to hear, when we have you here again, that you've met some really nice boys in the Lake District, but don't despair if you haven't because there are going to be hundreds and hundreds of them running after you at College. I wouldn't be surprised if you're not married and in a home of your own in a couple of years' time. Lots of girls don't finish at College, and I always thought at heart you are a *natural* girl and not a bluestocking. The vicar thinks so, too. We don't listen to what your father says, bless him.

I've been quite dizzy again since I received the letter from Eustace. I've been put on stronger tablets (the same ones as Mrs Ainsworth). News about Eustace's engagement has got all round the Lonsdale somehow, but certainly not through me. Everyone is so sorry for you, dear.

I shall write tomorrow again, but this is just to say I think of you all the time and send you my very great sympathy, darling. It's really dreadful being a woman, isn't it?

Mummy.

An hour later, a couple of Johnson's *Lives of the Poets* noted and memorised, Hetty went briskly downstairs for supper and saw three big dead rabbits lying on the back-kitchen stone, their big eyes dull, their fur matted with blood, their paws outstretched as if they were running still. An envelope was propped against them addressed to Hester Fallowes.

By the range was the omniscient back of Mrs Satterley.

'For me?'

'The rabbits is for the pot.'

'The note?'

'So it says. I didn't see 'im come, I was int' dairy. He gave a wave to Mr Satterley from t' gate.'

'What does it say?'

'Do you think I'd read it?'

The note said: 'I wish to talk to you. I shall be in the Meeting House. Come at once. As soon as you've had supper. I need you. I shall stay there till nine. It will not be locked.'

'It's nothing,' she said. 'Just chitter-chatter.'

They sat to supper and afterwards Hester took her time helping to clear up. She watched the sharp brass pointer of the grandfather clock almost static across the face of the rosy-painted moon. She hung about. She sat on the fender. She waited for nine to strike.

I will not be commanded, she thought. As I will not be pitied or manipulated.

All the while she saw the black eyes and the dark look. She thought of him sitting there in the Meeting House along the lane.

At a quarter-past nine she said she was just going out for a bit to get some air and, before there could be any comment about it, slid out of Betty Bank into the dark. By the time she reached the high protecting wall of the Meeting House she guessed it must be half-past nine.

I do the thing there is no point in doing, she thought. I suppose it's fear. Or madness.

Inside, the Meeting House was as still as it always was. She sat down, near the door. Not a mouse stirred. Not a board creaked. There was no blur of white upon the table to suggest a note – 'I waited until nine.'

Hetty sat on, bewildered by her lunacy in coming only when she knew she was too late. She longed to cry. 'But I will not, I will not.'

She sat for an eternity and the moon shone in through the long window, across the benches and the plain, plain table, where she saw that a book was lying. It was *The Perfumed Garden*.

She dropped it quickly. Then she longed to take it up again and stroke it, hide it under her coat, take it home. She sat on, listening for him to come back.

Quite soon she heard the door in the wall around the Meeting House open and close and footsteps come lightly down the path.

He is here. He knows that I am here. He reads my mind though

211

I can't read it myself. He knows me. If he wants to make love to me, so be it. He is the most marvellous creature I have ever met, will ever meet. He will be everything to me for ever.

The door opened and a little torch swung quickly here and there and someone stepped inside. It was the old woman with the bonnet and the long black dress. 'Hallo?' she said. 'Hallo there. Who is it? You. From Betty Bank. I'm sorry – I'm just locking up. I come every night though I don't think there's any need. The duty pleases me and I enjoy the walk from the post office and up through the fields. If you are wanting silence, then let me leave the keys and you can put them under the stone by the gate.'

'Oh, no. No, thanks. I have to go back now.'

'For one moment I thought it was last year and you were Mrs Stonehouse.'

'I beg your pardon?'

'Oh, she was a visitor. She sometimes came here in the dark. Sometimes I think she sat here with a friend.'

'I must go.'

'Is this your book?'

'Oh, no. No. It isn't. It was here already.'

'Someone must have forgotten to put it back.' She put *The Perfumed Garden* on the shelf between *The Journals of George Fox* and *A Book of Quaker Saints*, where it was later found, to considerable surprise.

At breakfast next day there was another note. It mentioned no tryst but said only: 'We are going away for the weekend, Patsie, Mabel and I, to my hovel on the Solway. Would you think of coming too? Saturday morning. Please say that you will. Rupert.'

Mr Satterley came in from milking and they began their breakfast.

'He wants me to go with them to somewhere on the Solway.'

'That's to his own place. It's a castle. It's down the south-west by the sea.'

'He says for the weekend and Patsie and Mabel will be there.'

'I understood that was the day you'd be leaving us. Home to your mother. You've stayed extra already.'

'Yes . . .'

'None of my business, of course.'

They all ate their porridge.

Mr Satterley, in time, noticed a feeling in the air. 'Is something amiss?'

'She's invited to the castle. By Rupert. Well, she knows what I think.'

'But what's wrong with him?' Hester shouted. She banged down her knife and fork. 'Nobody tells me.'

Mr Satterley looked at her. His face held the unworried depth of peace of the old cradle Quaker. He said, 'There is a lot right with him.'

'Then mayn't I go?'

'It is not for us to say.'

'It's my opinion you should ask your parents,' said Mrs Satterley.

'If you'd seen the letter my mother's just sent me . . .' Hetty yelled, jumping up, then bursting into tears. She ran to her room and slammed the door, 'so you could hear it over Saddleback', Mrs Satterley said later, though she had gone on drinking her tea.

Mr Satterley said, 'All that could happen is she'd find out he could never be serious.'

'At eighteen that can be bad enough,' said Mrs Satterley, 'especially for Hetty.'

Dear Mother,

I've just read your letter. I am sorry, but I can't be doing with it. How *dare* you think that I care about pathetic Eustace. Can't you see beyond your silly bloody head and your ghastly friends' silly bloody heads in the Lonsdale Café? I only kept seeing him because I knew he made *you* feel good, being the type you used to know before the first war, a real old left-over creep. None of my friends would go near him. Poor Brenda, he's all she'll ever get. Of course he was soppy over you. All these vaguely homosexual men go for old women. He was terrible. Pa thought so but he didn't want to upset you since he can't offer romance himself, or anything else because of the war, which you never even noticed going on. That's the only reason Pa and I put up with him – you feeling so thrilled by him.

And how *dare* you tell your friends! Of *course* you told the Lonsdale. I'll be getting bottles of grapefruit any minute. And the vicar! You can't have had the self-control not to tell the vicar. You have no reticence. Everything I tell you or have ever told you is immediately all over the town. Why is Pa so peculiar? Because you have no real fidelity to him and he can therefore tell you nothing. Because he has had to give his married life to the Lonsdale and the vicar – and *you*, Ma. There. I have told you.

You and your imaginary illnesses and psychosomatic complaints. Your ignorance. Your patronising of women's education. Your fear of me being a 'bluestocking', when you don't know the meaning of the word. You don't know what my education means to me. Its first purpose is to get me away from you. Do you think I want to end up like you? Unable to do anything but bake cakes – cakes you are too obsequious to let even your vile friends buy?

I'm staying on here. Sorry about the calendar. You'll have to turn the page over. From 'The Wilderness' to 'The Sea of Galilee, Sudden Storm'. You don't even know where the Sea of Galilee is, which country it's in. I'm going away on Saturday instead of coming home. I'm going for the weekend with a man I've met here. He has his own castle. I'll send you a postcard.

Don't *ever* write to me like that again about my private life.

Yrs, Hester Fallowes.

'I'm going to the post,' she shouted. 'Down to the station.'

'It won't go till tomorrow,' Mrs Satterley shouted back. 'Can it not wait for the postie? He'll put it in his bag here.'

'I want it in the post *now*.'

She ran without a jersey into the near-dark, along the lane, passing through the invisible table, the quick way through the woods. At the point where she had staggered out of the cornfield over a month ago, the cornfield now bare of stooks, she found Mabel sitting on a stile chewing a bit of binder-twine.

Mabel got off the fence and walked beside her down the field.

'I'm only going to the post,' said Hester, springing furiously ahead. Mabel lumbered behind her.

At the lower lane Hetty stopped, looked both ways and then made off to the right.

'It's along here. To the left. You post it at the shop, but it'll be shut.'

Hetty swung round and marched left. Mabel marched behind her.

'Are you coming on Saturday?' Mabel called. She had a growling voice, low and resentful.

'Yes, I am. Could you be quiet? I'm thinking about something.'

'Is it about what's in the letter?'

'I'm telling them at home. Yes. That I've been invited. I suppose you don't want me to come.'

'I do want you to come,' Mabel said, tramping up alongside and walking in step. She was a four-square, stocky, unsmiling girl. A drag. 'If you don't come I'll be all alone with Patsie and Rupert,' she said.

'Don't you like that?'

'I hate them.'

'But they're your cousins.'

'We're *sort* of cousins. We're all some sort of cousins in that house. They think I'm a slug. Do you play tennis?'

'Well, I wasn't in a team or anything.'

'There's a tennis court at the castle. Have you said yes? I'll tell them yes if you like.'

Hetty as she marched had been thinking more and more about the letter. She found that she wasn't letting herself recall exactly what it said. Here it was in her fingertips as she walked along.

They came upon the village shop that had no village. There was a post-box in the wall saying: FIRST POST TOMORROW, 9 O'CLOCK.

'It always says tomorrow, nine o'clock, but it's always after four.'

'Do you write a lot of letters, then, Mabel?'

'What else is there to do here? I do have friends at my school, you know, but Caversham's too far for most of them to come up here. We write letters to each other, yes. School starts next week. Are you coming on Saturday?'

215

'It was Rupert who asked me.'

'Oh, Rupert will ask you, all right.'

'Nobody thinks much of Rupert, I notice.'

'No. He messes people up. He's mysterious. I'm telling you – though I shouldn't because I'll be spoiling it for him – he's terribly good and terribly bad, is Rupert. But, look, I want you to come.'

'Why? Why do you like me?'

'Because you said you'd come and play with the puppies. I just *like* you,' and she came up and leaned against Hetty and breathed on her with a bubble-gum breath.

She's like a dog, Hetty thought. I hate dogs. Oh, not another weirdo. She could get as heavy as Eustace with his long turkey-neck. She thought of ludicrous bold Brenda. Then of her mother and kiss-kiss in the kitchen. Oh God! Once she and her mother had laughed together. They would have laughed together once about Eustace and Brenda. Her mother would have loved to hear and talk all about Mabel and the others here. Oh, they had talked and chatted so much once. Oh, I wish I was a child again.

But, by God, she's overstepped her territory. Does she think I'm still a child now? No. She has tried to inhabit my soul, live my adult life, experience everything I experience, experience my love affairs: a vile, unforgivable liberty. An immaturity, a lack of taste that cannot be forgiven in a mother.

'You've gone red-hot,' said Mabel, leaning close. 'You're angry. What is it? What is it, Hester?'

'You don't ask your elders what they're thinking.'

'I do.'

'Then I'm not surprised you're not popular. You ought to learn finesse.'

'What's finesse?'

Hetty remembered that Mabel was eleven years old. 'I don't know where you were brought up,' she said, tossing the letter in the box in the wall with a flick, 'but you haven't many social graces.'

'In China,' said Mabel.

'Oh? Oh, goodness, were you in prison too?'

'No. Ma brought me home before the war. She left Patsie with

Daddy. My father went in the Army – he went off fighting and left Patsie.'

'So Patsie was in the camp alone?'

'Oh, she ran the place. It wasn't a torture place, it was only a camp. She ran the PT classes even though she was a kid. Well, I don't know what else happened to her. She never speaks to me. Maybe she blames me for Mother coming home. I wasn't much to go home for.'

'I'm very sorry, Mabel. It's, you know, like a film to me. I'm glad you had your grandparents.'

'Yes. Grandpa's all right. And Grandma's not the fool she makes herself out to be.'

By the time they had begun to climb back up the denuded cornfield it was completely dark. You would not have guessed the ring of high mountains. Mabel led the way into the lane again and they trudged along.

'This lane, I don't like it,' said Mabel.

'No. It's a bit scary.'

'Could I hold your hand?'

'Oh, don't be silly.'

But they held hands like children until a light began to show, swinging towards them, lighting the black branches of the unceasing trees. A rackety car was coming.

'There couldn't be a car along here,' said Hetty.

'It'll be Ursula,' said Mabel. 'She'll be out looking for me.'

The person who was not the fool she pretended to be stopped her green car two feet from them and they jumped to either side of the headlamps.

'Mabel? Mabel? Wherever have you been? Whoever are you with? Oh yes, the Satterley girl. Well, thank goodness for that. You know you're not meant to go off like this. What were you sulking about? *I* don't know. We've been worried to death. We will not *have* these moods.'

Ursula climbed carefully out of the car and ran and hopped like a woodland animal towards Mabel and put her arms round her.

'Now, thank you so much, Valentine.'

'Valentine?'

'No, I'm sorry, dear. You remind me of someone we know called Valentine. I can't think who she is now, but she's a girl with a charming mother. Everything connects together somehow, you know. Hilda Fletcher tells me your mother is one of the sweetest people she knows.'

'Granny, come *on*.' Mabel led Ursula back to the car. 'Can I drive home?'

'Yes, of course, dear. Off we go. Can you manage to walk home, dear . . . er . . .? It's hard to turn the car. We can get back only if we drive on, if you see what I mean. Mabel's a wonderful driver.'

'So, you're coming?' Mabel's face was heavy, chin on the edge of the rolled-down window. *'Please* will you come?'

'Yes. Yes. Thank you,' said Hetty. 'I'll have to. I have sent the letter.'

She tried now to walk lightly along the lane, back to Betty Bank, as the car roared off behind her in the dark. She whistled. She kept her eyes upon the pale blob in the darkness ahead that surely must be the farm gate that led to the kind Satterleys, her books, the lamplight and the kitchen fire. She kept her mind off the letter.

It was time I asserted myself. It will make a difference. She'll realise now that I can't just be pushed around and discussed with all her friends.

'It had to be,' she told herself in bed. 'And soon.'

Then she got out of bed and said her prayers in the way she scarcely ever did now, at the bedside, down on her knees. She prayed specially for her mother, and began to weep.

Oh God, if only we were on the phone. Two or three words would put it right.

She lay thinking about her home, the womb of the house, enclosed and warm. She thought of Rupert and the miseries of love. She didn't think of Eustace at all. She waited gravely for sleep. I will after all go home, she thought.

But in the morning the sun shone so cheerfully that the summer seemed to have returned, and she began to think of arrangements for her weekend with Rupert at his castle.

218

25

On the day in late September that Una brought back to the library the books Miss Kipling had recommended, Miss Kipling looked at Una from her stately height and asked her to accompany her for a moment into the reference room and as they passed in together Miss Kipling hung a notice on the door saying ENGAGED.

'I want you to give me half an hour of your time, Una. I want to leave you with this letter I have received from Lieselotte.'

'You've had a letter? Everyone's had a letter except me.'

'This letter is written at random. It has nothing to do with me. You know her well.'

'I don't,' said Una. 'Nobody did. Now she can't stop writing letters except to the ones she spent any time with.'

'Please may I leave you to read it.'

Dear Miss Kipling [read Una, and with increasing shock],
I am writing as you see from California, where I have had an offer of adoption by my great aunt, the sister of my father's father, and I have accepted her proposal. I have now been resident in her house eleven days.

At first I was able only to sit here on this affluent shore beside the Pacific Ocean in my small back bedroom where servants run the house and my aunt plays Bridge with three friends every day in the large main room that fronts the sea. I am spending my time using up the supply of writing-paper in the room and some I brought from the ship. My aunt had me travel here First Class. I am trying to write to everybody who has been so kind. I haven't yet written to friends, but draw near to this now, in writing to you.

To thank you first for your help over the years in getting me German books through the library, which can't have been all that easy during the war in a place like Shields East. These did not only comfort my thirsty soul with the language of my birth but were the most considerable help to me in getting me in to Cambridge to do Modern Languages.

I shan't forget our first meeting over the library counter and your immediate understanding. I shan't forget your later encouragement and insistence that it must be Cambridge I try for – you did the same for Una, I know – and nowhere else. Certainly the teachers at the High School would never have thought of it. Sometimes I believe they thought that after the war I'd be going back to Hamburg. Your time at Cambridge you showed me to have been the cream of life. You have been a huge influence on my fractured spirit.

But now I have to tell you something maddening and despicable and this is my decision to come to the United States. In a fit of madness in my new home in London with marvellous people which was arranged for me, I'm not sure yet why, by the Jewish authorities for my vacations when I started at College, I made the discovery that I had not been informed of the death of all my family in Hamburg. My father had worked very hard to get me out. He and my mother a year later it seems went to the gas chambers in Auschwitz, in one of the batches of 2,000. I had always really known this when their letters of the first few months ceased, but of course one hopes. The knowledge, the confirmation, persuaded me to madness and I (thanklessly to my new friends and old) got myself to the last remaining member of my family in the world. My aunt being very rich and the Polish refugee I had met on the streets of London having great panache and resourcefulness, and, I have to admit, myself having made arrangements for a visa earlier this year after seeing films at the Palace about both Belsen and the Wild West and Deanna Durbin's happy life in America – I did it all as in a dream.

Now I must write down what has happened to me today, one hour ago, before it fades from me and I don't believe it, and it is a great comfort to me to see you as you read this in the public library, seriously smoothing out the pages on a beautifully cloudy, rainy day with a sharp and wonderfully cold east wind off the sea, direct from the North Pole. I see you frowning with surprise seated at your desk, the public about to arrive. You will say that you are not the one to tell, but Hetty is away somewhere in a Lakeland place and my friend Una is I believe in love. But soon . . .

This I have to tell you.

Today I was allowed out for a walk. I am treated as something between a nurse and a servant and also as a royal creature who must learn to be a little more American and perfect her appearance before going about California. But today I was told I might go down through Belvedere, our village, and leave orders for groceries. I did not come straight home, but walked and dawdled in the sunlight, several miles beside the sea, and then up into what I suppose they call 'the countryside' which is scrub upland that has pushed itself in among the despoiled forests. There are deep, deep forests here and they range along for miles and miles.

I began to walk downhill through them towards the sea on a winding path I saw through a gap, narrow and muddy. I came to a wooden house that stirred something from my early childhood, though I can't tell what or when or where. Then I went down and down further, and came out on a little beach that it seems is private though nothing had said so, and there in a big hammock lay a big old man asleep with a book on his chest. He rose from the hammock and quoted Shakespeare at me.

We walked back together to the timber house up above the forest and he asked me precise and forcible questions and I found myself compelled to answer him exactly, eye to eye. Almost from the start – did I tell you he is German? – we spoke

221

in German. Like you, he is a graduate of Cambridge University. It was long ago, he said, but 'I still have a little influence there'.

'You think I must return?'

'I most certainly think so. Have you renounced your place?'

'I haven't yet written.'

He said, 'That is most interesting.'

Then he said, 'The Law of Coincidence,' to which I replied, 'There is no Law of Coincidence,' and he said, 'There are many theories about the roots of coincidence' and was I to read Philosophy? I said no, Modern Languages, and he said, 'Consider reading Philosophy. I suspect your languages are already excellent. Tell me about your aunt.' And so I described to him my aunt's life here and its possible inheritance by me. And also the possible inheritance of her estate, as the last relative, if she can change me to her ways, I suppose. He said, 'What money have you now?' and I said, 'None. I gave her back the change from my expenses on the journey.'

'This is not life, but the abeyance of life,' he said and shut his eyes and shuddered.

Then he said, 'Would you let me see your papers? Your passport and entry documents? If I can arrange a passage home, could you be ready quickly?' and I said, 'Yes'.

He said, 'I don't suppose you have any papers with you now?' and I said I had and I took them out of the travel wallet that Carl the Pole had given me saying never let them out of your sight. I laid them down on the table where we sat among his grandchildren's paints and puzzles. It is a grand and glorious muddle, this playhouse: piano, a guitar with trailing bright ribbons, gramophone, books, books, books, and half-eaten bits on paper plates and Coco-Cola, and thick comfortable dust. It did not look like Hamburg but I felt I somehow knew it. As he read my papers simultaneously he was reading my thoughts. He is a very large, loose, quiet man about sixty-five years old. He said, 'I am from South Germany where we are not so neat.'

He gathered my papers and passport together and put them in a rough bundle in his jacket pocket. I could see other bits of paper there already. His jacket was old. I should say very old. It looked like a Scottish tweed.

'Come here to this place every day,' he said, 'It is never locked. There is plenty to read. There is an electric fire for when it gets cold, but please take care, for it is rather faulty. Everything here is yours, for you to find your identity again.'

'You have my identity in your pocket.'

'Not for long, I hope,' he said. 'Trust me.'

So we climbed up the path together through the trees and were standing beside his car at the roadside of the upland heath. I saw that the car was small but very wonderful, and also strewn about with things like newspapers, a tweed hat, chocolate, old good shoes.

Then he said, 'All I have to insist upon is that you will make yourself quite ready to go at one moment's notice,' and I promised. Then he said, 'Please be certain of what you are saying. I am German. German born, bred and a lover of my country, and I am not a Jew. I shan't be offended if you don't want to shake my hand.'

I shook hands with him, and he said, 'You are remarkable.'

I said, 'I'm shaking hands because you are yourself, not because you represent Germany,' and then I walked away down the hill road back to my aunt's house. I heard his car swoop off in the other direction.

There was nobody in when I arrived back. I realised that I had given up the papers, passport, visa, everything Carl had told me not to let out of my sight, to a man even whose name I did not know.

This is the state of things at present.

Very sincerely,

Lise.

Post Scriptum

Last night I asked my aunt as I put her to bed (arranging her wig on a wig-stand like an eighteenth-century baroness, for she has begun to trust me – at first she denied the wig, which isn't surprising because underneath the head is a pale skull) – I asked her if she knew someone with a house in the woods and she said, 'It is the banker, Henkel, one of the most influential men on the western seaboard, but nobody ever sees him here. He keeps the place for his family. He is very kind to his children.' I thought, God be thanked that he has taken me as his child.

Miss Kipling was standing over her as Una finished the letter and they looked at each other until Una gave a huge sigh.

'She's made it all up,' she said. 'She's gone off her rocker at last. It's a dream. Crickey Bill. It is like a film.'

'It is very surprising. The whole thing – writing to me about it . . .'

'You represent Cambridge to her. I think you must be a sort of safety valve. She knows you'd be so pleased if it were all true. I mean – Freud. Dreams. She's dreaming. Oh, poor Lieselotte.'

'Yes. I think it's fancy,' said Miss Kipling, and sat down sadly, and took the letter and folded it away in its envelope. 'I don't think we'll hear of her again.'

26

They were late, of course. Hetty remembered how twice before they, first Rupert and then Patsie, had not turned up.

'That castle's a few miles off,' Mrs Satterley had said: 'you'd best be ready early,' and so she had been up at seven. After breakfast she packed her books in the haversack with the notes she'd made, her mackintosh tied to the top with her one pair of heavy shoes dangling by the laces. In the zip-bag she packed her clothes for the weekend visit, wishing she owned one thing, one single thing, she liked. Her best thing was Joyce Dobson's cardigan. She would be coming back to Betty Bank for Monday night, home on Tuesday. The Satterleys had already arranged for her to be taken to the train in the farm cart. 'We'll have no more with taxis.'

She wondered whether to take the sheets and pillowcases off the bed. It was their day to be changed, but she'd only be here for one more night.

Mrs Satterley came sweeping in with the new linen. 'Friday's sheets day. We'll not have you in a dirty bed the night before you leave. We'll have those curtains down to wash today as well and scour the bed-china and wash and poss the rug off the floor. Leave your book-bag. Oh, and bring down the Gosse.'

'Gosse?'

'The ornaments.'

Hetty picked up the Present from Maryport's lid before she took it downstairs with the rose-pink candlesticks. The shreds of

Eustace's last letter had been removed.

'What time did they say?' Mrs Satterley asked Hetty in the kitchen, about eleven o'clock.

'They just said "early".'

'That'll be Rupert, then, gone off in a world of his own. Patsie's more reliable, but not much. Is Mabel going?'

'Yes. I think I've been asked to amuse Mabel.'

'More than likely. Well, make the best of it. It's historic, or so I'm told, though there'll never be one of his to inherit it. It may well go to Mabel; she's closer than Patsie. She's legitimate. Rupert will never be able to be a father.'

'But he looks quite well?'

Mrs Satterley said nothing.

At midday there was still no message and Hetty had to sit down to Betty Bank dinner, humiliated and not hungry. There was disapproval in the air. She could have been on the train home by now. Home to Shields East. Her mother on the station platform, overflowing this time with happy tears.

'Your curtains down and your floor swilled and the mat's on the line. I don't know where you're going to sleep tonight, Hetty, if they don't decide to come for you. We've a party coming.'

'A party? I thought you'd shut up for the winter. We've been so nice and empty.'

'There's usually those comes for a final bit of tramping before the right cold sets in. Well, there's ower the cow-house, a single room, if you're stuck here after all. It's habitable.'

'I think something's coming.'

Through the window Mabel was opening the yard gate.

'Hetty!' A bellow.

'How that child shouts when she does open her mouth. What sort of a boarding school does she go to? She's like a farm servant.'

'Goodbye, Mrs Satterley. Oh, and thank you so much. So much for the lunch. And for everything else. And I'll be back for my last night. I'm sorry you don't like me going off now.'

'We've grown fond of you,' said Mr Satterley.

'And they're none of your world,' said his wife.

'I don't know what my world is yet.' She wondered whether to embrace Mrs Satterley, but had to field a ferocious glare as she approached. 'Goodbye, then. I'll tell you all about it on Monday morning.'

'It's to be hoped you'll be ready to. Look you, Hetty, he'll be no good to you.'

Hetty put down her zip-bag to wave to them from the gate, but Mrs Satterley wasn't looking out and Mr Satterley had gone dipping sheep.

Patsie, it seemed, was driving Rupert's car today, and Mabel and Hetty were to be in the back. Rupert sat in front because of his long legs.

'His wonderful legs,' said Patsie. 'Make sure we all know about them. You and Marlene Dietrich.'

Rupert laughed. He hadn't greeted Hetty, had made no gesture of getting out to open the car door. He stared ahead; but his awareness of her, her awareness of him, was thick in the air.

'Comfy in the back?' asked Patsie.

'Yes, thanks.'

Mabel said nothing. They were far from comfortable. Underfoot it was cluttered with tennis rackets and a massive, prickly tennis net made a roll that brought their knees nearly to their chests.

'The dickie's full up,' said Patsie, 'with Rupert's stuff, of course. Rifle and other killing gear. He's the angel of death.'

'I thought the castle was on the sea?'

'Hetty, dear, Rupert shoots anywhere. He'd shoot fish from an open boat. It's not on the sea, it's *near* the sea.'

Hetty saw Rupert watching her in the mirror and was surprised to find that though his eyes were bright they weren't as splendid as she'd remembered. Seeing her watching, he said, 'I'm glad you could come, Hetty.'

His voice was beautiful, though.

They swung out of the Lake District, westward, leaving the mountains in heaps behind them and the countryside ahead opening out green and mild. Yellowhammers flitted in the hedges

227

that ran round the fields of winter wheat. The plain became warm, almost balmy, and fuschia bushes and late phloxes shone in gardens. Farmhouses quite suddenly were built of dark pink sandstone with white painted sills and scarlet front doors. After the whitewashed stone of the Lakes they looked foreign. Huge Dutch barns with red struts were packed so full of hay that it stuck out down the open sides, like stuffing from a mattress. Straw stacks with pepper-pot tops stood on springy beds of hedge branches. All the farmers were out roofing the stacks with silver cornstalks, embroidering and stroking them into place with handmade straw ropes. Their bodies were splayed across the stack-tops, ladders propped below. 'They look like black butterflies pinned out,' said Hetty. Nobody spoke.

'I hope you didn't bring a lot of clothes,' said Patsie. 'There's absolutely nothing to do at the castle except play tennis and there's nobody to see us but Nanny.'

'And Nanny doesn't exactly follow fashion,' said Rupert, and he and Patsie laughed.

Mabel said, 'Shut up about Nanny.'

'We keep Nanny in a cupboard,' said Rupert, 'and feed her bread and water. Let her out on a lead. So Mabel says.'

'You could pay her a bit more.'

'Mabel, how do you know what I pay her?'

'She tells me.'

'*I* don't know what I pay her. She should ask me. It won't be for much longer, anyway. Granny will be taking over.'

Patsie took a corner far too fast and nearly ran into the back of a farm cart. 'God,' she said, 'why can't they get tractors? They've all got more money than we have. They behave like it's old Tin-Sin round here.'

Nobody spoke for a time, glad to be still alive.

They ran out along the treeless Solway plain and began to go through mining villages, each a long street of narrow houses like side-on matchboxes painted different colours. A chapel, a bus stop, a smithy, a shop to each place. Children, very dirty, sat in the gutters. Poor women, their clothes in holes, leaned against their doorposts. There was grit in the air, grey washing on lines, but, all

228

around, fields of almost luminous green under a huge sky.

'It's wonderful,' said Hetty.

'Well, it's not romantic any more, thank God. You get cloyed in the Lakes. Well, I suppose the castle is romantic in its way.'

'No, it's just old,' said Rupert. 'It's pretty ugly really. A heap of pink stones. Looks like a decaying orchid.'

'With Nanny all alone in the dungeons,' said Patsie, and he laughed and touched Patsie's knee.

'But just you wait till you see the wonderful tennis court, Hetty-Hester,' he said. 'Here we are.'

They were all at once in a small eighteenth-century market town full of pubs and people. Inn signs swung. There was a market cross, a great many poor small shops. It felt far away, not English, hard, set apart. Hetty thought, I'm going further and further away; it's further than London here. There's nobody knows me here, nor ever will. There was a shop with faded, curled-up greetings cards in the window, and a post-box on the street outside. Men leaned against a wall, smoking. They wore spotted scarves round their neck. They had black eyes and dark, almost reddish skin and high cheekbones. They looked at the car distastefully.

'Could you stop?' said Hetty.

'Stop? Don't stop here. We're *persona non grata*. They're out-of-work miners.'

'I want to buy some cards,' and she jumped out and ran into the post office, where on the counter she found some coloured picture postcards of what must be Rupert's castle. It did look like a dead pink flower. She wrote one to Una and one to Lieselotte via the Stonehouses, saying PLEASE FORWARD; and then, after she'd bought stamps and stuck them on, she wrote one to her mother: 'Just arriving and having a wonderful time. Sorry for everything. I love you. Home soon. Hetty.' She put them in the box outside. Two languid miners watched her, not standing aside.

'Oh sorry,' she said. 'Excuse me.'

They seemed to glare, but one said, 'Now then, you're all right, marra.'

'You were bloody ages,' Patsie said, starting the car again. 'Picture postcards? You haven't seen the place yet.'

229

At the end of the street stood a green mound and on top of it a tumbling sandstone pile. One end of it seemed to be missing. There was a part of the town around the foot of the mound that had obviously been built hundreds of years ago from tumbled stones above. 'My rose-red ruin,' said Rupert, 'half as old as time. The Romans built it, the Normans pulled it down and tried again. People have been trying to get rid of it ever since, or improve it, but if ever a place was haunted, this one is haunted.'

'Why do you keep it, Rupert dear?' asked Patsie. 'As the Irishman said of the dying dog.'

'Shut up being cruel about dogs,' said Mabel.

'I shall present it to the Order,' he said. 'Though they'd be fools to take it.'

Round the hump they drove, a full half mile, and then through red sandstone gates and up a weedy drive.

The gravel of crumbled, pink sandstone had stained several metres of the banks around. The grass, the flowers, looked thick with rust. At the top stood high broken castle walls with a tired house growing out of the side of one of them. It had an important Norman doorway and rows of sandstone mullions. There was a coat of arms with the top corner missing, but the rest of the house had given up trying, like an old broke courtesan hanging on to her last French hat. Hetty thought that it was the nastiest house she'd ever seen.

'Do we go and see Nanny first, or play tennis?'

'It's going to rain,' said Rupert. 'So, tennis.'

'D'you want to go inside first, Hetty? There's a loo on the ground floor. Dump your bag. Mabel and I'll get the net up. The court's in the keep.' Patsie was dragging the net from the car, and then the rackets. 'It's clouding over already.'

Inside the front door was a square hall, a dirty marble floor and a Jacobean staircase. And silence. She found the WC, which was ancient and decorated inside the cracked bowl with garlands of grey flowers. There was an overhead chain and rusty cistern and the toilet paper was squares of newspaper threaded on a string. It's like a bus station in the middle of the war, she thought. She went out into the hall and sat on the bottom step of the staircase to do up her gym shoes.

The hall was dim and suddenly became much dimmer as, low in the sky, clouds dragged themselves over from the west. A wind was blowing. It began to bang about the house. Hetty felt the huge weight of the sandstone ruins above her head and thought, I could have been back home by now. Her mother would have made a chocolate cake and had the trolley all laid. She'd have had it all ready this morning, before she came to the station to meet her.

She saw her mother's face reading the wire saying Tuesday. She couldn't have got the letter yet. No. Surely not. Not yet. It'll be all right. I'll send another letter. She'll get the card tomorrow – or Monday.

I don't like it here. I don't like them and I detest Mabel, she thought. I'm scared of Rupert. Patsie only asked me so I could make up a four at tennis. She told Rupert to ask me, just to get me here to get Mabel out of their way. It's a most horrible town and a beastly house, and I'm here for two nights. Oh, please God don't let me have to stay two nights. Please God! Why did I come? Why did I think I had to? *Please*, God.

She went out looking for the tennis court and heard the others calling somewhere up in the weedy ruins, and she climbed up some broken steps that lay crooked in the grass, and found the keep.

A tennis court was marked out there. The new net was almost in place. There were no sides around the court, which was bounded by the high broken towers that seemed to lean inwards all around it. They were like the rubbery petals of some prehistoric flower. A poisonous flower, she thought.

'You must lose a lot of balls,' she said. (I must try to be calm.)

'Thousands,' said Rupert. 'They fall as rain on the townsfolk below. Who resell them in the market-place.' He smiled slowly, appreciatively, at her. She couldn't help looking up at him and they stood, looking at each other as if they were alone.

'Oh, come on,' said Mabel. She was scarcely four feet high and square as a box. Her mouth was set now, turned down at the corners, her brow like thunder. She is a monster of a child, thought

231

Hetty. Patsie across the net was bouncing a ball up and down between her racket and the ground, and the ball was becoming dirty pink. She had tied back her black and yellow hair and now smiled over at Rupert. 'Your very last game,' she said, and looked sly. She watched the tennis ball again. Bounce, bounce, bounce.

They began to play and Hetty understood why she was partnering Mabel. Mabel played like a tank engine, like a professional, like a small muscular man. Her solid arm swung back, the ball swung away from it with the force of the hammer of a bronze bell. The ball flew an inch above the net, touched the ground and spurted, invisible and out of reach. Only occasionally could Rupert hit it back and Patsie didn't even try.

'We're on form today,' he said, 'Mabel the fable.'

Hetty stood idle. Blinking. 'I needn't be here,' she said.

Mabel gave her a black, Olympian glance. '*Now* you see what I am,' it said. '*Now* you know who I am,' and her lips curled with pride.

But the better Mabel played, the less she seemed to be enjoying it. A game ended. Then another game. No one but Mabel had gained one point. Mabel twirled her racket and stood staring at it, waiting for the next kill. Then she bashed her service right at Rupert, where it bounced and hit him in the eye.

'Could you just let up a bit, Mabel?'

'He won't be playing again for ages,' said Patsie. 'Not now. He certainly won't, with one eye.'

'And it's not being a lot of fun for Hetty,' said Rupert. He walked over, one eye closed, and stood by Hetty. Then he hugged her and rocked her.

She felt, This is joy! Oh God, how marvellous! Yet it was not. It was fright.

Mabel returned from some evil country, looked around at everyone and said, 'Oh. Sorry. Got carried away.'

'You're not in the Public School Championship now,' said Patsie, 'though you do look just about butch enough.'

Mabel began to cry, and, crying, picked up one last ball and bashed it against the side of the peel tower. It flew high above Patsie's head and disappeared over the top of the masonry and out of sight, somewhere loosening a stone that sent up a puff of pink smoke.

'Last day in the old home,' said Rupert.

'Oh, come on back, Mabel,' he shouted, for Mabel now had thrown her racket on the ground and was away, stamping through the keep and out of sight, running furiously back into the house.

'She is what is known as our little problem,' said Rupert.

'She is a little shit,' said Patsie. 'The purest poison.'

'I'll go after her,' said Hetty.

'No. Please don't. We're hardly started.'

'It's going to rain. I'll go after her.'

She picked up Mabel's racket – a most beautiful red and cream Slazenger – and ran after Mabel into the house.

'Where are you? Mabel?'

There was no answer and so she walked about, opening doors. There was a melancholy dining room with a dozen chairs standing about, an unloved mahogany table, a black marble chimney-piece with a gold clock standing under a glass bell. Another room was cluttered with gilt chairs with broken claw feet and dirty blood-red silk brocade. The kitchens were slaty caves of silence, taps dripping somewhere out of sight in ice-cold sculleries.

She went everywhere, upstairs, into all the bedrooms, into fungoid bathrooms where lead bath-tubs on feet were stained seaweed-green in long smears beneath the taps. Spotted deep-sea mirrors. At a bend of the stairs was the marble bust of a man in a marble wig with little eyes. Like Rupert? There were portraits of similar people along the walls, dark eyes in luminous skin, but all too dirty to be properly seen. An attic staircase led to empty attics. Maids' rooms with no traces of maids. Not a chair, not an iron bedstead. Pink dust only. Rain rattled hard against the windows now. Back again she went, down the main staircase, where the wind through all manner of holes and gimmels was making blinds and even some of the paintings tap, tap, tap.

Then she heard coal being flung on a fire, and voices rise and fall, and stop. At the end of the half-landing a door stood partly open and Hetty pushed it and went in, to find Mabel, streaked with coal dust, heaving a bucket about. Across the fireplace was sitting an old woman with her feet in a tub of hot water. She was playing patience, a cigarette at a card-sharper's angle growing long ash. Hetty thought of how she had wanted to tell her mother about the old family Nanny of the great house.

The old creature sniffed and looked at Hetty with half-closed eyes, through the cigarette smoke, and the ash fell into the foot bath. Mabel paid no attention to Hetty in the doorway but wiped her face clean of coal with the back of her hand and then walked round and arranged a shawl about the old woman's shoulders.

'So what's this?' The old woman peered through smoke.

'Oh, I'm sorry,' said Hetty, not knowing why she should be.

'This is Nanny. I want to talk to her.'

'Now then, introduce me, darlin', and let me apologise for me feet. It's the damp. Hot water and mustard, nothing unpleasant.'

'Yes. I see.'

'The only hope, dear, incarcerated out here. And what's your name?'

'She's Hetty.'

'Well, now, sit down and we'll have a hand of cards.'

'I'm sorry, I don't play cards.'

'Well, that's a shame. It's a blunder. Now Mabel's very good, she could teach you lovely. Are the others on their way up, do you happen to know? I'm not just an ornament in this house, though they tend to forget it since I stopped smacking their little bottoms.'

'Rupert came specially,' said Mabel, 'to say goodbye.'

'Let's see if he remembers me now he's here. It's long enough.'

Downstairs a door slammed and a telephone began to ring in long jangly chimes. Soon it stopped.

Hetty said, 'Excuse me. Are you on the phone here?'

'And so we are, me darlin'.'

'Oh. Oh – please. I should so like to use the phone. Could I ring Miss Fletcher? Mabel? Please. It's the nearest phone to my home. Do you know the number?'

'Who is she? Oh yes, I know. No. I don't know the number. But Granny has it at home. We could ring Granny for it, if you like.'

'Oh, do you think I could? Or – oh, please – I could ring Directory Enquiries. I've not talked to anybody at home for over a month.'

'Why do you want to ring Miss Fletcher?'

'Just to make sure my mother knows when I'll be home. On Tuesday. I've made a bit of a muddle. Oh – and to send love!'

Patsie's light voice came floating up the stairs, and she came slinking in, hair now hanging sexily against her shoulder.

'Hi, Nanny. Feet bad?'

'They's a torment from bloody hell. Who was that, then, Patsie duck?'

'No one. Wrong number. Someone wanting to speak to a Miss Fallowes, so I told her to look again.'

'I am Miss Fallowes,' said Hetty. 'I am *Hester* Fallowes. Who rang?'

'Some bit of egg and cress called Una Vane. Very forceful, she was. I said to think again and goodbye. Oh! Are you called Fallowes, Hetty?'

'I don't believe you, Patsie,' said Hetty with a great voice that turned everyone to waxwork. 'There is absolutely, indisputably no way in the world,' she said, 'that Una could know I am here. *There is no way.* It is impossible. You've had an hallucination. It must be a call for someone else and it came through by some sort of . . . oh, I don't know. Una doesn't even know my address at Betty Bank.'

'Well, now, my duck, let's face it,' said Nanny, lifting out a greyish foot and shaking it dry, 'this is not what you'd call a usual house. Thing go on in this house we try not to think about. The soldiers had it in the war. Their hairs turned white overnight. And some of them strapping great land-girls packed and left when they saw the Roman legions drawn up out on the front lawn by the keep, only their top halves, not their feet. Their feet will be under the ground. It's rubbled up higher since Julius Caesar. Well, there've been soldiers here in a lot of wars. I should know, stuck here all alone with my rosary. There's a lot of nasty— And there's them that *attract* them. They can't help it. There's some attract the dark,' she said, looking at Hetty.

235

'Look,' said Hetty. 'I don't attract the dark. I don't believe in the dark. I am Hester Fallowes, and my friend is Una Vane and she cannot, *cannot*, have telephoned here.'

Everyone looked at Patsie, and Patsie smiled, showing her little square teeth, and then Rupert came in and everyone but Hetty turned towards him.

27

Miss Kipling left Una in the reference room, thinking about Lieselotte. She walked to the desk. Then she returned. 'Una, I think it is true. I think that Liese has imagined the fairy-godmother element, but I think that most of it has a basis. Even though she may have been going to films.'

'It does sound like a film,' said Una. 'I expect you get infected with them in California, but it's amazing Lieselotte did. She had no imagination at all. And she was always so serious.'

'Well, dear, there's absolutely no chance of her coming home, I'm afraid. There would be formalities. Legal considerations. And the visa – it would have been given for a minimum of three months, I'm sure. I remember when we went to Chile. I and my Communist friend. Do you suppose it is true that she hasn't informed Girton? That is very lax. Very lax. The College will not be pleased. She could not get back in time now – not unless she knew someone very high up in the system.'

'Well, she ought to come back. She must have been mad.'

'She agrees with you, Una. Will you tell me if you hear any more?'

'Well, I'm going away on Saturday on my bike. To the Lakes.'

'Isn't Hetty about there somewhere?'

'Somewhere, I'm not sure where – Betty Something. Betty Bank. I'm just going youth-hostelling.'

Miss Kipling stood in the doorway. 'Is this to be in company with the railway employee?'

'Could I go and get my library tickets back, please? I'll need them next vacation. I probably shan't see you again till then, so thanks so much.' Una came up to the reference room door to get by, but Miss Kipling stood her ground. 'You've made me so much better-read,' said Una. 'Especially the Jung and Freud.'

'Una, are you going away with Ray?'

'Yes, I am. I did before. My mother let me.'

'Oh, do be careful, child.'

'I'm sorry. This is my choice, Miss Kipling. I'm nearly eighteen.'

'It could wreck you. It could finish you. You could get pregnant. You don't know a thing.'

Mrs Brownley, who was listening round the Romantic Fiction, padded quietly nearer, into Modern Poetry, and listened harder.

'I do beg you not to risk your time at Cambridge. Una, Cambridge is what women had to fight and fight to get. It is the time we all look back on as the cream of our life. As Lieselotte says.'

'I'm not going with an innocent,' said Una, scarlet and furious.

'I'm sure that's true. But I beseech you . . .'

But Una had fled and the library sank back into its usual torpor, and Mrs Brownley padded on, into Children's Books, which were as usual being perused by several old-age pensioners.

'Good morning, Miss Kipling,' she said at the desk as an assistant stamped up *Swallows and Amazons*. 'Was that Una? Such a clever little girl after all she's had to bear.' Old sour-puss, she said to herself. Cambridge isn't the only saucer of cream.

'I had a letter from that nice little Jewish girl,' she said. 'So friendly and refreshing. From America. Near Hollywood, somewhere. How they all do get about these days.'

From the top step outside she watched Una biking away in the opposite direction to her home.

Una was angry. Until seeing Miss Kipling she had been all for letting the Lake District weekend get forgotten. She hadn't seen Ray since saying goodbye after High Dubbs, but she'd had a letter from him arranging dates for their next outing. The place was to be Rack Hanna Moss in Cumberland and the time 7 a.m. on the railway station, Shields East, bringing bikes and food for two days. They were to take trains as far as Penrith, on the edge of the Lakes, then ride forward and into the mountains.

But as the next fortnight passed, Ray had gone to ground and Una had put the whole thing out of her mind as she gorged on Tolstoy and Darwin and *The Interpretation of Dreams*. After returning the books, she pedalled about the town, seething. How dare the old bag talk about her getting pregnant! Even her mother never spelled things like that out.

On the Friday evening, although she had not heard from Ray, she packed her things for the weekend into her saddle-bag and hung about the house, not facing the reason why. She cleaned the windows of the salon, idly inspecting what was passing up and down the road. Nothing much. She washed down all the window-sills and rearranged the pinned-up notices about Marcel waving. No bike, no patient Ray with his argumentative sharp nose, balancing his foot against the kerb as he read his *Daily Herald*.

At about nine o'clock she decided to go and find him. She knew it was Muriel Street at the other end of the town and that he lived with his Mum. She didn't know the number.

She had never been down Muriel Street. They were miserable houses there, front doors on to the pavement, yelling kids, women shouting on doorsteps, washing hung out across the street, no men in sight, for they were either gone off somewhere since the war or sitting in the back or in the pub. There were no bathrooms in Muriel Street and only one communal lavatory down the end. Kids there often had no shoes, even with the war finished, and they still looked sick even after all the orange juice.

The only traffic in Muriel Street tonight was the coal cart, which stood empty, the scrawny black horse munching from its coal-black nosebag. Black coal sacks lay tidily folded on the flat platform back, fastened down with ropes against thieves. The hoop over the top of the car swung a painted wooden sign in green and gold saying BLACK DIAMONDS. The coal cart was a feature of the town, as was the woman who drove it about, a grimy, smiling widow woman parcelled up front and back in sacking tied in the middle with string, a man's cap back to front on her head. She had a smile and a wave of the horsewhip for everyone, a character of the town. Now she emerged from the one house in the street that looked freshly painted and hauled herself up on the cart, wagging her head at Una like an old pal.

'Off to his shed,' she said. 'Are you after our Ray?'

'Oh. Well. He lives round here somewhere, doesn't he?'

'Number nine is his and mine. Born and bred in it. Not that he's at home except for bed. It's work, work, work. Union and night-school. He's a good boy. He's away on some course this weekend.'

'A course?'

'Politics,' she said. 'But he's a grand son.'

Una pedalled home again and unpacked her saddle-bag.

Her mother, returning from *Snow White* again, said, 'So it's all off?'

'I don't know.'

'Has he chickened out?' and she began to make clucking noises and flutter about the kitchen.

Una tried to look haughty, but failed.

'That's better. Nice to see a smile. That Karl Marx wasn't doing you any good. I'm glad it's out of the house.'

'I'm not smiling, I'm fairly furious.'

'They're all alike,' said Mrs Vane. 'We're the creative ones. We're the productive ones. Cluck. Cluck,' and she sat down in the rocking-chair, where a cat catapulted from beneath her. 'Whoops,' she said. 'I've laid an egg.'

'Oh, Ma. Please. Look, I may be going. It's a point of principle because I suggested it. I don't see why I shouldn't go on my own if he doesn't turn up, do you? We were going to Rack Hanna.'

'Wherever's that? It sounds like somebody's carcass.'

'It's the Lake District. He was looking up all the trains – well, he knows them all by heart anyway. It's a bit remote, so we were meeting up at seven o'clock tomorrow morning.'

'And not a peep out of him? He's probably scared. They do get scared. Well, I should just go your own self. Quite right.'

'I haven't worked out the trains. I mean, it's his job. His mother says he's overworking himself at night-school.'

'I didn't know you'd met his mother.'

'Well, not formally.'

'She has an original style in millinery,' said Mrs Vane. 'I didn't know you'd realised Black Diamond was his mother,' and she put the tea-cosy on her head and twirled an imaginary whip.

'I didn't know. How did you?'

'I know most things. I'll tell you what, Una, I wish that Hetty would get herself home. I think there's trouble there. I don't know why, but I fear it. I saw Mr Fallowes this morning. There's something wrong.'

'Should I just stay home? Perhaps Miss Fletcher could telephone her. Telephone the people she knows up there. She found her the place, after all.'

'No. But you go. Have a nice fling. The only way to live life is by living.'

Not with any great pleasure, however, did Una set off at six-thirty next morning to the station, where, most unexpectedly, her heart gave a great leap as she saw Ray waiting for her. He was astride an enormous motorbike.

'Put your bike int' luggage office, I've got the key. Then get up ont' back, and hold tight.'

'Is it yours?'

'Aye, it belongs to a fellow member. I'm beginning to need faster transport.'

'Where are we going?'

'To Richmond, then Penrith on the A66. I've got the map. We could be on the track for Rack Hanna be five o'clock. Trains don't fit: 7.35 Darlington, 9.35 Newcastle, overt' top for Carlisle, and then there's only 6.53 Workington, stopping 7.42 Cockermouth, then Keswick 8.13 and we're still not on the mountain. Grab hold.'

'Yes. All right.'

'I'm cold,' she shouted over his shoulder as they rounded Scotch Corner.

'I'm freezing,' she screamed over Bowes Moor.

They stopped and ate some dreadful food at a black inn on a black moor, looking westward into a rainy sky.

'How much further?'

241

'A fair way yet. Tek me woolly.'

'Your what?'

'Me woolly. Me Mam knit it.'

'It's very . . .' she nearly said 'clean'. 'It's very bright.'

'Our house is bright,' he said. 'It's like the rainbow, our house. You never saw such polish as in our house.

She thought, He's making something clear.

'You'll be coming round?' he said. 'She's taken a fancy to you.'

'I'll think about it.'

They reached the Lake District frozen but on time, found a billet for the bike at an inn called The Fat Lamb and looked up the stony track of the mountain. Soon it grew gravelly, steep and rough, and it was a hard pull. They were not great walkers. Una's seat was numb from the bike and her hands were blue with cold. Ray stamped forward.

'Did you book us in?'

'No,' he called back. 'No need this time of year. Season's over now, and it's the most remote youth hostel int' British Isles. and the smallest. There's no warden. It's quite impressive to say you've even been here.'

'Have you been, then?'

'I've heard about it. It'll be a better do than High Dubbs.'

'How high is it?'

'Oh, two thousand. Three thousand. D'you want a push?' He stopped and waited for her and laid a hand against her back. The mountains rose ahead and around them like contemplative, moving creatures. As Una and Ray climbed higher, the mountains grew softer-coloured, and seemed more plastic, more mysterious, melting as evening came on.

'See yon stars?' he said. 'Coming out? Wandering stars, they're called, some of them. I guess you'll be on with wandering stars at Cambridge. With Physics and that.'

She thought, He sounds rueful, and she felt surprise. She felt loving then and caught him up and took hold of his hand. 'Will . . . we really be alone all night?'

'I'd say so. It's the end of summer. It closes down soon for

242

winter – snow and that. It's famous for loneliness and snow.'

'I thought you'd forgotten,' she said, as they rested their backs against a rock. The tiny fields below still glimmered white on the valley floor. 'There's a lake – look. Which one is it? It's glassy still. Where does the light come from?'

'That'll be another thing for your Physics. You'll be able to tell me by Christmas.' They stood on, side by side, as the lake blackened and the stars came out. He said, 'You'd do for my life, Una. You know that.'

'We'd better get on,' she said.

Round the next great gable-end of rock she said, 'Hey. I can hear something, can you? Is it water running?'

'I'd think, maybe. It sound talkative. Water can sound talkative at night.'

'There wouldn't be that much water running up here. Ray, it's people. It's talk. There's a light. It must be Rack Hanna. Oh! There's somebody here.'

Slowly now, they drew nearer to the light and saw that it flowed out through three adjacent doors of a long shed on the fellside. There was the smell of cooking, a clash of cook-pans. Squeals and shouts, and Lancashire voices.

'Eh, but it's full up, lad,' said a fat old man in shorts with a gleaming red face. There were five or six other people about. 'Full up, lad. It only teks six and we're eight.'

'Is there an outhouse or something?'

'There's not. We book in here this week every year, this group. Yer out of luck. There's places back down int' valley, plenty of them.'

As they turned back down the mountain someone called, 'You'll get in anywhere down there; it's not six o'clock yet.'

But it was slow going down, darkening and dangerous, and they felt very tired and hardly spoke.

They found the bike, climbed aboard again, the saddle horribly familiar, harder than before.

Ray said, 'Sorry, Une. I should have booked. My fault, I've been busy.'

'No. We'd not have got in. They booked last Christmas. Don't people live funny lives?'

'They could have let us sleep on a floor.'

'I wouldn't want to sleep anywhere near them,' said Una.

'Just because you don't know someone—'

'Oh Ray! To sleep on their floor! Hearing them coughing and making noises.'

'Well, so where do we go? Do we go looking round this god-awful lake, then?'

'Hetty's round here somewhere. It would be wonderful if we could find her. It's called Betty Bank. It's a guesthouse. This is the lake. I know that. But there must be thousands of guest-houses.'

'What's it near?'

'I don't know. I don't think there's even a village.'

'We'll coast about a bit.'

The motorbike attacked the nonchalance of the mountains and they roared off round the lake. There were no villages, though there seemed to be a railway line.

'Here's a station,' said Una, 'but it looks dead. Go on a bit further.'

The bike swung along the lane from the station and came to where it divided. The lane uphill to the left was marked by a wooden board and an arrow. It said TO BETTY BANK.

'It's it! It's here! Oh Ray. Oh Ray, Ray – hurrah, we've found it. Oh, and we'll see Hetty! She'll drop dead.'

He let the bike nudge its way upwards until the lane turned back on itself along the higher level. The headlamp lit up trees on either side, and bramble bushes. The eyes of small animals were close on either side. They disturbed some young pheasants, pale as little ghosts, who made for the undergrowth with extended hysterical necks, making noises like gas-rattles. They stopped the bike and walked through the white gate to Betty Bank as the silence reassembled itself, and saw a grave woman standing in a lamplit window.

She was wearing a broad criss-cross white apron and seemed to be examining something in her hands. Steam came up around her from pots on a fire.

'We've just one room free,' she said, 'and it's a single only and not dry yet from the last guest who's just gone. We've another owert' byre, but that's a single only, too. Yes, there's plenty of supper. There's always that. We're full tonight with a party of six, they're regulars at "Back-End". You could both cram in one room at a pinch, but I'd have to see your marriage lines.'

'The one that's gone,' said Una, 'it's not Hetty, is it?'

Mrs Satterley was not one to look amazed but she stood now, looking at Una seriously. 'It is Hetty,' she said. 'It is Hetty. She's been here the month and left only this morning, the weekend. She'll be back Monday before she goes home. She's been no trouble, no side, and we'll miss her. You can have her room if the young man will be happy with the cow-house.'

Ray said neither yes nor no.

'Come in,' said Mrs Satterley. 'I'll find you your suppers, but there's something here.'

'Something?'

'It's just now arrived.' She held a telegram out to them.

'Delivered all the way from Ambleside. Just come. Addressed to Hetty. Do you think it should be opened? It's providence you've come.'

Mr Satterley materialised from beside the range and put his hand on Ray's shoulder. 'You look fashed, lad. I'll get you some tea.'

'We must open it,' said Una. 'I'll take responsibility,' and she tore open the orange envelope and read: YOUR MOTHER VERY ILL IN HOSPITAL SUGGEST IMMEDIATE RETURN Fallowes Telephone Fletcher.

'Where is she? Where's she gone? Her mother's in hospital.'

'Didn't I say? Didn't I say? She knew what I felt. That Rupert is the death of happiness. She's gone off with them from the Hall.'

'What's the Hall? Is there a telephone?'

'Yes. The Hall's beyond the lane. You go through the gap and down, but it's difficult night-time. It's quicker by road.'

'We'll go by the road,' said Ray. 'Left or right?'

245

She told him, 'Avoid the lane, now.'

'I'm so sorry,' said Una. 'I can't say when we'll be back. It shouldn't take long, but perhaps you'd better not expect us. I must find Hetty. Though, oh – I can't think we can go much further tonight.'

'That you must. Find her and leave it all to Lady U. It doesn't matter how late. Hetty'll be in a right state. Well, she has been in a state – shredding letters and putting them in pots.'

'I am the friend of Hester Fallowes,' Una announced to the funny old woman who was putting some turkeys to bed in a shed.

'Wait a minute, my dear, while I see to the crowdie bucket. I'm so sorry. I didn't hear you exactly. What a splendid motor-bicycle.'

'Hetty Fallowes. I am her friend. I have to find her. There's been a telegram to Betty Bank, but she's not there. Mrs Satterley says she is away somewhere with some people from here.'

'Oh my dear, yes. Little Valentine. She's at my grandson's house near the Solway Firth.'

'Oh, please, is there a phone there? Her mother's very ill. Oh, please, could you help?'

'Of course there is a telephone both there and here. Come along.' She passed Ray the bucket and led them to the house, and across the high saloon.

'Hallo?' said Una when the phone at length was answered in the castle. She turned back to Ursula and Ray and said, 'But they say they don't know her. They just rang off.'

'Rubbish. That would be Patsie. She's an introvert and still suffering from being in prison and because her cousin is about to go into a monastery.'

Ray suddenly dropped the crowdie bucket on the marble floor and left the room.

'Ring again,' said Ursula. 'At once. Tell whoever answers the phone that I am on my way and Hetty is to be ready to come with me. I'll put her on a train for Darlington from Carlisle. Yes. And do you know Hilda Fletcher? Girl Guide? Were you a Guide? Oh, splendid. Ring Hilda: the number's on the pad. Say to be ready to hear what train to meet tonight depending what hospital it is – she will have to find out. I shall ring from the castle when I get there. Now, can you manage? I'll just tell his lordship I'm leaving. It's scarcely more than fifty miles. Now. Ask for Valentine *in person*, dear, and don't be put off by anyone else who answers, especially if it's Nanny, because she's mad as a hare.'

'Do you think I ought to tell her – tell Hetty – exactly what the telegram says?'

'Most certainly. She is eighteen years old. Goodbye, my dear. Do tell your husband to get himself a whisky: he looks exhausted.'

'Hetty? It's Una. Yes. I'm at someone's house. A mansion. She's gone off in her car and she's coming to wherever you are to fetch you away.'

'Una, how on earth—?'

'Hetty. This old woman here, she's going to drive you to Carlisle tonight. OK? Could you sit down somewhere? All right? Please hold on to something, right? There's been a telegram, sent to Mrs Betty Banks, and I turned up there . . . Yes, I know. By accident. A telegram had just arrived for you from your Pa to say your mother's ill in hospital.

'Hetty? Hetty, listen. Ray says they can get you home tonight as there's a night train to Darlington, but a stopping train, so it'll be slow. Miss Fletcher's going to meet you somewhere. OK? I've rung her. The old – the lady here is going to ring her too, when she gets to you, wherever you are. All you have to do now is sit down and wait.'

'Una.'

'Hetty.'

'Oh, Una!'

'I'll be home tomorrow night. I'll see you then. I'll come straight round. OK? Listen—'

'Una. Oh, God. God, God. Oh!'

'Listen. *It's not your fault*, OK?'

'I didn't say. I didn't write. Oh, I wrote a terrible—'

'Stop it. Think of your mother. She taught you to say prayers. Goodbye, Het.'

247

'Una. Thanks. Oh, Una.'

'Ray? Where are you?'

Una looked about the unlikely, shadowed room. Tall windows against the black night. A little light gleaming here and there on a huge chandelier above, on wine glasses and decanters, the faded silks on chairs and sofas, a swag of shabby tartan.

'It's *Anna Karenina*. It is old, old Russia. Wherever are we now? Ray?'

She found him in one of the rooms that led out from this one, where a small fire was burning in a massive grate. He was deep in conversation with an old gentleman, and they were both drinking whisky.

'Oh, good. There you are,' said the old boy. 'So very sorry to hear about your friend, Hester. I remember her from last week. Knows a lot about cattle. Lives with the Satterleys. Well, Ursula's gone, but I hope you're both staying the night with us? Dinner is about ready, I think. I'm afraid it's in the kitchen, to save fuel, but there's someone to see to it, and to your bed. I heard Ursula putting you in Lady Anne Clifford's bed.'

'I hope she won't mind.'

'No, no. She's not been here since 1616.'

Over grouse hash he listened with interest to Ray on the subject of the possible decimation of the railways and agreed that this would be suicide.

'After victory in war,' said Ray, 'a country is often tempted to suicide. Historically speaking.'

His lordship said that that was very true.

'I've met you both before,' he said, 'haven't I? Wasn't I at your wedding?'

28

After Una's message, Hetty put down the rattly black daffodil of a receiver in the hall of the horrible castle. She sat down on a gawky armless leatherette chair. She sat there straight, and for a long time.

Patsie came out of Nanny's room and called down: 'Hi? Hetty? Are you there? Sorry I got your name wrong. I'd forgotten.'

Her head over the banister disappeared and Hetty sat on. She thought, I'd better ring Miss Fletcher, but Una had remembered that and done so. Ursula would ring Miss Fletcher again when she arrived. Anyway, there was really nothing to be said.

She heard footsteps coming through the porch and into the hall. They were Rupert's.

'Hetty? Is that you, sitting all alone there? You're unhappy. What is it? Hetty?'

He got down on his haunches and his eyes were level with hers. She noticed the insecurity of him behind the blasé face. She noticed that this was the only moment since she had met him that he might not be trying to be loved.

'We shouldn't have invited you. It was Patsie's idea. I never would have done so . . . unless I could have had you to myself.'

She looked at him and thought, He says nothing. He is nothing at all.

'You think I'm nothing at all.'

'I fell in love with you as soon as I saw you,' she said. 'There's something – maybe you're very bad. Or very good. I don't know.

Are you dying? They all go on about you doing things for the last time.'

'Everyone has their ideas for me. You're not a Catholic?'

'Oh, good heavens, no!'

He looked disdainful. As they often look, Catholics, she thought. Elite, patronising, only a little sorry that I'll fry. And suddenly she thought of the rolling, thundering, fearless Anglican vicar at home. I wasn't fair to the vicar, she thought. I was jealous.

She said, 'Rupert. There was something wonderful about you when I first saw you, something better than body or soul. Spirit.'

'What d'you say?' He was looking profoundly uncomfortable. 'Let's not get too intense.'

'Spirit. I think we have the same sort of spirit, Rupert.'

He looked very uneasy indeed.

'Some sort of thing sort of floated between us,' she said. 'But I think I was mistaken. Maybe you are not really wanting women at all. You're just wanting to be . . . sort of amazing in some way. Like going into a monastery and all that stuff.'

Now he looked very angry.

'Maybe you're just wanting your childhood back. And the wondrous Fergus.'

'You're out of your depth,' he said, and stood up and walked across the dirty flagstones of the hall and with his back to her examined the vast, dead fireplace. He said, 'D'you know what happened to Fergus?'

'How could I?'

'He was my rear gunner and we were shot up together over Holland.'

'Weren't you captured?'

'No. We got home. Just. I got her down on the edge of Lincolnshire. We kept her flying by hypnosis or something, with the tail shot to bits.'

'But you got Fergus out. I'd guessed that's why you were a hero and got decorated.'

'Nobody got Fergus out, he wasn't there. Well, they hosed out what was left of him. It was two years ago.' He paused. 'I'm sorry to upset you,' he said, looking at her face.

250

She seemed hardly to have heard.

A door opened and shut. Feet pattered. Mabel stood on the landing.

'Rupert, Patsie wants you. Nanny wants fish and chips for supper and someone has to go and get them from the shop and there's a flick on at the Empire, it's good. It starts at eight. Hetty can't go because Ursula is coming to get her.'

'Ursula's coming? Here?'

'Yes. She's taking Hester away, and I'm going too.'

'Tonight? Nobody told me this.'

Mabel stood staring and Rupert looked down at Hester. 'Going? We've upset you. I'd better see Patsie about all this,' and he went to look for her.

Nearly an hour passed, but still Hester did not move. The nanny came down the stairs hanging on to the fat banister.

'God love us, look at you sitting in the dark. Are they gone for fish and chips? There's not a whiff of them. Now then, will you be playing Racing Demon, later on?'

Hetty sat. Time crawled. At length Mabel came downstairs in a coat. She stood beside Hetty and said, 'I'm coming with you and Ursula. Rupert's up with Patsie. She's always been weird about Rupert. They're both in bed, I think. Hester? Why're you sitting there? Sometimes I actually think that she hates Rupert. Hetty? What's happened? I'm coming with you, whatever it is. Whatever it is, I'm coming with you.'

'I heard a car,' said Hetty.

Ursula came through the door in a minute, in mid-sentence.

'. . . taken into hospital. Must just check which one, with Fletcher. We must get along quickly, dear, if we are going to catch the train from Carlisle.'

'I'm going with her.'

'Yes, dear. Why not? I think that would be a good idea.'

'I'm afraid I don't,' said Hetty, standing up. 'I'm perfectly able to manage alone.' She let her gaze wander about over Ursula, Mabel and the grotesque nanny grinning on the stairs. She saw herself as a full-scale person. In control. 'I shall deal with this myself perfectly well,' she said.

But, 'Now, come along, my dear,' said Ursula. 'Leave everything: we'll see to any luggage. Take a coat off the peg; the trains will be unheated. We must get a move on. I have rung Fletcher and she will be there at Middlesbrough, I think.'

Rupert and Patsie were nowhere to be seen as she put on her coat.

'Granny? Can I drive?'

'No, dear, not tonight. If we were caught it would make us late, though I know you drive faster than I do.'

Hetty never even looked up the stairs to see if Rupert might be there.

Ursula put her foot down to the ground in the little car. The Roman road north to Carlisle was silky and moonlit, quite empty. Above them were the wandering stars. At one point Mabel in the back leaned forward and half-strangled Hetty, arms tight around her neck.

'Get *off*!'

'Yes, do let Hetty alone, Mabel.'

'Granny, can I go on the train with her? I could stay with Miss Fletcher.'

'Yes, dear, if you like. I'd feel happier if Hetty had someone with her.'

'Thank you. I prefer to be by myself.' (How they presume, these people. How they command!)

But it was now Carlisle, and Ursula was buying two tickets, one single, one return.

'I do not want her,' said Hetty to Ursula. 'Can't you understand that I want to be by myself? Thank you very much, but I *must* be by myself.'

'No, dear,' said Ursula. 'I do not understand. Not at present. You must just this once be guided by an elder. Now, ring me up from Fletcher's, Mabel. Be a good child.'

'I always bloody am,' said Mabel.

In the cold night train Mabel slung herself into an empty carriage across from Hetty, who had retreated into a figure of wood, her face turned to the window, regarding the night. Mabel fiddled with the ashtray on the side of the carriage. You could tip it over and tip it back. Old cigarette ashes tumbled out. She did it again and again. She began to work on the leathery window-blind next. She pulled it tight to the bottom, level with the big brass press-stud that might secure it, then let it go, to watch it fly up again to the top of the window with a malicious snap.

'Will you *stop* it?' Hester yelled, soon.

'OK. Is your mother very ill?'

Hester tried to hit her, and saw that Mabel's dark eyes were not only miserable, but innocent.

'I don't remember much about my father,' said Mabel. 'I expect my parents are pretty well certainly gone now for good.

'I only *asked*,' she added.

Hetty watched her and thought, How plain she is. 'I don't know, Mabel. I think so. I think she's very ill. From what my friend said, my mother's very ill.' Listening to her own words she accepted them.

'Was it Mrs Satterley sent Ursula to find you?'

'I don't know. I think so, maybe.'

'Because, if she did, I think your mother probably is very ill. Mrs Satterley has a sort of gift for spotting things. I'm terribly sorry.'

'Thanks, Mabel.'

'Hetty?'

'Yes?'

'Could I ask you something?'

'Yes, all right.'

'D'you remember the book?'

'Book?'

'The one on the table? In the lane? The day you came to Mrs Satterley's? *The Perfumed Garden*, by someone called Burton. You threw it down and ran away. Did it make you feel, you know, sort of awful?'

'Mabel,' said Hetty, 'how d'you know I saw it?'

'I was watching you through the hedge. I saw you walk all round the table and put your bag down and pick up the book at the place where I'd just been reading about that sexy stuff and you looked so scared and your mouth fell open and I couldn't decide whether you were a grown-up or, you know, a little girl.'

'What are you talking about? Let's not talk rubbish just now, please.'

'I was just sort of taking your mind off . . .'

Disdain registered on Hetty's white, withheld face.

'Hetty?' Mabel's flat eyes yearned at her. 'Hetty, do you think we have to learn about all that?'

The train rocked, clattered, clanked, steamed along in the dark.

'Yes,' said Hetty, 'I do. But don't fuss. You're only eleven.'

'Thanks, Hetty.'

'Mabel,' she said later, 'I thought it must be Patsie's book. Where did you find it?'

'Oh, Rupert, of course. He's got lots of stuff like that, most not even funny. I thought *The Perfumed Garden* was rather funny sometimes. I kept going back over bits of it. It's rather fascinating. I told Ursula about it.'

'You told *Ursula!*'

'Yes. She just went on picking flowers. She said that Rupert isn't quite like other people because of the war.'

The train was certainly a stopping train. It stopped and it stopped. Again and again. You'd never have thought there could be so many stations on one line. You could have walked between them as fast. Once, they had to get out and change and sit on Newcastle station on a long bench. One old man in a ticket kiosk nodded over a newspaper. Much later, Hetty found that they were on another train, rocking steadily, remorselessly, along towards Middlesbrough, and there on the platform stood Hilda and Dorothy in full Red Cross regalia. Hilda wore the ribbon of the Légion d'honneur from the 1916 French trenches. Oh, I must tell Mum, thought Hetty before the gulf swept her away.

Away in the sweeter air of Betty Forest someone from the kitchen was leading Una and Ray to their bedroom along stone passages, up and down staircases, into the old part of the Hall, which was Tudor with low-beamed ceilings, oak floors, portraits on wood, heavy oak furniture.

'Lady Anne's room's the warmest,' said the servant. 'There's bottles in, too, and the incubators make a difference.' She was carrying a candle that blew in the wind down the icy eighteenth-century corridors and when they came to the Tudor bedroom she set it down. 'There's no electrics in the old wing, on account of the risk of fire. The incubators is paraffin, but don't let them upset you: there's scarcely a fume.'

From a contraption in a corner came the sharp picnic smell of a paraffin stove, and a dim glow.

'What does she mean, incubator?' Ray asked Una. 'What are they incubating? Smallpox?'

'I don't know. It smells more dangerous than electric light.'

They looked quickly at the bed on which Lady Anne had lain in 1616. It had four fat carved posts and a canopy, and hanging down its back a tapestry embroidered with coats of arms and mottoes. Any bed cover had been removed and the bed stood high, narrow and puffed-up, like rising bread. It was rather a short bed.

'I expect she was quite small,' said Una. 'They were then.'

'We're quite small,' said Ray.

They stood looking gravely at the bed. Then they began to unpack their night things from their saddle-bags. The bathroom was about a mile away. They'd been shown it on the way. They were alone in this silent, dreaming part of the old house. They put on their pyjamas and did up the buttons and climbed into the bed respectfully, one from either side. The feather mattress sank slowly down beneath them. There was a very hard bolster for their heads.

'There's a rock down here,' said Una.

'There's another my side.' They filched up two mighty stone hot-water bottles from near their feet and examined them. 'They're like beer kegs,' said Ray. 'Hot beer. Will they explode, eh? I'm dropping mine out; I'm risking nothing.'

'I'll hold on to mine,' she said, 'till I warm up.'

Over against the noble fireplace there was a plopping and singing from the stove, a rustling and a tiny tapping.

'Some might say ghosts,' said Una.

They lay side by side in the filmy dark. Soon Una let the stone keg crash down on the floor and cast herself all at once upon Ray's Viyella chest.

'Oh Ray, oh Ray!'

He began to feel for the buttons on her pyjamas.

'Oh, Ray, no! Not yet. I can't stop thinking of Hetty's mother,' and she buried her face in him and took him in her arms. At once he wrapped his own round her. Slowly they grew warm together.

Much much later he said, 'You can't live anyone else's life for them. I've told you before. We're living ours now. There's a time and place.'

Again, long after, she said, almost asleep, 'Yes. It's you and me.'

In the morning she found herself with one arm stretched up high above her head stroking the carved bedpost, her fingertips tracing feathers and beaks and feet of little birds; leaves and grapes and tendrils of a smooth old crafted vine. She thought, Other fingers have done this.

And this too, she thought, turning yet again towards Ray, tracing now with her fingers the line of his cheek-bone, his ears, and his mouth, which soon she began to kiss once more.

When the sun eventually reached the lattice window of the Lady Anne, she at last got up, went across to it, opened it and hung out into the shining autumn morning. Ursula's vegetable garden sparkled with dew. A rabbit was calmly at work on the cabbages. Red berries were thick on the rowans.

'It could be dew or it could even be frost,' she said. 'It's a marvellous sharp cold smell. The sun's brilliant. You can't tell from in here.' She looked back at Ray on the bed and they smiled at each other.

'Can you remember yesterday?' he asked.

'I'm trying not to think yet. Not about tomorrow. Not even about today.'

'What are the creepy noises, Une? Elizabethan rats? They're in here somewhere.'

She went across to the stove, which stood attached by tubes to a deep glass case, like a jeweller's counter.

'Oh, crikey!' she said. 'Oh, my God! Look! It's eggs. Hundreds of eggs and things are coming out of them.'

He sprang across the room. There was a sort of holding of breath within the case and then in a corner something yellow, alert and fluffy was present. Another egg broke in two nearby, and a beak followed by a small bundle came out of it. Other unseen beaks were tapping.

'They're incubating eggs!' she said. 'In here. The guest-room. Think of it. It's the craziest thing yet. The mad aristocracy.'

'They're not weird,' said Ray the Bolshevik. 'That old guy was all right and the old woman got things done.' He was watching life begin. 'Hey, they're cute, Une. They're great. Aren't they a miracle?'

'Ray, you don't think they're a sort of . . . omen?'

'Omen?'

'I mean . . . Miss Kipling warned me about it. You know . . . getting pregnant before Cambridge.'

'I'm not silly.'

'I'm scared, Ray. I didn't care last night. Now I do.'

'Don't be daft. And hell – I went to Timothy White's.'

'Boots are better known.'

'Boots are Roman Catholic.'

'Oh, Ray – not in Shields East? You didn't go to the Timothy White's in Shields East? Everyone'll know. It'll be round the Lonsdale. Oh *no*!'

'D'you think I'm an imbecile? I went to the Middlesbrough branch. I'd an hour between trains.'

'Did you go in your Guard's uniform?'

'Whatever's that got to do with it?'

'I don't know.'

He looked sternly at her, but then they started laughing. They laughed and held tight to each other and soon were back in bed, Timothy White's, the Lady Anne, Mrs Fallowes, Hetty and Miss

Kipling all forgotten. Inside the warm glass frame the little noises went on and chickens opened their eyes to the world, like the flowers of the forest.

'Please?' Hetty begged as they reached the hospital. It was the middle of the night. Not a car in the car park; hardly a light in the squalid old building. 'Oh, please,' she asked pitifully. 'Let me go in alone.'

'We'll just take you as far as the ward door,' said Hilda.

'D'you know where to go?'

'We brought your father up this afternoon. Mabel, I think you should stay in the car with Dorothy.'

'I'm coming with Hetty.'

'Hetty prefers to see her mother by herself. I'm sure you must understand that.'

'No,' said Mabel.

They trooped, dazed, into the hospital, in the middle of the night, and at the swing-doors of the ward were stopped by the Archangel Michael, with blazing eyes.

'*Whatever* is this? I cannot have my ward disturbed at this time of night. This is an outrage. The Red Cross has no place here, not while I am in charge.'

'It is for Mrs Fallowes. Her daughter has travelled two hundred miles.'

'Then she must go home to bed and come back in the morning. Mrs Fallowes must *not* be disturbed. She is asleep. It is vital.'

Behind the Sister's head-dress, down either side of the ward, were two rows of iron bedsteads and upon each lay a neatly arranged patient, like a rolled-up pancake. In the middle of the ward was a big coke stove with a chimney going up through the roof and a ruffian was proceeding down the ward from the other end towards it. He was hissing and grumbling as he tramped along in his boots, with a hod of coke on his shoulder. He scraped back the metal lid of the stove, dropped it with a clang, and the coke thundered in, some of it scattering about on the floor.

'This is like Sebastopol,' said Fletcher.

'I *must* have quiet!' roared the sister.

'I shall report you,' said Fletcher. 'There was nothing like this at Arras.'

'Is this a relative, then?' asked the Sister, looking at Mabel, and blanching a little.

'I'm a lot of people's relative,' said Mabel. 'But Hetty must see her mother. *Now.*'

'Every one of you should be turned out,' said the Sister, 'and I shall call for the night porters'; but a sad small voice was heard calling from down the ward.

'Hetty? Is that Hetty? It can't be Hetty! Oh, so you did get home! Oh, I hope you didn't come back specially. They shouldn't have told you. Whatever time is it?'

Hetty stared the Sister in the eye. 'Please?'

'Well, very well. The rest of you must go. One minute only. Your mother is to have complete rest. The next few days are critical. You must never tell anyone. It is half-past midnight.'

'I'll just be sitting here,' said Mabel, bringing forward a chair from the Sister's office. 'To see Hetty back to the car.'

'Then I shall go back to Dorothy,' said Miss Fletcher, and Hetty moved down the ward in the direction of her mother's voice.

At first she did not recognise the woman on the bed and thought there must be a mistake. It was a thin, small person and one side of her face was different from the other. It was an old woman, one eye closed, the other open and wildly excited. One arm lay still, the other was raised from the elbow, its fingers questing the air.

'Oh, Mum. Oh, Mum!' She knelt by the bed and laid her face against her mother's cheek. 'Was it the letter?'

'They won't let me read my letters. I think they're on the bed-table. Read it to me, Hester.'

She could see the letter standing unopened among other letters and she reached for it and put it in her pocket.

'Well, tomorrow, then. Keep it, dear. I keep all your letters. I've kept everything you've ever written, even your first little essays. Read it to me tomorrow.'

'I'll write you lots more.'

'Well, of course you will. From College. I know you will. I just have to get over the next few days.'

'Oh, Ma!'

'Did you have a nice time?'

'Oh, I wish I'd stayed at home.' Hetty sat up and looked into her mother's face. She didn't seem there. Even the voice was different.

'Oh, this would have happened anyway, dear,' came the croaky whisper. 'I felt it coming along. Such queer surges. Very like poor Mrs Black, you know, and Ada Fisher.'

'Mum.'

'I can't feel anything down this side, Hetty. Hetty, let your father go his way.'

'What d'you mean? He always did.'

'Hetty. Remember, *you* have to go your way, too.'

'Go?'

'To College. Promise me you'll go to College, whatever happens.'

'Yes. Of course. But I can't do without you, Ma.'

'You'll never be without me.'

'Mum, I don't want to go home tonight without you.'

Feet were coming across the war. A patient coughed and coughed, and another one moaned.

'I quite like hospital, dear. Everybody's so kind.' The one rolling eye was looking over Hetty's head. 'And who is this?'

'Mabel, will you *go!*'

'Who is she, dear? What a funny little person. What a very nice smile.'

'You simply must go now,' said the Sister, her shoes sounding like galloping horses crossing the floor. 'I have to insist on perfect quiet. You *must* leave your mother *now*.'

After another moment or two, kissing her, nuzzling her, trying to embrace her, Hester left the bedside.

Three steps away her mother gave a little cry.

'Mum?'

'There's a cake in the green tin.'

29

The day of the funeral there was the inevitable north-east wind off the sea, but light streamed over the sands and the town and to the hills inland, bathing the crematorium in glory. There had been an earlier service in Church, but nobody had tolled the bell. The smiling, enigmatic grave-digger had been quite ready to do so, but the vicar had vetoed it as inappropriate in the widower.

Afterwards, at the wake, the sun shone into every corner of Kitty Fallowes's house, lighting places which had grown dusty the past fortnight, and which she would never have countenanced. It shone on brasses and mirrors and pictures and clocks, and the calendar of the Holy Land, which nobody had moved on to October (The Garden of Gethsemane). It shone on the gate-leg table, inherited, and polished for two centuries with beeswax. Crowds were present. There were affectionate greetings and desperate laughter and a few people sitting silent. Hetty ran among everybody like a bride, trying to make everyone comfortable. Her father had come to the church but then disappeared. No one knew where he was. Una and her mother had surprised the town by taking charge of the tea and Mrs Vane was being rather noisy in the kitchen with the kettles and the washing-up. The vicar passed through. His Anglo-Catholic cloak with the silver chain swirled. Someone else had taken the service as there was a meeting of the town council that day and the vicar was a councillor. It was being said that he could have sent apologies to the council. Hetty caught his wretched glance before he swirled away.

'Come home with us,' said Una. 'Go on – leave them all. Just come.'

But Hetty was Kitty's daughter and had to stay until the last one had gone. She stayed alone in the house that night, in her own bed.

The Lonsdale group met up the next morning and the sun still shone, on and on. Mrs Lonsdale had moved their table a little apart from the others so that they could talk privately. She herself was still in her black from the funeral with even more gold chains, but the friends of the deceased were in everyday attire again, their black gloves back in tissue paper in various chests of drawers.

They talked. To meet and not talk was not in them.

'There's not one of them,' Hetty's father had always said, 'that can come into a room without saying something,' and Kitty had always said, 'That is not kind, Malcolm.'

Beneath the chatter today, however, there was a sense of uneasiness, as if waiting for an honoured guest who they knew would not turn up. They stirred their coffee and dropped little saccharine tablets into it.

'Will she go, d'you think? It's next week, isn't it? She could never leave her father so soon.'

'I'd think she could get permission to arrive late.'

'I don't think Malcolm Fallowes cares one way or the other. I was in just before the funeral, and do you know what he was doing? Spreading a little tray cloth on the table, one of those she used to embroider with lazy-daisies, and setting out a knife and fork on it. One. And one spoon and one glass and one pepper-pot and a salt. Just for himself. "I'll be fine on my own," he said. "Fine," he said! I don't know where Hetty was. Away in that churchyard, someone said, where they all used to do their exam revision. Morbid, really. And not anything to do with Kitty. Malcolm Fallowes seemed quite jovial – but, of course, he's an actor. I always thought he was an actor.'

'As to jovial, what about Hetty?'

'Shameful, if you really want to know! Shameful. You'd have

thought it was a wedding party. Mind, she was always deep. Not an open girl, though she was all smiles. She doesn't give a thing away – which reminds me, Kitty always promised me that print of the Malvern Hills where we went with the Mothers' Union.'

'It looks like Hetty and Malcolm have always wanted to get free. And Kitty doted on them. She doted on them both,' said Mrs Pile.

'There were plenty of wreaths. My word. Did you take a look? There was a nice one from that officer. He was there, you know, at the funeral. I saw him talking to Hetty a minute. Yes, on his own. I think that the other girl didn't work out. And did you see that Ray sitting at the back with Una and Mrs Vane in gold earrings with that smart woman? She reminded me of someone, in that bandana-style scarf. And a lovely black costume. You know, that officer let Hetty down.'

'I wonder how he knew about the death, then?'

'They put it in the *Telegraph*. Malcolm Fallowes is well-connected. However left-wing they are, they always put it in the *Telegraph*, these intellectuals. Well, he's right away from them all now, I don't know why he bothered. I don't think he will even miss her, he's so peculiar.'

'There are many who will,' said Dorothy. She had left Hilda holding a handkerchief against her mouth and nose, staring at the sea.

'Those were Ellison's pies,' said Ada Fisher. 'At the wake.'

'Of course they were Ellison's pies. The most beautiful pies. They saw us all through the war, Ellison's pies. Two of their great long pies.'

'They say that Ellison's wouldn't take a penny for them.'

'Ellison's are top-notch people,' said Mrs Brownley. They sat on. They were unwilling to go.

'D'you know,' said Joyce Dobson, 'I believe Kitty baked that sponge herself. I could always tell a sponge of hers.'

'She *never* did! Oh, but that's dreadful. I know she always had everything planned ahead, but . . . it's awful really. Eating her sponge.'

'It wasn't as fresh as usual,' said Vera Robertson.

'Well, I am afraid there's one thing I won't forget, and it's made a difference to me. The way Hetty was so bright. I didn't care for it at all,' said Mrs Stevens. 'She might at least have pretended to be upset – I mean, for *our* sakes.'

Dorothy said she was going home now to Hilda, and she rose quickly from the table and walked back the promenade way, thinking of camp-fires before the First World War, of knots and bandaging and songs of Empire. How between the wars in the Guide Hall all the little girls had made promises to God and the King beneath the Union Jack, and she thought of Kitty's sweet smile and her plait of chestnut hair.

30

Hetty found herself somehow living with the Stonehouses a couple of days after the funeral, and coming down the stairs on the third morning she called out, 'Oh, please stop. Don't iron for me, Mrs Stonehouse. You're so kind, but don't iron for me. You see, I can't go. I can't go to College.'

'I see.' Mrs Stonehouse lifted the heavy iron filled with a bar of hot clinker. These old irons saved electricity and ironed so smooth and well. She looked at the base of it, intently. 'But I think that you promised your mother?'

'I did. But she meant the opposite. She must have done. She was asking too much. It's too soon. She would have realised, if she'd been well.'

'Yes. It is very soon. Have you told Una?'

'No. I'll go round now.'

'I think she is coming here, to see you. I've laid your breakfasts!'

'I couldn't eat anything. I haven't eaten anything yet. I can't, until I've told Una.'

'I expect you have already told your father?'

'I don't think that he would take it in at present. He says he's going away somewhere. To someone we've never heard of. To do with the First War. I think it's a . . . female.'

'Look, Hester. If so, what is there for you here?'

'Oh, to go on living. As Mother did.'

'That is what she always prayed you wouldn't do.'

'That's what she *said*. Subconsciously she knew she was living the right way. She wanted me to marry locally and . . . well, just live. Well, you have, Mrs Stonehouse. You never wanted to go away.'

'Here is Una,' said Mrs Stonehouse, looking out of the window with her big pale eyes.

Una came swinging round into the neat seaside garden on her bike with her hair in a strange lump over one ear.

'It's a hair-piece,' she said. 'Mum's latest. Hetty, she wants to give you a perm.'

'Oh, thanks. That's OK. No.'

'"For London", she says.'

'No. Una. I've something to say.'

Mrs Stonehouse set down the Ovaltine.

'If it's that you won't go, forget it,' said Una. 'I've been and got our rail tickets, through Ray.'

'I'll pay you back. Look . . . could we go out somewhere?'

They walked the wide sands, looking at starfish in pools.

'I've something to tell you, Una. I wrote my mother a terrible letter. At first I thought it was what must have given her the stroke, but when I got to the hospital the letter was there by the bed, unopened, and so I took it and burned it, even the envelope.'

'Well, that was wonderful. You must have been so thankful. So relieved.'

'Yes. But now I'm wondering. I'm wondering if it maybe *had* been opened and then stuck down again. She knew me, you see. I'll never know, because I burned it. I didn't look at the flap. The ward was so dark, I couldn't have seen.'

'Of course it hadn't been opened.'

'She said it hadn't. But that was funny. Why did she bother to tell me she hadn't opened any of her letters?'

'Of course she hadn't.'

'I don't know. She was looking sort of . . . forgiving. And . . .'

'And what?'

'Well, sort of triumphant, too. Almost – it's an awful thing to say, but almost – complacent. As if she'd had something enormous to forgive and forget. Sort of pleased with herself for being able to, almost, dupe me. Get the better of me.'

'Oh, come on. You know they said she could hardly see anything by then.'

'She could. She saw Mabel.'

'Hetty, stop it. This is morbid guilt.'

'I'll never know. I'll never know. Una, I'll never know.'

'Well, frankly, I don't think it matters,' said Una on the dunes. 'She knew you. You were always sounding off at her like that, and it never lasted. I bet you sent a postcard ten minutes later apologising. She knew you loved her.'

'She never had the postcard. It arrived just before the funeral.'

'Oh, for hell's sake,' shouted Una.

They wandered the sands, the sandy wind blowing.

Then, on the way back by the side streets, for Hetty didn't want to be seen yet:

'I *can't* go, Una. Not yet. She's with me all the time.'

'Yes, I know.'

'Whatever I say, it's to her. Whatever I do, she is watching. When I pick up my toothbrush she says, "Now, did I pack your toothbrush?" She sent my trunk off to College a month ago while I was at Betty Bank. She sent all the presents from the Lonsdale gang. Doilies and a coffee-pot, and a chip-pan. I ask you, a chip-pan! I argue with her twenty-four hours. She's here. She's here now. Here on the sands. She's everywhere. I can't live without her, Una. It would be treachery. We were far, far too close to be ever without each other. I almost hate her.'

'This is what has to stop.'

'Oh, it would be so cruel to her to leave her!'

'She's being cruel to you at the moment.'

'Well, maybe I deserve it. I've no interest in going to College. I've done all the exams I ever want to do, and won a big award. I'll always have that. And I've met all the people I ever want to meet. More than enough.'

'I met some of the ones you met. I slept in one of their beds. But

I want to meet more, and so will you again, when you're yourself, Het.'

'I should have stayed at home.'

'No. You shouldn't. You should have left your books at home and gone somewhere with someone for some fun.'

'That wouldn't have been fair to Eustace. I was a fraud. He'd have found me out. I only got in because of him. I had to read.'

'Hetty, he didn't do a thing for you. He went off with Brenda Flange. Anyone who could go off with Brenda Flange after you . . . But I gather that's all over. I saw him at the—'

'He only loved Ma, anyway. And who would I have been able to go and have fun with?'

'I'd have come with you.'

'You had Ray. Well, you have Ray. Don't you? You do still have Ray?'

'Yes. I have Ray. Actually, I'll marry him.'

'What? But he's the first.'

'Yes. First and last. But I'm going to Cambridge, and you're going to London. I'll be round on Wednesday night. We're both to sleep at the Stonehouses', and then Hilda and Dorothy are driving us as far as York.'

On the Wednesday morning they waited in the Stonehouses' sitting-room for Hilda and Dorothy to arrive and the Stonehouse dahlias were rich in the sandy borders.

'My Pa's coming to live here for a bit,' said Hetty to Una. 'He's going to help with the garden.'

'Shall we have a bit of silence?' said Mr Stonehouse.

Una squirmed, but then the silence flowed across them all.

At last they stirred, and all shook hands.

'How is your mother, Una?'

'Oh, fine. Dancing about.'

'Does she mind you going?'

'Oh yes, dreadfully. But she's got herself ready for it. Years ago, probably. I don't believe she'll even write to me. But Ray will tell me if she's more doolally than usual.'

'I'm sorry she won't be writing to you,' said Mr Stonehouse.

'Oh, she's pretty ruthless, Ma. She wants me to be "honed as steel".'

'Dear me.'

And here were Hilda and Dorothy coming up the path. They were in Girl Guide uniform today. Dorothy was wearing ankle socks and mittens for her circulation. Farewells. Then across towards the Vale of York they went, keeping clear of Hetty's house, for fear of seeing the grave-digger working passively in his garden. In time they crossed the railway line in the Wolds, where long ago, from the selfsame car, Lieselotte's papers had blown away, though nobody knew it. There was a man in the signal-box now, reading a newspaper and looking bored, as if his job was far from the Western Desert.

At York Hetty said, 'Miss Fletcher, I'm terribly sorry but I'm afraid I can't get out of the car. I'm not able to go.'

They were in good time and so they all sat patiently waiting, not speaking, in the car in the station forecourt. At length, Hetty got out.

There was a fluster, when the train came in, about the disposition of Una's bicycle, which had done very well on the first part of its journey, expertly attached to Miss Fletcher's car roof by a round turn and two half-hitches. The guard's van needed adaptation.

Then Una and Hetty found seats and Hilda and Dorothy stood to attention and gave the Guide salute as the train drew out. It was an hour before the travellers said a word.

'Una?'

'Yes?'

'I'd better tell you now. I'm absolutely serious. I have been from the first. I can't do this. It's asking too much. I can't do it.'

'What shall you do, then?'

'I'll have to tell them. At the College. When I get there. I should have done it at once, by letter.'

'Yes. You should. Anyway, you could have let them know what's happened.'

'Yes. I'll go and see the principal tomorrow. I'll apologise, of course.'

'And then?'

'I shall go home again.'

Una looked out of the window.

'I mean, I can't stop talking to my mother. All the time.'

'Shall we go and get a cup of tea?'

They joggled along in the dining-car.

'I mean, I talk to her day and night. Night and day.'

'Het,' Una was peering forward at the dreary Midlands, did you ever hear of someone called Lady Anne Clifford?'

'Born 1590; died 1675,' said Hetty, her face a mask. They'd reached Stamford. She observed unseeingly all the great pale churches. 'Wrote a diary. Quite important. Went to Queen Elizabeth's funeral, only she wasn't tall enough to see much, she was thirteen. Lived through the Commonwealth and the Restoration. Hated Catholics but told Cromwell where to get off. Mad on Spenser. Is that who you mean?'

'You do know a lot, Het. Is she well known – sort of First Eleven?'

'No. She kept to herself. Had a marvellous tutor and governess and . . . mother. Couldn't read French and neither could her mother, because the men in the family didn't let them, not liking France. Any more?'

'Please?'

'Two marriages. Rotten husbands. Crazy about her daughter – and grandchildren, etcetera. Never stopped.'

'Never stopped?'

'Lived for ever. Bashed on and on. Fought for her inheritance but not a hope since she was female. Got it in the end at sixty. Queen of the north for twenty-eight years and never went south again. Loved possessions, rooms, furniture, doing places up. She had five castles. Built almshouses for the poor and everyone visited – servants up to dukes and duchesses. Very religious, very generous.'

'Did she like beds?'

'I expect so.'

270

'She sounds tough.'

'Strong constitution. She used to be seen year after year with her horses and servants and pikemen stamping about the mountains between one property and the next, all weathers, terrible roads. When she got old she went around in a sort of bed on poles.'

'So she did like beds. Was she beautiful?'

'No, not a bit.'

'Did she have a romantic side?'

'How will we ever know? I'd think there might have been something with the tutor; she built him a tomb. She was passionate and grand and busy. Una . . .'

'Yes?'

'You are pathetically manufacturing a distraction for me.'

'No, I'm not. I'm impressed. I didn't know you knew all that.'

'You can have a run-down on Thomas Carlyle if you like.'

'No, thanks. Het, all that knowledge! You can't let it all go.'

'Anne Clifford never went to College, Una. You are being transparent. I don't want a scene at the end. You have to accept it. *I don't think I can possibly go.*'

'OK,' said weary Una, 'OK.'

Another hour. They were approaching London. Hetty had not spoken. She was staring, staring at the long, long suburbs.

'Una, what is it? Look, don't worry any more about me. I'm perfectly calm now. I know what I must do. Una?'

'I'm not even thinking about you. I've lost interest.'

'Oh. Oh, yes, I see. I'm sorry.'

'I'm just missing Ray a bit, that's all. He is the only person in my life, if you really want to know.'

'I'm sorry. Oh, I'm *terribly* sorry! I'm being so insensitive. Oh, how could I think only of myself?'

'You're sounding just like your mother. Listen. You're not the only one with a dead parent, you know. It'll all have happened before at the College many a time – someone's mother dying. The principal's not going to be all that interested. She's not the Lonsdale. You'll be just another student.'

'How do you know all this?'

'I know a lot more than I did. It must be because I have a lover.'

They sat in silence as the train rushed on; began to slow down.

'You mean a *real* lover?' said Hetty. 'In the technical way?'

'Yes.'

And so Hetty, as the train swept into King's Cross, realised she was more alone even than she had thought.

'What do we do now, Una?'

'I'm supposed to be taking you to the College; it's nearby. Then I'm getting a taxi to Lieselotte's old lodgings, where she was before America. Ma found them, don't ask me how. Ray gave them the train time and said I'd be getting to them after tea. Then tomorrow I go to Cambridge. By myself.'

Hetty stood on the platform, dignified and chill.

'There's absolutely no need for you to come with me now, Una. I don't want to put you out. I've obviously been a great deal of trouble to you.'

'Too right you have.'

'Una . . . oh, Una!' and Hetty began to cry. There on the station for the first time, she began to cry, Una taking no notice but staring down the platform. Oh, how she cried among the rushing people, nobody taking any notice at all, not of a girl bereft of her lover nor of another girl awash with mourning tears.

Una then put her hand on Hetty's arm and said, 'Look! *Look*,' she said: 'Standing at the barrier. Who's that?'

Behind the gates stood a small old man with a fine hat held against his chest, a tall black-haired boy with a twitch, and a sharp, bright girl in high heels and lipstick, waving and calling.

'It *can't* be Lieselotte! She's smashing! She's lost stones. Whoever are the men?' and Una ran down the platform, for the moment forgetting even her bike.

The three of them went looking for a tea-shop. Hetty did not have to sign on at the College until six o'clock, in time to change for dinner, and it was only half-past four and the College a short walk away. Carl said he would take Una's luggage to Rillington Mansions, disregarding the cabbie's doubts about the bike, which had to stand in the open front with the one wheel over its shoulder, dreaming of the Yorkshire moors. Carl helped Mr Feldman into the back of the cab.

Then Mr Feldman got out of the taxi again, removed his hat and opened his arms in order to deliver a short speech. He informed the station forecourt that the three girls were all his children, that Rillington Mansions was Hetty's home if she needed one while she was in London, that Mrs Feldman was about to purchase a camp-bed from Army Surplus, that this was the longest journey he had ever made since 1939, that the Feldmans were now upon the telephone and here is the number; and that he would expect all of them, at any time they wished, and would suggest tomorrow.

Carl twitched and looked Una and Hetty appreciatively up and down with Polish eyes. Then he jumped in beside Mr Feldman and the taxi disappeared.

The three girls went looking for a Lyon's Corner House and Hetty thought she would die among the tall buildings and the awful traffic.

'I'm sorry about your mother, Hetty,' said Lieselotte.

'Oh, thanks.'

'It's a good thing you can start the term right away.'

'Have you really been to California and back, Lieselotte?'

'I suppose I have. Look.' On her finger was a cube of amethyst set in gold.

'Wow! Is that an engagement ring?'

'You are still so very romantic, Hester. No. It's my inheritance from my painted aunt. It might have been a lot bigger. There was more than the ring. Had I sold my soul.'

'You can always flog it,' said Una, 'and we could all go to Paris in the spring.'

They had reached Baker Street, where there were a good many establishments called Milk Bars, but everybody inside them looked terribly ill under the new fluorescent lighting. They walked on, therefore, towards the College and came to a wine bar with latticed Tudor windows.

'Here,' said Una.

The wine bar had a sign hanging outside, all vines, grapes, a flagon and flourishing writing.

'Will they let us in here? Three girls?'

Lieselotte said that they were all just about eighteen now.

'Yes. But they don't like girls alone in bars in London.'

'Let's see,' said Una, and they went in and set Hetty's suitcase down upon the floor and looked around. The little room was empty and dark but there was a good coal fire in the grate.

A waiter came up. He didn't seem to mind that they were girls but looked askance at Hetty's suitcase, once the grave-digger's in his carefree Oxford years but which for over half a century had been used as a store for sexton's appliances. 'I can put that thing round the back,' said the waiter.

'We shan't be staying very long,' said Una. 'We just want a coffee.'

'I'm sorry, we don't serve coffee, only wine. What wine would you like? A bottle? A half bottle?' He went off with the suitcase.

Nobody liked wine, and silence fell. Una said, 'I expect it's our Yorkshire accents.'

'I didn't know we had them. We didn't at school, compared with the rest.'

'Here they will think we have them.'

When the waiter returned, Lieselotte said to him, 'Well, now, Ah'm a spirits drinker, but I don't mind if we open a bottle of red and I'll take a glairse or two.'

The two girls looked surprised and the waiter went off for a wine list, Una saying, 'I didn't know you could do American like that, Lieselotte. My mother would go crazy to hear you.'

'I'm a student of Modern Languages,' said Lieselotte.

The wine list arrived and bewildered them. The waiter hovering near was fully aware of it.

'I suppose you don't have any *crème de menthe*?' asked Una.

'We do serve *crème de menthe*,' said the waiter, 'but not often at this time of the day.'

'Three *crème de menthes*,' said Una, and when they arrived looked with disbelief at the size of the glasses.

'It's in thimbles,' she said.

'And they're half a crown each,' said Hetty. 'It must be a try-on. Yes, I bet it's because we're from the North.'

Lieselotte sipped from her thimble and then took it all down in a gulp.

'I think it's spirits,' she said. 'Tastes just like peppermint creams. It's gone so fast. It's a wonderful colour,' and she ran a scarlet fingertip round the rim.

'I feel wonderful inside,' said Una. 'We'd better leave at once or we'll have Hetty arriving at the College rolling. It wouldn't be a good beginning.'

'Una, Lieselotte,' said Hetty looking down into the oily green eye in the bottom of her glass, 'could I go back with you both now to those people? That marvellous old man? I'm being perfectly calm and sensible. Una, tell her. I've known for a long time I can't go through with this, Lieselotte. College is asking too much of me. Please.'

They paid, retrieved the suitcase and went out into Baker Street, where, across from Regent's Park, they could see the College lights shining through the trees.

'Could you just make this one, last try?' asked Una; and Hetty, as they stood amid traffic on an island in the middle of the road, thought, She does look tired.

And so they walked on, and reached the park in the blue and golden autumn evening with transparent smoke going up from the piles of bonfire leaves in the grass, other leaves drifting down, scratching the paths. Along a side road, the traffic noise faded and black-painted iron gates stood before them wide open, joined overhead by a black and gold scroll, that made Una think of the coal cart. But on this scroll were Latin words. Under the scroll they went and the windows of a library came in view, shadowy girls all reading at desks.

'Miles of books for you, Hetty.'

'Yes,' said Hetty. 'Fine.'

Down an avenue of towering plane trees they went, the grave-digger's suitcase knocking against Hetty's leg like a tiresome puppy. The trees were very high above them with clusters of black round fruits dancing against the night. Side by side the three marched on, up two shallow steps between the urns; and here were the College doors.

'Well, thanks masses, and goodbye,' said Hetty.

'We're coming right in,' said Una.

There was a block of wooden pigeon-holes on the wall outside the porter's office and it was obvious at once that the one marked F was packed solid. There were even letters overflowing along the shelf above, where a dubious package had been stood in a saucer. Something inside it seemed to have broken and there was citrus juice about.

'Everything in F seems to be for you,' said Lieselotte.

'It'll be the Lonsdale. They are so terribly kind. Mum's friends . . .'

'I hope they're from friends of your own,' said Una.

'Oh no,' said Hetty sententiously. 'Ma was the one with friends.'

Una looked stony and said, 'Well, thanks.'

The porter approached. He looked like somebody's butler. 'Ladies? Ah yes, Miss Fallowes. Your haversack has been forwarded from the Lake District and your trunk has been here for some time. They are up in your room. Will you follow me a moment, please? You *are* Miss Fallowes?'

'Yes. I'm Hetty Fallowes. Hester Fallowes. *Hestah*,' and she disappeared with him into his office and Una and Lieselotte stood stalwart outside, watching a procession of assorted women still marching as to war, some others, still schoolgirls, queuing beside a phone on the wall to ring home. There were yet other ones from the previous year, reuniting with shrieks.

'Nice building,' said Una. 'Good as Cambridge. Parquet flooring and central heating. She'll be cosy. *If* she stays.'

'But what's happened to her? Where's she gone? Mrs Feldman wants to fit me for a dress. It's yellow satin: just the thing, she says, for Cambridge. I wonder. Look, we must go,' said Lieselotte.

Then Hetty came out of the porter's office carrying an enormous bunch of flowers and her face was very still.

'It must be Eustace again,' said Una. 'Oh God. I thought she'd got away.'

'Maybe it's from someone she's met since.'

'There wasn't anyone in Cumberland. I saw the place. Nobody under ninety. All she did was read books in a peasant dwelling and go off for one weekend playing tennis with some nobs.'

Hetty walked up to them and held out the flowers. 'They're from my mother.'

Una and Lieselotte took three steps back. Students rushed around them, calling and squawking like birds.

'Could you take them? I don't want them. There've been so many flowers.'

Una and Lieselotte took another step back.

'She ordered them from Moyses Stevens in Oxford Street last month. To be delivered today, with a note she wrote.'

(The note had said: 'Always in good time, darling!! Welcome to your new life. I'll *never* stop thinking about you', but Hetty didn't tell them this.)

'I could give them to Mrs Feldman if you like,' said Lieselotte. 'She'd love them.'

'Yes, do. Thanks. Now, I'll see you to the gates.'

'Hetty, are you sure? Shall we come and see your room?'

'No, thanks. I'm sure. Come on.'

When they all reached the urns, though, Hetty stopped and said goodbye. They looked back up at her nervously as she stood on the top step, hands on hips.

'Macabre, wasn't it?' said Hetty. 'I won't come down to the gates with you, on second thoughts, if you don't mind. I'll have to change for dinner and that, though God knows what into. Can you see your way through the trees? It's going to be foggy.'

The two looked down the avenue of planes and then back up at Hetty. They didn't move.

'Oh, *go!*' said Hetty. 'I'm fine. I'm staying. Go. I haven't your phone numbers, so you'll have to ring me. If you've time. I'll tell you something, in case you don't know. In the end things get hosed out. OK?'

Still they stood.

'We'll ring tomorrow.'

Still they looked anxious. Still they wouldn't move.

'*Go!*' said Hetty. 'I love you both very much, but go. There's a lot to be seen to.'

She watched them moving uncertainly between the trees, Una, Lieselotte and the huge bouquet. The bouquet was dried-up golden-rod and joyless asters. I'll bet she never ordered asters, thought Hetty. Oh, poor old Ma.

She turned from the trees to the College buildings behind her, where all the lights were blazing. Young people were running and shouting and laughing inside. Above the roofs, the London sky was rosy, not with sunset but with the lights of the great city.